The Adventures of Adathir

The Jewel of Numenera

Paloma Earnheart

AUTHOR'S NOTE: This is a work of fiction. Names, characters, places, and incidents are either the product of the author's imagination or used fictitiously. Any resemblance to actual persons, living or dead, business establishments, events, or locales is entirely coincidental.

ISBN 979-8-9881339-2-6

The text of this book is set at 10-point Libre Baskerville

Printed and bound in Kansas City MO, U.S.A.
10 9 8 7 6 5 4 3 2 1

First edition

To Isaiah, Victoria, and David Earnheart, my favorite siblings.
Without you three, this wouldn't be possible. None of these characters, worlds, lore, or scenarios would exist without you. Each of you plays an important part, not just in the stories of Susan, Roi Gurri, Caroldus, and William, but in my story as well. I wouldn't be who I am today if I wasn't your big sister.
Thank you. It has been my honor to see you guys grow up into amazing people. I hope you're as proud of me as I am of you.

Table of Contents

The Adventures of Adathir

The Jewel of Numenera

Prologue

Susan Wellns was a teenage girl with big dreams and a small chance of accomplishing them. She had been living on a small farm in Kansas with her guardian, Mr. Norman, for as long as she could remember. She didn't know much about the real world, but she knew one thing.

She had been living a lie her entire life.

She was told by Mr. Norman her parents had died in an airplane crash when she was about a year old, which is why she barely remembered them. Whenever she asked about the diamond-shaped scar on her neck, Mr. Norman would always say she was born with it. But Susan never believed him.

Mr. Norman was a marine biologist, and he spent most of his time locked up in his study, or at some sort of conference in another state. He never took Susan anywhere, and rarely talked to her unless he had a special announcement about the work he was doing, or if he was introducing her to a new concept in her schoolwork. It was a very boring life.

When Susan wasn't doing schoolwork or tending to the house, she would sneak out of her bedroom window and roam the woods, trying to remember her real father and mother. The only thing she could remember was a flashing light followed by a burning sensation on her neck.

When she forced herself to look back, Susan thought she could remember her mother. When she did, she didn't like the expression her mother had; her emerald green eyes were dim, her face white with fear, and her golden hair wild. Then there was a flash, and she was gone. When it came to her father, she could only remember his gentle brown eyes.

The reason she had to sneak out was that Mr. Norman never wanted her to leave the house unless she took him with her, even though there was no place she could go. Susan wasn't particularly fond of Mr. Norman, and had never understood why he was keeping her away from the 'eyes of the world'. He always said there were dangerous people looking for her, but Susan never believed him. She had never known anyone besides Mr. Norman, so how could he possibly know she was in danger without her meeting someone else? All she knew was she was special, and something about her wasn't normal. Something about her was inhuman. There was something about her Mr. Norman was afraid of.

Chapter One
The World Beyond The Earth

One bright New Year's afternoon, Mr. Norman paid a surprise visit to Susan's room, which was small for a teenager, with faded pink walls. She hadn't been expecting him, but she didn't jump in surprise when she heard the knock on her door. At this point in her life she knew only Mr. Norman could ever be at her door, despite her fantasies.

She opened the door to see Mr. Norman's face gleaming, his grey hair combed back, and dressed in one of his three-piece suits. He smiled somewhat warmly at her, though the young girl knew there was a lot more behind the smile.

She already knew from the looks of it he was going to another conference and decided she would spare him another one of his announcements.

"I already know," Susan stated.

Mr. Norman looked confused. "You do?" He asked with genuine surprise. "I thought I had hidden it well."

"You did. I wasn't expecting you to leave so soon after the last one. So where is your conference this time? Washington? New York? L.A?"

He chuckled and wrapped his arm around Susan's shoulder, causing her to stiffen in discomfort.

"You're a smart girl. I am going to a conference but that's not what I came to talk to you about."

She frowned. He rarely ever talked to her about anything besides work, or how she needed to take better care of the house, which always got her mad. He saw the surprised expression on her face and smiled.

"Don't you remember?" He asked. "Today is your seventeenth birthday."

Susan pinched herself and frowned. She had forgotten, and somehow he remembered. How did she forget her own birthday?

"No," she whispered as she looked down at her feet. "I forgot."

"Well then, I must make sure you don't forget again. Follow me."

Susan followed him out of the small, light grey house, whose paint was chipping, with a wrap-around porch. She paused and looked around the house, trying to see beyond the acres upon acres of leaf barren woods. But, as usual, there was nothing new to see. The house stood in the center of five hundred acres, and all around were woods, with only a singular path for Mr. Norman to drive on.

It was another snowless winter thus far, void of beauty or hope of the spring to come. Winter was only tolerable when the white, powdery pieces of heaven fell from the sky. Unfortunately, the heavens wouldn't be blessing the farm with its beauty for another month or two, leaving Susan to wish for the cold, grey sky to be covered in heavy clouds.

"You should be wearing a jacket," Mr. Norman said to Susan as he stepped off the porch, wrapping his arms around himself and shuddering despite his heavy coat and boots.

"You know I have a high tolerance for the cold," Susan said, the bite of the wind not even giving her goosebumps.

Mr. Norman shook his head in disbelief as Susan followed him to a dark brown monitor shed that stood beside the house. When he flipped on the lights Susan was pleasantly surprised to find it clean and tidy. Usually, it was full of old gardening tools that were thrown about because they didn't have a proper place, old feed for animals they didn't have, or storage for the things Mr. Norman brought back from his trips.

But what surprised Susan the most was to see that the shed had been built into a stable, and inside of the stable stood a magnificent stag. Its fur was a beautiful dark cinnamon color, almost the color of rich dirt, its antlers reached far and wide like tree branches, and it had a pure white star-shaped spot on its forehead. Susan looked back at Mr. Norman, a confused look on her face.

"He's for you," Mr. Norman said proudly as if he was the best father figure on Earth.

Susan was skeptical. Not once had Mr. Norman bought her something so extravagant, and definitely not on her birthday. It was always overlooked, so she hardly remembered herself. And a stag? Why a stag?

She cautiously approached the stag, lifting a hand to allow the beautiful creature to sniff her hand before putting it on his forehead. She felt a tingling sensation around her, and a faint memory surfaced in her mind. She saw the stag leaning over her, and rubbing the side of his face to her once-baby body, a small giggle coming from her lips. She snapped out of her trance and looked into his eyes.

"White Star," Susan thought. *"That's his name."*

The name didn't feel random like how most children and teenagers would name their pets. It came to her mind in an instant, an instinct told her this was already his name.

"Susan," Mr. Norman said in a gentle tone. "I'm leaving now. I'll be gone for about a month. I have to get to the airport on time."

Susan nodded, keeping her gaze on White Star. She seemingly ignored the man in the room, but she could feel the dark, angry energy emitted from him onto her. It was an aura of hatred, and it seemed to dare her to turn around and look into his eyes. She feared that if she turned he would attack. She resisted the shudder that wanted to crawl down her body, and she heard him starting to walk out.

"Thank you, Mr. Norman," Susan managed to say, despite her bad feeling. "This is the best birthday present you have ever given me."

"And the only one," she thought with a frown.

Mr. Norman smiled as he walked away, smirking when he was out of her view.

"Goodbye, for now, Susan Wellns," Mr. Norman thought as he disappeared like a phantom.

Susan continued to stare at White Star, wondering why she felt like she had seen this stag before. There was the memory she thought she had a moment ago, but it couldn't be. She had never once seen a deer so close up before.

"It could've been a memory from when I was very young," she thought. *"But then again, I would've forgotten that memory by now."*

Susan groaned and placed a hand on her head as her mind twisted and turned, trying to wonder why she remembered him from somewhere. He looked too familiar, it was like an answer was shouting into her ear, but she refused to hear. It frustrated her, and the mental pain started to increase.

"Dang it," she muttered, pressing a hand to her temple before looking up at the large stag.

He looked down at her and winked before stomping a hoof. She peered at him and took a small step back, not knowing if a deer winking was unusual or not. To her, this was all new, and she was starting to wonder why Mr. Norman left her with the deer by herself anyways.

"Is he really stupid enough to leave me with an animal alone?" Susan wondered.

"Did you just... wink at me?" She asked White Star, the question mostly to herself, not thinking he would actually answer.

White Star nodded as if he was saying yes. Susan started to tremble in shock, her body inching backward again. She was both frightened and curious about having a deer that could understand her. Then again, maybe it was a coincidence. She knew deer couldn't understand humans, it just wasn't possible. She scoffed at her thoughts before laughing.

"Come on Susan, you're seventeen," Susan thought. *"Just because you've never seen a deer up close doesn't mean you didn't learn about this kind of thing."*

She turned to walk out, but White Star bumped against her as if trying to get her attention. She stumbled, looking back at White Star with a small frown.

"What do you want?" She asked, regaining her composure.

White Star raised his hoof and he drew in the dirt, making lines. Susan raised a brow and walked over to stand next to him. She gasped when she saw he wasn't just drawing, but in fact, writing. He stepped back, allowing her to look at the message.

"*Hello,*" the message simply wrote.

Susan cautiously looked up at White Star.

"Alright," she said shakily. "So you *can* understand me. Does Mr. Norman know you can understand us?"

White Star nodded again.

"Why that-" Susan muttered before she cut herself off.

"He knew?" She thought. *"Then he must know about other supernatural things and never told me. That means... he really has been lying to me my entire life. I've been lied to my entire life."*

Susan dashed outside and to the garage. She looked to find the car was still there, but Mr. Norman was nowhere in sight. She looked all over the house and land, calling for him till her voice was hoarse, but he had disappeared without a trace. She eventually gave up and made her way back to the stable.

She walked over to White Star and he looked down at her. She thought of a million stupid questions to ask him but decided it best not to.

"Besides, who knows what he might do if I offend him? I don't know how high magic stags think of themselves."

"Is your name White Star?" Susan asked, wondering if her instinct was correct. White Star nodded, her frown deepening. "How did I know that?"

He let out a snort in response as if saying he didn't know either. She sat on a stool and began to think about everything that was happening.

This was strange, and not your everyday average strange. This was ridiculously strange. Impossible. It wasn't real. Or at least, it wasn't *supposed* to be real. Susan peered at White Star, looking for anything unusual, but he looked like a perfectly normal stag, except for his unusually large build. But there was some sort of glow about him, something she couldn't understand. It was like something was shouting the answer to her, again, but she didn't have the mind to comprehend it. She shook her head and rubbed her eyes.

"Maybe it's my imagination."

But when she looked back at him he still had an eerie glow. She blinked and fiddled with her necklace, unsure of what to do.

"Okay Susan, you're all alone with a stag that can magically understand you, Mr. Norman is mysteriously gone, and you have no one to turn to. Great. I have no idea what's going on, but something's about to happen, I can tell."

White Star decided he was hungry and started chewing on the straw next to him, making a crunching sound echoing in the once-silent room. He looked over at Susan as he ate, observing her as she thought to herself. She was smaller than he had expected. That was the main thought in his mind above all else, surprisingly.

"She looks like her parents," White Star thought. *"But compared to them she is tiny in height and build."*

Susan looked over to see him staring at her and she sighed. She didn't know what to do, the only thing she was certain of was the sound of the straw being chewed was irritating her.

White Star looked up at Susan, lifting his hoof and pointing it at her. Her brow lifted and she stood up.

"Do you need something?" She asked.

White Star shook his head and nudged his head towards her.

“Then what is it?” She asked again, annoyed he couldn’t just speak to her.

White Star snorted in irritation, but he guessed it would be hard for her to understand him. He walked over to her, and she felt small compared to the stag’s intimidating form. She stumbled back but stopped when she realized he wasn’t a threat to her. He nudged his head against her neck, where her scar was. She gently touched it with her fingertips as he backed away from her. She remembered the burning she felt when she tried to remember how she got it. And the voice that came with it... The voice Susan believed was her mother, crying out.

“No! Please!”

She looked down, a sad aura surrounding her. A thought came to her and a smile broke out on her lips. She looked up at White Star.

“Do you know how I got my scar?” She asked.

White Star nodded and made a sort of smile. Hope flooded throughout her entire being. For the first time ever, someone actually knew about her.

“Did you know my parents?”

White Star nodded frantically and stomped his hooves around as if he was excited she finally got it. She was almost speechless, her mind racing with so many ideas and questions. But she was able to ask one more question before her mind went completely blank.

“What are you?”

White Star grunted and stomped his left hoof. A blinding light engulfed him and Susan backed away in fear. When the light dispersed, White Star was no longer a normal stag. His whole body had grown significantly, he was three times the size of a stallion. His antlers grew so that they reached the roof of the barn, his hind legs turned into that of an eagle, and wings appeared on the sides of his body. They stretched out longer than the length of the barn, so he couldn't fully expand them. Long, beautiful white and cinnamon feathers draped behind his legs and dragged onto the floor.

Susan stumbled backward and fell to the ground, speechless and trembling violently. White Star snorted and touched the ground with his antlers, and from the spot appeared a scroll, sword, shield, and key. Susan cautiously approached the objects and picked up the scroll, opening its seal. Her eyes scanned over it slowly, reading over every word carefully. The scroll read,

"To Susan Aldist Amaria Wellns, Daughter of Marcus and Defestri Wellns, in the Milky Way Galaxy, on the planet Earth, in the nation United States of America, in the state of Kansas.

You are hereby summoned to appear at the Kingdom of Zudanum, to the capital city of Mandem, on the planet Zudanum in the Phirun Galaxy.

White Star will provide you with your key, sword, and shield. Do take heed of the Winter Guardians that guard the door of Mestmin, which is the door to the city of Mandem. Prince Roi Gurri Lepon Sunar Drago will be there with the Winter Guardians waiting for you. The reason you have been called will be explained to you when you arrive.

Sincerely, his highness King Regel Formon Lepon Drago and her highness Queen Sharmon Luin Forton Drago of the Kingdom of Zudanum."

Susan stared at the message, baffled.

"Kingdom of Zudanum?" She thought. *"The Planet Zudanum? Phirun Galaxy? None of this really exists though... Does it?"* She looked up at White Star. *"Of course it's real, there's a stag with eagle legs and wings standing in front of me. Anything is possible now."*

She looked down at the sword, the mysterious metal shining in the light. She picked it up carefully and started to examine it, her arms shaking from the weight. The blade was a sharp metal she didn't know, and the handle was decorated with a dozen precious stones, many of them unrecognizable. In the center of the pommel was a glowing purple gem. She was mesmerized by it, as the inside swirled and glowed with unknown power. White Star bellowed and she moved on to the next item.

She picked up the key and the sword's metal scabbard, examining each of them closely. The key looked ancient, long, and gold with a small leather band wrapped around the end. The scabbard was as extravagant as the hilt of the sword, covered with patterns of various jewels. The waistband was made of fine leather and was uniquely designed.

She strapped on the waistband and placed the sword in its scabbard. She stumbled as she tried to get used to the weight. She picked up the shield and examined it, her arms holding the heavy metal the best she could. The metal glistened in the sunlight that streamed through the window, blinding her. She smiled as she examined the large, roaring amethyst griffin that was painted in the middle of the shield. She looked up at White Star as she slipped her arms through the straps in the back of the shield and gripped it.

"How do we get there?" Susan asked.

The idea of finally leaving this place thrilled her, even if she was nervous. But if he knew her parents, the people who wanted to see her probably did too. And that alone gave her all the courage she needed to move forward.

"Or maybe they're still alive."

She was now very eager to go, her adrenaline running already. White Star walked up to her and pressed their foreheads together. She shivered, and a second later they evaporated out of sight.

They reappeared in a lush, snowy forest. Susan jumped at the suddenness. She looked around the forest, which she could tell was far from Kansas. It started to snow around them as White Star huddled closer to her for warmth. White Star tapped the ground with his antlers and a fire, with water and food, appeared out of nowhere. Susan gasped, shocked! She looked at White Star in awe. He truly was mysterious.

"Are we going to be traveling very far?" Susan asked.

White Star shook his head.

"Are we waiting for someone?"

He nodded.

Susan slipped her arms out of the straps of her shield and set it down next to her as she sat on the ground. White Star decided to lie down, resting his head on her lap as his eyes closed. Susan couldn't think of resting, even if she wanted to. Her eyes wandered all over, admiring trees and birds in the winter wonderland she had fallen into. It was like a fairy tale forest, with an air of mystery. A bluebird flew onto a branch close to her and she smiled.

"Well, hello there," she said to the bird.

The bird tilted its head, peering at the strange girl. The bird fluffed its wings in response.

"Do I look strange to you?"

It tweeted and ruffled its wings. Susan giggled, and the bird tilted its head.

"Can it understand me?"

White Star glanced up at Susan but didn't make any sort of gesture. Susan looked up and closed her eyes.

"I've never been so far from home," she thought. *"But it's worth it. Because for the first time in my life, I feel alive."*

She daydreamed for what seemed like hours, just listening to the wind and the birds singing in the trees.

She jumped when she heard the snap of a twig from behind her, her mind instantly awake and alert. White Star also heard it and quickly got up, Susan following his action. The bluebird flew away, having been startled.

Susan grew worried as she heard footsteps come closer to them. She turned to see five men step out of the bushes. They were dressed in green and white camouflage clothing, and masks covered their faces.

"Who are you?" Susan asked, her voice shaking with fear.

"None of your concern," one of the men snapped harshly, and Susan flinched.

She knew right away these men were not the Winter Guardians her letter had spoken of. These men had a dark presence about them and she didn't like it. She glanced down at her shield on the ground, wondering if she could grab it in time, but decided against it. She pulled out her sword and held it in front of her, her arms shaking from the weight. The men hesitated as they looked at the sword, but not for long before they burst out into laughter.

"I'll bet the deer you've never used that," said another man.

She couldn't tell if he was talking to the other men or her, but she wasn't going to risk it either way. White Star stepped up next to her and lowered his antlers towards the men, ready for a fight. She looked from him to the men. *He* may be ready for a fight, but she certainly wasn't. The men started to advance towards them, weapons and ropes in their hands.

Susan was now shaking with fear, not knowing what to do next or how to defend herself. She started to lift her sword farther from her but decided to put it back in her scabbard since she didn't know how to use it.

"Surrendering already?" The leader asked, smirking as he walked towards her. "Smart move."

"Who says I'm surrendering?" Susan asked.

The man laughed as he stood in front of her. "Now let's be reasonable. You can't fight, and the deer can't protect you and himself at the same time. So, why don't you just come with me, and I'll take good care of you."

He brushed his hand against her cheek and she stiffened.

"He's not a deer."

The man raised a brow. "What?"

"He is a peryton. A deer-like creature with wings."

"Are you lecturing me?"

He brought his face closer to hers so they were only a few inches from each other. She nodded, before clenching her fist and punching him in the nose as hard as she could.

He stumbled back and gripped his nose, groaning in pain as he felt warm blood dripping down his face. He looked back at Susan with his eyes now full of anger and frustration.

"That went better than I expected," Susan commented, shaking her now throbbing hand.

She looked over to see two of the other men advancing toward her and she backed away. She looked over at White Star to see he was struggling to get rid of the ropes around him, but the other men had a good hold on him.

"Run," a voice echoed in Susan's head, but before she could react, one of the men punched her.

She fell back and was grabbed by another, who twisted her arm behind her back. The one who struck her started to punch her in the stomach and face, causing her to cry out in pain. The men let go of her and she dropped to her knees, gasping for air as she gripped her stomach and winced in pain, She heard the men laugh around her.

"Still feeling tough?" One of the men taunted Susan, the girl looking up with a mischievous twinkle in her eyes.

She started to laugh as she slowly climbed to her feet from her kneeling position. The two men frowned.

"What's so funny?"

She slowly stopped laughing and looked into the man's eyes.

"I may have only known one person all of my life, but I find it funny that a man will beat a woman to cover a mistake he made," Susan snapped.

The man growled as he grabbed her hair and raised her off of the ground. Her teeth gnashed, and she couldn't stop her cry of pain.

"Why, aren't you a brave one?"

He threw her to the ground and she scrambled back up onto her feet, only to have someone hit her on the head with a hard object. She cried out as she fell onto the ground, feeling warm liquid running through her hair and down her neck. She slowly looked up to see the leader get up, walking over and grinning as he saw her state. He grabbed an ax and lifted it over his head with a murderous look in his eye she knew couldn't be tamed.

"Well, it was fun while it lasted," she muttered as she held her hands to her face and closed her eyes, waiting for the blow.

She heard several pairs of footsteps coming closer and her eyes squeezed closer together, thinking it was more of these men. She heard a loud commotion around her, the sounds of metal clashing and men yelling filling the air. She realized these men were different but didn't dare open her eyes as she curled herself into a ball. The fight went on for a few minutes before it all stopped, and the only sound was the wind.

"Ma'am?" A voice asked, and Susan's eyes flickered open.

Chapter Two
The Prince of Zudanum

Susan cautiously looked up. In front of her stood several giant men, in loose-fitting white clothes and masks that matched the snow. Swords and quivers full of arrows hung from their sides and backs. They all looked identical, except for the man in front of her.

He wore an entirely black outfit, from his boots to his gloves, except for a snow-white cape that hung from his shoulders. He had dark brown hair, deep sea blue eyes, and an intense gaze. His sword and shield were also different from the other men, they looked similar to Susan's. His sword had different gems and markings than hers, the glowing gem on his pommel was emerald green, and his shield bore the mark of an emerald lion in mid-roar.

"I-I'm Susan Wellns," Susan stuttered. "Please don't hurt me."

The leader's expression softened and he shook his head. "We're not here to hurt you," he assured. "I'm Prince Roi Gurri Drago, and these are the Winter Guardians. I apologize for our late arrival. We had no idea they would attack you."

"It's alright. I'm fine, really."

Roi Gurri looked at her surprised. Large bruises were starting to form on her face, blood partially soaked the blonde braid falling down her back, and blood covered the back of her neck.

"This is the girl my father says will defeat A'Vaddon?" He thought.

He pulled out a white handkerchief and handed it to her. "Your head is bleeding."

Susan took the cloth and reached back, wiping the blood from her neck before dabbing it at her head wound, wincing.

"Thanks," Susan said.

Roi Gurri offered a hand to her and she stared at it cautiously.

"He has no reason to hurt me," Susan thought. *"Besides, his father is the one who called me here."*

She slowly accepted Roi Gurri's hand and he helped her up.

"Follow me," he said. "Unless you feel like staying here."

Susan picked up her shield and made sure her sword, key, and letter were secure. She looked over to find White Star freed from his bonds, a smile coming to her lips.

"Trust me, I don't," Susan replied as she and White Star followed Roi Gurri and the Winter Guardians away from the site.

They lead her through the forest, stepping with caution over patches of ice and fallen trees. Susan heard a tweet and looked up to see the bluebird from earlier, its head turning as it tweeted at her. She smiled and tapped Roi Gurri's shoulder.

"Can it understand us?" She asked, pointing to the bluebird, her eyes wide in curiosity.

He looked at the bird and gave a ghost of a smile, as he saw how fascinated she was.

"Most likely," he replied in a soft voice. "All animals can understand us in some way, they just don't know how to tell us sometimes."

They continued walking, Susan's smile wider than before. The bluebird followed them until they reached a big wooden door in a wall of uneven stone. Susan looked at the wall curiously, raising her hand to touch it.

"Don't touch the wall," Roi Gurri snapped, and she jumped as she turned to him.

"Sorry."

One of Roi Gurri's men approached her, holding out his hand.

"Your key, please," he said.

She pulled the key out of her pocket and handed it to him. He slid the key into a small slot in the door and it quickly flung open, a bright light shining through. She held her hand up to her eyes, letting them adjust. The guard returned her key before standing at attention and nodding at Roi Gurri. He nodded back at the man and motioned for Susan and White Star to follow him through the door.

Susan was in awe as she stepped through the door and warm air met her. They had stepped out of the winter forest and into a sunny flower garden surrounded by walls, a cool spring breeze meeting them. She gasped as she breathed in the air. She was instantly alert, and the fuzziness of her head wound cleared like it didn't even exist. Her mind was sharp and aware, and her lungs filled with sweet air like it was her first time breathing.

"What the-" she breathed out and Roi Gurri grinned.

"Our world has more pure oxygen than Earth does," he explained. "That's why you feel a lot more energetic.

Also, we have an ice barrier around the planet that protects us from UV rays."

Susan looked up at the sky to find it glistening like a crystal. Hints of aqua green, pink, gold, purple, and white streaked across the sparkling blue ice in waves.

"That explains why you're all giants," Susan said, still in awe of the unique sky.

"Compared to people on Earth, and to you, I suppose we would be considered giants," Roi Gurri said.

"No kidding. I feel like a midget."

They both laughed and she followed him and White Star further. Susan was awed as she looked around. Flowers of all kinds covered the grass, and stone paths trailed through the gardens, dividing them into different sections. She walked closer to some camellia bushes, gently brushing her hand over one. They were at least three times bigger than the ones on Earth, and ten times more alluring.

"Keep up!"

She looked up at Roi Gurri as he started to walk away from her. She quickly ran to catch up with him. Small children ran towards White Star and started to pet him, giving him handfuls of food and grass to eat. He gratefully accepted the treats he was given and allowed the children to touch his antlers.

Susan smiled as she looked over and saw the children. They looked to be the ages of five to nine but were the sizes of middle school students on Earth.

"I've really been kept in the dark," she thought.

Their smiles and carefree spirit reminded her of how she played alone in the fields when she was a child, pretending she was carefree as well. But, she never had the luxury of having real friends or a carefree spirit. She did her schoolwork online and had never seen any other children. She was strictly monitored about what she watched and listened to. It wasn't a very happy childhood, but she was grateful for the many books she had to keep her company

But, before she forgot, she took a quick look back, only to see the wall they had entered through was mysteriously gone.

"Magic?" She thought, but she shook her head at the thought.

Magic didn't exist and she knew it. If it did, then perhaps some sort of magic would've helped her as a kid. Maybe magic could've saved her parents if it existed.

Roi Gurri glanced back at Susan to see her smile had dropped and she was crying. He raised a brow in confusion since the last thing he had seen her doing was smiling at the sight of children playing.

"That's a strange thing to frown and cry at," he thought. *"But then again she was raised on Earth."*

She blushed as she looked up to see him staring intensely at her and quickly wiped the tears away.

"Why do you seem sad at the sight of children?" He asked.

"No, it's not that," she said, shaking her head. "The children make me happy. I wish I could've had a happy childhood like them."

"What do you mean? How was your childhood so horrible?"

"Well... because I didn't have any friends, or know anyone for that matter. I didn't have any freedom. And until today, I've only known and talked to one human being my whole life."

Roi Gurri stopped dead in his tracks and he looked back at Susan.

"You never knew anyone until you met me?" He asked, uncertain that what he heard was true.

"Well, I did know Mr. Norman!" She quickly spoke, but the sadness was still clearly in her voice.

"Who's Mr. Norman?"

"He was my guardian. Wouldn't you know who he is? Weren't you the ones who placed me on Earth?"

Roi Gurri looked troubled as he thought for a moment.

"Oh boy, this will not go well," he mumbled, but she clearly heard it.

"What do you mean?"

"You were placed with the wrong guardian. I'm afraid he may be a spy."

She frowned. "For who?"

"My father will explain it to you."

As they approached the castle Susan couldn't help but be in awe of how enormous it was. It stretched so far wide she imagined it would take all day to circle it, and so high she thought it might be touching the clouds. It was entirely made of smooth, tan-colored stone that glistened in the sunlight. The castle was surrounded by three-story pillars of the same stone, making a porch of sorts before they entered the real castle.

Susan made sure to stay close to Roi Gurri as they approached a pair of guards. The guards looked at Susan curiously as they entered but didn't dare say a word with Roi Gurri by her side.

Inside, the castle's walls and ceiling were painted with gold and lined with jewels. The walls were covered in tapestries that depicted wars and great achievements of long ago.

Soon they were outside a large pair of gold doors with diamond and emerald designs. Roi Gurri looked down and gave her a stern look.

"Don't talk until he talks to you," he warned.

Susan raised a brow. "Who is *'he'*?" She asked with a hint of fear in her voice.

"You'll know when you see him."

Roi Gurri gave her a small, reassuring smile before he pounded on the door twice with his fist and it swung open.

Susan's knees buckled as she entered a magnificent throne room. The walls were covered in silver and gold, and beautiful jewel patterns all along the walls created images and scenes of hunts and beautiful pictures of nature.

She couldn't help herself, she walked to a scene that was close to her. Surprisingly, it wasn't too hard to tell what it depicted, even though it was created with jewels. It was a picture of a golden waterfall, and two people sat near the edge of the pool.

Roi Gurri gave a fake cough and she flinched as she turned back, blushing in embarrassment.

"Sorry," she said, as she went back to him.

She followed him towards two large thrones standing at the back of the room. He walked to the bottom of a flight of stairs leading to the thrones and knelt down. Susan froze as he knelt down, not knowing what to do. She knew this wasn't how you greeted a normal person, but on the other hand, she didn't really know how to greet people normally in the first place. Her first greeting into this world was by being attacked, but then again, that's probably not a normal way to greet someone. She also knew the people they were greeting weren't normal people.

"Father," Roi Gurri greeted, his tone filled with respect, but not much warmth.

Susan was in awe as she looked up at the two people, now finally realizing they were the King and Queen of Zudanum.

The king was very tall, taller than nine feet for sure. He had a dark brown beard, and a head full of curly hair, none of it white. He was well built and had no blemish, and his body didn't appear like one of an old, or even middle-aged, man. Strong muscles climbed from his legs to his shoulders. Susan could tell he was a hard worker from the calluses on his hands. Scars showed on his hands, and arms, and some were even on his neck and face. His long, strong fingers were adorned with beautiful jeweled rings, magnificently gleaming in the bright lights. He wore long emerald robes and a flowing gold cape that looked to be made of liquid gold.

The queen, though shorter than the king, was still taller than eight feet. She had no flaws on her face, no wrinkles or blemishes of any sort. Her knee-length hair truly was magnificent, silky red strands with abnormal braids of raven black mixed in. Her body was that of a goddess, one that many women on Earth would envy! It was like that of a young woman, except for the eerie golden glow of wisdom that surrounded her. A beautiful jade necklace wrapped around her chest. Her hands were covered with soft, white silk gloves. She wore a floor-length emerald green dress that flowed around her figure, the ends laced with gold.

Large spectacular crowns sat upon their heads, far more magnificent than any of the jewels worn by Kings and Queens of Earth. The crowns were too elegant to describe, except for the fact they looked extremely heavy. They were the most amazing jewels Susan had ever seen.

Susan snapped out of her daze as she remembered the names of the king and queen from her letter. King Regel Drago and Queen Sharmon Drago. King and Queen of the Kingdom of Zudanum. She quickly knelt next to Roi Gurri and began shaking, praying she hadn't offended them or done anything wrong. Queen Sharmon smiled softly, sensing her fear and nervousness. King Regel waved his hand, his expression showing a bit of amusement as he saw her shaking. She sensed it and growled quietly to herself.

"This isn't fun," Susan thought. *"I look like an idiot. At least your wife is more respectful towards a fearful stranger."*

"Both of you, get up," King Regel ordered.

Susan and Roi Gurri both stood straight, but she didn't dare look up at King Regel and Queen Sharmon. Roi Gurri looked up into his father's eyes confidently, his back and shoulders straight.

"Father," he greeted. "This is Susan Wellns."

Susan finally looked up at them, doing her best to keep her head straight.

"Why do you have bruises?" Queen Sharmon asked her.

Susan was surprised, but she cleared her throat and looked down in respect.

"I was attacked, your majesty," she answered quietly, her voice shaking as fear still lingered.

"She actually sounded like she was worried!" She thought in wonder. *"Worry... Something Mr. Norman never did for me. Knowing someone actually feels worried for me feels strange."*

"By whom?" King Regel asked.

"She was attacked by Sudan and his men before we got there," Roi Gurri spoke for Susan, knowing she wouldn't know the men who attacked her.

"I see."

King Regel looked at Susan, who was still looking down. He stood from his throne and started to make his way down the steps. She heard his footsteps and looked up at the grand man coming towards her. She felt the urge to step back, intimidated by his height and build, but resisted it.

"Are you alright, Susan?" King Regel asked.

She was taken aback. His tone was soft, caring, almost father-like. A king and queen of another planet were worried about her?

"Yes, your majesty," she replied quietly. "I'm fine now."

"Very good. Now, the reason you were called here was that A'Vaddon is back, and we need you to finish him off for good. Now that you are older, you will be able to send him off to sheol. You will be provided with the necessary armor, of course, and anything else you might need."

"Father-" Roi Gurri interrupted.

"Not now. You will also be able to bring White Star with you if you wish. I believe it will be easier if you bring him along."

"Um... your highness?" Susan asked quietly, scared he wasn't going to like what she had to say.

"Yes?"

"I'm sorry, but I have no clue who A'Vaddon is. I've never heard of him."

King Regel was taken aback.

"Were you not taught anything about your homelands?" Queen Sharmon asked gently.

Susan's head snapped up at her and she frowned. Her shaking stopped as she suddenly grew more confident.

"This is not my home," Susan stated. King Regel and Queen Sharmon were taken aback by the abrupt statement. "I have lived on Earth my entire life, what do you mean? I only came here because White Star said he knew my parents. And also, you and your son are the first people I have ever met or talked to in my life, besides Mr. Norman. Besides White Star, I have no ties with this world."

King Regel looked at Roi Gurri, anger written on his face, but not intentionally directed at his eldest son.

"She has no idea?" He asked, outraged.

Roi Gurri nodded, not flinching at his father's reaction. King Regel balled his hands into fists, and Susan stepped back. He raised his hand and blasted the wall with some sort of green energy, causing the walls to shake. Susan stumbled away from the infuriated king.

She subconsciously raised the shield strapped to her arm, her body reacting in case it needed to defend itself. Queen Sharmon quickly rushed down the steps and stood next to her husband, gently touching his arm. King Regel looked down at the calm expression on his wife's face and started to relax. He looked over at Susan and laughed dryly as he noticed her raised shield.

"Do you really think that metal shield can stand up to my power?" He asked, gesturing to her shield.

She looked down at it and then back at him.

"He's right," she thought. *"There's no way I could possibly beat him. What was I thinking?"*

She brought her shield back down to her side, and King Regel sighed as he looked down at Queen Sharmon.

"I guess we'll have to put Susan into one of the patrols to be trained until she is ready to face A'Vaddon," he said. "Roi Gurri, take her to the Groon. When he decides what patrol to put her in please escort her to it. Afterward, you may go back to your patrol."

Roi Gurri nodded and motioned for Susan to follow him.

When the golden doors closed behind them, Roi Gurri walked towards the nearest wall and punched it as hard as he could. The wall was all of a sudden covered in vines and foliage, crawling out of the spot where his fist made contact. Susan took a step back in fear and pressed her back to the opposite wall. She hadn't processed it when Regel used his supernatural powers in front of her, but when Roi Gurri did, it shook her to the core. She could even see how the skin of his fist turned a shade of green when he used his power.

Roi Gurri looked back at her and took his hand off of the wall, the vines and leaves retracting back into his hand. He noticed her fearful expression and sighed.

"Sorry," he apologized, "I just get frustrated when my father talks down to me. I mean, obviously, I know what to do with you and where to go, he had no reason to say it."

"What are you?!" Susan screamed, her heart racing in her throat. "You and your father! How- how did you do that?"

Roi Gurri smiled warmly and started walking down the hall again. Despite being scared, his smile had her quickly running after him.

"I'm anti-natural," Roi Gurri explained. "Anti-naturals are people with special abilities, like me. On Earth, I believe you call them powers, and the people who possess them... *superheroes*."

"What are your powers?"

"Nature and healing. Healing is one of the rarest powers anyone could have, might I add."

Susan couldn't help but chuckle lightheartedly. It must be rare for Roi Gurri to brag about his abilities since everyone around him must know how special it is by now.

"What's the rarest?" Susan asked, out of curiosity.

"There are quite a few rare ones, but the first to come to mind is Gemstone. It's a strong ability, and if not controlled it can cause a lot of damage. You'll find out what your powers are soon enough, if you have any. Trust me."

She thought about what King Regel had said about placing her in a patrol, and she started to wonder what it meant.

"What are patrols?" Susan asked.

"It's like a school," Roi Gurri explained. "If a child in Zudanum has strong abilities, is a noble, or of royal blood, then the Grand Council will place them into the hands of the Groon, who will place them into a patrol. There are four patrols, and each targets different abilities within a person that will help them in a future career. For example, those in Warrior Brave often become soldiers, the Cobra Cave become diplomats, the Owl Perch go into business or law, and the Kindness Keep go into agriculture or medicine. Of course, not everyone goes on those paths, but those are the most common. The patrols all have an animal guardian that represents them. There's a wolf for the Warrior Brave, a snake for the Cobra Cave, an owl for the Owl Perch, and an eagle for the Kindness Keep. Once someone is placed in their patrol they are taught and trained to protect the core values of their patrol, and how to best protect Zudanum with their abilities and personality."

Susan's eyes filled with wonder as a smile broke out on her face. "You're in the Warrior Brave Patrol, aren't you?" She asked.

"How did you know?"

"Each animal you said symbolizes something specific in my world. A snake, for example, usually symbolizes hidden wisdom and craftiness. An owl symbolizes mystery, ancient knowledge, and sometimes magic. An eagle has always symbolized honesty and justice, and a wolf usually represents guardianship, loyalty, and spirit. By taking all of those traits, what I know about you, how you dress, and how I've seen you act, I guessed you would be in the Warrior Brave Patrol. I'll admit though, I thought for a moment you might be in Cobra Cave."

Roi Gurri raised a brow and grinned. "Are you saying I'm not wise or peaceful?"

"No, I didn't say that!"

"I'd place you in the Sloth Patrol if there was one."

Susan rolled her eyes. "I'm not slow."

"Compared to me you are. And you're also very short." Susan groaned and hugged herself. Roi Gurri laughed. "Don't worry Little Legs, I've seen some four-year-olds around your height that you can play with."

"Hey!"

She hit his side and he laughed.

"Were you trying to tickle me?"

She groaned in mock frustration. "Are all people like you? I just want to mentally prepare myself."

"No one is like me, but many are worse."

They both chuckled as they continued walking down many halls. Soon he had led her to a large wooden door with no markings, and no door handle.

"This is the Groon's room. He's the one who will place you in a patrol."

She nodded, but before she could step closer to the door, he placed a hand on her shoulder.

"Susan, what's about to happen, don't question or resist it," Roi Gurri said. "It'll make things go faster that way."

Susan raised a brow, wanting to question it, but she simply nodded instead. "Alright," she agreed.

Roi Gurri pushed open the door to the Groon's room. Susan blinked a few times to adjust to the darkness as they walked in. She looked over to see a man standing in the middle of the room. A dim light shone on him, revealing his features. He had dark, black skin. His body would have blended into the room if it weren't for the light coming through the door. He was well built and about the same height as King Regel, possibly taller. He wasn't dressed in armor or jewels, but in what to Susan looked like normal clothes.

Roi Gurri motioned for her to walk toward the man as he walked to a corner of the room, leaning against the wall. Susan looked at the man she assumed was the Groon and took a deep breath.

"Am I really about to let this man decide my fate?" Susan thought. *"If I'm placed in a patrol, then others will lay my life out for me. My life will never be mine again if I continue. But then again, my life was never mine in the first place. And, if these people want me to defeat a man named A'Vaddon, then there's no chance they'll let me walk away. I have to do this, I guess."*

Susan walked closer to the Groon until she stood in front of him.

"You are here to find out which patrol you belong to, yes?" The Groon asked.

Susan nodded, looking up into his soul-piercing eyes as they twinkled in the light.

"Yes, I am," she affirmed.

"You are not from here."

"I know."

The Groon lifted his hands and held them a little ways away from the sides of her head. "You have the same sense of humor as your father."

Susan's breathing abruptly caught in her throat. "My- My father?" She breathed out.

But before anyone could say anything else, her eyes snapped closed and she collapsed onto the stone floor.

Roi Gurri didn't even flinch as her body slammed into the stone, but he did make a small cushion of leaves for her head. He knew this was the process of finding out which patrol one belonged in, but he also knew how much his head hurt after he went through it.

Susan's whole body remained completely still as she lay on the stone floor, a thousand thoughts wanting to run through her mind, but none could as she felt the Groon enter her mind. She wanted to get up and make him leave her mind, but she couldn't. Her mind and body were being weighed down by a force, and she felt if it wasn't stopped it would soon crush her.

"Don't resist it," Roi Gurri whispered, seeing her struggling expression. "Remember, don't question or resist."

His voice echoed into her head, but it didn't calm her.

"I've never liked the idea of someone going through my thoughts," Susan thought. *"And I don't like the feeling now."*

She shivered as a tingling sensation came into her brain. It felt as if a cold, strong hand was wandering through her thoughts. The hand reached into her brain and grabbed her memories, causing her to gasp and tense as she felt fingers run through her brain.

"Who are you?" Asked a voice, causing her to shudder. "So, you're Susan Wellns. This is very interesting, I haven't seen a Wellns in a very long time.

"Should I put you in Owl Perch where the wise gather to learn? Where they seek knowledge beyond their understanding. Where they grow up to serve justice, and to govern the people who need to be led. Where they fight for justice and freedom for themselves and others.

"Should I put you in Kindness Keep, where the kind gather to learn to cure the sick and harvest the field? Where they learn to tend to the soil and heal the wounds of others. Where some learn to fight for peace and harmony.

"Should I put you in Cobra Cave, where the crafty and wise gather to learn? To become spies and sorcerers who search out the truth. Where they grow to receive information and defend the hidden wisdom they so desperately crave.

"Or should I put you in Warrior Brave, where the brave and the strong gather to learn? To become warriors and honorable men. Where they grow to defend those who cannot defend themselves. Where they go on adventures, and journey through the most dangerous passes."

"I don't care which one you put me in," Susan thought. *"Just get out of my mind."*

"I see you are strong in each of these places. But in one, you have the most strength. In one, you will go through your best and worst experiences. In one, you will grow. In one, you will suffer. In one, you will thrive. You are who you are, and I cannot put you where you don't belong. Your mother was in Kindness Keep and your father was in Cobra Cave. I knew your parents well. They would've been proud of you at this moment. I have made my decision. Get up. Now."

Susan felt herself climbing to her feet, but couldn't tell if it was really her moving or not. Her limbs were weak, only moving as if they were connected to a string. Something, or someone, was controlling her limp limbs. She didn't like it. Her eyes fluttered and she looked up to come face to face with the Groon. Her eyes adjusted to the lighting of the room, and she looked back at Roi Gurri as she felt the strings connected to her limbs release.

"You are to be put into the Warrior Brave Patrol," the Groon stated.

Her head snapped back up to him.

"Warrior Brave..." She mumbled to herself.

"Would my parents really be proud of me getting into a patrol neither of them was in?"

"Are you sure?" Roi Gurri asked as he stepped forward. "No woman has ever been in Warrior Brave. It's nearly impossible."

"Only *nearly*, young Highness," the Groon said. "It has never been done before only because no woman has had the heart to be chosen into Warrior Brave. But Susan here has the heart of a true warrior. Her Patrol name is to be Adathir."

Roi Gurri nodded and walked out, Susan quickly following him without another word. She wanted to stay and ask the Groon about her parents, but she thought it better not to hold up Roi Gurri, or possibly upset the Groon. She took one last glance at him as the door closed, wondering if she'd ever get a chance to ask him about the parents she never knew.

Chapter Three
The Warrior Brave Patrol

"Why did he give me a patrol name?" Susan asked Roi Gurri as he led her down the hall. "What is it for?"

"It's a name that represents a part of ourselves," Roi Gurri explained, "That's what the Groon says anyways, but he doesn't expand on it. We call each other by our patrol names when we're training, in danger, or on patrol. It's like a code name to conceal our identities."

"What's your patrol name?"

"Terra, which means 'Earth' in one of your ancient languages."

"It's Latin. Mr. Norman had me learn it, as well as a few other languages."

"Knowing languages is a useful skill, but have you ever noticed how quickly you were able to pick them up? Did you ever notice you could translate the words without even studying?"

Susan's head tilted. "Yes, I did. Why?"

"Long ago the Zudanums invented a chip that would expand the portion of our brain used for memorization and language comprehension. It lets us memorize any language almost instantly. After years it became a genetic trait and the chips were no longer needed."

"That's so cool!"

"By the way, we have always had a small room separate from us boys just in case a girl did make it into our patrol. You can stay there so you don't have to deal with all of us."

Susan laughed, but her expression suddenly turned grave.

"Why do you think I won't survive in the Warrior Brave Patrol?"

He frowned down at Susan. "How do you know what I'm thinking?"

"I asked you a question first."

Roi Gurri sighed. "Because it's the toughest patrol. We've been put through trials all of the others have not, and will not, be put through. All patrols have physical trials, but none are as dangerous or severe as the Warrior Brave's training procedures. And if the others did go through what we did, they would probably drop after the first trial."

"Are you saying I can't do what you can?"

"I *know* you can't. Look at our size differences and think about it. If the trials are harsh for me, they'll kill you."

Susan's spine emitted shivers down her back and she frowned.

"I'll survive," she stated confidently.

"What makes you so sure?"

"I don't know. I just feel like soon I'll have a reason to keep going. I don't have a reason now, but I'm not going to *not* try just because I don't feel a reason to live yet. I've been given a whole new world, a chance to restart. A chance to become stronger and better than I ever was on Earth. I feel as if something is going to happen soon that'll be my sign... and until that happens, I'm not giving up."

"Strong words, for a short girl who's never worked a day in her life,"

"Says who? Who are you to say you know who I am? Who gives you the right to say you know me?"

Roi Gurri's mind went blank, taken aback.

"I am the son of the king."

"Not my king."

He stopped in his tracks and she turned to him.

"That's treason to say."

"It's true, for me at least. Your father is not my king, and Zudanum isn't my home." She started walking again, but stopped and turned to him. "And furthermore, you're no 'Prince Charming'."

The rest of the walk to the Warrior Brave Patrol was silent, neither Susan nor Roi Gurri wanting or needing to speak. They were soon outside of a tall and thick oak door built inside of a stone wall. The door was carved with scenes from a forest, almost as if the door was a painting in itself. She stared at the door in awe and Roi Gurri smiled in amusement.

"It's beautiful, isn't it?" He asked her.

"Yes," she agreed. "It is."

Susan looked up to see the words "*Warrior Brave*" carved into the door.

"Ready to meet everyone?"

She took a deep breath and nodded. "Sure."

He opened the door and led her into a large living room filled with several men, some younger than others, but most looked to be teenagers and were definitely taller than Susan. The older teens sat in the comfortable, large leather chairs, and others stood on the cold stone floor, talking and laughing. The younger boys yawned and started to head over to the sleeping area. Roi Gurri fake coughed and a few of them looked over and noticed Susan. They all immediately stopped what they were doing.

"Now now," said one of the men, "Who is this beautiful young lady?"

Susan froze. She wasn't used to being put in the spotlight, especially not by a bunch of giants.

"I'm going to guess a very young child," one of the men said, laughing.

The older men joined in the laughter. Susan glared at the man and placed her hands on her hips.

"For your information, I'm seventeen," she stated and some of the men laughed.

"Seventeen?" One of them asked. "Have you not grown at all since you were born?"

Susan groaned and Roi Gurri laughed.

"Everyone, this is Susan Wellns," Roi Gurri introduced. The room went silent, and the boys glanced at each other. The Wellns name was known well. "She just came from Earth, and since their atmosphere is different she didn't grow as much as we did. She has now officially joined this patrol."

All of the men laughed, even the younger boys.

"You can't be serious," one said.

"I'm being very serious. Her patrol name is Adathir. The Groon chose her to be in Warrior Brave. I was there."

All of the men gave each other knowing looks. They glanced at each other's scraped and bruised skin in comparison to the pale, now very bruised skin of Susan, causing some of them to shake their heads.

"Well then," said another man, who wore a metal mask that covered his entire face up to his eyes, and his neck. "We must give the first woman to be in the Warrior Brave Patrol a proper welcome." He walked up to Susan and extended a large hand toward her. "I'm William Sumander. My patrol name is Silentium, and I'll be your tour guide for tonight."

Susan firmly shook his hand and decided right away she liked him. From what she could see he had soft, beautiful honey-brown eyes, and buzzed brown hair. She couldn't see any of his other features, but she noted that the metal mask looked hand-made, several different colors of metal were welded together to make it. His eyes smiled as he noticed her observing his mask. She also observed he smelled like oak wood.

"Sorry about the mask, but I have scars and I don't necessarily like to show them," William explained.

"Of course, sorry if I was staring," Susan apologized.

"It's fine, lots of people do. Anyways, the door in the back of the room leads to the sleeping area, and in the back left corner of that room is your room. The door on the right over here leads to the equipment room which is where we sometimes work out and sharpen our weapons. The kitchen is over there on the left. We only eat there for breakfast though, we eat lunch and dinner with the other patrols. Caroldus over there is the one who makes breakfast. Of course, his food sucks, so we only eat it when we're starving or if we skipped dinner the night before."

"I heard that!" Caroldus yelled.

Susan and the other men laughed.

"I'll make sure you don't starve tomorrow," Susan assured.

"Why do you say that?"

"Because I'll make breakfast for you instead. If you train as hard as I hear you do, you shouldn't be skipping meals."

"Are you sure you won't burn it?"

"Or make it explode in your face?" Roi Gurri muttered, but they still heard it, causing them to laugh.

"I've been cooking since I was very young, I think I've got this," Susan assured.

"Looks like you might finally get replaced, Caroldus!" William called. "Anyway, our restroom and shower room is that door over there, and yours is in your room."

"And now, we must sing the Warrior Brave Patrol song!" Caroldus called from across the room, the men groaning in unison.

"A song?" Susan asked.

"It's a tradition Caroldus made," Roi Gurri explained with an eye roll. "It's stupid, but he does it for some reason."

"It's not stupid!" Caroldus protested as he stepped forward. "It's fun!"

Susan looked up at him to see he was very handsome, with very dirty blonde hair and greyish hazel eyes. He looked to be Roi Gurri's height but was leaner than the young prince.

"For you at least," one of the men said to Caroldus. "It makes the rest of us look like idiots."

"Fine, then I'll do it by myself."

The other men started to laugh and cheer for Caroldus, chanting his name.

"Do not despair fair gentleman!" Caroldus said dramatically, as he jumped up on a wooden table in the middle of the living room. "I am here to sing!"

Susan bit her lip to hold in her laughter, while the other men laughed freely. Caroldus placed a hand on his heart and cleared his throat.

"Now you're new to the Warrior Brave Patrol," he sang, looking at Susan and she smiled as she crossed her arms.

"So you may have heard we're brutal, violent, and even crazy! And that may be slightly true, but when we get the cue... we're a lot more than swords and gore!"

He spun on the table and did a few dance moves with his feet.

"So come with me, take my hand, and I'll show you the other side of a wolf guardian's heart!"

The other men started clapping a beat and Caroldus danced to it on the table. Susan smiled as he walked to the edge of the table, in front of where she stood, and held his hand out to her.

"As soon as you cross this table, as soon as you start singing with me, you become a guardian of the wolves' heart and cave!"

Susan confidently took his hand. The men cheered and Caroldus smiled warmly as he pulled her onto the table next to him.

"If you want to survive the ride then stay with me. I'll show you how to survive till we get to the other side! So if you want to survive the patrol that guards the wolves' heart, then stay with me until you can handle the ride on your own!"

Susan smiled and squealed as Caroldus spun her around the table, the men clapping and cheering.

"Now it's your turn to sing!" He said to her, and her expression fell.

"What?!" She exclaimed, taking a step back. "No no no, you don't understand, I can't sing at all."

"You don't have a choice, Ms. Wellns."

Caroldus grinned and the other men laughed, starting to chant her name.

"Fine, fine, fine!"

Susan pulled in a deep breath as she thought of words to sing.

"I see now there's more to the Warrior Brave Patrol than I've been told."

She sang sheepishly, causing Caroldus to smile.

"I thought I'd die the second I walked in since I'm so small and fragile compared to all of you."

The men laughed and she smiled as she started to sing louder and become bold.

"But now I see there's more to the feared Wolf Patrol than meets the eye. Now I've never been out in the world, but if you're so brave that you'll jump up on a table and burst into song, then I was placed in the right patrol!"

The men cheered as Caroldus and Susan bowed, laughing together.

"You were right," Caroldus said to Susan, "You can't sing at all,"

More laughter prevailed and Susan shot a playful glare at Caroldus as she hit his side.

"I told you!" She exclaimed as she and Caroldus jumped off of the table.

"Now, now," William said. "If Susan is to join Warrior Brave then she must go through *my* initiation as well."

The men cheered, but Roi Gurri frowned.

"William," he said, his tone low, but William raised a hand to silence him.

"You know we have to. If Caroldus gets to sing his stupid song then I get to do this."

"Hey!" Caroldus exclaimed before hitting William's side.

William's eyes grinned at Caroldus before turning to Roi Gurri.

"Come on, I'm your best friend! Surely you trust me with Susan."

"Wait, I thought *I* was his best friend," Caroldus countered.

Roi Gurri rolled his eyes at Caroldus's comment and gave Susan a worried look. She nodded at him, trying to assure herself she was willing to go through with whatever William's form of initiation was. She wanted to be a full part of the Warrior Brave Patrol. If that meant proving herself, she was willing to go through with anything. She turned back to William and stared into his eyes confidently.

"Bring it," she challenged, both her and William grinning.

The boys 'oohed' and cheered.

"Alright then, Wellns," William said, "I hope you're mentally stable and have a strong back. Come with us, we're going somewhere else."

She nodded as they, and some others, walked out. She followed William to the roof of the castle and her heart started racing.

"Heights," she thought. *"Is that what William's initiation is going to be about?"*

She looked over to Roi Gurri for help, but only found he was at the very back of the crowd of men. Despite him being in the back of the group, she was calmed knowing someone she knew was close by. She was pushed onto the roof, skeptically looking up at William.

"Come with me," he said, placing his hand on her back.

He led her over to the edge of the roof and she started shaking. She tried to stop, knowing William would feel it, but she couldn't help it.

"Don't be afraid," he whispered to her. "Look into the horizon. Tell me what you see."

Susan's gaze swept over the Zudanum horizon. This was the highest she had been in her life, no tree could dream of reaching the top of the castle. No tree could dream of having this view either.

"I see the forest," Susan said quietly. "I see the city and glistening nights. I see the crystal-covered sky."

"Good. Don't worry, it'll be over soon." His calming voice helped her nerves. "Now, stand on the ledge."

She hesitantly obeyed. She climbed onto the ledge and looked back at him.

"What now?" Susan asked.

He looked into her eyes, calm and collected. They were so close she could see small flecks of gold in his irises. A murderous look suddenly appeared in his eyes and Susan's heart raced. His cold, metal mask brushed over her cheek as he leaned close to speak to her.

"Die," William whispered in a dark tone.

Susan's heart jolted. Before she could react he pushed her off of the ledge and she went toppling off of the castle. She screamed as she fell. The wind swirled all around her, rushing away as if it was trying to escape being crushed. Her heart palpitated as she fell farther and farther away from the top of the castle. All of her senses were clouded, fear stopping them from working. His laughter disturbed her.

"Why is he-"

Her thoughts were interrupted as she abruptly bounced from the ground back up to William. She gasped.

"What's going on?"

"Look down!" William called, laughing.

She looked down to see a plant under her, which caused her to bounce. It had thousands of small, blueish, rubber-like leaves that caused her body to shoot up upon contact.

"What is this?!" Susan asked.

"It's a Dormotilist!" Roi Gurri called down. "It's a bouncing plant!"

She relaxed and started laughing. It was gentle at first but quickly turned hysterical. Both William and Caroldus jumped off the roof to join her, Caroldus grabbing her hand so they'd stay close.

"How do we get off of this thing?" Susan asked him.

"Someone will have to pull us off!" He replied, "And who knows when they'll do that!"

She gasped and he laughed.

"Caroldus!"

***

Around eleven o'clock at night, after they had had their fun, they all started to make their way back to the Warrior Brave room. Susan's breathing slowed, and sweat dripped from her red, happy face.

"That was amazing!" She exclaimed to Caroldus.

"I know!" He said. "Did you really think William was going to kill a beautiful girl like you?"

She shrugged and blushed. "Who knows? Compared to what I know about Earth, this place is crazy."

"I'm sure."

They both laughed as they entered the Warrior Brave room. Caroldus flopped down onto a couch, pulling Susan down next to him. She laughed as she landed halfway on the couch and halfway on him. She leaned against his side, positioning herself so she was comfortable. Neither of them noticed the glare Roi Gurri sent Caroldus's way.

"This night has been amazing," Susan said quietly. "I just hope it doesn't all turn out to be a dream,"

Caroldus looked down at Susan, a sorry look on his face. He couldn't imagine what she must be going through, but he was determined to make her feel as at home as possible. With that thought in mind, he grinned.

"Does this feel like a dream?" He asked before whacking her with a large feather pillow.

Susan squealed before falling off the couch, and the other men laughed. She glared at him, got up, grabbed a different pillow, and smacked him with it.

"No one smacks me with a pillow and gets away with it!" Caroldus cried dramatically.

"You started it!"

Susan giggled as they started hitting each other with the pillows. Roi Gurri leaned against the wall and chuckled, watching the two. William stood next to him.

"Caroldus will never grow up," William muttered.

"Probably," Roi Gurri agreed. "You may not either."

"I'm more mature. He's a bit childish. There's a big difference."

"So, your prank of an initiation isn't considered childish?"

William shrugged. "My grandfather started the tradition for the Warrior Brave Patrol, and I intend to keep it alive."

The door abruptly swung open and they looked over to see their physical trainer walk in.

"Alright everyone, time for the lights to go off!"

Everyone else turned towards the door to see a very dark, muscular woman standing inside the doorway. She loomed over all of the men and was at least nine feet tall. She was built like a warrior, and a large scar ran down the left side of her face, very close to her eye. She wore a leather outfit that showed her curves and muscular build. Her long, dreaded black hair was laced with many silver strands.

The woman looked at Susan, her face expressionless. Susan set down the pillow she was hitting Caroldus with, stood straight, and looked into the woman's dark brown eyes with respect.

"I'm Scadrin and I'm your instructor," she said. "Whatever I say goes. I will not tolerate disobedience. Do you understand me?"

"Yes ma'am," Susan said, her voice firm.

"You will begin training the day after tomorrow with the others. You will not be off to the side just because it will be your first day. And, I don't care if you are smaller or weaker than all the men, you will be doing *all* the training exercises they do."

Roi Gurri, William, and Caroldus were alarmed as they looked at Scadrin.

"But Scadrin!" Caroldus protested. "She won't-"

"She won't survive!" Roi Gurri cut off Caroldus.

William and Susan exchanged glances. Susan sighed. William didn't speak up because he knew Scadrin wouldn't change her mind, no matter who protested. And also, when Caroldus sang his song, he did say he would help her until the end of the 'ride'. William applied that part of the song to himself as well. So, it didn't matter what Scadrin said, he would help Susan get through the trials.

"I'm not changing my mind," Scadrin stated firmly as she glared at them. "Susan will be training with us, whether you like it or not. You can help her if you like, but let me warn you, babysitting a girl while trying to train will take a lot of time. It'll be hard to keep up, and remember you have trials coming up soon."

Roi Gurri growled in frustration. "But she's the Chosen One!" He protested.

"Then she should be able to easily keep up, shouldn't she?" Scadrin shot at Roi Gurri, who shut his mouth. "Now, it's time to rest. Tomorrow is the day of rest, and I'm sure you all will want your energy."

The men nodded, some heading towards the sleeping area.

Susan cast her eyes to the ground as she turned and started to walk towards the back door, feeling her friend's eyes on her. She knew she would only slow them down if they tried to help her, but she secretly hoped that they would help her anyway. She knew she wouldn't survive without their help.

"I guess I'll have to try to keep up on my own," Susan thought sadly. *"I'm sure their equipment is bigger than mine, but I'll have to do my best."*

William glared at Scadrin before he quickly followed Susan.

"Hey, Susan," he said, placing a hand on her shoulder. She turned and looked up at him. "Don't listen to Scadrin. I'm going to help you train, I promise. Besides, I don't mind spending two extra years in the Warrior Brave Patrol if I fail trials."

"I don't want to hold you back, William," Susan responded. "If you have a chance to speed up and leave me, then take it."

William shook his head. "You're going to make it, I promise. Do you doubt me?"

Susan smiled. "No, I guess not. You seem to be a trustworthy guy." The two chuckled. "Good night, William."

"Good night, Susan."

She walked towards the door leading to the sleeping area. When she opened the door, she saw several bunk beds and dressers, all of them organized and without clutter.

She looked at the wall on the left and saw a small door she assumed led to her room. She hesitated to turn the doorknob. She looked back at the men, wondering if when she woke up it would all be a dream, just part of her imagination, and she would be back in her room on Earth.

"Please don't let it be a dream," Susan whispered to herself.

Scadrin frowned as she saw her muttering.

"Is something the matter, Adathir?" Scadrin asked her.

Susan shook her head, not looking in Scadrin's direction. She walked into her room and was greeted by a large bed along the wall, a dresser, and a desk and chair.

"It looks comfortable enough," Susan thought, quickly noticing everything was larger than anything she was used to.

She climbed onto her bed, exhausted from the night she just had with the guys. She smiled as she thought about the first time she actually laughed with a group of friends, just like in her dreams. With that thought in mind, her eyes shut and she fell into a sleep so deep she didn't even dream.

In the living room, some of the men continued to yell and be wild in the now dark, but Roi Gurri, William, and Caroldus headed toward the sleeping area for their beds. They were some of the oldest and most mature in the Patrol. They knew the importance of sleep.

"Susan is quite the girl isn't she, Roi Gurri?" Caroldus asked the man beside him, looking over to see his reaction.

Roi Gurri nodded but didn't say anything to give away what he was thinking.

"She's pretty, too," added William as he walked over to his dresser drawer and pulled out some night clothes.

"It's a shame she won't survive Warrior Brave," Caroldus mumbled, following William's actions.

"She *will* survive," William whispered, almost to himself, but the others heard.

"How would you know that?" Roi Gurri asked.

"Because I'm going to help her train, and I'll keep her safe from the trials the best I can. She won't be able to survive on her own, but if some of us help her, she might just have a chance. Besides, if she really is the Chosen One we have to help her if we want A'Vaddon gone."

The other two men nodded.

"I agree with you," Roi Gurri said as he walked over to his bed. "It'll be good for Susan to be around some people."

"Why do you say that?" Caroldus asked, raising a brow as he changed his shirt. "I'm sure she had lots of friends on Earth."

"No, before she came here she only knew one person her entire life," Roi Gurri explained.

"What about her parents?"

"She was too young, she probably doesn't even remember their faces. We're the only friends she's ever had, if she even considers us friends."

Caroldus looked shocked, not able to imagine life without his friends. The ones he placed all of his trust in, and the ones who always had his back. William had no response as to how he felt, and no one could read his expression with the mask on.

"How?" William asked.

"The person who was taking care of her never let her see anyone and never let her talk to anyone," Roi Gurri explained.

Both William and Caroldus frowned.

"But guardians aren't supposed to be like that," William protested as he climbed into his bunk above Roi Gurri's.

"She was placed with the wrong guardian."

William and Caroldus froze as they looked at Roi Gurri.

"What?" Caroldus asked. "How?"

Roi Gurri shook his head. "I don't know, but hopefully my father is looking into it."

"Roi Gurri, you know what that means, right?" William asked. "That man could've been a spy."

"I know," Roi Gurri nodded.

Caroldus sighed. "Hopefully Scadrin will take it easy on her," he said quietly.

"We all know that's not going to happen," William said. "Scadrin never takes it easy on anyone, not even if they have a sprain or a broken bone."

"She might not need it anyway," Roi Gurri said, relaxing as he sat on his bunk. "Before the Winter Guardians and I got to her and White Star, they were attacked by the Forest Loons. She had the guts to fight Sudan and one of his other men before we got there. She actually gave him a bloody nose and a few bruises. He did worse to her, but she quickly shook it off."

"I do have to admit, Sudan is pretty tough, but Sudan's not quite as tough as... Well, you know, A'Vaddon. He wiped out legions of soldiers and over a dozen anti-naturals, and Susan doesn't look like she's trained a day of her life."

Roi Gurri shuddered at the sound of the name of A'Vaddon, memories and thoughts racing through his mind. A'Vaddon was a demon everyone feared, even King Regel, though he didn't admit it.

"Yeah, that's true," Caroldus said as he sat on his bunk, which was across from Roi Gurri's. "But if Susan was able to somehow scare A'Vaddon away for all these years, she could probably scare him away for good. Or, better yet, defeat him once and for all."

"We can only hope that day comes soon," William muttered.

"There's something else," Roi Gurri said. "When the Winter Guardians and I came out to face Sudan and his men, I noticed Susan's ears perked at the sound of our footsteps before we even came out."

"And?" William asked.

"Well, wouldn't you think Sudan and his men would've heard us if Susan was able to? Because she was raised most of her life on Earth, she didn't grow the same way all of us here on Zudanum did, which means her senses didn't either. But the fact she seemed to hear and sense us before Sudan did surprises me."

Caroldus thought about that for a moment.

"You do have a good point," Caroldus said. "Do you think Susan may have super hearing?"

Roi Gurri shook his head. "No, Susan isn't anti-natural. I know an anti-natural when I see one. I think she may have a special ability, though. Like how I have the ability to never forget, but it isn't considered an anti-natural ability."

William and Caroldus both nodded.

"Yeah, that's most likely it," William agreed. "What do you think her ability is?"

"Enhanced senses, for sure. But every person who has had the ability of enhanced senses can be compared to an animal. What I want to know is what animal Susan's senses are compared to."

"Yeah, same," Caroldus agreed. "We'll have Scadrin test her."

"Yeah."

There was silence for a moment, and Caroldus looked into Roi Gurri's eyes.

"Should we talk about him?" Caroldus asked.

No one said a word. Roi Gurri's eyes fell to the ground, and his hands gripped his bedsheets as painful memories surfaced in his mind.

"No," Roi Gurri whispered. "Not now."

Caroldus nodded in understanding, but he felt the itch in his chest to relive the past. He felt the words threatening to run past his lips, but held them back. If Roi Gurri wasn't ready, neither was he.

"Good, now let's get to bed," William said, relieving some of the tension as he lay down. "I'm actually excited to see what Susan makes for breakfast. Hopefully, it'll be something better than your cooking, Caroldus."

Caroldus rolled his eyes as he lay down. "My cooking is just misunderstood," he insisted, dramatically placing a hand on his heart.

"Last time you tried to bake bread it exploded in my face and I had goo in my hair for a month," Roi Gurri snapped with a grin.

"Thankfully, I *heard* it before it exploded," William said.

The men gave a quick laugh as they closed their eyes.

Chapter Four
A Day in the Market

Susan abruptly woke up as she was hit by a cold wind. She shivered and groaned, slowly sitting up. She rubbed her eyes and looked over to see she had kicked the blankets off the bed in her sleep.

"No wonder I'm so cold," she mumbled, yawning as she undid her braid and let her hair loose.

She looked around the room to find it was dusty. A cold draft came from somewhere, but she couldn't tell where.

"Hardly anyone has been in this room for about... Twenty years I would say," she thought as she jumped off of the bed.

She placed the blankets on the bed and turned to the door to see a pile of clothes and toiletries in front of the door. On top of it was a small folded note with her name written on it.

"Queen Sharmon thought you needed some new clothes and some personal toiletries.

-Scadrin."

She cracked a small smile.

"Queen Sharmon... She seems awfully concerned for me. I wonder why."

Susan looked down at the things on the floor. Several pairs of clothes and a pair of combat boots were folded neatly, along with three cloaks. She lifted one of the shirts and compared it to her size.

"Looks like she had clothes made that would actually fit me. Or they're children's clothes."

It felt nice for someone to be concerned about her personal hygiene and welfare like a mother would. She quickly changed and got ready for the day before walking out to test her new shoes.

"They're a pretty good fit. A tad bit small, but better than having them be too big and making me stumble around."

Susan walked over to her sword lying on her bed, strapping the scabbard to her side with the leather strap. She grabbed her shield and quietly walked toward the door, slowly opening it.

She peeked through the door to see all the men still resting peacefully. Roi Gurri and William's bunk was right in front of her room. Caroldus slept next to theirs, closer to the door that led out. She quietly slipped out of her room.

"Don't wake up, don't wake up," she repeated in her head, walking out as quietly as possible.

She remembered Scadrin had mentioned something about today being a day of rest, so she didn't want to disturb anyone. She managed to get out of the room and let out a breath.

"They looked like they were sleeping pretty deeply. Hopefully, they sleep a little longer and let me get some time to myself."

Her ears perked as she heard heavy footsteps and the sound of wheels coming toward the room. Her nose twitched, smelling a pleasant aroma.

"Whoever it is, they're carrying food."

She heard grunting from the other side of the door and walked over to open the door for the person. She looked up to see a man looking down at her in surprise. He had midnight black hair and very bright chestnut eyes. His skin was smooth and pale, with barely a blemish on it.

"Do you need help?" Susan asked, eyeing a large amount of food and drink in a small cart behind him.

"Uh, yeah- yeah, sure."

He looked very surprised to see a woman in the Warrior Brave Patrol.

"I'm new," Susan explained, opening the door for him as he brought the cart in.

"But you're so small," the man blurted out, his eyes widening as the words left his mouth.

Susan smiled and shook her head. "Oh really?" She asked sarcastically and he chuckled.

"Sorry,"

"It's fine. I grew up on Earth, and the atmosphere there is different, so I grew differently than you guys do."

"That makes you Susan Wellns, right?"

Susan froze as she looked up at him. "Yeah, how did you know?"

"Word gets around pretty fast in this castle. Besides, if the King wanted to keep you a secret then he would. Over a quarter of the planet probably knows about your arrival to Zudanum."

"Oh. I didn't realize I had that effect on people."

The two of them chuckled as they finished placing the food and drinks on the table in the kitchen.

"So, does someone bring food for breakfast for all of the patrols every morning?" Susan asked.

"Yeah, I deliver food once a week. All of the patrols eat breakfast in their own rooms, and then lunch and dinner they eat together in a grand hall."

"I see. I guess it's less chaotic that way."

"Definitely. Well, I have to go now, but it was an honor meeting you, Adathir."

Susan raised a brow, and then she remembered the Groon had given her that name.

"I guess that's what others are supposed to call me now," she thought.

"Thanks." The man turned and started to walk out. "Wait," she stopped him. "I never got your name."

He smiled. "My friends call me Legion."

"It was nice to meet you too, Legion."

Legion smiled and nodded as he walked out of the room.

Susan let out a breath and turned back to the kitchen. She looked at all of the food in front of her and sighed.

"I guess you need a ton of food to feed a ton of giant men," she muttered.

Spotting a stool in the corner she grabbed it so she could reach the shelves and see what could be made with the food in front of her.

***

About forty-five minutes later Roi Gurri woke up to the smell of fried bacon and eggs. He groaned as he slowly opened his eyes, adjusting to the dim light in the room before sitting up. He looked around seeing the others still asleep.

"They wasted most of their energy last night fooling around," Roi Gurri thought. *"They'll be asleep for two more hours at least unless someone wakes them up. Caroldus and William will be asleep for maybe twenty more minutes."*

He walked to his dresser and silently changed, remembering the times he wasn't the first one to be awake. Good times. He walked out into the kitchen to find Susan making breakfast like she had said she would the night before. He noted she was wearing a new outfit and her hair was done neatly.

"Sharmon is probably behind that," he thought, knowing his stepmother well.

He looked down at the eating table to see the table set with equal amounts of round bread, bacon, and eggs on each plate, full with a considerably good-sized portion.

Susan glanced up to see Roi Gurri, smiling softly in acknowledgment. She was glad to see a familiar face, it was refreshing after meeting Legion.

"Good morning Roi Gurri," Susan said softly.

"Morning," Roi Gurri replied in the same tone, offering a smile. "Did you sleep well?"

"I think it was the best sleep I've had in all seventeen years of my life. I slept like a rock."

Roi Gurri looked down at Susan, surprised she didn't sound as nervous as she did the day before.

"She gains confidence pretty quickly," Roi Gurri thought to himself, keeping a mental note.

"That's good," he said. "I thought you would have trouble, considering it's a new place."

"Me too, but I guess I was pretty worn out because of the jumping last night."

"Makes sense. Caroldus and William can be draining sometimes."

Susan chuckled and shook her head. "Nah, I like them."

"That makes two of us."

There was silence for a moment until Susan cleared her throat.

"So is today a holiday or something?"

Roi Gurri shook his head. "No. Once a week we have a day of rest, to honor our God, Jehoyam, who made everything in seven days. He rested on the seventh day, so we rest on the seventh day as well."

Susan abruptly stopped and looked up at Roi Gurri. "You believe in Him too?"

"What do you mean?"

"I just thought... I never thought people *not* from Earth would have a God who made everything in seven days."

Roi Gurri smiled. "You believe in Him?"

"I think I do," Susan said hesitantly. "But I'm still not sure. Mr. Norman never told me otherwise, except for what was written in school textbooks. But the logic in those books just didn't add up to me."

"Why?"

"A lot of people on Earth have some... interesting theories about how Earth was created, to say the least."

Roi Gurri raised a brow before he burst out laughing.

"I'm sorry," he apologized, recomposing himself as Susan chuckled. "I've studied some of Earth's culture, and I agree with you."

"I don't blame you."

The two laughed, and Roi Gurri looked over at a large clock hanging on the wall.

"It's almost eight," he thought.

"Should I wake up the others?" He offered, Susan nodding as she finished setting the table.

"Sure, I'm almost done anyways."

Roi Gurri turned to leave when he spotted two empty pans next to her. He grinned, and she chuckled as she saw a gleam of mischief in his eyes.

"Do you need those?" Roi Gurri asked.

"Knock yourself out."

He grabbed the pans as he went back into the sleeping area. Susan shook her head.

"Men," she muttered to herself.

Roi Gurri walked into the sleeping area and smirked as he stood in the middle of the room, a pan in each hand.

"They're all going to kill me, but it'll be worth it," Roi Gurri thought as he started banging the pans as hard as he could against each other.

Several men fell out of their bunks in surprise, while others sat up too quickly, banging their heads on either the top bunk or the ceiling.

"What in the name of King Fumin?!" Caroldus exclaimed as he banged his head on the bunk above, throwing his blankets off.

Roi Gurri burst out in laughter at his friends' reactions, setting the pans aside.

"Breakfast is served," Roi Gurri said in a sing-song tone, smirking. "I'm not sure why I've never done this before. I'll be doing this on random mornings since I now know this is the reaction I'll get."

William sprang out of his bed and threw a pillow down at Roi Gurri who easily dodged it and laughed.

"You throw like my little sister, William."

A few of the other men also threw their pillows at Roi Gurri as they quickly changed and walked to the kitchen.

William paused when he saw Susan was there. His breath caught in his throat, and Susan glanced up at the sound. She noticed William was looking down at her in surprise as he sat down to eat. She just smiled at him, thinking he was surprised she actually made food.

"I'm sure he'll adjust to the fact I live here within a day," Susan thought to herself.

William had almost thought last night was all just a dream, but no. It was real. The supposed Chosen One was standing before him, and she didn't even know a thing about her family or her homeworld. It was like a nightmare in a dream come true.

"She knows nothing..." William thought sorrowfully. *"I'll have to teach her then, I'll have to be the one to tell her everything, won't I? It'll be like having the little sister I always wanted."* He smiled fondly at the thought before relaxing.

Susan smiled warmly as the men entered the kitchen, walking out into the living room so they could have their privacy. Roi Gurri looked over to see Susan walk away, assuming she had already eaten. He walked over and sat between William and Caroldus.

"This is the best food I've ever had," Caroldus said through a mouthful, causing William to twist his mouth in disgust. A small panel opened on William's mask, an opening where he could eat.

"I couldn't agree more," William said after the first bite. "She's a way better cook than you, Caroldus. But then again, anyone and everyone is better at cooking than you."

"Shut up, William," Caroldus said as he hit William's arm. "Doesn't your patrol name mean silence?"

William sent Caroldus a playful glare, as the panel on his mask closed again.

"Speaking of patrol names, I think your name should've been 'Loud Mouthed One' instead of 'Crystal Heart', since you're so keen on talking all the time."

"Then maybe yours should've been called 'The Party Killer One'."

William growled and Roi Gurri laughed, but he didn't comment on anything.

"Roi Gurri's patrol name is the only one that makes sense," William stated and Caroldus nodded.

"Terra is a fitting name for someone who has nature powers," Caroldus agreed. "But maybe the name 'Earth' should've been given to an anti-natural who has Earth powers,"

"He *does* have earth powers, you idiot."

"No, Roi Gurri controls *nature,* not 'earth'. Nature is plants, earth is rock."

As the two started another debate about Roi Gurri's power, Roi Gurri glanced out to see Susan sitting on a chair reading a book. He looked a little closer at the book which was titled, *The Patriarch of Justice*. Roi Gurri smiled.

"So, she found the books about the Kings," Roi Gurri thought to himself. *"It looks like King Aldist intrigues her. Well, it's really no surprise. Everyone loves to study her."*

"Susan!" William called, causing Roi Gurri to flinch.

Susan looked up to find Roi Gurri staring at her and he quickly looked away, a slight blush dusting his cheeks.

"Susan!" William called again. "Get over here so we can give you a medal."

The other men laughed and hollered for her to come over. She quickly got up and walked over to them, her blushing face frozen with surprise, but she felt glad the men enjoyed her food. William motioned for her to come to sit down next to him, and she shyly sat between him and Roi Gurri.

"I've never had that kind of compliment before," she said, still blushing. "Come to think of it, I've never really had a compliment."

William laughed and gave her a reassuring look since she couldn't see his smile.

"If you train as well as you cook, then I can assure you that you'll be getting that a lot," he assured.

"Do we have training today?" Susan asked, a bit excited.

"No, we don't have training on a day of rest." He looked at Caroldus and Roi Gurri, then back at Susan. "I have to let you know, last night Roi Gurri, Caroldus, and I had a little talk about you."

Susan looked at him, surprised. "Why?"

"We were talking about how you likely won't survive the Warrior Brave Patrol and the trials," Caroldus said.

"So we decided we are going to help you train," William explained. "Hopefully, you can pass the trials and one day defeat A'Vaddon."

"I've been meaning to ask you something," Susan said, nervously fumbling with her hands. "Who is A'Vaddon?"

She didn't like the sound of his name, and a bad feeling came over her whenever she heard it. Roi Gurri looked down at Susan, his eyes were dark with anger and sorrow.

"A'Vaddon is the most powerful anti-natural in the Realm," Roi Gurri explained, his tone serious. "The only ones who are supposedly equal to him are your family, and the only one he fears is my father. Almost seventeen years ago he tried to take over the kingdom. My father had several powerful anti-naturals go up against A'Vaddon, but either they turned to his side or he destroyed them. My real mother was one of those who was killed trying to fight him, even though my father tried to stop her from fighting. A'Vaddon was also the one who killed your parents." Roi Gurri looked away from Susan so she wouldn't see the tears in his eyes.

"But, for some reason, he couldn't kill you," Roi Gurri continued, forcing himself to turn and look down into Susan's eyes. "He tried, but he couldn't. Ever since then, he's been hiding, until a few weeks ago when he was spotted in the Pradosion Mountains. So, we sent White Star to fetch you, hoping you had some knowledge of who you are, and that you'd be ready to fight him. But, I guess you ended up with the wrong guardian, which means that A'Vaddon has a great advantage at the moment."

Susan looked down, trying to comprehend what Roi Gurri had just told her.

"How am I supposed to destroy A'Vaddon when I don't even have any powers?" Susan asked. "What if I don't have any powers? And I don't know anything about this place. Not how anti-naturals work, who or what A'Vaddon is, I don't even know anything about my own family."

Susan's hands clenched, and William placed a comforting hand over her fist.

"We'll train you," Caroldus assured, "Hopefully soon you'll gain your powers and take down A'Vaddon. I know you'll be able to do it one day, especially if you have us train you!"

Susan smiled at Caroldus, and she nodded.

"How many people have powers?" She asked. "Is it common to have them?"

"No, not very many people have them," William said. "Roi Gurri is the only one who has powers in Warrior Brave so far. There are two who are anti-natural in the Cobra Cave Patrol I think, three in Owl Perch, and two in Kindness Keep."

"That doesn't sound like a lot of people," Susan commented.

"It isn't," Caroldus agreed. "But word has it that A'Vaddon has quite a few anti-naturals who are willing to fight for him, so King Regel has been looking for anti-naturals too. He hopes that A'Vaddon doesn't have all of them."

"Hopefully he doesn't, I can't fight several anti-naturals at once, at least not now. Maybe not even ever, if you're all giants."

Caroldus chuckled and William nodded.

"Yeah, we're all giants," William agreed. "A'Vaddon is rumored to be taller than King Regel."

Susan was horrified, letting out a shaky breath.

"T-Taller than King Regel?" Susan asked, and the three boys nodded. She chuckled nervously, gripping the hilt of her sword. "That's pretty tall."

"Yeah, it's even tall for us," Caroldus said.

William shot him a look that told him to shut up.

"Well, good to know I guess," Susan said.

She nodded at the boys as she got up and started to clear the men's dishes. Roi Gurri quickly got up to help her, causing Caroldus to grin knowingly.

"Thanks," Susan said to Roi Gurri.

He nodded at her and politely smiled. They walked to the sink and washed and dried the plates. Once they were done, William motioned for them to come to sit with him and Caroldus. They walked over to see

Caroldus had a piece of paper, and he seemed to be making plans.

"What's going on?" Susan asked, sitting next to Caroldus and looking at the paper he was writing on.

"He's making plans for what we're going to do today," William said.

Caroldus was too focused to respond. Susan giggled, looking at the serious expression on his face as he continued making plans, seeming not to hear them.

"Why does he look so serious?" Susan asked Roi Gurri.

"He takes his day off very seriously," Roi Gurri responded as Caroldus stopped writing and looked up at them.

"All done!" He exclaimed, standing. "First, we're taking Susan to the Black Unicorn tavern in Gartington, then we'll go to the Gardens of Queens where we can tell Susan some history about Zudanum, then-"

Susan giggled, and Caroldus snapped his head down to look at her. Susan blushed.

"Sorry, you're just taking this so seriously," she said.

William and Roi Gurri nodded in agreement.

"This is our chance for you to look around and learn some things about Zudanum," Caroldus explained. "It's a day you hopefully won't forget."

"I'm sure I won't forget, no matter what we do," Susan said reassuringly.

"Good, now let's go."

He took Susan's hand and led her out of the Warrior Brave Patrol room. She laughed as she tried to keep up with him.

"Come on Roi Gurri, let's make sure he doesn't wear her out," William said.

"Yeah," the prince agreed, shaking his head.

Susan paused as a growl startled her. Caroldus stopped and Susan turned to see a large, metal wolf growling at the two of them. She pressed herself closer to Caroldus, who smiled at the wolf.

"Don't scare our new recruit, Lucas," Caroldus said to the metal wolf.

Susan looked between the two of them. Lucas let out a raspy, metallic mutter, and he looked at Susan, seeming to relax. She looked into his eyes and shivered. His eyes had no pupils, and no color besides the iron color of the metal he was made of.

"You're a Wellns," Lucas stated.

Susan stood straight as she looked into his eyes. "Yes," she responded. "How did you know?"

Lucas gave Susan what looked like a smile, the smile of a wolf that is.

"Though neither of your parents was in my patrol, I know a Wellns when I see one. You have your father's eyes and your mother's nose. I can put two and two together."

Susan smiled, then she raised a brow. "*Your* patrol?" She asked.

Lucas nodded as he lifted his head with pride. "Yes. I am the Guardian and founder of the Warrior Brave Patrol."

Feeling that he deserved respect, Susan bowed.

"It's an honor to meet you," Susan said, and Lucas chuckled.

"Stand straight, I'm not a king or god. There is no need to bow to me." She nodded as she stood straight and smiled. "Now go have fun. I know it's the day of rest."

"Thank you, Lucas."

Caroldus took her hand again and led her down the hall. She laughed as she raced to keep up.

"Caroldus, slow down!" Susan squealed.

William and Roi Gurri snickered as they quickly followed the two. They were on their way to the town Caroldus had spoken of, Gartington.

"Is there anything special about this town?" Susan asked.

"Not really, but it's full of many shops," Caroldus explained, "There we'll be able to show you what kind of things we create in this world."

"I'm excited, but kind of nervous. This is my first time going to a town."

"Don't worry, we'll be there," Roi Gurri assured.

"True, I have three giant men protecting me against evil threats."

"Most people will probably think that you're a child," Caroldus commented. "Hopefully they don't think you're one of ours."

Susan laughed as William and Roi Gurri looked at each other in horror.

"Don't worry," she said. "The man who brought the food for breakfast this morning told me that most of the planet knows about me now."

The three men nodded.

"I'm worried that you might get some hate," William commented as they approached the town.

"For what?" She asked.

William exchanged glances with the others.

"Political stuff," Caroldus said with a shrug as they entered the town through large wooden gates. "But for now, just take in the sites!"

Susan's eyes filled with wonder as they entered the town, and her heart leaped in her throat.

"It's okay Susan," she thought to herself. *"You managed to keep your cool when you entered the Warrior Brave Patrol, so surely you can walk through a town right?"*

Her thoughts quickly changed as she looked at the people in the town. They were all giants, like the men she was with. Some were even taller than them! What else should she have expected?

"Right, their atmosphere is different from the one I'm used to on Earth," she reminded herself.

When the people in the town saw Roi Gurri and Caroldus they quickly bowed their heads in respect and moved out of the way for them. Roi Gurri and Caroldus nodded back in acknowledgment.

"I understand them being respectful towards Roi Gurri," Susan whispered to William. "But why Caroldus?"

"He's the son of King Regel's head general, Jemdi Fridink," William explained. "His father is considered one of the most powerful generals of all time, and most of the people fear him, so they respect Caroldus and his siblings."

"Should people fear the one who leads them into battle? Who else would have an opinion when deciding battle plans, then, if they feared him and his decisions?"

William grinned under his mask and resisted the urge to laugh.

"I think it's more like they fear his power. I've met him before, and while he *is* intimidating, he's a nice man when you get to know him."

"Interesting, I hadn't thought of it that way."

"Generals are always intimidating. It's what gives them power, it's how they protect people who are close to them. When people fear you, they tend to not want to mess with you."

"You know from personal experience?"

"... Yeah, somewhat."

Susan sensed that his experience wasn't from being intimidating, but from being intimidated. She touched his arm tenderly, causing him to tense up.

"I think you'll be a General one day," Susan said confidently with a smile.

William's eyes smiled fondly. "Thanks, Susan. That means a lot to me."

They hastened to catch up with Caroldus and Roi Gurri.

People in the town looked down at Susan, some eyes widening as if they recognized her, and others raising a brow as if they were wondering why a child had such a teenage-like face. She felt uncomfortable under the eyes of everyone around her, and let out shaky breaths.

"They all recognize me somehow. I need to make sure I don't get-" She paused as she stopped and looked around.

None of her friends were by her side.

"Lost..." Susan breathed out, completing her thoughts.

She quickly looked around but didn't see any of the three men she was just with. She started to run in the direction she thought they were heading, slipping past people and running past shops.

"William!" Susan called, her heart almost as loud as her voice as she ran through the crowd. "Roi Gurri! Caroldus!"

She winced at the noise of the crowd, her ears sensitive to noises that were too loud and near her. In response, she started to run away from the crowds. Surprisingly she found that she could run pretty fast, and without getting a stitch in her side for that matter.

"Must be because of the atmosphere. The air already makes me feel very energetic, so I guess it makes sense for my running ability to be better than it was on Earth."

"William," she breathed out as she ran down the streets. "Roi Gurri, Caroldus, where are you guys?"

***

As she was trying to find the three men, they still didn't realize she was missing. They were talking and laughing, when William paused.

"Why hasn't Susan said anything?" He thought, quickly looking behind him to see she wasn't there.

He stopped in his tracks.

"Roi Gurri! Caroldus!" William called out to the two who had walked a bit in front of him. They turned to him, Roi Gurri raising a brow. "Susan is missing!"

Both Caroldus and Roi Gurri immediately looked around to realize William was right.

"What do you mean Susan is missing?" Caroldus exclaimed. "Weren't you with her l-"

Before Caroldus would finish his sentence William turned and took off running where they had come from. Roi Gurri sighed and Caroldus growled.

"Leftor," Caroldus cursed.

"We'll never be able to catch up with the second-fastest guy in all of the patrols with a head start," Roi Gurri stated as they watched William disappear into the crowd. "Caroldus, search the back alleyways on the east side of town. I'll search the west side."

Caroldus nodded as they split up.

***

William was retracing his steps to where he had last spoken to Susan. He tried to move his way through the crowd without causing a commotion but didn't look back or apologize if he bumped into someone. His mind was too focused on finding her.

"Please let Susan be alright," William thought. *"I won't be able to live with myself if she's hurt..."* He stopped as he looked around, biting his lip under his mask. *"This is the exact place where I last saw her."*

He looked down at the ground for any traces of her footprints, but too many people had come and gone since then. He looked up to see a familiar vendor near him, rushing over to him.

"Excuse me, Kleris," William said, "Did you happen to see a very short blonde-haired girl a few moments ago?"

The vendor glanced up at him, his eyes widening a bit when he saw the masked teenage boy.

"She took off running towards the west side of the town, William," Kleris replied. "It looked like she was heading towards the back alleyways."

William nodded. "Thank you!" He exclaimed as he ran towards the alley.

"Susan, don't you know that alleyways are dangerous?"

He paused and looked down, recognizing her tiny footprints leading deeper into the alleyway.

"William!" A scream echoed throughout the alleyways, and William's heart leaped into his throat.

"Susan!" He cried.

***

Susan was in a position she never wanted to be in. She was backed into a corner, two men in masks in front of her. Her heart raced, and her hand itched to reach for her sword under her cloak.

"Not yet," she thought. *"I need an opening, an opportunity."*

The two men each held a claymore sword.

"So you're the Chosen One?" One of the men asked with a smirk. "You're shorter than I thought you'd be."

The two men laughed and Susan frowned.

"A'Vaddon will probably be putting a price on her head soon," the other man commented. "We should take her now before other bounty hunters start looking for her."

Susan's heart threatened to burst.

"No, I can't face A'Vaddon! Not now, I can't!"

The sound of footsteps reached her ear and her heart filled with hope. She subconsciously sniffed the air and the smell of oak wood hit her.

"William."

"William!" She screamed and the bounty hunter immediately lunged for her.

"Get her!" One said to his companion.

Susan's legs reacted on their own as she ran at the two and drew her sword.

"I'm not going to attack, I'm not ready for that. I'll only defend and stall until William gets here."

Susan's sword clashed with one of the bounty hunter's claymores and she cried out in pain. Her arms trembled as she tried to push the man's sword away from her, but it was no use. Her arms were weak, her sword was extremely heavy, and the bounty hunter was at least five times stronger than her. He pushed his sword down on Susan's, and it came closer and closer to her shoulder. Her legs trembled as she tried to keep her footing, and she let out a cry as she tried to push the sword away from her one more time. The other bounty hunter laughed as his companion placed his arm around her neck.

Susan gasped one more time for air before the man started to choke her. She dropped her sword and tried to claw the man's arm away from her. He winced, but his grip didn't loosen, the other bounty hunter chuckling as he placed his sword back in its scabbard.

"William..." Susan breathed out with her last breath, her body starting to go limp.

"Don't kill her, just knock her out," the other bounty hunter said.

"It's not my first time choking a child."

Susan's blood began to boil.

"It's not my first time choking a child."

Those words rang through Susan's head and she snapped. She placed her hands on the bounty hunter's arm and he laughed.

"Going to try fighting again?" He asked as he tightened his grip on her.

Her eyelids became as heavy as bricks as dark spots started to cloud her vision, her lungs burning. Her legs were about to go limp when the smell of oak wood hit her again, this time a lot stronger

"Leave her alone!" She heard the voice of William cry.

Susan slowly lifted her head to see William running at her and the two bounty hunters, drawing his sword from under his cloak. The man let go of Susan and she fell to the ground, gasping for air.

Her head started throbbing and her lungs pulled in air as fast as they could. She heard the sound of a punch and feet running around, prompting her to look up. She quickly rolled out of the way as one of the hunters was about to fall on her.

"Susan, run!" William ordered.

She looked up to see him locked in a fistfight with the other bounty hunter. She quickly ran over to her fallen sword and picked it up from the dusty ground.

"William! Susan!"

Susan turned to see Roi Gurri running toward them, relieved that he was here to help Willaim. Her ears perked as she heard footsteps running at her from behind. She quickly turned to face the bounty hunter that was running at her. She gripped her sword, ready to defend herself as the man reached her.

"Susan, don't try to take him on!" Roi Gurri cried as he reached his hand out.

Vines shot out of his hand and past Susan, hitting the bounty hunter and pinning him to the wall.

"Duck!" Roi Gurri ordered as he ran at her.

Susan obeyed and quickly knelt on the ground. He jumped and easily bounded over her, running at the bounty hunter who was now pinned to the wall. Susan got up and looked over to see William knock the claymore out of the other bounty hunter's hand and hold his own sword to the man's neck.

"What are you doing here?" Roi Gurri demanded to know, asking the bounty hunter who was pinned to the wall.

The bounty hunter smirked and chuckled dryly.

"You know why we came," the man stated, looking over at Susan.

Roi Gurri turned to her and she locked eyes with him.

"They wanted to take me to A'Vaddon," Susan gasped.

Roi Gurri frowned and turned back to the hunter. "So you know where he is?"

"No one knows where A'Vaddon is," the bounty hunter responded. "Not even the best of us bounty hunters can find him."

"Then how would you make contact with him once you had Susan?" William asked, his sword still on the other bounty hunter's neck.

The bounty hunter held by roots laughed, William and Roi Gurri glancing at each other in confusion.

"Oh no, we wouldn't make contact with him," the bounty hunter explained. "*He* would make contact with *us*. A'Vaddon knows everything fellas, there's nothing you can hide from him. A'Vaddon sees and hears everything. He's probably even watching us right now."

Roi Gurri, William, and Susan exchanged worried looks, and the bounty hunter laughed.

"He'll get you sooner or later *Wellns*," he said, looking at Susan. "In no time, hundreds of bounty hunters from all twelve realms will be here, all of them hoping to collect the reward that A'Vaddon will offer for your head."

Susan bit the inside of her lip softly. "What's the price?" She asked.

"A'Vaddon hasn't sent out a word yet. But believe me, he will."

Susan tensed and her hands trembled. The bounty hunter grinned as he turned his head to look at Roi Gurri.

"You can't protect her, *oh mighty* prince," he said. "Not you, not anyone."

Roi Gurri growled and his vines pressed against the skin of the bounty hunter's neck.

"We need to turn them over to the Zudanum Guard," William reminded, ignoring the hunter's comment.

Roi Gurri nodded but didn't keep his eyes off the bounty hunter.

"I can do that," the voice of Caroldus called.

Susan turned to see the young man coming up from behind them, and he placed a hand on her shoulder.

"Are you okay, Adathir?" Caroldus asked Susan and she nodded.

"I'm fine," she said.

"Good. I'll go get the guard, Terra," Caroldus said to Roi Gurri as he turned and ran back down the alleyway.

Susan turned back to the bounty hunter that was pinned to the wall and walked up to him. She stopped and looked him in the eye, thinking for a moment.

"Who is A'Vaddon?" She asked, but it sounded more like a demand.

"No one knows, sweetheart," he said, not once breaking eye contact. "No one."

Her heart skipped a beat as she read the man's eyes. He was telling the truth.

The rest of the wait for the Zudanum Guard was spent in silence. Susan leaned against the stone wall, thinking about everything that just happened with the bounty hunters, and what they had said.

"No one knows..."

Those words rang through her head, echoing off of the walls of her mind. Susan had always welcomed the unknown, she had always wished for an unknown force to take her away from Mr. Norman. But not knowing about the man who was supposed to be her greatest enemy terrified her.

"Hey." Susan looked up at Roi Gurri as he placed a hand on her shoulder. "I won't let any bounty hunter take you, ever. I promise."

Butterflies fluttered in her stomach as she saw the sincere look in his eyes. She believed him, so she nodded.

"I'm going to hold you to that," she said with a small smile.

Soon, Caroldus came running back with six guards.

"Are these the bounty hunters, Caroldus?" One of the men, who looked very much like Caroldus, asked.

"Yes, father," Caroldus responded, the other guards quickly stepping forward and taking the bounty hunters.

Roi Gurri and William stepped back as five of the guards took them away, their commander staying behind.

"Your Highness," Caroldus's father greeted Roi Gurri, who stood at attention.

"General Emerald Serpent," Roi Gurri greeted. "I didn't expect you to show up personally."

"King's orders," General Emerald Serpent explained. "Anyone going after the Chosen One gets special treatment."

"Do you recognize those two?"

"No, but I'll look into it." He turned to Susan. "Are you alright, Adathir?"

"Yes sir," Susan responded.

"I can handle things from here, Terra," General Emerald Serpent said to Roi Gurri. "But, I expect a full report of the incident by tomorrow morning from you, Silentum, and Adathir."

Roi Gurri nodded, and he turned to the others. "Let's move out," he said.

As they walked away, William reached down and grabbed Susan's hand. She raised a brow as she looked up at him.

"Just to make sure that you don't get lost again," William explained, and she nodded.

They walked around the town for the rest of the day, Susan's eyes always wide in fascination.

When they finally decided to go back to the castle it was starting to get dark, and Susan was drained. William's features softened as he looked down at her to see her eyes start to flutter.

"Tired?" He asked, and Susan gave a small nod. He knelt down. "Get on my back."

"Don't you drop me," she muttered as she climbed onto his back.

"Don't worry, Susan, I've got you."

***

The next morning was the same as the last, except no one was sleeping in. Susan woke up at six o'clock and walked out of her room to see the men were awake and getting ready.

"Oh, right. There's training today."

She went back into her room, brushed her hair, grabbed her sword and shield, and walked back out. She went into the living room to see Roi Gurri and William already ready.

"Morning sleepyhead," William commented. "Training is in an hour."

She nodded and headed to the kitchen, hastily making breakfast before the other men came out. She noticed Caroldus was nowhere to be found.

"Where's Caroldus?" She asked, and the two men chuckled.

"Probably trying to figure out a way to skip training today," Roi Gurri said.

"He doesn't like training?"

"Not in the slightest," William replied.

"Of course he doesn't."

Susan grabbed two pans and walked toward the Warrior Brave room. Roi Gurri and William grinned as they followed her into the sleeping area. She stood over Caroldus's sleeping form, a grin spreading over her lips as she raised the pans over his head. She started to bang the pans together over and over again, causing Caroldus to jolt awake and yelp. She stopped hitting the pans and burst out into laughter as he looked up at her, glaring.

"Why did you have to do that?" Caroldus snapped.

She started laughing hysterically.

"Oh don't be such a baby, Caroldus," William said, causing Caroldus to flare up at him.

"Why must one of you always disturb my slumber?"

"Wake up already," Susan said as she walked out and back to the kitchen.

Roi Gurri followed her to the sink, where she started to clean the dishes, so he decided to help her.

"You don't have to," Susan said.

"It's fine," Roi Gurri assured. "I just need something to distract me right now."

"Alright."

Roi Gurri barely looked at or talked to her as he started to dry dishes, causing her to think maybe she had done something wrong. It wasn't because of the silence. She knew sometimes no words had to be said, but there was something about the aura coming off of Roi Gurri. He avoided eye contact and snatched plates out of her hand more forcefully than he needed to. She turned and looked up at him.

"What's wrong?" She asked gently. Roi Gurri turned to Susan, puzzled. "Why do you seem to look at me or act like I'm something you hate? Did I do something? Since yesterday, you've given me these looks that I tried to ignore but I just can't anymore. Do you have something against me?"

"It's not like that at all," he replied, looking into Susan's eyes and sighing. "It's just that... you remind me of two very important people who were in my life."

"Oh, I'm sorry. Can I ask who?"

"Our mothers."

Susan almost dropped the plate she was holding.

"I was young, but I can never forget anything," Roi Gurri explained. "It's a strange and somewhat depressing gift I was born with. My mother was my best friend for the three years I knew her. She did everything with me, and she loved me with all of her heart. It was the same with your mother. Before she gave birth to you she took care of me when my mother was away doing her duties as queen. My mother trusted yours because they were best friends. After you were born she started taking you to my quarters when she came to see me. I remember looking at you and wondering who you were." Roi Gurri chuckled. "It was a fun two years.

"Your eyes would always sparkle whenever you were playing with me or your mother. Then a year later...

Everyone was gone. Both of our mothers were dead and you disappeared. I had no one until my father got remarried to Lady Sharmon and gave birth to my brother Johles. But we never really connected. So, whenever I look into your eyes, I don't only see your mother, but I see mine as well."

She felt sorry for Roi Gurri, yet jealous he knew her mother that well.

"Oh how I envy his ability to remember everything," she thought.

"Roi Gurri," she said softly, placing her hand over his. "I will do everything I can to make sure that A'Vaddon pays for what he did to both of us. His crimes will not go without punishment."

"Yeah, but first you need to unlock your powers. And who knows when that'll happen, if ever."

She sighed and her head lowered. There was silence for a few minutes before she finally decided to speak again.

"Roi Gurri, who was my father?"

Roi Gurri looked up at the clock. "It's time for training."

She frowned, clearly perceiving what he was doing. "You can't end a chapter like that, Roi Gurri. One day, you will have to tell me who my father was."

"I didn't know him, so there's not much I can tell you. And don't bother asking anyone else who he was, you'll just get the same results as you will with me. Your father was a shadow, you forgot he was there unless you saw him."

She looked into Roi Gurri's eyes, not blinking. He returned her stare. She was deciding whether to believe him or not.

"You don't know me Roi Gurri," she said quietly, her voice cold. "I may not have lots of experience with people, but I'm going to figure out how to get what I want out of whomever I want. I can do things most humans can't do, I can expose pressure points. One learns a lot when you're isolated for seventeen years. I will find anything, and I mean *anything* that I'm looking for."

"Watch your tongue, *Wellns*. It might get you killed one day."

"Perhaps, but I don't plan on dying anytime soon. I plan on finding what I'm looking for, and you can't stop me," she tiptoed up, her lips dangerously close to his. "No one can."

Chapter Five
Training With the Devil

Roi Gurri was about to argue, but Susan quickly put her shield on her back and walked outside where all of the other boys and girls, girls from other patrols, of course, were heading outside. She started to speedwalk so Roi Gurri wouldn't say anything else to her, but he easily caught up.

"Who was my father?" She asked as they stepped outside. "If you're going to walk with me then at least answer my questions."

Roi Gurri sighed. "I told you I don't know who he was, okay?" He snapped. "I only met him once. Can't you be satisfied with the fact that you have no living relatives?"

Susan abruptly stopped walking and stared up at Roi Gurri in shock. He also stopped and looked down at her, his expression softening when he started to realize the words he had just spoken. He immediately knew he had screwed up. He had pressed one of Susan's buttons, one that hadn't ever been pressed, and one that should've never been.

"He didn't just say that," She thought, tears brimming her eyes.

"Who the hell do you think you are?" Susan growled as her fists clenched, her eyes darkening. "You may be royal, but you're no prince or king to me, Roi Gurri! You're barely even my friend, and now you've crossed the line! Who even says things like that?"

Several people had stopped to watch the confrontation, some staring in shock at such a small girl rebuking the Prince of Zudanum. And even worse, she was speaking of treason by not seeing him as the heir prince. But Susan didn't care, nor did she know it was treason.

Her tears were threatening to spill over at any moment, her hands shook, though they were clenched in tight fists, and her teeth gritted. Roi Gurri didn't know what to do, especially when he noticed the way her eyes darkened, a tint of purple covering them.

"Susan, I'm sorry, I don't know what came over me," he pleaded quietly when he finally realized what he had said, and the way it was impacting her at that moment. "I know I said something I should've never said. I don't know what else to say, I wasn't-" He cut himself off.

He was too late, he could see it in her eyes. He wasn't going to be forgiven.

"You're *sorry*?" Susan spat, her whole body starting to shake in anger as her knuckles turned white. "Well, I don't forgive you. For what you just said, I will *never* forgive you. Now leave me alone, before something we both regret happens."

She turned and started to run, knowing something bad would happen if she was close to him for too long.

***

William noticed Susan run past him, her whole body shaking with anger and her eyes flashing purple, the purple gem on the pommel of her sword flashing as well. The small detail did not slip past his attention. He turned to see Roi Gurri heading in his direction, a guilty look in his eyes as well as on his features. He looked horrible. William frowned and stopped to wait for the young prince.

"What did you just do?" He asked in a low voice, though it sounded more like a demand than a question.

Roi Gurri looked down, finding it hard to tell his friend what happened, especially since William had become so attached to Susan already.

"I said something I shouldn't have," he finally answered, not wanting to offer any other explanation.

Unfortunately for him, William was persistent.

"Tell me exactly what you just said to her, Roi Gurri, don't play games with me," William snapped. "You know I can see through lies better than anyone."

Roi Gurri looked into William's eyes to see anger, knowing he was most likely going to punch him if he told the truth. William naturally had a brotherly and gentlemanlike personality, making it impossible for him to ever react the way Roi Gurri had just reacted to Susan.

"William-" Roi Gurri went to protest, but William saw it coming and cut him off.

"Roi Gurri."

"I asked her if she could be satisfied with the fact that she has no living relatives."

William's eyes narrowed and he let out an angry growl.

"You. Said. What?" He asked, saying each word slowly, each one filled with venom.

Roi Gurri's body stiffened and he looked away from his masked friend to the dirt ahead of them. "William-" He went to say.

Before the prince could continue his sentence, William punched him in the face, causing everyone around them to look. William's fist shook with anger as he grabbed Roi Gurri's shirt and pulled the prince closer to him.

"Let's hope she is still willing to fight for you," William spat before he ran in the direction Susan went, hoping to calm both her and himself down.

***

Susan passed a group of other boys and girls running to the same place she was, and a few of the boys started to run next to her. Some congratulated her, and others were asking if she remembered what A'Vaddon looked like.

"I guess no one has ever seen him before," she thought when she was first asked. *"No one in my generation at least."*

Susan would say no to this question and just keep going. She didn't want to discuss the man who killed her parents, and she didn't want to remember what he looked like. Besides, with what Roi Gurri, William, and Caroldus told her, she had a pretty clear image in her mind.

As Susan ran she tried to not look at the man who was beside her, but it was hard not to. He had skin so pale he'd burn within five minutes on Earth, and hair that was snow white. His eyes made goosebumps crawl up her arms, for they were ice blue with no light in them. He was shorter than Roi Gurri, but still significantly taller than Susan.

She tried to sprint ahead of him, as she did with Roi Gurri, but he always caught up with her. She eventually stopped running and started jogging, not wanting to walk or stop so that the others didn't think she was weak.

"Hello," the man said, his voice cold and smooth. "I'm Subaron Tugar, also known as Thunder Shadow. I hear you're the new girl at Warrior Brave. Congratulations, you've made history." Susan couldn't tell if he was being sarcastic, so she decided to try her best to ignore him. "I'm from Cobra Cave. We'll be doing some of our training together. It'll be nice for a member of Cobra Cave to win a game of Swarbus in record time."

"We'll see about that," Susan replied.

"Oh, will we? I thought you came here from Earth, a planet literally named dirt. Didn't you live with a *human*? How long have you known you were really born in Zudanum? Your parents should've known what was best for them and joined A'Vaddon while they had a chance. But instead, they got what they asked for, death."

Susan stopped, reached up, and grabbed Subaron's shirt collar. She pulled him down to her, making him look her in the eyes.

"Say that again," she dared, her voice low and cold.

Subaron laughed and his friends surrounded her, ready to fight.

"Face it, if your parents would've just joined A'Vaddon, even if they were faking it, then they would still be alive and you would've been a lady of the court. They would've never kept you with them if they had been with A'Vaddon, but you would've been raised in the palace with the other royal children. Not on a filthy place like Earth."

Susan's fists clenched, her urge to hit Subaron becoming stronger with every passing second. But, deep down in the pits of her heart, where things she didn't want to admit lurked, she knew part of what he said was true. It made her stomach ache at the thought, but she kept her face emotionless so Subaron wouldn't know he had won.

"I wish I could stay and fight you," Susan said, her grip on his shirt loosening. "But, I think I should go and catch up with my patrol."

Subaron glanced over to see that most of the Warrior Brave Patrol were gone, and he nodded.

"Well then, go. I'll see you later. Make sure you don't die before we have a chance to fight."

Both Subaron and Susan glared at each other, their menacing looks causing the others around them to shudder.

"I'll count on it," Susan whispered as she let go of Subaron's shirt and ran to catch up with William and Caroldus, leaving Subaron's thoughts running as she ran away.

***

"Why didn't you beat her to teach her a lesson?" One of Subaron's friends asked him.

"I did," he said.

"I don't see how you did."

"Then you weren't listening. One day you might understand, but for now, you just watch and listen."

The friend shut his mouth and nodded, Subaron's gaze turning back to Susan as she ran.

"Let's see what the Chosen One is made of," he muttered.

***

Susan quickly caught up with the rest of the Warrior Brave Patrol, finding William and Caroldus in the crowd.

"William! Caroldus!" She called out to the two, and they turned to her.

"How was your time with Subaron?" William asked as Susan stood next to him.

"Horrible," she replied, frowning at him. "I can't believe you left me there with him and his friends."

"I guess we forgot to warn you about the small 'gang' in Cobra Cave," Caroldus said, chuckling as he scratched his neck. "They're the nasty sort you can say. They pick on all of the other patrols, but they say they're trying to make us stronger through it. And they go after the so-called 'weak ones' in Warrior Brave. But thankfully not all of Cobra Cave is like that. Some are pretty nice. It's mostly that small group that causes trouble. I hate to say it, but I'm pretty sure you're their next target."

Susan sighed and shook her head. "What do they do that's so bad?" She asked.

"Beat up weaker people, cheat at games, compromise machines, and they have 'accidentally' killed people in Swarbus."

Susan shuddered. "What's Swarbus?"

"It's a game we play mostly in the Warrior Brave and Cobra Cave Patrols. Two people fight with their weapons and the first person to bleed at the torso loses. And if after five minutes nobody bleeds then it's a draw."

"Ouch."

"Yeah. I have a few scars from it, but few people have beaten William and me."

"And why is that?"

"Even though the Cobra Cave works more on their speed and quick thinking than the Warrior Brave Patrol does, we have brute force to go with that training as well. William is one of the few people in Warrior Brave who trains with the Cobra Cave, so he knows a lot of their tactics. He is naturally very fast, but he's not a natural tactical thinker. I'm just the opposite. I'm not naturally fast, I had to work for it, but I'm one of the best when it comes to making tactical decisions. So I help him work on his tactics, and he helps me with my speed."

"That's good, you help make each other stronger."

"Yeah," William agreed, looking ahead as they reached the training facility. "Welcome to sheol, Susan Wellns."

Susan bit her lip, hearing William as she looked up at the large building with a glass dome overhead. As the three walked into the dome, not a word was spoken.

"If the God who made everything in seven days can hear me," Susan prayed in her head. *"Please give me strength."*

Susan was amazed as they walked into the dome, William chuckling as he saw her expression.

"Don't worry," he said. "We'll make sure you stay alive."

Susan let out a breath and relaxed, feeling determined to not let nerves get in the way of her doing her best today.

"Calling members of the Warrior Brave and Cobra Cave Patrols, as well as all those who have physical training in Owl Perch and Kindness Keep!" Scadrin called from the center of the training center.

"Hey, I've been meaning to ask, why is Scadrin in charge of training us?" Susan asked.

"Only cause she's the toughest Zudanium in history!" Caroldus explained excitedly.

"Legend has it that she was the one who ended A'Vaddon's reign until you were born," William explained.

"Really?" Susan asked in awe. "I thought no other women had been in Warrior Brave before."

"Scadrin wasn't in Warrior Brave, she was in Owl Perch."

"Really?"

"Yeah, she's a real inspiration," Caroldus said, almost giggling with excitement. "Legend says that in the Battle of Foxes, she fought off a whole legion of soldiers by herself! Her battalion was the last line of defense to protect King Quintor, and she ended up being the last survivor. In one ground-breaking move, she ended up driving off all of A'Vaddon's army, and even managed to fight the man himself!"

"Wow... What move did she use?"

"No one knows for sure, A'Vaddon was the only survivor to witness it, and apparently it's such a dangerous move that it's being kept top secret."

"I can't believe she took out a whole legion and even managed to survive fighting A'Vaddon. How'd she do it?"

"By listening to my instructors, instead of swapping stories with my friends."

The trio flinched, looking behind them to find Scadrin peering down at them, a coy smile on her lips.

"Sorry, Scadrin," Caroldus apologized.

"Maybe today's lesson will teach you to pay attention when I'm speaking. Do you agree, Crystal Heart? Silentum?"

"Yes, ma'am." The boys both echoed.

"Good." She looked down at Susan. "It was more like two legions, actually."

Susan felt distressed.

"How on Earth am I ever going to be on Scadrin's level?" Susan thought worryingly. *"I can't fight A'Vaddon, let alone a whole legion of soldiers!"*

"Now then," Scadrin said, as teens and children from the four patrols started to gather around her, "let's begin training. Today, we will have tests of endurance."

Many of the teens in the patrols groaned. Susan's face grew pale and she tensed.

"On my first day?" She internally screamed as she did her best to keep a straight face, biting her lip in anticipation. *"She's doing this on purpose. She wants to see what I'm capable of. Fine then. This is going to go all wrong for me, I know it, but bring it."*

"I have only faith in one person to complete this task though," Scadrin continued. Susan's ears perked. "And that person is Susan Wellns, but known to you all as Adathir."

"What?" Susan whispered as everyone looked down at her small form, her body freezing as she stared at Scadrin with a very confused look.

"Am I right, Adathir?" Scadrin asked.

Susan's scared expression fell completely as she remained silent.

"Let her test me," she thought. *"She knows that if I fail today, then none of these people will follow me into battle one day. They'll eat me alive like wolves. Say nothing, act like it's nothing. I may be small, but let's see what I can do. Maybe working on a farm all those years will help me."*

"Very well," Scadrin continued, looking away from her. "First, we'll start with running. Follow me to the track."

All of the children of the patrols quickly followed Scadrin, some muttering things amongst themselves. Susan was able to hear some of their conversations.

"She's so small, she won't be able to run very fast," one boy said to another.

"What if she has a speed ability?" Another asked. "Speed would be handy to have to defeat A'Vaddon."

"Perhaps. It could be possible, but wouldn't you think her body would've developed longer legs if she had a speed ability?"

"That's true. Abilities do tend to affect the physical form of someone. Looking at her, she doesn't have a speed or strength ability."

"Well, that's useless."

Susan walked a little faster, not wanting to listen to any more of the conversation.

"Hey, Susan."

She looked up to see Caroldus. She smiled softly at the familiar face.

"Hey, Caroldus," she replied.

"Sorry about Scadrin, but if she sees potential in someone, she tends to single them out."

"Or if a prophecy says there's potential in me," she said somewhat bitterly.

Caroldus frowned, but he understood where she was coming from.

"Prophecies tend to be right," he responded calmly.

"But they can also be wrong."

"That's why you have faith."

Susan looked back to where they were walking. He made some sense, she knew that, but believing it and then admitting it would prove to be more difficult.

She became anxious they finally arrived at the track. The track stretched out at least a human mile, if not more, and many obstacles stood in the way. Walls with ropes, lava pits with ladders hanging over like a bridge, certainly not any normal running track you'd find on earth.

"Wow..." Susan breathed out.

"The best time for this course is three and a half minutes," Scadrin announced. "Adathir, choose a partner from the barrel, and let's see if you can beat the best."

Susan's hands shook as she approached the barrel full of names, her heart thumping rapidly in her chest as she reached down and drew one of the pieces of paper.

Terra.

"Roi Gurri," Susan breathed out.

"Say it louder, Adathir," Scadrin ordered.

"Terra."

She turned and looked back at the crowd to see Roi Gurri step out. He didn't look nervous at all, the opposite of Susan's pale expression. The two exchanged looks, Roi Gurri silently telling her he was sorry, Susan telling him she was terrified of failing.

"Terra, Adathir, only one of you needs to cross the field to win, but a minute will be added if you don't finish at the same time," Scadrin explained, Roi Gurri and Susan nodding in assent. "Begin."

Roi Gurri immediately grabbed Susan by the wrist and ran straight into the course.

"Hey!" Susan snapped, quickly doing her best to keep up with Roi Gurri's long strides.

Because of the atmosphere of Zudanum, she wasn't out of breath and felt as if she could run for hours, but she knew this wouldn't be the case for long. Her leg and arm muscles weren't developed enough for a course this challenging, but she had to try. The first part of the course was a five-hundred-meter dash, which Roi Gurri practically dragged her over, his long strides able to complete it very quickly.

"First thing you need to know, Susan," Roi Gurri said from over his shoulder. "Is, when Scadrin says 'begin', she means right away."

Susan nodded as she struggled to keep up with Roi Gurri, thankful he was still keeping a tight grip on her wrist as they ran. Up ahead were what appeared to be steel monkey bars hanging over a large lava pit. A bit cliche from Susan's perspective, but terrifying nonetheless. Roi Gurri looked down at her hands and panic flooded him. She wasn't wearing any gloves, not knowing about the obstacles they'd face.

"Oh no," he thought as he looked from his gloved hands to her bare ones.

If she touched the metal, her hands would immediately burn and she'd let go and fall. Even his healing powers wouldn't be able to work at that point.

"Susan, whatever happens, you can't focus on anything else except getting across," he said.

"Roi Gurri, my skin will melt off!" She exclaimed, horrified.

He groaned as he thought quickly and picked her up, moving her in front of him and having her legs wrap around his hips and her arms around his neck. Susan's face flushed.

"Just hang on," he assured her as he jumped up and grabbed onto the metal bars, quickly swinging across the bars, skipping one at a time.

Susan hung on for dear life. "Roi- Roi Gurri," she stuttered quietly. "I'm not going to survive this. I can't defeat A'Vaddon."

He glanced down at her with a soft expression, which quickly faded when he turned back to his task of getting them across. Her scared state was making her vulnerable, even though she was mad at him a few minutes ago.

"You're not going to do it alone, Susan, always remember that," Roi Gurri replied with a grunt, sweat dripping down his brow as he reached the end. "Just remember, I'll never abandon you."

As soon as Roi Gurri's feet hit the ground she let go of him and he threw off his gloves, grabbed her wrist, and continued to run, not having time to catch his breath.

Next was climbing a wall with long spiked ropes down the side. Roi Gurri jumped up and grabbed onto one of the ropes, throwing Susan up with his other hand. She gasped in surprise as her hands latched onto one of the ropes instinctively. She hissed as she cut her hand, instantly drawing blood.

Susan looked down to see Roi Gurri pulling himself up, quickly taking initiative and climbing up to the top. She looked down to see White Star at the bottom of the other side, a saddle strapped to his back and a quiver full of arrows attached to the saddle. Roi Gurri immediately jumped onto White Star's back. Susan followed him and grabbed the bow that was beside her. White Star sped off. Susan gripped the back of Roi Gurri's shirt to keep her balance.

"Shoot at the targets!" Roi Gurri demanded. Susan turned to see several targets behind them. "Now! Before they get out of range!"

She quickly took an arrow from the quiver at her side and turned her body to aim behind her, shakily letting go of the arrow and hitting the end of the target.

She shot off several more, none of them hitting the center of the targets, but they didn't miss either. She pulled out the last arrow to see a rope attached to it, looking forward and seeing what seemed to be a large whirlpool up ahead.

"Get ready to hold your breath, and stay close to me," Roi Gurri said back to her, and she nodded in understanding.

She took the rope from the arrow and tied it to both her and Roi Gurri's waists, Roi Gurri smiling in approval of the initiative she was taking. White Star bucked up his hind legs without warning, throwing them both into the water. Susan took in a deep breath before they hit, but the sudden force of being tossed around almost knocked it all out of her.

Roi Gurri grabbed Susan by the waist and pulled her small body back into his chest, both of them waiting out the bumpy ride. As the swift current carried them along, he felt her struggling and clawing at his arms. He turned her to see fear prominent in her eyes as multiple air bubbles escaped her lips. He knew she was running out of air, her small lungs weren't able to hold as much as his since he had run this course multiple times. He pulled her forward and pressed his mouth to her own, pushing some of his oxygen into her lungs. Her face turned beet red, but she didn't complain now that she had more air.

In an instant, the two shot up and surfaced. Susan coughed up water and gasped for air, letting go of Roi Gurri, who went to his knees as he gasped for air as well.

"Well done, Terra and Adathir."

The two looked up to see Scadrin, and Susan looked down to see they were lying in a puddle-like body of water.

"I didn't notice that before," she thought.

"Three minutes, was your time," Scadrin announced.

Susan was shocked as she looked at the other children of the patrols. They looked both surprised and impressed.

"Never underestimate a partner who is smaller or weaker than yourself," Scadrin said as Roi Gurri and Susan stood out of the water. "Adathir may have not been able to complete the trials on her own, but she trusted Terra and followed his orders. Know when to submit."

Some of the students murmured "yes ma'am", while others remained silent as they watched Susan and Roi Gurri fall into place with them. The Prince of Zudanum and the Chosen One had just broken a record together, and neither was hurt nor did they argue. They had trusted each other and created a bond. It was a symbol now. Maybe, with their next king, this small girl could really become someone great.

"Now, let's continue."

Chapter Six
Playing Games With Thunder

Susan placed her hands on her knees, sweat dripping down her face and her breathing heavy. Caroldus chuckled as he stood beside her and placed his hand on her shoulder. She glanced up at his smiling face.

"So what's your first impression of training?" Caroldus asked.

"You guys are superhumans," she breathed out and he laughed.

After the training course, there were several other physical tests, in which Susan didn't have Roi Gurri dragging her along, so it was definitely more of a challenge.

"So, Scadrin mentioned that we're playing Swarbus today?" She asked.

"Yeah," Caroldus affirmed. "Hopefully, you won't have to play because you're new."

She frowned but understood. She had barely been in Zudanum for two days, and this *was* her first day of training. She knew they still considered her a weak link, which wasn't entirely untrue. She may have grown up doing farm work, but she could never fathom being on the same level as these men. They had been training for years, she had been training for hours.

"If I do play, I hope I go against Subaron," Susan muttered coldly, which had Caroldus frowning.

"I hope you *don't* go against Subaron," William said as he walked up to the two. "He's one of the best in Cobra Cave. He'll have you bleeding, if not dead, within thirty seconds. Plus he's had ten years of training, whereas you've had about four hours."

"He insulted me and my family," Susan said. "I don't care if I have to bleed a little to show him I mean business."

Caroldus sighed and lazily placed his arm on her shoulder as they walked.

"Well if you do fight him, it was nice knowing you," he said in a joking tone, which had Susan giving him a playful glare.

"Are you saying you don't think I can hold my own for even a little bit?" She asked.

"Maybe, anything is possible. But as William said, Subaron has years of experience and is fast as sheol. But not faster than me, of course."

"He's might be stronger than you, though," William pointed out.

Ignoring his friend, Caroldus abruptly grabbed Susan by the hips and lifted her small frame up onto his shoulders.

"Hey!" She squealed, grabbing his hair to steady herself.

"If I can carry Susan on my shoulders, then Subaron doesn't stand a chance against my strength," Caroldus countered with a playful smirk.

Susan gasped in mock hurt and tugged his hair.

"I'm not *that* heavy!" She protested with a pout, the two men below her laughing.

"You're right," William said. "I bet even the young princess could carry you."

Susan crossed her arms and huffed. "You two are mean."

Caroldus burst out laughing and William shook his head.

They were inside the training center, a place full of equipment, arenas, and obstacle courses for the students to train on. It spanned about two acres and was divided into five sections. One for heavy lifting, one for aerobics, one for bladed weapons training, a shooting range for both arrows and firearms, and the other for resistance training.

"Caroldus put me down now," Susan said as they walked into the area for bladed weapons training, the man nodding as he lifted her off of his shoulders and set her down on the ground.

"Boy, you sure are a workout!" Caroldus teased as he stretched.

"Sure, whatever," she said with a grin, playfully slapping Caroldus's arm as he jogged up to Scadrin.

William went to follow, but Susan grabbed his arm and held him back.

"I'm sorry, William, but I need to talk to you about Roi Gurri," she said.

"What's the matter?" He asked, worried.

"Well, I had asked him who my father was. And then he yelled at me as if he was mad. Or a better explanation, he wanted to avoid the subject."

William tugged his arm out of Susan's hand and looked her in the eye, surprising her with his sudden movement.

"He's just sensitive about topics of the past. I would be, too, if I could remember what he went through at such a young age. Now please, promise me you're not going to look into this too far. It's okay to want to know about your family, but your focus should be on the present, not the past."

Susan looked down at her sword and sighed. "Alright, I promise."

She crossed her fingers.

"I'm sorry, William," She thought. *"But I have to know my past in order for me to know my place now."*

They saw Scadrin standing in the middle of an arena, so they raced toward her. They stood next to Roi Gurri and Caroldus who were whispering to each other, but they stopped when Susan came up to them. She frowned and clenched her firsts. She was mad, mad enough that the others started picking up her dark vibes.

"What are they keeping from me?" She thought. *"It has to do with my father, I'm sure of it. But what?"*

Caroldus smiled down at her, the small girl not being able to help but smile back.

"Does anyone know why Subaron hates me?" Susan asked, trying to lighten the mood.

"It's because he was born a day before you," Roi Gurri explained. "The day you were born had a special prophecy with it. It was along the lines of;

"'Whoever was born on the day of the new year, that year, would be the key to the end of an age of evil. The path between worlds, both physical and spiritual'.

"That's the part everyone knows at least. No one knows what the full prophecy is."

"Spiritual?"

"Some aren't quite sure what that means. But most have concluded that you will be able to communicate with angels and demons, and be able to perceive them."

Susan laughed and shook her head. "The day I see an angel will be the day I die."

"Warrior Brave and Cobra Cave!" Announced Scadrin, causing them to look over. "Today you will be facing each other in Swarbus. You will be picked depending on if I pull your name out of this box or not. You all should know the rules, and if you don't, watch and learn." Scadrin pulled two pieces of wood out of the box. "Crystal Heart and Poisonars!"

"That's me," Caroldus said, drawing his two double-edged swords with a grin. "Wish me luck, Poisonars is pretty good. Maybe I can taunt him by using his real name."

"What is his real name?" Susan asked.

"Meludisoris." The boys all said at the same time.

Susan held in a laugh as Caroldus grinned and walked out into the arena with complete confidence. He stood a little ways away from his opponent, a tall, strong-built dark teen.

Scadrin blew a horn and Caroldus reacted a split second afterward, catching Susan by surprise with his amazing speed. He rushed at Poisonars and went to slash at his torso, only to connect with his ax and cause him to be pushed away. Caroldus quickly ducked as Poisonars' ax came towards his head, almost decapitating him. Susan gasped in alarm.

"Aim for the torso, idiot!" Caroldus snapped before he rushed again.

Poisonars lunged at him, but he quickly moved to the side and dodged the attack.

"Caroldus is fast," Susan remarked in awe, the boys next to her nodding simultaneously, both in the same state of awe she was.

"When it comes to fighting, Caroldus is the fastest out of all of us," William whispered. "He relies on his speed more than his physical strength. Even anti-naturals have a hard time keeping up with him."

Caroldus rushed towards Poisonars and quickly lunged one of his swords at him. Poisonars blocked the sword with his ax, and Caroldus kicked him in the gut. Caroldus rushed forward and punched him in the nose, causing him to stumble back and allow Caroldus to cut his stomach. Blood darkened his green shirt.

"Crystal Heart wins!" Scadrin announced.

Caroldus put his swords back into the scabbard on his back and cheekily bowed as Warrior Brave cheered. He walked back toward Susan, William, and Roi Gurri with a victorious smile.

"I almost got decapitated," he remarked with a light laugh. "Poisonars always wants to decapitate me though, so nothing unusual there."

"For a short fight that was pretty intense," Susan remarked.

"It always is. If a fight isn't interesting it means neither are giving their all, or they're tired."

"What's the point of this game?"

"To focus on your attack point. It teaches us to aim for the kill spot, the abdomen, for when we go into a real battle. No matter what species you are, the abdomen is the safest place to attack if you're looking to take them out."

Susan hummed and nodded, thinking about that for a minute. Scadrin continued to pull names out of the barrel.

"Serpentila and Poison Cloud! Silver Streak and Golden Warrior! Silver Scar and Scarlet Snow!" And so on.

Soon everyone had fought except for a few people, including Susan and Subaron.

"Adathir and Black Mamba!" Scadrin called.

Susan frowned at not hearing Subaron as her opponent, but Caroldus just laughed and shook his head.

"What's so funny?" Susan asked, looking back at Caroldus before she stepped into the arena.

"Black Mamba is my little sister," he replied, "Her real name is Eloziah."

"Sorry if I cut your sister," Susan quipped with masked confidence.

Caroldus shook his head and smirked. "Yeah, good luck with that."

She rolled her eyes but agreed with him in all seriousness. She turned to see Eloziah pull out two large spiked wooden clubs. She was definitely over six feet, her long beautiful chestnut hair tied up to keep from getting in the way. Susan wasn't sure how old Eloziah was, but she looked younger than Caroldus, who was the same age as herself. The two locked eyes, neither smiling nor feeling lighthearted.

"She seems a lot more serious about this than Caroldus did," Susan thought and quickly drew her sword and shield as she took her position in front of Eloziah, her heart racing.

"Oh, dear God. I'm going to die fighting a six-foot woman with two spiked clubs bigger than my head."

Susan firmly gripped her shield and her teeth started to gnash together as she tried to think of a strategy to defeat Eloziah, though not too many ideas came to mind. She didn't have any sort of advantage.

As soon as Scadrin blew the horn Eloziah charged at her, reaching her within a few seconds and catching her off guard. She swung her clubs at her torso, but Susan held up her shield and blocked the attack.

"Crap," Susan thought as Eloziah repeatedly hit her shield, causing her to start sliding back. *"She's not giving me time to react. I'm going to be cornered into the wall at this rate!"*

Eloziah's attacks on her shield continued, though the strong metal held up. Susan struggled to keep herself from sliding backward, but her legs were already so sore she wasn't sure how long she could keep them up.

Susan pushed Eloziah away from her with her shield and swung her sword, just barely missing her chest. Eloziah thrust one of her clubs at her, and she turned just in time to avoid it, but the spikes cut open her left arm. Susan let out a cry and used her shield to bash against Eloziah's wrist, knocking the club out of her hand. Eloziah kicked Susan in the stomach, the wind being knocked out of her lungs as she fell back, her sword flying in the air as she let go of it. Eloziah raised her arm to hit Susan with her other club, but Susan rolled out of the way in time. Eloziah pounced on top of her and they started wrestling in the dirt. Susan knocked Eloziah's club away from her and Eloziah wrenched her shield out of her arm. Eloziah raised the shield and brought it down on Susan, hitting her in the face with the end of it. Susan cried out as the end of the shield created a deep gash on her face.

Roi Gurri flinched as he heard the pained cry.

"This is getting bad," he observed, one of his hands resting under his chin.

"What are you talking about?" Caroldus asked. "This is amazing! This is probably the most entertaining fight between two women I've seen."

"Are you really saying that right now?"

"Of course I am. This is only Susan's third fight, right? And she's actually managing to hold her own."

Roi Gurri nodded and turned back to the fight to see Susan kick Eloziah off of her, jumping up and running toward her sword. Eloziah scooped up her clubs and ran at Susan. Susan picked up her sword and she turned just as Eloziah was about to hit her. She brought her sword up and managed to slice one of Eloziah's clubs in half.

Everyone in Cobra Cave gasped, and the boys in Warrior Brave cheered, William's eyes smiling.

"I didn't expect Susan to last this long," Caroldus whispered to Roi Gurri.

"Neither did I," Roi Gurri admitted. "Eloziah is pretty tough, I should know."

As he said this Eloziah knocked down Susan and quickly used her remaining club to roughly cut her stomach.

Susan cried out and squeezed her grip on her sword, her teeth gnashing together from the pain. She didn't want to seem weak in front of all of the men, so she did her best not to scream, or for that matter cry. The people of Cobra Cave cheered for Eloziah as she made her way back to them.

"Black Mamba wins!" Scadrin announced.

Susan slowly got up and made her way back to Roi Gurri, sweat pouring down her face and blood seeping through her wounds.

"Are you alright?" William asked, placing a hand on her shoulder.

"I think so," Susan said shakily, putting her sword back into the scabbard. "But the wound on my stomach is pretty deep, and my head is throbbing."

"Let me take a look," Roi Gurri offered.

She nodded, lifting up part of her shirt to show them the wound, wincing.

Caroldus was surprised when he saw the wound. The cut was very deep, and it went from her side down to near the middle of her stomach.

"You must've really irritated her," he remarked.

"You think?"

"Last time she cut someone that deep was when my brother and I covered her room in goostic slime."

Roi Gurri gently placed his hand on Susan's wound and mumbled a few chosen words, his breath blowing on her skin and making it warm. She shivered as a cold feeling came over her, looking down to see a gold, eerie glow come from Roi Gurri's hand. Her head tilted as she watched. When Roi Gurri removed his hand the wound was gone, the only thing left was a nasty scar.

"I remember you telling me that you have healing powers," Susan commented, looking down at Roi Gurri as he nodded.

"Really comes in handy when you're in a patrol that gets injured all of the time," Caroldus said with a smile. "We're lucky to have Roi Gurri in our Patrol."

"Yeah, we are."

Susan felt a warm feeling inside of her, looking away from Roi Gurri as her cheeks warmed. But then she remembered what happened with him earlier, causing her heart to harden. She made a fist, the pink in her cheeks immediately leaving, along with the light in her eyes. Caroldus noticed Susan's expression change, and his face went from smiling to worried.

"Are you okay?" Caroldus asked quietly.

"I'm fine," Susan snapped, catching him off guard, but he thought it better not to ask her anything.

"If she wants to talk about it, she can," he thought, nodding to her.

Susan looked up to see Eloziah coming toward them.

"Heard I cut you too deep," Eloziah said, looking at Susan and smiling sheepishly. "Sorry about that."

"It's no trouble," Susan replied, smiling. "And I'm pretty sure I'm going to be getting a lot more scars here."

"Trust me, you will. I'm Eloziah Fridink by the way."

She held out her hand and Susan shook it.

"I'm Susan Wellns. Caroldus told me you're his sister."

"Yeah, but only Jehoyam knows if we're *really* related or not."

"Hey!" Caroldus whined, elbowing his little sister lightly in the ribs. "That's no way to talk about your big brother."

Caroldus stuck out his bottom lip in a pout, but he eventually gave in to a smile when everyone started laughing.

"I have to go," Eloziah said, looking back toward the Cobra Cave Patrol. "But I have to say, Susan, you are a natural at the sword. If you train hard enough you'll definitely defeat A'Vaddon."

She turned and jogged towards her patrol companions, leaving Susan with a big smile.

"She should've been placed in Warrior Brave," Susan mumbled.

"Maybe," Caroldus said with a shrug, "But I think she was placed in Cobra Cave because she's more clever than most in Warrior Brave. And she's very sneaky. That's what Cobra Cave's known for, being sneaky and clever with their words. That's why they're often chosen to become spies."

"And we're proud of it."

Roi Gurri, Susan, and William groaned in unison as they turned, already knowing it was Subaron.

"What do you want, Subaron?" William asked, annoyed.

"I just wanted to congratulate Susan on her fine swordsmanship," Subaron responded as if it was no big deal.

"And?" Susan asked, placing a hand on her hip. "I'm a natural, big deal. And you hate me, so why would you congratulate me?"

"So we're enemies?"

"You can say that again. You insulted me and my family name, nothing like that gets past me."

"Why are you offended? It's not like you even knew your family."

"At least I bring honor to their name."

"Do you really?"

"More than you ever will for your family."

"Want to put that to the test?" One of Subarons' friends asked as he drew his ax.

Susan and William quickly drew their swords and shields, stepping forward in acknowledgment of the challenge. Roi Gurri and Caroldus took a step back.

"Should I get Scadrin?" Caroldus whispered to Roi Gurri.

"You can, I want to see this," Roi Gurri replied, his eyes not leaving the four ready to fight.

Caroldus shrugged and gave Susan and William a worried look before he jogged off, not wanting any of his friends to get hurt.

Subaron didn't take out his sword, causing Susan to eye him suspiciously. Subaron grinned as he lifted his right hand toward her. In an instant, a flashing light came out of his hand and shot straight at her.

She wasn't fast enough to react in the slightest, the electricity hit her in the chest and blasted her a few feet away from William. She cried out as she fell to the hard ground, a sharp pain pulsing throughout her entire body.

"Susan!" William cried as he put his sword back into its scabbard and ran to her.

Subaron gave a crooked smirk and went to approach Susan, but Roi Gurri stepped in front of him.

"You're going too far, Subaron," Roi Gurri stated coldly, his fists clenched.

"I disagree."

Roi Gurri growled, turning at the sound of Susan's groan, his eyes widening in worry.

"Are you alright Susan?" William asked Susan, placing a hand on her shoulder.

She groaned and twitched, a bit of electricity running down her body before it disappeared.

"I'm good," she breathed out as William helped her sit up.

"That was a strong blast," Roi Gurri said in a serious tone as he knelt next to Susan. "Are sure you're alright?"

She nodded. "My body just feels sore, that's mainly it. A-And my heart is-"

Roi Gurri interrupted by placing a hand on her shoulder, his hand starting to glow once again.

Susan shuddered and gasped as she felt her heart rhythm return to its normal pace, the lighting strike having disrupted it, and her body relaxed again. When Roi Gurri was done he stood up and turned to Subaron. His eyes burned with rage.

"That could've killed her you son of a dog!" Roi Gurri snapped.

"If you think that was my full power, you're a fool, Drago," Subaron snapped.

"You may not have used your full power on her, but I'm going to use mine on you."

"Enough!"

Roi Gurri and Subaron looked over to see Scadrin and Caroldus walking toward them, an angry look clearly on Scadrin's face. She first walked to Susan and knelt beside her.

"Are you alright?" She asked.

Susan nodded and William wrapped one of his arms under her shoulders to help her up.

"I'm good," Susan mumbled, leaning onto William.

She was clearly tired from more than the lightning blast. William nodded at Scadrin, indicating that he would watch Susan. Scadrin turned back to Roi Gurri and Subaron.

"It's dangerous for you to use your powers on people who have not yet unlocked theirs or don't have any," Scadrin scolded Subaron. "You could've killed Susan, which would have ruined our chance of defeating A'Vaddon. Do you know what would've happened then?"

"We'd all be dead," Subaron quipped, earning himself a slap.

Susan gasped, but the others around her acted like they'd seen this before. Subaron's head snapped back to look at Scadrin, and their eyes locked in a dead stare.

"Don't talk back to me, Subaron," Scadrin snapped at her student. "Your mouth will end the life of you, and your friends." Subaron's eyes hardened. "It's time for riding now. I'll speak to your father later." Subaron's face fell and he growled. "You're dismissed."

Scadrin turned and walked back toward the castle. Roi Gurri glared at Subaron.

"Don't look at me like that, Your Highness," Subaron snapped before turning and walking away, his friends following him.

Roi Gurri frowned and turned to see Susan standing more on her own, but William steadied her so she wouldn't fall. He walked towards them and gripped Susan's arm.

"Careful, you were just struck by lightning," he warned.

Susan shook her head and laughed.

"What's so funny?" William asked.

"I just can't believe it's only my third day on this planet and I've already been struck by electricity," Susan explained.

"I guess that is something to laugh about," Caroldus said as he walked over to the three. "Now come on, we have to show Susan where riding is."

The men nodded and helped Susan over towards a large field where dozens of horses, unicorns, and pegasi were standing. Susan was amazed, as she saw the 'mythical' creatures she read about when she was on Earth.

"These are our companions," William explained to her. "Everyone has one, but sometimes they aren't one of these. There have been rare occasions where someone's companion is a dragon, peryton, or griffin."

"How rare are they?" Susan asked in curiosity.

"Dragons and perytons are very rare, but griffins even more so. People aren't sure if they even exist anymore."

"Just pick a horse or something that hasn't been mounted yet," Caroldus said to Susan before heading towards a brown pegasus.

Before Susan had a chance to look at the other horses, Scadrin came up to her, a pearly white pegasus following her. Susan looked up at Roi Gurri and William, but they were both heading toward their companions already. She looked back at Scadrin and the pegasus, her eyes locking with the pegasuses. A flicker of a memory passed in her mind and a shudder ran down her spine.

"I want you to ride-" Scadrin went to say.

"Pearl Bolt," Susan interrupted, her eyes not looking away from the pegasus.

"How did you know?"

She paused and frowned. "I... I don't know." She approached Pearl Bolt. "It feels like a memory of some sort, or an instinct. Like from when I was little. The same thing happened with White Star actually."

Scadrin stared at Susan for a moment, not quite sure how to approach this.

"I see," Scadrin murmured thoughtfully. "Can you tell me who owned her before you?"

Susan thought deeply for a moment. She pressed her hand on Pearl Bolt's head and looked at her side to see that she had a large scar, which triggered something in her memory.

She felt a burning pain pressuring her entire head, and let out a cry as she fell to her knees, a vision flashing through her mind.

***

She saw Pearl Bolt circling around her, her mother riding her, and she was holding a long mace in her hand. Her mother was facing a tall man who was riding a large, inky-black, scaly dragon with large bared teeth and fiery amber eyes. The man looked down and spotted Susan, and she heard a baby's cry come from herself. She couldn't tell who the man was, but she knew she was terrified. She tried to move in her vision, but nothing happened, it was like she was frozen in place. Her mother looked down at her, her face turning white.

"Susan!" She cried, her beautiful emerald eyes full of fear. "A'Vaddon, please don't!" She pleaded.

The man, who Susan now knew was A'Vaddon, lowered his hand towards Susan and shot a shining black bolt of lightning at her. She heard her mother's scream before she felt a pain on her scar and she let out a blood-curdling scream.

***

Scadrin cautiously approached Susan, who was now on the ground, her head in her hands. Tears were streaming down her face and her hands were shaking.

"Susan?" Scadrin asked.

Susan looked up at her through tear-filled eyes.

"Pearl Bolt was my mother's," she choked as Scadrin knelt next to her.

"What happened?" She asked, placing a hand on her shoulder, trying to calm her.

"I just had a memory. I remembered a time when A'Vaddon and my mother were fighting. And I think it's when he gave me my scar."

"Are you alright?"

Susan nodded. "It just hurt. I could feel everything as if I was there right now."

"There are few who can remember like that. But don't let this deter you from remembering your family. For in order for you to become the Chosen One, you must know who you are, and where you come from."

Susan felt relief from Scadrin's words. It was encouraging for an elder to tell her it was okay to look into her past, especially after William had practically begged her not to.

Scadrin helped Susan stand, and she walked over to Pearl Bolt, who knelt so she could mount her.

"Remember, Susan," Scadrin said. "Pearl Bolt and White Star are from your family line. They are your companions."

Susan nodded. As soon as she mounted Pearl Bolt, the pegasus flapped her wings and flew into the sky. Susan felt as if all her organs had leaped into her throat, her eyes widening in wonder and fear. Her memory was now far from her mind as she looked down to see she was high above the ground.

"First timer," Caroldus joked as he flew beside her, his companion a brown pegasus.

Susan glared at him and gripped Pearl Bolt's mane tightly.

"Did you do any better when you first started riding?" Susan shot back.

"Truth be told, I broke my arm *and* nose. I flew up way too high and fell. I grabbed onto a flag but it ripped. Though it did break my fall enough so I didn't die."

"Hopefully that doesn't happen to me."

"Yeah, it hurt like a club to the face."

"I'm sure it did. Can I ask you a few history questions?"

"Take your best shot! Although I must warn you, I don't do very well when it comes to history. My brother is better at that."

"I'll take your word for it, but I think that this one might be easy. Where did you all first come from? Are you aliens? Or some version of a human?"

"We're *technically* human."

"Then why did Subaron say that I grew up with a *human* as if you weren't humans?"

"Well after living on this planet for a few hundred years we stopped classifying ourselves as Humans, and instead as Zudaniums. Especially since after living in this environment for so long, our bodies have adjusted differently. Lots of people also believe that anti-naturals are superior to other people. He's just disgusted that you're a mutt."

"Mutt?"

"That's what ignorant people call those who aren't from a full line of anti-naturals. Believe it or not, your mother wasn't anti-natural. She was normal, just like anybody else on Earth and most people here."

"Then why did she go against A'Vaddon?"

Caroldus's face fell at seeing Susan's hurt expression.

"Because she was strong, and could point out weaknesses, from what I hear. Even in anti-naturals. She apparently took down lots of them in her time."

Susan tilted her head. "Took them down?"

"Well, not all anti-naturals are on our side, unfortunately. Your mother was a trained assassin."

"And yet she came from the Kindness Keep Patrol?"

"Just shows that there's more to the other patrols than meets the eye."

Susan couldn't help but smile. Her mother sounded like a badass, and it made her excited to learn more about her.

"Thanks, Caroldus," Susan said.

"I'm your friend, it's what I do."

Susan was glad to have a friend. "If you aren't aliens, then where did you come from?"

"Over ten thousand years ago some people, our ancestors, discovered a portal to here. It just showed up out of nowhere and would disappear as soon as we went through. Here we found magical animals, large plains, minerals, and we discovered some of us were anti-naturals. We used our newfound 'gifts' to build our kingdom. Soon we became one of the most powerful civilizations in our galaxy. We've developed gadgets, a strong army, and powerful allies with other life forms."

Susan's eyes never left Caroldus as she listened in wonder.

"Wow, you've done great," she complimented.

"Tell me about it."

"What are William and Roi Gurri's companions?"

"Roi Gurri's is a unicorn, and William's is a mare. Here, we should go back down and join them."

***

William was petting his mare, Stellalux, when he saw Roi Gurri coming toward him. He saw the serious expression on his friend's face, so he mounted his companion and rode to meet his friend.

"We need to talk," Roi Gurri said as he brought his unicorn, Pure Lighting, beside Stellalux. William only nodded, allowing Roi Gurri to continue. "The way you hit me this morning is a blatant form of disrespect. If my father hears of it, and he will, he could call for your head."

"Pardon my treason," William said through his teeth.

Roi Gurri reached out and grabbed William by his shirt to bring their faces close to one another. "Do you not understand how serious your actions are?" He hissed.

"I understand. I also understand that if you continue to drive Susan away there is no future for Zudanum. If she is not on your side, Roi Gurri, who do you think she will turn to? Not your father, nor I. But I can think of a vulture who would do anything to swoop down and steal her away from you."

Roi Gurri's expression softened as he leaned back from William and let him go. He knew his friend was right, yet he still feared the wrath of his father.

"If the king calls for you, tell him exactly what you've told me," Roi Gurri finally said. "He will take your side, I'm sure. But, William." The masked man's eyes rose to meet his own. "Next time I behave foolishly, correct me in private. Whether I like it or not, the people around us will one day have to look to me as king, and I'd rather their image of me not be the times you've publicly humiliated me. Do you understand?"

William nodded and he hung his head. "I'm sorry, I wasn't thinking." He lifted his gaze. "I will support your reign till the very end, Roi Gurri. I won't let you down again."

"Thank you."

The two men shook hands to seal their apologies. Just then, they heard the sound of horses from above, and looked to see Caroldus and Susan circling above them.

"Hey guys, how does it feel to not fly?!" Caroldus called in a jesting voice. "Why don't you come fight us in the air?!"

"Caroldus!" Susan scolded as she brought Pearl Bolt down beside William.

"Face it, Susan, we have the advantage! We should challenge them!"

Susan's expression was apologetic as she looked over at Roi Gurri, but he was bearing a wide smile.

"He should know better," Roi Gurri said as he raised his hand.

In an instant, a giant root shot out of the ground, came up to Caroldus, wrapped around his body, and lifted him off of his pegasus!

"Hey!" Caroldus cried as he attempted to break out of the root's hold, but it was to no avail.

"I'm sorry, I can't hear you over my anti-natural abilities!" Roi Gurri taunted as he commanded the roots to bring Caroldus back down to the ground.

William and Susan laughed as Roi Gurri set Caroldus on the ground beside them, and the roots returned to the ground.

"Must you ruin my fun?" Caroldus asked as he dramatically fell onto the ground.

"Always," William said, his eyes smiling. "How else are we to amuse ourselves?"

Chapter Seven
A'Vaddon

Thousands upon thousands of light-years away, halfway across the galaxy, is the planet of Vorimar. This is the hiding place of A'Vaddon. On the northern half of the planet, in the quarter of Malidus, are the deadly mountains of Durondrus. Inside one of the many tunnels, in a secret chamber, a crystal ball rests.

A man covered in all-black armor stood in front of the crystal, his eyes staring intensely into its core. But, he wasn't looking at just anything, he was in fact watching Susan as she was laughing at Caroldus. His blood boiled at the sound of her laughter.

He slammed his fist onto the stone table, causing it to shake and the people sitting around it to sit straighter. They didn't dare say a word as the man threw his chair against the wall. Some of them flinched as the chair shattered into pieces when he struck it with black lightning, one of the main powers of the most powerful beings in the realm. A'Vaddon.

He looked back at the fifteen people watching him. His stare pierced them all, even though they couldn't see his eyes. A dragon stood in the corner behind him, glaring.

"She's back," A'Vaddon hissed, looking at each of them through his mask. "That *little* girl always appears when I'm on the verge of attack."

"But, A'Vaddon," one of the men calmly said. "Perhaps she has no knowledge of her powers, they may have placed her with the wrong guardian."

In a split second A'Vaddon turned towards the man and raised his hand towards him, using his telekinesis to lift the man and bring him towards himself. The man went flying out of his chair and towards A'Vaddon until he was only centimeters away from his masked face. A'Vaddon saw the fear written all over his follower's features, cold sweat dripping down his face, his mouth wide open, and his hands trembling as he gripped A'Vaddon's wrist in a feeble attempt to make him release him.

"Do you think Regel is that stupid?" A'Vaddon growled in a low, menacing voice, causing shivers to go down everyone's spines.

It wasn't often that A'Vaddon lost his temper, but when he did, it was highly suggested to run. Unfortunately, none of his followers could run at the moment.

"Don't waste your strength, A'Vaddon," a calm voice called from behind, causing his eyes to harden under his mask.

A'Vaddon let go of the man currently in his grip, and swiftly turned, only to face a man in a long hood that only left his mouth and chin visible.

"You'll need your strength to defeat Susan," the man continued. "That is, if you can."

A'Vaddon sneered, insulted at the idea that he *couldn't* defeat Susan. He stood straight and looked down at the man standing a few feet from him.

"Akuma?" A'Vaddon questioned. "Unless you have some useful information, you might as well get out."

He turned back to his council, caring little about what his informant had to say.

"Susan was placed with the wrong guardian~," Akuma said in a sing-song tone, catching A'Vaddon's attention. "Your plan worked. She has no idea what her powers are, or if she even has any. She also has barely any idea who you are, and I've seen to it she never gets any deep information about you."

At the sound of this news, A'Vaddon grinned.

"Anything else?" He asked.

"Yes. King Regel is going to call on her today, but I'm still not sure why."

"Come back once you've found out."

The man nodded and turned, disappearing down a hall.

A'Vaddon turned back to the crystal ball and stared at it once again, but now Susan was back on the ground having a conversation with Scadrin.

"You don't see me, but I see you," A'Vaddon whispered into the crystal as if he was speaking to Susan.

At that same moment, Susan heard those words echoing in her head, causing her eyes to widen and shivers to crawl down her spine. She looked behind her, expecting to see William or Caroldus playing a prank on her, but no one was there.

A'Vaddon laughed to himself as he watched her freak out.

"A'Vaddon," a woman at the table said. "If I may, why don't you just kill her through the crystal?"

A'Vaddon looked at her coldly, but he didn't get angry. It was a valid enough question for a new recruit.

"I very much wish I could do that," he admitted. "Then I would've been able to kill Regel long ago. But this crystal doesn't work like that. And I wouldn't kill Susan if I could anyway."

"Why?"

"Because she could be the best ally I've ever had, if I can convince her to join us. I need to break her, and hard. Too bad her mother is dead, she would've been just the thing. But, for now, all I can do is watch and prepare." He looked at the other people at the table. "If any of you touch Susan Wellns without my consent then you'll have to answer to me."

All of the followers nodded, the fear of punish- ment driving their agreement. A'Vaddon swiftly left the room, the large black dragon following him out.

They walked down large halls, made to fit a dragon of course, then entered a room full of furniture and many books. Five shelves full of ancient texts, with more piled on desks. All were filled with knowledge and most had unreadable titles.

A'Vaddon reached his hands behind his head and lifted his mask slowly, letting the cold air of the room cool his face from the heat of the mask. He tilted his head back, closed his eyes, and sighed.

"Being human is tiring," he thought as he opened his eyes and set his mask on a desk.

He had two large scars on his face, one going from just below the left temple down to the bottom of his cheek. The other scar went across his jaw, and several smaller ones were scattered all across his face and along his neck. His oil black hair glistened with sweat, and dark circles bagged under his eyes.

He walked over to the other side of the room and sat on a cushioned chair, rubbing his dark amber eyes. The dragon walked up to him and rubbed his head against his side.

"Don't worry, Furiton," A'Vaddon assured his companion, rubbing its neck. "This time I won't just scare Susan. I'll make her join us or I'll kill her. She won't have any other choice. Soon she'll have no memory of her friends."

"How would you know?" Furiton hissed.

The dragon looked into its master's amber eyes, patiently waiting for an answer.

"Do you doubt me?"

"I doubt everyone. I make no sudden conclusions,"

"What's one thing you would add to my plan?"

Furiton grinned, well, a dragon grin that is. He had been waiting for this question.

"Send your war General, Judez, to be placed into one of the patrols. Let him use his 'influence', to sway Susan over to our side. She'll never see it coming."

A'Vaddon approved of this suggestion. "You are wise beyond your years, Furiton, but you have a flaw in your plan. How would you get Judez into Zudanum? He's not going to want to go back."

"You can leave that up to me. Just make sure he is ready."

The dragon turned and walked out of the room. A'Vaddon put his helmet on and stood, waiting. A tall, burly man walked into the room, his arms folded, a mask covering his face.

"Judez," A'Vaddon greeted. "I have a task for you."

"If this is about Susan Wellns I'm not going," Judez snapped. "I said I'd never go back to Zudanum and I meant it."

"Yes, it is, and yes, you are. I need you to go back and use your charm to sway her. I need her on my side, and you're the key to that. I trust that you won't fail me."

Judez didn't say anything as his eyes glanced at a random book.

"I don't want to do this," he said.

"This isn't open for an argument. I need Susan, and I need her *now*. Prove your loyalty to me and win her over. If not, I'll send you back to the sewers where I found you. So either tolerate staying on Zudanum for a few years or stay there forever."

Judez sighed before reluctantly nodding. "I'll bring her."

"Good, because time is valuable right now. Grab your weapons and go. Furiton's waiting for you, he has a plan to get you into Zudanum."

"Since no one knows I'm alive this should work out perfectly."

Judez was about to walk out when A'Vaddon stopped him.

"I need her alive," he reminded. "It's the only way I can get the Jewel of Numenera. Do you understand? I need the jewel."

"Don't worry about it."

***

Susan and the others were about to put their companions away when they heard yelling on the other side of the field.

"Give that back, Subaron!" Cried the voice of a little girl, which is what first caught Susan's attention.

"It's not yours!" The voice of Subaron scolded.

William, Susan, Caroldus, and Roi Gurri raced to the girl, just as Subaron took off into the sky with his companion.

"What happened?" Susan asked the girl as she jumped off of Pearl Bolt.

"Subaron stole my crystal ball," she explained, her eyes glistening with tears.

Susan's heart softened towards the girl but turned as hard as stone when she thought of Subaron. She barely noticed Roi Gurri's hard expression as he knelt down and wrapped his arms around the girl in a comforting manner.

"I'll get it," Susan said.

She jumped back on Pearl Bolt and flew up to Subaron. She flew up in front of Subaron and his pegasus, a pure black stallion.

"Give that back Subaron," Susan demanded, trying to steady her voice. Considering that they were a few hundred feet in the air, she thought she was doing well. "I thought you were above stealing from kids."

"Clearly you don't know what this is," Subaron said as he held up the ball, which appeared to be made of crystal.

"I don't care, give it back!"

"Go get it," Subaron said as he threw the ball down.

Susan didn't hesitate as she jumped off of Pearl Bolt and free-fell towards the ball. Subaron looked down as she fell and shrugged.

"I didn't see that coming," he muttered.

Everyone was yelling and pointing at Susan as she fell. Roi Gurri looked over to William, who was watching Susan with a horrified expression.

"Holy Jehoyam," Caroldus gasped. "Are we going to have to catch her?"

"What choice do we have?" William asked. "Roi Gurri, come on, we've got to get under her."

"Right," the prince agreed.

Truth be told, Susan barely knew what she was doing. Her body seemed to have moved on its own, but she didn't know what to do after she jumped. She barely moved toward the ball, so she dove to go faster.

She reached out her hand and grabbed the crystal ball.

"You're so stupid," Susan thought. *"Now what are you going to do?"*

She looked to her left to find Pearl Bolt flying near her. She twisted her body beside the companion, lifted herself onto Pearl Bolt, and hung on tight.

Pearl Bolt swooped up and stopped her from crashing into the ground just in the nick of time. She cried out when her grip loosened, letting go of Pearl Bolt and crashing onto the ground. Pearl Bolt landed in front of her as Roi Gurri ran up to her.

"Are you alright?" He asked, helping her stand.

She nodded, dusting herself off and wincing as she felt several scrapes and cuts on her body.

"I'm fine," Susan replied, before watching Subaron as he landed. "You did that on purpose," she growled at him. "I could've died."

"Wouldn't have been funny if you did," Subaron said in a serious tone.

"Then why did you provoke her?" Roi Gurri snapped. "I guess the Chosen One would be dead because of you then, isn't that right?"

"Oh shut up!" Subaron snapped. "Shut up about the stupid prophecy, about a stupid girl being the Chosen One, and about her being so special. Susan doesn't even have powers! Let me ask you now, how is this weak, pathetic mutt going to destroy the most powerful demon in history, who has thousands of years of experience?"

Roi Gurri's face turned red with anger, and everyone gasped.

"Susan's a mutt?" People started getting into arguments.

"He's lying."

"No, he's not, I read about her bloodline in the library,"

"You're stupid for an Owl Perch. How can a mutt destroy an anti-natural?"

"Her mother did it. And how would a Kindness Keep know anything about the Wellns bloodline?"

"Her mother happened to be from *my* patrol, you know."

"I heard that she isn't even anti-natural."

"Another stupid suggestion."

Susan lost it. "Everybody shut up!" She screamed. Everyone immediately stopped talking and looked at her. "It's true, I'm a mutt. My mother was a normal person, just like most of us. And if you've heard that I'm not anti-natural, then you've heard the truth. I don't have any powers."

Whispers started to break out again, and Susan sighed. No matter what she said, or how many times she could try and prove herself, someone would always find something against her.

As she was thinking, Scadrin marched up to her and slapped her, causing her to stumble back into William's chest. Susan was shocked and confused as her cheek throbbed in pain.

"What in the name of King Regel were you thinking?" Scadrin scolded. "Jumping off of Pearl Bolt that high in the air?"

She leaned over Susan, getting in her face. Susan wasn't quite sure what to say.

"I believe I did the right thing," Susan defended herself, trying to not let her voice shake as she stood up straight again.

"And why is that?"

"I stood up to someone who thinks that he's bigger than everyone else."

"And who might that be?"

Susan glanced at Subaron before she looked back at Scadrin. "Oh, I think you know who I'm talking about."

The little girl ran up to Scadrin and tapped her leg. Scadrin swiftly turned around but lost some of her steam when she saw her.

"She saved my crystal ball from Subaron," the girl said, her voice soft and sweet like a melody.

"You took a very big risk asking Susan to do that," Scadrin scolded, still very angry.

"I didn't ask her to, she volunteered. And, I am very grateful for that."

She walked up to Susan and smiled. Susan looked in her hand, saw the still-intact crystal ball, and handed it to the girl.

"Thank you very much!" The girl said as she ran off.

Susan looked up at Scadrin, her head held up high, and her shoulders straight.

"You got lucky this time, Adathir," Scadrin said. "But what you did was very dangerous. Go to the throne room, the king has called for you and Terra."

Chapter Eight
Forced Arrangements

Susan turned to Roi Gurri as he came over to her.

"Do you need help getting to the throne room?" He asked.

She blushed and nodded, embarrassed that she had forgotten the way. Roi Gurri sighed and grabbed her hand, pulling her away from everyone else.

Susan wasn't sure if he was pulling her because he was angry or annoyed at her. But either way, he had an iron grip that did not come off as friendly.

He pulled her away from the training grounds, which were behind the castle, past gardens, down hallways, and soon they were in front of the tall golden doors that lead to the throne room.

Susan yanked her hand out of Roi Gurri's, finally having enough of being dragged, and gave him a cold look.

"Did I do something wrong?" She snapped, annoyed.

"You almost killed yourself, so yes," Roi Gurri snapped back, annoyed as well that she didn't already know this.

"Were you going to do anything? I'm not going to stand around while Subaron acts like a jerk to everyone he sees. Including me!"

"That's what your mother felt about A'Vaddon, and look where it got her!"

Susan did everything she could to keep a straight face and not lash out, but it was very difficult.

"You know what, I don't have to take this from you."

She tried to walk past him, but he moved in front of her.

"We are *not* done with this conversation," he growled.

"Oh yes, we are. You crossed the line when you brought my mother into this, *Drago*."

Roi Gurri's arm lashed out and he grabbed her arm, which was Susan's last straw.

"Do not touch me!" Susan snapped.

She slapped him, tore her arm out of his grasp, and swung open the two golden doors.

Roi Gurri barely noticed the action of the doors opening and grabbed her wrist roughly, yanking her back to his side. She winced and turned and twisted his hand. He let out a cry and knocked her onto the floor. She swiftly got up just in time to dodge a hit from him. She tried to kick him, but he grabbed her foot and flipped her over. She pulled her foot out of his hands and kicked him in the face. He moved back in shock, now angered. She got up and stood in front of him, her fists held up.

"Do you really think that your fists are going to stop an anti-natural?" He asked her challengingly.

"Let's find out," she spat.

He shot thorny vines out of his fingers at her. She quickly leaned back and the roots flew over her. She pulled out her sword and sliced the roots and branches that he shot at her, desperately trying not to get hit.

Although she tried hard, he did manage to hit her with a vine and pin her to the opposite wall. Susan cried out in pain as a root pressed hard against her abdomen, thorns threatening to pierce through her shirt and into her skin. She held her breath so her stomach didn't expand, trying to think of a way out of this position.

Roi Gurri pointed an accusatory finger at Susan and went to yell at her when a cough echoed through the room. The two looked over with wide eyes to see that the large golden doors were wide open, and King Regel and his chief advisor were watching the two closely.

Roi Gurri's expression dropped, quickly releasing Susan and standing at attention in front of his father. She fell on her feet but leaned against the wall for support as she pulled in deep breaths. She picked up her sword, placed it in her scabbard, and stood next to Roi Gurri, her eyes fixed on King Regel.

"What was that?!" King Regel boomed, an angered look directed at Roi Gurri.

There was silence for a moment as Roi Gurri glanced down at Susan, but she refused to look up at him.

"I'm sorry, father," Roi Gurri finally replied. "I overreacted, and I apologize."

King Regel stroked his beard thoughtfully and looked over at Susan.

"Susan, what did he say to make the both of you overreact?" He asked.

Susan glanced up at Roi Gurri, and he looked down at her. She knew she had started the physical fight by slapping him, but the look he was giving her seemed to convey to let him take the fall. She acknowledged to herself that she overreacted before looking up at King Regel.

"I provoked him," she replied. "I take the blame."

Roi Gurri was relieved and grateful that she didn't tell his father, allowing himself to relax.

"You're lucky, Drago," Susan thought as the two kept silent, waiting for King Regel's response.

He finally nodded, but he didn't seem satisfied with the answer.

"Very well," the king said. "Roi Gurri, leave us now, but wait by the door." Roi Gurri nodded and closed the golden doors behind him as he walked out. "Come here, Susan."

Susan walked up to King Regel and bowed, but he waved his hand in dismissal.

"None of that nonsense now, we have very important things to discuss."

"With all due respect sir, what things?" Susan asked. "I've barely been here for three days."

"I know, that is the reason we have so many things to discuss." King Regel got off of his throne and walked over to the small table his advisor was standing at. "Susan, this is my chief advisor, Sondman."

"Nice to meet you," Susan greeted him.

"Yes, very nice to meet you as well," Sondman said to Susan with a nod of his head. "Bring your sword over here, Susan." She took off her scabbard, and set it down on the table. "Now, look very closely. Do you see the bright gem on the end of the handle?"

"I see it very clearly," Susan said. "Does it have a meaning?"

"This sword is a very rare sword, known as a Necto Blade. There are twelve of these blades in all, and each one has a Phantom Gem on the handle."

"What is a Phantom Gem?"

"Each gem is the embodiment of a unique force of nature. Legend has it that if the owner of the blade takes out the gem and presses it to their heart, they will have the unlimited power of the Phantom Gem."

"So they can give you powers?"

"In a sense."

"What are their powers?"

"Light, sound, mind, fire, water, earth, speed, electricity, healing, gravity, strength, and hope."

"Hope is not a physical power, so what good can it do?"

"That is what most people think, but you must look on the inside."

"Sounds like all of that sloppy stuff I heard about when I was a kid," Susan said bitterly.

"You never believed in any of those things?" Sondman asked.

"Why should I? I have no family, I have no real home. Even if this was my parent's home, I know nothing about it."

"I completely understand, but now that you are here, you must think of us as your family."

"It's not that easy, Sondman."

"Susan, your parents wanted you to become as strong as possible, so now we will do all we can to fulfill that wish."

"Has anyone put a Phantom Gem up to their heart?" She asked, changing the subject.

"Yes, but no one has been able to do it in a thousand years. Not all Necto Blade holders are worthy."

"Which gem do I have?"

"You have the gem of Hope."

"Of course, I'm stuck on a planet I know nothing about, I had a family I know nothing about, and I was given a 'powerful' weapon to defend myself and even ***that*** *is useless."*

"Who else has a Necto Blade?" Susan asked.

"Roi Gurri, who has the Necto Blade of Earth, and A'Vaddon, who has the Necto Blade of Fire. The other Necto Blades are scattered among the twelve realms."

Susan reflected upon everything she had just heard. Powerful blades didn't sound as bizarre as anti-naturals and A'Vaddon, but it was still a hard idea for her to wrap her mind around. She had the intrusive thought to pull the Phantom Gem out of her blade, but she quickly pushed it away. She looked to King Regel.

"I sense this is not the only reason you brought me here," Susan said.

"Of course not," King Regel affirmed. "But before I continue, I must ask you, do you have any skills that might help you in battle?"

"I don't know much of anything. But I found out earlier today that I'm decent with a sword."

"Have you unlocked any abilities yet?"

"No, none. But I'll let you know the minute I do."

"Grab your sword and come over here."

Susan drew the sword from her scabbard on the table and held it to her side before following Regel to the open floor.

"Fight me," King Regel ordered.

Susan froze in place, stunned. She didn't want to fight King Regel, especially when she knew that he was a very powerful anti-natural user. But she assumed that he was testing her.

"Why should I?" Susan asked.

King Regel lifted his hand and shot Susan with a blast of green energy. She went flying across the room and hit the wall behind her harshly, knocking the wind out of her. Her body ached and her muscles involuntary clenched to keep her from moving.

"Did his blast just paralyze me?"

"Fight me!" King Regel commanded again.

"You are paralyzed. You can't get up."

"Yes I can," Susan groaned. "I have to get up. 'Cause if I don't, what am I worth to these people?"

She slowly stood and looked the king in the eye, still barely able to move.

"Impossible," Sondman breathed out.

King Regel was thinking the exact same thing.

"I can arrange that for you," Susan said to King Regel as she gripped her sword.

She started to run towards him, her heart racing and her legs burning as she desperately tried to keep her mental concentration.

King Regel shot another ball of energy at her, but this time Susan was ready. She dodged and ran, not sure what she was doing, only knowing that if she wanted the fight to end she had to hit him hard enough. She avoided and blocked energy blasts with her shield as she ran toward him. She took her shield and used it to push him, but he didn't budge.

He grabbed her shield and twisted it, twisting her arm as well. She cried out and pulled her arm out of the shield grippings. She swung her sword up at him and barely missed his beard. He dropped Susan's shield and shot a ball of energy at her. Susan wasn't fast enough and was stung by the energy, falling to the floor. She felt even more pain, her heart palpitating, but she kept going.

"You can't get rid of me that easily," Susan panted.

She stood and grabbed the end of her shield, standing still. King Regel shot another blast of energy at her, but this time Susan took her shield and used it to redirect the energy back at him. He didn't move in time and was struck by his own power. He fell with a groan and didn't get up. She ran up to him and stood over him, her sword hovering over his neck. Sweat poured down her face and her body ached badly.

Badly enough that she couldn't react when King Regel blasted her with his energy from under her. That blow was the final straw for Susan's body. She immediately collapsed onto the ground, unable to even think about moving. King Regel stood, as if unaffected by his own power's blast.

"Pathetic," the king murmured. "Roi Gurri!" He called.

Roi Gurri came rushing in and knelt beside Susan, putting his hands on her shoulders and sending his healing energy into her. As soon as Roi Gurri had untensed all of her muscles Susan took in a big, long breath of air.

"Oh my God," Susan gasped, rolling onto her side and coughing.

"Are you okay?" Roi Gurri asked, keeping a hand on her back and continuing to heal her.

Susan held in a laugh as she nodded. She knew Roi Gurri had been watching the fight the whole time.

"I'm good," Susan rasped. "Help me up."

Roi Gurri obeyed and practically lifted Susan off the ground, holding her up as she regained her strength.

"I am still disappointed in you two for fighting," King Regel said to the two teens. "You must learn to get along, it's important that you do."

"Would it be the worst thing in the world if Roi Gurri and I didn't get along?" Susan asked.

"Yes. Because as of today, you are betrothed to each other."

The two teens looked at each other, both embarrassed and quickly looking back at the king.

"But-But I'm not anti-natural," Susan pointed out shakily. "I don't have any powers. I couldn't even beat you!"

"Well, you must have something, because you survived black electricity. Few people have survived that. And fewer have been able to move after taking on one of my paralyzing blasts."

"Black electricity? That doesn't exist."

"In this world, it does. Black electricity is one of A'Vaddon's powers."

"What are his others?

"We're not sure. There are lots of records saying he has a wide variety of powers and many claims he has over a dozen. Though, we doubt it. It's very rare to have more than five powers."

"What does it mean if you have more than five?"

"Then your body is very resilient. Anybody, no matter what race, can only take so much power. Perhaps you'll break that cycle. After all, you're destined for great things."

"But there is nothing special about me. My parents may have been great, but I'm not. You are mistaken to choose me for Roi Gurri, please, he deserves someone much greater than I! I can't even tell you who the first King of Zudanum was, that's how new to this I am."

"You have animal instinct," Roi Gurri pointed out.

Susan looked up at him with her brow raised. "What do you mean?"

"I've seen the way you've trained, Susan. I've never seen someone move with such precision, or have such high levels of senses on their first day. Your levels of seeing, hearing, and touch are incredible. That may be the only thing you think is 'special' about you, but don't disregard it as nothing."

"I always thought it was normal. But from now on, I'll do my best to improve that skill."

He smiled and she returned it.

"You are dismissed," King Regel said as he waved them away. "The arrangements have already been made, my word is the law and will not be revoked. On Roi Gurri's twenty-third birthday, you will wed."

Susan and Roi Gurri looked at each other and bowed to King Regel before walking out.

The silence between the two was awkward as they walked, both of them stealing looks at each other.

"It wasn't my idea," Roi Gurri muttered.

Susan looked up at him and nodded. "I know," she replied calmly. "We should try to get along anyway."

"Yeah, it wouldn't be good if the king and Chosen One were constantly fighting. I'm sorry for what I said earlier. I just want you to stay safe."

"I suppose I can forgive you."

He looked down at her with a small smile, but she had turned her nose up to hide her blush.

"Thank you, Susan. And by the way, the first king of Zudanum was Aldist Drago."

"Really? I started reading about her yesterday. I noticed that Aldist is one of my middle names."

"Your parents probably really admired her."

Before Susan could ask him more about the king, she heard footsteps following them. The two turned to see that Regel's advisor, Sondman, had followed them out into the hall.

"There is one more thing I must show you," he said to Susan. "It is something that once belonged to your father, and I must now give it to you."

Susan glanced at Roi Gurri, who nodded, and she turned to Sondman.

"Lead the way," she responded and he smiled.

He led them down to the east wing of the castle, and into an empty, dark hallway.

"There's nothing here," Susan observed and Sondman chuckled.

"Thousands of years ago," Sondman started to explain, "when this castle was first built, King Doral had secret passages placed inside of the walls. Most of them were in case the castle was overthrown by an enemy, but some lead to secret rooms that hold the most valuable and powerful objects in Zudanum. What I'm about to give you is one of them."

Sondman walked over to a brick and he pressed on it with the palm of his hand. Susan was sure she saw a marking on the brick, but it was too high for her to see. A hiss echoed in the hall and a secret door in the wall opened. Her face turned pale as she looked through the door to see nothing but darkness.

"Fire doesn't scare you but this does?" Roi Gurri asked, amused.

Susan shot him a glare and he raised his hands in surrender.

"It just surprised me," she protested.

"Whatever you say."

"Follow me," Sondman motioned for them to follow him into the passage.

The door quickly shut behind them. Susan shivered as they entered the cold, stone passageway, a draft flowing through the hall. She observed the small amounts of light coming in through cracks in the stone. Water slowly dripped down onto the floor, the sound of the droplets echoed along with their footsteps.

Sondman led them down several mazes of halls, taking many turns and even climbing down a few stairs.

Finally, he opened an old wooden door to a room. In the room was a stone table, and resting on it was a small blood-red jewel. It was smaller than the palm of Susan's hand.

"What's so special about this jewel?" Susan asked, admiring it.

"This is the Jewel of Numenera," the advisor explained. "It was entrusted to your father, before he died. It is now to be passed down to you. And one day, you will pass it down to the offspring you think worthy. It is told to have untold power, and death will come to you if you touch it."

"How?"

"Those very few who *have* survived no longer live to tell. But we believe the stone torments your mind, taking control of you like a puppet, and finally, the person's mind has enough and quits. It is now your duty to take the stone, and to protect it."

Susan stared deep into the jewel, as if she was expecting it to show her something. She felt that the jewel was alive and could both see and hear her, which was creepy.

"Can any good come of this stone?" Susan asked.

"Those that did touch the jewel, and lived to tell, wrote that if the stone allows you to hold it you'll be unstoppable," Sondman explained. "Of course, that hasn't been done in centuries."

Susan sighed in reluctant agreement. Roi Gurri handed her a handkerchief, and she wrapped the stone in it before putting it in her pocket.

"I'll guard it with my life," Susan promised. "But first, I need to learn how to do that. I need to get back to training. Thank you, Sondman."

"It is my pleasure, Susan."

Susan nodded and turned to follow Roi Gurri out of the tunnels. But as she left she thought that Sondman's eyes flashed from blue to red. And, to add to her suspicion, he gave a smile that made her think of Subaron.

"Did you enjoy the fight?" Susan asked Roi Gurri, his eyes widening.

"How did you know I was watching?" He asked.

"I noticed that the door was cracked open."

They both laughed, their cheeks turning pink.

"Are we good now?" She asked, looking up at him.

He looked down at her and smiled. "Yeah. Just don't do anything stupid from now on."

"No promises."

"I see I'm going to always have to be on my toes with you, Little Legs."

***

"How was your free time?" William asked when Susan and Roi Gurri walked out to join them.

They looked at each other and silently agreed not to say anything about their betrothal.

"It was alright," Roi Gurri said with a shrug. "It was more like a history lesson."

William chuckled and Caroldus raced up to them.

"You guys just missed it," Caroldus said, "Scadrin yelled at Subaron as if he had killed the king! It was so funny."

Susan laughed as she imagined it, but paused as she looked down to see the little girl from earlier looking up at her.

"I forgot to tell you my name," she said. "I'm Sutan, I'm Roi Gurri's little sister."

Susan smiled in delight as she looked from Roi Gurri to Sutan. She had the same vibrant red hair as the queen and the same sea blue eyes as Roi Gurri.

"It's nice to meet you, Sutan." Susan said. "I'm Susan."

"You don't have to tell me," Sutan said. "I knew who you were right when I saw you."

"How?"

"Only a Wellns can ride Pearl Bolt. She bucks off everyone else, except me of course. I'm a natural when it comes to animals."

She laughed and ran off towards a small pack of baby unicorns, who immediately greeted her with neighs. Susan laughed and looked up at Roi Gurri.

"You don't want to tell them?" She whispered, referring to their arrangement.

He sighed. "They'll find out sooner or later," he said. "Word spreads really fast around here. And I don't want to talk about it. At least, not now."

She nodded and walked towards Scadrin.
"Are you still mad at me?" She asked.

Scadrin folded her arms and glared at her.

"What do you think?" She asked. "You almost died. That would've been on my hands."

"I'm sorry, and I'm ready to get back to training."

"Aren't you still recovering from the energy that King Regel shot at you?"

Susan shook her head. "Roi Gurri healed me, I don't feel any effects. Wait, how do you know that happened?"

"Word spreads fast, a servant happened to be watching. It seems that you have learned that the mind is stronger than the body."

"For a little while, it was. But King Regel's strategy was better than mine, which is why I have to get back to training."

Chapter Nine
The Hot-Headed Father

Susan wanted to find the library as soon as she could but had to wait a month before she had the time to do so. Scadrin had been making sure to keep her busy with training and learning everything she could ever need to know about Zudanum, but Susan needed to find the library for a different purpose.

It was late, most of the Warrior Brave Patrol was asleep, including William and Caroldus. Susan thought she had successfully escaped the room without being noticed, but was quickly proven wrong.

"Hey." Susan flinched at the heavy voice of Roi Gurri, quickly turning to face him. "Is everything okay?" He asked.

"Yeah, I just want to go to the library," Susan explained. "There are some things I want to look into that I haven't had the chance to do yet."

"Oh, okay. Have you been to the library yet?" Susan shook her head. "Then I'll show you the way. Try to remember how to come back, because I won't be able to stay."

"That's okay, thank you, Roi Gurri."

He nodded and wordlessly led her to the library. The castle was built like a maze, meant to confuse any enemy that would dare to enter. You'd have to have lived in the castle for decades to be able to expertly manuver through it.

Besides being the home of the Drago family, it held all of the patrols. The four patrols had their own wing, away from the ballrooms, private quarters, war rooms, and so on. This was so the children who were training could be closely monitored, and also close to the biggest ground army force in case of an attack.

It was also full of many wonders, such as talking statues. Each of the patrols had one main guardian, and a second that the main guardian could awaken when they needed extra protection. Lucas, the metal wolf, guarded the Warrior Brave Patrol with a stone knight. A metal eagle and huge stone wild-cat guarded the Kindness Keep Patrol. A huge metal cobra and a stone hare guarded the Cobra Cave Patrol. And a metal owl and stone mouse guard the Owl Perch Patrol. Susan had never met the other guardians, because they were always at the door to their patrol, and she had never entered the other patrol's dorms.

Susan was in awe of the library's size from the moment she stepped in. Dozens, no, hundreds of bookshelves were completely full of holographic records and books dating before the reign of Chief Roi Gurri the First, the great-grandfather of King Aldist the Patriarch of Justice. The data of the holographic files were stored in books with yellow glowing spines, and when opened all of the folders in the drive would pop up. The files could be moved and touched, but would always return to the book once it was closed.

"Do you know what you're specifically looking for?" Roi Gurri asked.

Susan didn't want to lie to him, but she was worried about what he'd say. The last time she had brought up this subject it almost ended in disaster.

"I'm looking for records on my parents," Susan quietly admitted.

Roi Gurri didn't say anything, he only nodded. He made his way to the heart of the library, and Susan followed.

"This section is dedicated to past soldiers," Roi Gurri explained, motioning to the shelves. "Both of your parents were employed by the castle for at least fifty years. You'll find their records here."

Susan was surprised. "I thought you didn't want me to look into my family."

"I've come to realize I was being selfish. If I were in your shoes, I would want to know about my parents too. I think sometimes I forget that I think and remember things differently than everyone else. I have no right to tell you that you can't look into your parents when I knew them better than you."

Susan was glad, and relieved, about Roi Gurri's change of heart. "I thought you couldn't forget anything," she jested.

He chuckled and shook his head. "I hope you find what you're looking for. If you get lost on the way back, call for Lucas, he'll come to find you."

Susan nodded in affirmation as he left the library. She immediately searched through the holographic files until she found the ones labeled;

"Marcus Wellns: Vulcan"
"Defestri Parphit Wellns: Aurora"

Susan brought them to the entrance of the library, which was full of tables to allow people to research and work. She was glad she was the only person in the library because a part of her felt like she was doing something she wasn't supposed to. Then she remembered she had Roi Gurri's approval and started with her father's file.

As soon as she opened the book she was met with a glowing picture of her father. He looked stern and serious, but still handsome. His hair was black as coal, but his eyes were bright and shining like amber. Susan could see a lot of her features in her father, like his nose and eyes. It was hard to believe her hair didn't end up black like his, but her mother's genes must have been very strong. She began reading his 'General Info' file.

"Count Marcus Wellns. The only son of General Karniss and Countess Falgide Wellns."

"I wonder why they only had one kid," Susan mused. "You'd think if you were alive for so long you'd at least want two."

"Born: Twelfth day, third month, year 10,733
"Patrol of Origin: Cobra Cave."
"Alias: Vulcan."
"Abilities: Pyrokinesis, flight, lightning manipulation (white)."

"Lightning manipulation?" Susan wondered aloud. "Like A'Vaddon?"

Susan paused. Just because her father had lightning manipulation, didn't mean he was related to A'Vaddon. Subaron had lightning manipulation too, and the Tugars had no biological relation to the Wellns or to A'Vaddon. Plus, their classes of lightning were different. A'Vaddon had control over black lightning, the most powerful class. Subaron has control over blue lightning, the middle class. White was the lowest. She moved on to his 'School Reports' file.

"Report: First day, first month, year 10,580

Vulcan shows tremendous strength. He has already developed a clear understanding of his Pyrokinesis, though he has a big head and temperament. He has begun to pick fights and make enemies with other students.

From the desk of Colonel Scadrin J."

Susan couldn't help but laugh. Her father sounded like a brat, and on his first day was making enemies! No wonder no one wanted to talk about him, he probably made enemies with King Regel himself, or maybe even those on the council.

"Maybe that's why they hate me too. Maybe it's not just because of my height and knowledge, but because my dad was a punk kid."

"Report: First day, fifth month, year 10,591

Vulcan has exceeded every expectation and trial I have put before him. Though, I will not allow him to graduate yet due to his issue with authority.

From the desk of Colonel Scadrin J."

"I wonder if my dad was dumb enough to talk back to Scadrin," Susan wondered. "Even Owl Perch knows not to get smart or have an attitude with her."

"Yes, they do," an unfamiliar voice said.

Susan quickly looked up to find a gigantic metal cobra slithering toward her! Her eyes went wide, and she didn't know whether to run or scream. He must've seen the fear in her eyes because he stopped and tried to smile.

"I am Tristen," the snake introduced himself. "I am the guardian for the Cobra Cave Patrol."

"Oh-Oh, that makes sense," Susan said with a nervous chuckle.

"I couldn't help but wonder who was in the library at this hour. Your father used to come here in the late hours as well, studying everything he thought would be even a little bit useful to him."

"Why?"

"Because he was a powerful boy, who wanted more power." Susan frowned. "Don't get me wrong, he was a good kid, but he was hot-headed and had an ego."

"I guess that's why no one wants to talk about him?"

"He wasn't exactly a people pleaser." Tristen slithered up to Susan's side and used his tail to scroll down Scadrin's reports. "But he did improve."

"Report: First day, twelfth month, year 10,593

I have successfully found no fault in Vulcan's training. He is a brave warrior, a brilliant tactician, and a good man. I believe he is finally ready to graduate, and his potential is being wasted in school.

From the desk of Colonel Scadrin J."

"Report: First day, second month, year 10,594

Due to the slow movement of the council, I will be graduating Vulcan and giving him the rank of: Knight, effective immediately.

From the desk of Colonel Scadrin J."

Susan couldn't help but feel proud of her father. According to the dates of Scadrin's reports, he was only twenty when he graduated, and most graduated at twenty-five.

"He was a fast learner," she remarked.

"Oh, yes. He was as bright as he was dangerous. Perhaps that's why your mother was attracted to him."

"When did they meet?"

Tristen thought about it for a moment. "They formally met in his eighth year of training, and her ninth. I think he only became interested in her when she began showing off her expertise in combat training."

"But she was in Kindness Keep?"

Tristen nodded and opened Defestri's file. "Correct."

Susan looked at the picture of her mother in awe. The picture was much more stunning than her foggy memories. Her hair was bright blonde, so vibrant and frizzy it almost looked like it was on fire, but her skin was dark and her eyes were emerald green. The pictures of her parents side by side really put into perspective how completely different they were.

"Wow," Susan breathed out. "She's..."

"Stunning," Tristan filled in Susan's thoughts. "And her beauty was only enhanced by her fighting skills. She was proficient in handling a mace but was just as skilled with a long sword. Yes, I think it was when she beat your father in Swarbus that he finally noticed her."

"I guess that's one way to fall in love," Susan remarked.

"I said noticed, not fall in love. No, no, he claimed to hate her for years."

"Really?"

"He was frustrated by her ability to beat him in combat despite not being an anti-natural. She knocked down some of his pride, and could've taken credit for him graduating early."

"So when did they fall in love?"

"Oh... I'd say a few years later. Defestri graduated at twenty-three, and when she became a knight she and Marcus were assigned to go on a mission together. I remember when they came back, and the look on their faces was priceless. Something happened, no one knows what, but something happened on that mission that changed everything. They went on hundreds of missions together, and every time I think they fell more and more in love. After seventy-nine years he asked her out, and when they were both a few years over a hundred when they got married."

"Why did they wait so long?"

"Things here on Zudanum work differently than anywhere else because of our incredibly long lifespan. People have time to get to know each other, really intimately and personally, before they commit to being together forever. It's a big decision to be together for almost a thousand years."

"Not all of us get to know each other that personally before getting married."

Tristen couldn't help but feel sorry for the girl. "You may not have as long as your parents did, but not everyone needs eighty-four years to figure out if they have a connection. I truly believe that no matter what, Roi Gurri will be a good husband to you."

"You know that, but I don't. We haven't fought in the past month, but we haven't really connected either. I know we have about three years to figure it all out, but it doesn't seem like enough time."

"You'd be surprised at how much you can learn about a person in three years."

"Why couldn't my father make a decision in three years?"

"You've read the reports, Marcus was a hot head who didn't pay attention to anyone but himself. He didn't take the time to get to know Defestri, but you have the time to get to know Roi Gurri. Don't let it go to waste."

Susan slowly nodded. "Thank you, Tristen."

"Of course. Now, my dear, it is very late. You want to get your sleep for your day of rest tomorrow, right?"

"I should, but I don't want to stop reading yet."

"Take the files with you."

"I can do that?"

"Of course. Just make sure you return them within sixty days."

Susan nodded, collecting her things before following Tristin out of the library. Despite wanting energy for tomorrow, she stayed up reading about her parents late into the night.

Chapter Ten
The Haunted Estate

The next morning, Susan was awoken by someone gently shaking her shoulder. She groaned and rolled over, trying to fall back asleep.

"Let me be," she moaned. "It's the day of rest."

"Trust me, you're gonna want to wake up," Roi Gurri's calm voice hazily flooded her head.

Susan sighed and rolled over, looking up into Roi Gurri's beautiful blue eyes. She got lost in them as she thought about whether to go back to bed or not.

"This better be important," Susan said.

"It is," Roi Gurri assured. "Get ready, I'm taking you somewhere special today."

"Do I get to know where?"

"No, not yet."

He left the room, allowing Susan to get dressed and pack a bag before meeting him in the common room.

"What time is it?" Susan asked with a yawn.

"Seven," Roi Gurri responded.

"Are you kidding me? Roi-"

"You're going to be able to sleep in the ship. Come on, I know you won't regret it."

"I guess I'm awake already, I might as well follow him."

Susan nodded, and Roi Gurri led her to the docking bay. There he acquired a small ship that was painted green, with his family symbol on the side.

"You guys have spaceships?" Susan asked in awe.

"Well, this one is my personal form of long-distance transportation, but yes, Zudanums have spaceships," Roi Gurri explained. "There's room for you to sleep in the back, it's going to take about an hour to get there."

Susan nodded and climbed into the back, while Roi Gurri handed her some pillows and blankets. When he was sure she was comfortable, he moved to the driver's seat and began their journey.

Susan still wondered where they were going, but it didn't take long for her to fall asleep. When she awoke they were still moving, but it was a lot brighter out. She made her way to the front of the ship, sitting in the co-pilot's seat.

"I was wondering when you were going to awake," Roi Gurri said with a smile. "We're getting close."

"Still not going to tell me where we're going?" Susan asked.

"That'd take the fun out of the surprise." Susan rolled her eyes but didn't press him. "There are some drinks in the compartment next to you if you'd like some."

"Thanks." Susan hydrated before leaning back against the seat and admiring the view. "Why are you doing this?" She looked over at Roi Gurri, but he only gave her a glance before looking ahead. "Do you still feel bad about what you saidlast night?"

"Yes," Roi Gurri admitted. "I was a jerk for trying to keep you from your family, I shouldn't have tried to do that. I'm just hoping this will help make up for that."

"You don't have to make up for anything, I already forgave you."

"Well, maybe you can forgive me again."

Susan realized the ship was landing and looked out to see they were in front of a giant black stone castle.

She would've called it a mansion if it wasn't so much more grand than one.

"Where are we?" Susan asked.

Roi Gurri stood and offered a hand to Susan. "Welcome home, Countess Wellns."

Susan accepted his hand and let him lead her out of the ship. They took their time approaching the castle, keeping on the gravel path. Susan didn't know what to think. This was her home? A castle with a gorgeous fountain in front? She looked up at Roi Gurri with a confused expression.

"I don't understand," she admitted quietly.

"This is the Wellns estate," Roi Gurri explained. "This is where your father grew up, and where he and your mother lived. I've had some people cleaning it for the past week, so you wouldn't come home and find it a mess."

Susan stayed quiet. To say she was in shock was an understatement.

"Come, let's go inside," Roi Gurri offered, leading her to the entrance.

He pulled out a set of keys and unlocked the door before holding it open for her. She walked in and stood at the entrance. The inside was covered in beautiful black marble and stone, which glistened in the light that shone through the dozen large windows. In the center of the room, two spiral staircases led upstairs, while the open floor stretched like a ballroom.

When Susan was ready to move she began exploring the ground floor, Roi Gurri following quietly behind. The ground floor was home to a grand dining hall, a ballroom, a kitchen, sitting rooms, and many rooms full of books and artifacts.

If it weren't for the lack of dust Susan would've had no doubt that no one had been in the manor since her parents died. The chillingly still air hadn't been stirred by a Wellns in over a decade. It was as if a museum was being visited by the very person its artifacts were made by.

A sense of reverie washed over Susan as she took her time exploring the sitting rooms. Books lined the walls, real paper books as well as holographic ones. Some books were even kept in glass cases to preserve them. Old jewelry and artifacts were displayed in the sitting rooms as well, preserved in crystal cases. Susan dared not open them in fear of ruining their state, but still admired them with awe.

Susan found herself drawn upstairs, which led to her finding several bedrooms. But only one was clearly the master bedroom, the biggest of all. The room held several dressers and a gigantic bed with a nightstand on both sides. Unlike the rest of the dark rooms, this room was painted with lighter colors, and the balcony windows were wide open, letting in the fresh air.

Susan walked over to the dressers and found the tops covered with pictures of her parents and her baby photos.

"This was my parent's room," she realized.

Susan picked up a photo of her parents embracing, both smiling like they were laughing. She couldn't stop the tears from welling up in her eyes. This picture told a much bigger, brighter story than the stoic ones on their files.

"They're real," she whispered. "They were really real."

Immediately Roi Gurri was by her side, wrapping his arm around her. She leaned into his embrace and clutched the photo in her hands. Reading about her parents and their adventures didn't feel as real as seeing them in these photos.

"I wish I could remember them like you," Susan admitted to Roi Gurri.

"I wish you could too," he said. "I wish you knew how much they loved you."

"Well, they did die for me. There is no greater love than to lay down your life for another."

"I agree."

"I just wish they could've waited a few more years to show that love." They both laughed and Susan wiped her tears away. "Thank you, Roi Gurri. You really are forgiven a second time."

"I'm glad to hear that."

"William, why are we here?" The faint, tired voice of Caroldus asked from downstairs.

Susan's eyes widened. "Caroldus and William are here?"

"Shoot, I told them to wait a few hours," Roi Gurri muttered. "I figured you didn't want to spend the day here with just me."

Susan laughed and shook her head. "Not that I would've minded too much, but you made the right call."

"This place is haunted," William's voice came, followed by a slapping sound. "Ow!"

"Shut up," Caroldus snapped.

Susan and Roi Gurri quickly made their way to the top of the stairs to find their two friends walking in separate directions.

"I told you two to wait for a reason!" Roi Gurri called.

"And why's that?" William snapped.

"Because I knew you two morning glories would kill each other."

William and Caroldus only glared at each other, and Susan couldn't help but laugh.

"There's a ton of beds here if you guys wanna get some rest," Susan offered.

"Pass," William said.

"I'm already up," Caroldus said with a shrug.

"Then let's explore the grounds," Susan suggested, already down the stairs and heading for the back door.

The men followed her outside to find a giant, shining marble courtyard surrounded by hedges. Susan stepped onto the courtyard and imagined that grand balls and parties were once held there. She could vividly picture the beautiful dresses and dashing suits as they danced under the four Zudanum moons.

Someone tapped Susan's shoulder, and she turned to see Caroldus smiling and offering his hand to her.

"May I have this dance?" He asked with a bow.

"I'd be delighted," Susan said, giggling as she accepted his hand.

He led her in a simple box step around the courtyard, spinning her occasionally to make her giggle and smile.

"You're quite the dancer," Caroldus complimented Susan. "Have you been practicing?"

"I wouldn't call this a difficult dance," Susan said. "But yes, Scadrin has been teaching me to dance."

"And why is that?"

"Because, 'balance, precision, and hand-eye coordination are best taught on the dance floor'."

Caroldus pretended to shudder. "Man, you sound just like Scadrin. Don't talk like that on my day off."

Susan threw her head back and laughed. "Okay, okay, I won't talk of Scadrin for the rest of the day."

"That sounds amazing."

"Excuse me," Roi Gurri interrupted the conversation with a smile. "I do believe it's my turn."

"But of course," Caroldus said with a grin.

He let Susan go and pretended to back away, before taking Roi Gurri's hand and beginning to lead him in dance! Both Susan and William laughed as the two men danced across the marble floor.

"The moons look lovely tonight, don't they?" Caroldus pretended to flirt.

"It's nine thirty a.m," Roi Gurri deadpanned, though he was amused.

"Shhh, don't ruin the moment, my love."

As Susan was laughing, William came to her and watched alongside her.

"Do you dance?" Susan asked William.

"Only on special occasions," William said. "I learned it for training, but I've never used it in any other situation."

"You haven't been to a party?"

"Not one that would be held in a place like this. My social status isn't as great as the two love birds over there."

"I wouldn't call us love birds!" Roi Gurri protested.

"Oh!" Caroldus cried dramatically. "You're breaking my heart!"

William snorted and Susan shook her head.

"Do you know if they do this at actual parties?" Susan asked.

"Only once, when we were kids. I heard about it from Caroldus, who said Regel threw such a fit that they won't dare do it again."

"Oh, I bet."

The two men finally stopped dancing and Caroldus walked over to the hedge.

"Hey, I think this is a maze!" He called. "We should go in!"

"It's got to be a mess," William insisted as he walked over to the entrance. "No one's been here in fifteen years."

"The paths will still be there, I'm sure," Roi Gurri said. "Let's see who can get out of the maze first."

"What's the incentive?" Caroldus asked.

"What do you think, Susan?"

Susan thought about it for a moment. "Whoever makes it out first gets to pick what we drink from the cellar."

"Bet!" Caroldus exclaimed as he ran into the maze.

"Hey, cheater!" William called as he ran after the blonde.

"Is that a good prize?" Susan asked, stunned by Caroldus's reaction.

"Your grandfather, Karniss, was known for his extensive wine collection," Roi Gurri explained. "So, yeah, I'd say so."

"Well then let's go!"

Susan took off into the maze, turning to the right while Roi Gurri went left. Her heart raced as she ran through the maze, but a smile stayed on her lips as she laughed. Soon her run slowed to a walk, and she began to intently search for the exit.

"Where are you guys?!" Caroldus called from across the maze.

"Wouldn't you like to know!" Susan called back.

"Yeah, what she said!" William called.

"Well, fine then!" Caroldus called. "Just know all of you are gonna lose!"

Susan laughed and kept walking. Hours passed, mostly in silence with the occasional taunt coming from Caroldus or William, but Susan didn't mind. Being at her own estate gave her a lot to think about.

How many times had her father and mother gotten lost in this maze? Did her father grow up exploring the hedges, letting himself get lost like she was now? Perhaps this maze had been here before her grandfather, Karniss. Maybe the roses along the path had been planted for her mother or grandmother.

A ringing sound began to echo in Susan's ears and pulled her away from her thoughts. The sound drowned out the noise of her surroundings, and wouldn't go away no matter how much she rubbed her ears or eyes.

"Do you ever wonder what else they're keeping from you?" An unfamiliar voice asked.

Susan quickly turned at the sound of the deep, raspy voice, but to her surprise found no one there!

"Do you really think they've told you everything now?"

Susan turned, but again, no one was there.

"Who's there?!" She called. "Show yourself!"

"What makes you think they're being honest with you?"

The sky turned black, and Susan watched as the passage she was walking down elongated and twisted. She tried to take a step backward but vertigo overcame her senses and she couldn't find her balance, causing her to stumble back into a hedge wall.

"You can never trust a friend," the voice echoed. "You can never trust a king."

"Help!" Susan cried, shaking and confused. "Caroldus! William! Roi Gurri! Help!"

"What makes you think they really care about you?"

Panic flared in Susan's chest as she watched a black figure morph out of the shadows and slowly approached her from the other end of the maze. She screamed and curled her legs close to herself, holding out her hands like that would stop the figure.

As Susan's heart trembled, so did the Jewel of Numenera inside her pocket begin to tremble and glow.

"Jehoyam!" Susan cried.

Instantly a ball of crimson energy surrounded Susan and created a forcefield. Her eyes widened as she observed the almost liquid form of energy. She could see right through it and see the dark figure still approaching, yet she didn't feel afraid.

Susan wasn't drunk, but the Jewel of Numenera using its power so close to her made her feel sober and clear-headed. She felt tempted to pull it out of her pocket, without any protection, but thankfully someone came to her aid in time.

"Susan!" A familiar voice cried before Roi Gurri came crashing through one of the hedge walls.

He turned toward the figure, his sword held firmly in his right hand. At the presence of Roi Gurri, the force field retracted back into the Jewel of Numenera, as did the soberness Susan had from it.

Another crash came from beside Susan and she let out a startled cry, closing her eyes and covering her ears.

"Susan, open your eyes, look at me!" The voice of William ordered with alarm.

As the ringing in Susan's ears faded away, she looked up to see the shining honey eyes of William looking down at her. She leaped forward and wrapped her arms around his shoulders, hugging him tightly.

"Who hurt you?" William asked, his voice so deep it was almost a growl.

"I don't know," Susan admitted. "I didn't even see him, but I heard him so clearly it was like he was right behind me. I saw an illusion, or maybe it was all in my head, and I didn't even think about fighting."

"It's okay, you're safe now."

"I don't see anyone here, or nearby," Roi Gurri reported as he approached Susan and William. "I can't sense anything through the hedges or vegetation either, besides Caroldus."

"I swear, something was here," Susan insisted.

"Maybe this place really is haunted," William suggested, looking up at Roi Gurri.

The prince stiffened and sent William a pointed look. "Susan, do you want to head inside?"

Susan nodded. Roi Gurri knelt down and lifted her with ease, carrying her bridal style.

"I'm fine, I can walk," Susan insisted, suddenly self-conscious of her weight.

"It's not a problem," Roi Gurri said, his grip on her tightening.

Roi Gurri noticed William's glare, but before he could remark on it Caroldus came crashing through the hedge.

"What's wrong?" He asked, his tone serious and a dagger held firmly in his hand.

"It's been taken care of," Roi Gurri said. "Susan experienced some kind of hallucination."

"Are you okay?" Caroldus asked Susan, walking forward and pressing the back of his hand against her forehead. "You're a little warm."

"I'm fine," Susan said, pushing his hand away. "I was just a little shaken. Maybe it was just a memory, I've had a few vivid ones since I've been 'discovered.'"

"Still, I'm going to search the grounds. William, cover me?"

The masked man nodded, and the two ran through the hedges.

"They won't find anything," Susan stated.

"No, they won't," Roi Gurri affirmed. "But better to be safe than sorry."

As Roi Gurri carried her out of the garden, she began to ponder. Was that really a memory? None of her memories had triggered a reaction from the Jewel of Numenera before. In fact, none of her fights or training sessions had ever triggered the Jewel of Numenera.

"What was it protecting me from?" She wondered.

Susan decided to find out.

***

The group had decided to spend the night at the manor despite the afternoon's episode. They ate, drank, and explored the manor well into the night. But the men hadn't noticed Susan was only pretending to drink, taking very small sips if any at all.

By the time the night came to an end, the men were all passed out in guest rooms with no chance of them waking unless startled. That's when Susan made her move.

She dressed comfortably, in loose clothes she knew she could run and fight in without worry. She strapped her sword to her side and slid on running shoes before leaving her room.

Despite knowing the men nearby were sound asleep, she used caution as she crept through the manor because she knew that William was a light sleeper. When she was finally outside she relaxed.

Susan approached the maze, her hand firmly gripping her sword. Dark clouds crept across the sky and thunder rumbled in the distance. The wind pushed against Susan's back, urging her to move forward. With a deep breath, she responded to the call of the wind and walked into the maze.

Every little footstep alerted the night to Susan's presence. She tried to walk quietly, not letting her heels touch the ground as Scadrin had taught her, but in the end, she gave up. If someone was actually there, they'd be trespassing on *her* land and she'd have every right to deal with them how she pleased.

An eerie ringing silenced all other noises in Susan's ear. It overwhelmed her senses, as if the sound was attacking her soul.

"You've returned," the same raspy voice from earlier said. "So you know what I say is true."

"I've come for my own benefit," Susan said, continuing to walk through the maze.

"What is it that you desire?"

Susan shuddered. She hated the word '*desire*.' "I want to know what you think the others are hiding from me."

Susan turned a corner and stopped at the sight of the black figure. He was the embodiment of the night, for no light touched him or dared to reveal his identity.

"What reason do I have to tell you what they've hidden from you?" The figure asked.

"If you didn't have a reason, you wouldn't be here."

He chuckled. "I am here under orders. You have walked right into my trap."

"Susan!" The distressed voice of William called. "What the sheol do you think you're doing out here?!"

Susan turned at the sound of William's voice, but he must've been outside of the maze. She decided not to respond to him, knowing he'd only start an argument. When she turned back to the dark figure it had moved closer! She drew her sword, holding it close to her chest.

"Don't come any closer," Susan warned the figure.

"What power do you hold to stop me?" The figure asked.

The pillar of darkness broke apart into ghoul-like creatures that crawled along the hedge walls and ground. They began racing toward Susan.

"Jehoyam!" Susan exclaimed as her heart trembled with the same fear she had felt earlier.

The Jewel of Numenera glowed and in a flash it's power surrounded her with a forcefield. The ghouls threw themselves upon the forcefield to break it, but as soon as they touched the orb they shrieked and ignited into flames!

The ghouls hit the ground, rolling in the dirt to try to extinguish the flames eating them alive. Fortunately, for Susan, the flames stayed lit. All she could do was watch as the monsters writhed and screamed in agony until they were nothing but ash.

The clouds moved from the sky, and the light of the four moons hit the maze. As soon as the silver rays fell upon Susan, the force field disappeared and she was alone in the maze. She felt anger and resentment swell in her chest.

"You can't shake me!" Susan screamed into the air, though her hands were shaking. "You can't touch my soul, foul demon!"

Susan took a deep breath and calmed her spirit, her hands coming to rest at her sides. If A'Vaddon thought he could send other demons to do his dirty work, he had another thing coming.

"Susan, what happened?"

Susan turned to find William approaching, and offered him a smile.

"I just needed to deal with an intruder," Susan explained. "It's been taken care of." She sheathed her sword. "Let's go back to bed, you must have a skull splitting headache."

"I can hold my ale just fine," William muttered as they made their way out of the maze. "You shouldn't be fighting demons alone."

"Well, thankfully I have a new ally on my side."

Chapter Eleven
Royenden

Susan trained hard for the next three months, trying to keep up with the men of Warrior Brave and Cobra Cave. The obstacles were the most intense of all, they were very difficult and deadly. She was lucky to have Roi Gurri, William, and Caroldus to help her. Indeed, if they weren't there she would've already been dead several times. Despite her obstacles, she was developing muscles and growing at an alarming rate.

Susan jumped out of bed and went to make breakfast when she noticed Roi Gurri wasn't in his bunk.

"Was he here last night?" Susan wondered. *"I can't remember..."*

"Good morning, Susan."

Susan was surprised when she heard Caroldus, turning to see him sitting up and stretching.

"You're awake?" She asked. "Willingly? This early?"

"Of course," Caroldus said. "Today is Royenden."

"Royenden?"

Caroldus raised a brow. "Susan, I told you what Royenden was. You can't remember?"

Susan blushed and shook her head. "No, not at all. Maybe it's because of those drinks we had last night."

"Lightweight." Susan looked over to see William awake as well. "Can't hold your ale?"

"Well it's not like I could casually drink on Earth," she retorted.

"Royenden is the celebration of the royal heir's birthday," Caroldus explained. "Today is Roi Gurri's twentieth birthday."

"What?" She asked. "But I didn't get him anything!"

"I'll put your name on my card," William said as he jumped down from his bunk. "Don't worry about it."

"But I'd still like to give him something."

"We have all day for that," Caroldus said as they headed for the living room. "There's going to be lots of booths set up today, I'm sure you'll find him something."

"Yeah. Why is he not in his bunk?"

"He slept in his royal chambers last night," William explained. "It's part of the tradition. The first person to wish him a happy Royenden will be someone in his family. Probably Sutan."

"So what do we do?"

"Skip breakfast and go see what's being set up outside," Caroldus said with a grin. "Come on!"

He headed for the door, and Susan and William followed. But before they could make it through the door, a guard walked in.

"Can we help you?" William asked.

"I'm here to bring Countess Wellns to Queen Sharmon," the guard explained.

"What?" Susan asked. "Why?"

"You are to partake in today's festivities with Prince Roi Gurri, of course."

Susan looked at William, who nodded.

"It's okay," he assured. "It's because you're betrothed to Roi Gurri."

"We'll see you out there," Caroldus said, patting Susan on the back.

"Alright," she said before following the guard.

***

Roi Gurri woke up on his own. Not to the sound of birds, or to the suns rising like he normally would. He almost thought he was dreaming when he woke up in complete darkness, but then he knew he was in his chambers. Royalty always had rooms deep within the castle, and without windows so they were less likely to be assassinated.

Roi Gurri stared up at the darkness, becoming lost in his thoughts.

"I'm twenty," he thought, though he didn't feel any different. *"I wonder when the change will kick in."*

He rolled over and expected to find the edge of the bed, but instead only found more bed. It was strange how different it felt to sleep here than it did in the Warrior Brave Patrol room.

"Maybe I can just stay in here all day," he muttered.

Roi Gurri loved his people very much, but he didn't like being under the strict gaze of his father for so long. He had to pretend that he was given love and affection from him when it certainly didn't feel that way. He felt more love from Caroldus, William, and Susan than he did from his own father.

"What a life," he mumbled.

But then he smiled as he remembered what had happened last year, and every year before that. He remembered the traditions, and how happy the people were when they saw him. He remembered how much fun he had every year, and his spirits were lifted.

Suddenly, the lights turned on, and a small body jumped onto the bed and onto Roi Gurri. Roi Gurri grunted and groaned, looking up to see it was his little sister, Sutan, who had jumped on his ribs.

"Happy Royenden!" She cheered with a big smile. "It's time to wake up and get ready!"

Despite his brief pain, Roi Gurri couldn't help but smile as he sat up. "Must you wake me so energetically, little highness?" He asked in a teasing tone.

"Yep! Today's a really big day, after all! You need to be wide-eyed and alert."

"Yes, your highness."

Roi Gurri grinned and began to tickle Sutan, who squealed and laughed in delight.

"Stop it!" She cried as she tried to tickle him back.

Roi Gurri laughed as he let go of her and moved his hand to ruffle up her hair. "Come on, I've got to get ready now," he insisted.

"Me too! Mom made me a really nice dress to wear today. I can't wait to show Susan!"

"Are you not excited to show me?"

"Yes, but I'm more excited for Susan to see it."

Roi Gurri gasped and pretended to be offended. "I'm hurt, little highness. Am I no longer your favorite?"

Sutan giggled and grinned. "Nope!"

And with that, she ran out of his room and down the hall. Roi Gurri chuckled and shook his head as he stood, heading for his closet.

"Happy Royenden, son."

Roi Gurri looked over to see his father in the doorway. He nodded politely to him.

"Thank you," he said.

"I wanted to tell you that Susan will be joining you in the festivities today," King Regel explained. "I expect you to be a teacher to her today. Show her what it will take to be a queen one day."

Roi Gurri nodded. "Of course. Why wasn't I told about this sooner? I would've liked to prepare her."

"It isn't needed. This will build character for both of you. I will see you soon."

With that, he closed the door and left. Roi Gurri sighed, and his expression turned into a scowl.

"Typical," he muttered, opening his closet door.

Traditionally, the heir was supposed to dress up to show off their wealth, to present themselves to the people in a grand way, but Roi Gurri preferred to do the exact opposite. He dressed down, appearing humble and human to his people. The only part of his outfit that was significant was the crown he wore. He hoped whoever dressed Susan would have the sense to dress her the same way.

When he was dressed, he figured he should go find Susan. With that in mind, he knew the first place he should look was Sharmon's quarters, which weren't too far from his. When he knocked on her door, it was quickly answered by little Sutan.

"It's Roi Gurri!" Sutan called back.

"He can come in!" Sharmon's voice called.

Sutan opened the door more and Roi Gurri stepped in to see dresses laid everywhere, each different sizes and shapes, but all emerald green.

"Welcome, Roi Gurri," Sharmon said in a sweet voice. "Are you here for Susan?"

"Yes," Roi Gurri said in a polite tone.

"She's trying on another dress. Personally, I think this is the one."

"I'm afraid these fancy dresses don't match what I'm wearing. It'll appear odd."

"It's okay for you to be dressed down, because you want to appear as a humble king, right?" Roi Gurri nodded. "Well, the people don't know Susan. They know of her as the Chosen One, as the queen-to-be, as the poor little Earth-girl. For her reputation's sake, she needs to appear more powerful than she really is. If I were to dress her like you, no one would see their future queen, they would see another one of your father's mistakes."

Roi Gurri was shocked at Sharmon's profound wisdom. He had known she was wise, but never took the time to have intellectual conversations with her. Actually, ever since she came into his life, he had always avoided her when possible.

"Well spoken," Roi Gurri simply said, looking away from Sharmon.

"Roi Gurri, Roi Gurri, look at my dress!" Sutan exclaimed excitedly.

He looked down at her and she twirled, showing off her poofy amethyst purple dress, which was adorned with many beautiful garnet jewels.

"Ah, now I see why you were so excited to show Susan," Roi Gurri said with a smile. "You look very pretty in her family colors."

"Queen Sharmon, I really don't think green is my color," Susan's voice interrupted. Roi Gurri looked up to see her stride across the room toward a mirror, seeming to not notice him. "I mean, I know it's the Drago family color, but we're not married yet, so does it matter?"

Roi Gurri couldn't help but be in awe of her beauty. Her long blonde hair, which was down for the first time since she had arrived in Zudanum, made her look feminine and youthful. While the dress, which he thought was definitely her color, was long, silky, and hugged her curves in the right way to make her look mature yet flattering.

"It's all about presentation, my dear," Sharmon said as she stood from her seat and approached Susan. "It's all about showing your best self for your people. Don't worry, I think the green looks stunning with your hair."

"I agree," Roi Gurri breathed out, unable to keep his eyes off of her.

Susan turned to him and immediatly turned red, embarrassed that she hadn't noticed him before.

"You look... elegant," Roi Gurri continued, slowly approaching.

"I feel completely overdressed, now that I look at you," Susan admitted.

"And I feel completely underdressed."

They both smiled and chuckled, feeling more at ease.

"I know that your father has a dress shirt that will match Susan," Sharmon said to Roi Gurri. "Wait here, I'll go get it."

Sharmon and Sutan left, and Susan turned back to the mirror.

"So, what exactly is going to happen today?" Susan asked Roi Gurri as she adjusted the gold sash around her waist. "Sharmon said that you would explain everything to me."

"I guess those drinks hit you pretty hard last night," Roi Gurri jested, earning him a glare from Susan. "Sorry. Royenden was a celebration started by King Fumin the Peaceful, who wanted to show off her children as a blessing after the cursed reign of her father and grandmother."

"King Asistom the Vengeful and King Elodist the Butcher, right?"

"Yes."

"So she wanted to show that her children weren't going to be like her dad and grandmom."

"Exactly. You catch on pretty quick."

"Well, I've learned from you, after all."

Roi Gurri smiled proudly. "Glad to see I've been a good influence on you." He looked her over before raising a brow. "Did you get taller overnight?"

"No, Sharmon gave me platform shoes so I appear taller."

"Heels?"

"Oh, Jehoyam no. They're running-type shoes."

"Good, because heels won't do you any good today."

"What do you mean?"

Before he could answer, Sharmon and Sutan came back into the room.

"We found it!" Sutan declared, running the silk green shirt up to Roi Gurri. "Go put it on, father is going to start the ceremony soon."

"Thank you, little highness," Roi Gurri said before patting Sutan's head. "I'll be right back."

He walked into Sharmon's closet and quickly changed shirts before walking out to the mirror, making sure he looked presentable.

"You guys really do match," Sutan said with a big smile. "It's adorable!"

Roi Gurri, Susan, and Sharmon all laughed and nodded their heads in agreement.

"You two are all set," Sharmon said, brushing some of Susan's hair away from her face. "I will have a change of clothes sent to the arena. Have fun out there today."

"We will," Susan said with a smile.

"May I escort you to the balcony, Countess?" Roi Gurri asked, offering his arm to Susan.

"Yes you may, my Prince," Susan said with a giggle as she accepted his arm.

He led her out of the room, making sure he wasn't forcing her to walk too fast and trip over her dress.

"You were saying?" Susan asked, continuing their conversation before they were interrupted.

"Today is the day where I'm shown off like a prize horse," Roi Gurri explained. "I have to perform tasks to show how strong and capable I am, so the people will trust me as their king one day. I will fight ten knights this year to show my strength and skill, for example."

"Do you think I'll have to do the same thing?"

"Yes, you'll do it alongside me. It was why I would've preferred you to dress down, but now I understand why you can't."

"Sharmon told me that the people would look down on me if I dressed down."

"She's right. Unfortunately, there's a lot of high expectations put on you."

Susan sighed. "I understand. It's just one of the perks of marrying you."

She gave him a reassuring smile, and he returned it with one of his own.

"Don't worry, I'm going to be here for you every step of the way," Roi Gurri assured. They approached a large balcony, staying far enough from it that they wouldn't be seen by the people crowded below. "First I'm going to be given gifts from the council and high nobles. Then the elders of Zudanum will pray over us before we go up against the knights."

Susan gripped his arm. "Alright. We've got this."

Roi Gurri smiled and laid his hand atop hers in assurance. She looked up into his eyes, and his chest fluttered.

“My son!” King Regel’s voice boomed, drawing Roi Gurri and Susan out of their trance. “And his betrothed, Countess Wellns!”

Roi Gurri led Susan onto the balcony and the crowd erupted in cheers, screams, whoops, and hollers. Roi Gurri smiled and waved, while Susan did her best to do the same. He could tell she was scared, but he tried to reassure her by firmly holding onto her hand.

"Another year passes, and my son grows stronger and taller than ever!" King Regel boomed, and the crowd cheered. "I can't think of a better man to be my heir or to be your king. Today, he shall prove once again that he is more than capable to stand in my place. Now, let Royenden commence!"

The people cheered and slowly began dispersing, while Roi Gurri led Susan back into the castle.

"You look stunning today, Susan," King Regel complimented as he followed the pair. "You look more like a queen than my son does a king."

"Thank you, your highness," Susan said. "But I think Roi Gurri looks like a mighty king. Perhaps his humble spirit is what makes him great."

Roi Gurri didn’t attempt to hide his smile, nor the blush that creeped onto his cheeks, and King Regel raised a brow. Susan wasn’t exactly trying to hide the shade she threw toward the king. He looked away from the two and strutted ahead of them. Roi Gurri snickered as they followed his father.

"Thanks," he said to Susan.

"No problem, I meant it," Susan replied with a grin. "Besides, he shouldn't be giving backhanded compliments to his son."

"How I wish you were here growing up instead of Earth, you could've put my father's ego in check long ago."

They both laughed as they entered the throne room. The room was full of nobles, councilmen, and anyone of high importance in Zudanum and their family. They all began applauding as the pair walked into the room. They kept their heads held high, smiling politely as they approached the thrones.

They stopped at the bottom of the stairs and bowed to King Regel and Queen Sharmon. The king and queen stood from their thrones and descended the stairs.

"Stand beside his throne," Sharmon whispered to Susan as they passed.

Susan followed Sharmon's instruction as Roi Gurri led her up to the thrones. Roi Gurri looked back at her to make sure she was okay, and she nodded.

They spent the next two hours receiving gifts from the esteemed guests. Along with gifts, they'd give an extended speech about how much they supported their future king and swore their allegiance to him. Roi Gurri would accept the gifts with gratefulness, consistently checking on Susan to make sure she was okay with standing. She would smile and nod at him, but he wasn't convinced. After the first hour, when one of the families had stepped down from the throne, Roi Gurri stood and offered his hand to Susan.

"Sit down," he offered quietly.

"I can't sit on the *king's* throne," Susan hissed.

"Sure you can. As your future husband, and future king, I have every right to offer you my chair."

Susan looked to Queen Sharmon, who subtly nodded. She ignored King Regel's disapproving stare, looked back at Roi Gurri, and nodded. He moved her to sit on the throne while he stood beside her.

Many murmured their opinions among themselves, but Roi Gurri was confident in his decision. He knew having Susan sit on the king's throne could strike up controversy, but in his eyes he was showing respect, not for just the Chosen One, but for his queen.

After every gift had been given and every speech was made, Roi Gurri and Susan knelt at the bottom of the stairs leading to the thrones. They were surrounded by the oldest and wisest elders of Zudanum, who laid hands on them. They began praying for Roi Gurri one by one, pleading to Jehoyam to keep him strong and healthy, to give him many blessings, to give him a strong large family, and so on.

Roi Gurri held tightly onto Susan's hands the entire time. He couldn't keep his shoulders from shaking and tears coming to his eyes at the elder's prayers. He knew better than anyone that their words were powerful, and their prayers would be heard.

"Guide my hands, Jehoyam," Roi Gurri whispered quietly so only Susan could hear. "Let me be a good king. A good brother. A good husband. Be my eyes, my ears, and my words. Don't let any of my loved ones fall to harm."

When the elders finished praying Roi Gurri quickly wiped his tears away and turned to Susan, who looked very concerned. He smiled in reassurance.

"It's okay," he said quietly. "It's just... a lot."

Susan could only nod. When he saw tears in her eyes he immediately wrapped his arms around her.

"I've got you," he whispered. "It's okay."

"I'm scared," Susan admitted quietly. "I can't do this, I can't be a queen."

"Yes you can, I know it. I'll protect you. And when I can't, Jehoyam will."

She nodded and he gently wiped her tears away. When they were both ready the elders dispersed and they stood.

"Now, on to the festivities!" King Regel announced.

The people cheered as Roi Gurri and Susan were escorted out of the palace by seven guards.

"What happens now?" Susan asked.

"We'll walk through the booths on our way to fight the knights," Roi Gurri explained. "If you see anything that catches your eye, don't hesitate to let me know." Susan didn't say anything, so he took her silence as refusal. "I'm serious."

"I know, but I'm not used to that," Susan explained. "I didn't grow up with a lot of things, so I never feel that I need a lot of things."

Roi Gurri nodded, but he didn't understand. He grew up as the firstborn, the current heir, everything he could ever want had been given to him within reason.

"Are you ready to face the people?" Roi Gurri asked, changing the subject. "This will be your first time facing them in a formal setting."

"I'm not sure," Susan admitted. "I know they have a lot of opinions and thoughts about me."

"Today's a day to prove that you deserve to be treated like a noble. I have no doubt in your abilities."

"But they do, which is why I have to give it my all."

"That's the spirit." They approached the castle gates, and Susan took a deep breath. "Are you ready?"

"Yeah, I'm ready."

The gates slowly swung open, and the couple were met with cheers and applause. Surrounded by guards they began to walk through the crowd, holding tightly to one another. The crowd was so big and dense that Roi Gurri feared they would crush Susan if he didn't hold on to her. So that's exactly what he did, he kept his arm wrapped around her waist and pressed her to his side.

A few small children ran up to the two and offered trinkets to Roi Gurri. He smiled and waved the guards aside before kneeling before the children.

"Well, hello," he said with a kind smile. "What do you have?"

"We made bracelets for you," a little girl said shyly.

"They're good luck for your fight today," a boy said.

"I would love some luck today," Roi Gurri said and the children giggled.

They began tying their handmade jewelry around both of his wrists. The ones that had been made too small he offered to Susan, which still delighted the children. Some even made bracelets just for her, and she accepted them joyfully.

"I'd love to know how to make these," Susan said aloud.

"I can teach you!" One of the boys quickly exclaimed. "It's easy, I promise."

"What's your name?" Roi Gurri asked the boy.

"Jumin, your highness."

"Meet us at the arena before the fight, Jumin. You'll have some time to teach her then."

"Okay! Bye, your majesties!"

The children ran off and the couple laughed before continuing through the stands.

"Do they do that every year?" Susan asked.

"Yes," Roi Gurri said with a smile. "The children very precious to me, and so are the things they give me. I have a box full of their trinkets in my royal chambers."

"How long have you been celebrating Royenden?"

"Five years. It starts when the king proclaims their heir, and I was proclaimed to be heir five years ago."

"Why not when you were born?"

"Because Zudanums live for so long that a king's firstborn isn't automatically the heir. I wouldn't be surprised if one day Sutan is declared as the heir."

"Why?"

"Because she's younger. Her youthfulness gives her more time to rule, especially if my father lives to a thousand. The line of succession in Zudanum is never clear, and to most is very confusing."

"I never thought of it that way. How old is your father?"

"Five hundred and fifty-seven years old. So he's still got a long way to go."

"So we may not even rule one day?"

"Yes. But we must prepare like we will, especially with A'Vaddon appearing again. Death waits for no man, including royalty."

Chapter Twelve
Stronger than One, Stronger than Ten

They changed the subject to something more lighthearted as they walked. Roi Gurri noticed Susan became distracted often, looking at the vendor's stalls, but when she didn't indicate what she wanted they'd move on. He began to realize she was trying to buy something for him and tried to act like he wasn't paying attention to her.

"This is gorgeous," Susan muttered, and Roi Gurri turned his attention back to her.

She was holding a sleek dagger, encased in a sheath made of gold. The pommel, a roaring head of a lion encrusted in gold, caught Roi Gurri's attention since it was his family's crest.

"You have a good eye, Countess," the seller complimented Susan. "There is no other dagger like this, for I made it just for today. Please, unsheath it."

Roi Gurri watched as she unsheathed it and twirled it between her fingers. He was proud of her growing skill in handling weapons. From swords and daggers, to bows and arrows, to firearms, Susan was a fast learner.

"We'll take it," Roi Gurri said, handing the vendor a handful of gold coins.

"Excellent!" The man exclaimed, bowing as he accepted the gold. "I promise you won't be disappointed. Please, allow me to wrap it."

Susan handed over the dagger before looking up at Roi Gurri. "You didn't have to," she said.

"Nonsense," Roi Gurri said with a wave of his hand. "I don't like to be the only one receiving gifts on my birthday. Besides, as my future wife, you should only have the finest weapons to defend yourself." He took the wrapped dagger from the seller. "It's no Necto Blade, but think of it as me defending you when you wield it."

He handed it to her, and she accepted it with a nod.

"I pray I don't have to wield it," Susan admitted quietly.

"I pray you don't have to either."

They took their time finishing their walk through the stalls and then mounted their companions, White Star and Roi Gurri's unicorn Pure Lightning, to ride to the First Arena. It was a battle arena that was a few miles out of town, meant for entertainment like Swarbus challenges and Royenden.

"Do we have a plan?" Susan asked Roi Gurri as they rode ahead of the crowd. "I'm not really prepared to take on the planet's top knights."

"The rules allow me to use my anti-natural abilities, so I'll cover you the best I can," Roi Gurri said. "For this game, we use weapons called neuron blades, which will phase through the skin but make contact with anything else. This way no one actually gets killed. You'll get your pick of what kind of weapon because there are a lot of varieties, but you can only have one."

"What about a shield?"

"No shield, unless you'd rather have that than a sword."

"I think your nature abilities will be more than enough for a shield."

"I agree."

"How do we win against them?"

"We have to bring them to their knees. And it's the same for us, if they manage to bring us to our knees, we lose."

"Is this a submission thing?"

"What gave you that impression?"

Roi Gurri grinned as Susan glared at him. He laughed and bumped her shoulder with his own.

"Cheer up, it's not going to be as hard as you think it is," Roi Gurri assured.

"You say that, then I remember we're going up against *ten* of this planet's best knights and your words don't sound so comforting."

"I know it's intimidating, but remember one thing."

"Which is?"

"I've been better than all of them since I was fifteen."

Susan laughed and shook her head. "I guess that is comforting."

They entered the arena to find the stands were already packed with people, eagerly waiting to see if their prince would finally be beaten this year. Roi Gurri led Susan to an area where they could pick their weapon, only to find the little boy from earlier was waiting for them.

"Now, how'd you manage to get past the guards?" Roi Gurri asked Jumin with a grin.

"That's a secret, your highness," Jumin said, looking down at the ground sheepishly.

Roi Gurri and Susan both laughed, dismounting their companions and approaching him.

"Come with us," Susan said. "You can show me how to make the bracelets while I pick a sword."

Jumin eagerly followed them into the weapons room, sticking closely to Susan's side. He and Susan sat on a bench and began working, while Roi Gurri searched through the blades on the other side of the room.

His go-to was always a long sword, something balanced and with range. He admired the faint silver glow coming off of the blade, indicating its uniqueness. Neuron blades were only used during the first few months of weapons training and sold as self-defense weapons for children. They may phase through the skin, but they leave a nasty shock when they do. Roi Gurri turned to inform Susan of the shock she'd be receiving, but what he saw made him stop.

Susan's gaze was completely on the hands of the Jumin as they gracefully wove pieces of string into a beautiful criss-cross pattern. They were talking and laughing about something, but Roi Gurri had tuned it out. For a moment he was reminded of his mother, and the way she would act toward the children of Zudanum. She used to interact and play with them the same way Susan did now, with patience and kindness.

Susan looked up into his eyes and he was instantly mesmerized. He had heard people say that brown eyes weren't beautiful, but at that moment he knew they were completely wrong. There was nothing more beautiful than her eyes, as beautiful as smoky quartz and as rich as freshly ground coffee. No other brown eyes could compare to hers.

"Your highness," an unfamiliar voice called. Roi Gurri snapped out of his trance and turned to see a guard at the door, who bowed. "The tournament will begin in fifteen minutes."

"Thank you," Roi Gurri said with a nod, and the guard left. He turned to Susan and Jumin. "It's time for us to get ready."

"Alright," Susan said, turning to Jumin and smiling. "I'm sorry, but you should go find a good seat."

"Okay," Jumin said with a smile, jumping up from his seat. "I'll be cheering for you, your majesty!"

He bowed lowly and kissed Susan's knuckles before running out of the room. Susan smiled brightly and chuckled as she watched him leave before standing and turning to Roi Gurri.

"Do you have any suggestions for me?" She asked, motioning to the weapons.

"Yes, I do," Roi Gurri said, picking a short sword from the wall. "This blade is a similar size as the Necto Blade of Hope, but it's lighter. That means your swings are going to be a lot more powerful because you won't have as much resistance. Try it."

He handed her the blade and she tested it out, swinging it and thrusting it a few times to get a feel for it.

"You're right," she said. "This is nothing compared to the Necto Blade."

"Just made sure you are in complete control of your blade, you don't want to overswing and leave yourself exposed. You really don't want one of these blades touching you, they leave a nasty sting behind."

"Really?" Susan asked before pushing her right hand through the sword without hesitation. Her eyes immediately widened and she loudly cursed, shaking her hand and dropping the sword. "Damnit, I shouldn't have done that."

"Yeah, you shouldn't have." Susan glared at Roi Gurri and he smiled. "Come here."

He approached her and took her hand, covering it with his own. His hands glowed and the pain in hers began residing.

"Thanks," Susan said.

"Don't mention it," Roi Gurri responded. "If you do get injured real badly try to let me know and I'll do my best to take away the pain."

"No, don't worry about me. We're going to be completely surrounded, we won't have time to worry about injuries. Besides, if we play our cards right this shouldn't take too long."

"You think so?" Roi Gurri asked, amusement in his voice.

"Yeah. You're a powerful anti-natural, and you've beat these guys before."

He shrugged. "Perhaps, but you'd be surprised at what these guys can do. Just don't get cocky, okay?"

"I won't."

"Good. Now, you should put on something more suitable for the fight, as well as some armor."

"Right."

Susan changed into the extra clothes Sharmon had prepared for her and tied up her hair before she and Roi Gurri suited up with leather armor. It would would allow them to move faster than they would with metal armor, while still being protected.

At the sound of a trumpet they walked into the arena. The crowd cheered so loudly Susan wanted to cover hear ears, but resisted the urge. Any sign of weakness and the crowd would judge her harshly. It was enough to be judged by her classmates, let alone a planet.

They walked into the center of the arena, and another trumpet blasted. Seven men and three women walked out of doors around the arena, surrounding Susan and Roi Gurri.

"Couldn't handle us alone this year?" A man with short blonde hair taunted Roi Gurri.

"I could take you all blindfolded," Roi Gurri clapped back. "You're lucky you're not fighting just her, Eludikai."

"Hah! I could step on her and not even notice. Good luck protecting that leech on your back, prince."

Roi Gurri's eyes shone with fury, drawing his sword from its sheath. Susan was shocked by the blatant disrespect toward his prince and future princess, and judging by the faces of the other knights they were shocked as well.

Susan eyed the men and women surrounding them. They were all tall, strong, and young. It dawned on Susan that they weren't fighting Zudanum's strongest *soldiers*, but its strongest *knights*, one of the most obscure classes in the military when it came to their job description.

Knights did everything from recon, to being ambassadors for Zudanum, to assassination. Still, they were one of the lower classes of military. Susan had been thinking she was going to be fighting people like King Regel and Scadrin, and thankfully she was dead wrong.

"You seem confident, shorty," one of the girls, olive skinned with bleached blonde hair, said, pointing her sword at Susan. "Don't worry, I'll knock that confidence out of you when I bring you to your knees."

Susan contained her laughter, but still smiled and tilted her head. "What's your name, soldier?" She asked.

"Elanda was the name given to me by the Groon."

"Elanda, do you know who you're talking to?"

"I'm talking to the dirt-girl, who else?"

Susan's amusement fled and her jaw clenched. Apparently, she hadn't made enough of an impression on the Zudanum people to be addressed by any of her proper titles, or be recognized as anything more than a 'dirt-girl'. She glanced at the other knights to see they looked appalled. Eludikai and Elanda wouldn't be getting much help from their teammates.

"Elanda is mine," Susan whispered to Roi Gurri.

"I'll take Eludikai," Roi Gurri replied.

"Deal."

"Begin!" King Regel's voice boomed, followed by the sound of a trumpet.

Strong, thick roots shot up from the ground and grabbed the knights by their legs, straightaway forcing four to their knees. Four managed to jump and avoid being ensnared, including Eludikai and Elanda, and the last two struggled against the vines.

"Take care of those two," Roi Gurri ordered Susan.

"On it," she replied.

A root lifted Susan into the air, putting her in front of the suns rays and in everyone's blind spot. She ran along the branch before jumping off.

She landed on the calf of the male knight struggling, successfully bringing him to his knees before he completely fell to the ground. She didn't bother to run to the other knight when she saw Roi Gurri's vines pull him to his knees.

Susan ran to aid Roi Gurri, only for Eludikai and one of the women to step in front of her. The look in Eludikai's eyes made her back away and draw her sword.

"Your prince won't be able to save you," Eludikai taunted. "Not with Elanda backing him into a corner."

"Eludikai, don't be disrespectful," the woman, with bangs and short auburn hair, snapped.

"Step aside, Rulitor, go help Elanda."

Susan glanced over at Roi Gurri to find him engaging with Elanda, who was using some kind of enhanced lung capacity to try to knock down his wall of roots and vines.

She wasn't worried about Roi Gurri, but she was worried for herself. Eludikai was packed with muscles, and there was not even a hint of mercy in his eyes. It gave her an idea.

He swung his sword, and rather than meeting it with her own strike, Susan backed up and batted his sword away with her own. He kept running at her, swinging at her chest and neck, but Susan only dodged and evaded his strikes.

Rulitor was hesitant to engage in the fight, looking between Eludikai and Susan with a conflicting gaze.

When Susan was sure Rulitor wasn't going to be joining in the fight she put her full attention on Eludikai. His swings came with more and more force each time, and eventually he closed the gap she was trying to put between them.

"Admit it, you can never hope to defeat someone as experienced as me," Eludikai taunted.

Susan didn't respond to his taunting, instead she focused on her plan. She had responded to taunts in her training, and it never went well for her. She couldn't afford to make a silly mistake on this day.

She led him to the center of the arena, where Roi Gurri and Elanda were fighting. Finally, she engaged Eludikai by stomp-kicking his stomach when he provided an opening by overswinging his blade. He bent over and clutched his abdomen, and Susan ran to Roi Gurri's side.

"Let down your wall," Susan ordered.

"Are you sure?" Roi Gurri asked.

"Yes, do it now!"

Susan tackled Roi Gurri to the ground and he let down the wall of roots.

The prince watched as Eludikai, who he hadn't noticed was charging Susan, was blown away by the force of Elanda's enhanced lung capacity! He hit his head against the area wall before landing on his hands and knees.

"Eludikai!" Elanda cried in alarm.

Roi Gurri used the distraction to summon shoot vines from his hand and wrap them around Elanda's legs. With one powerful tug, she collapsed and her face smacked against the ground.

Roi Gurri looked up to find Susan hovering over him, her loose hair frizzed and wild as it fell down her shoulders and brushed his face.

"Can I kiss you?" Roi Gurri asked Susan breathlessly.

Chapter Thirteen
Confessions Under the Stars

Susan's eyes widened in shock and horror and her heart pounded in her chest with anxiety. How could Roi Gurri ask such a question at this moment?

"Are you crazy?" Susan rebuked, unable to think of anything else to say.

Their awkward moment was interrupted by Rulitor and the last knight. Susan hadn't forgotten them, and she raised her sword to block the blow the male knight had aimed for Roi Gurri's head. She cried out in shock, her arm trembling from the force of the blow. Roi Gurri quickly raised his arm and his sword went through the knight's wrist.

The knight cried out before dropping his blade and clutching his wrist. Susan quickly stood, roundhouse kicked the back of the knight's knee, and sent him to the ground.

Susan and Roi Gurri turned to Rulitor, who made no advancement toward them.

"The actions of my fellow knights were not honorable, my prince, my lady," Rulitor stated. "I am truly ashamed of their actions. Therefore, allow me to swear fealty to you here and now."

Rulitor went down on her knees and bowed her head. The crowd gasped, shocked by the total surrender. Susan and Roi Gurri also found themselves shocked, yet grateful for Rulitor's acknowledgment of their high positions.

"Thank you, Rulitor," Roi Gurri said. "May your honor rest upon your head like a crown forever."

Rulitor smiled as she stood and bowed. "I will wear it proudly, my Prince."

A trumpet and the crowd's cheers sounded Roi Gurri and Susan's victory, though neither felt they could celebrate it.

"Susan, I'm sorry, I don't know what came over me," Roi Gurri quickly apologized. "I shouldn't have asked you such a question."

"No, it's fine, I was just surprised," Susan said, though the way she shied away from his reach said otherwise. "Just smile and wave, or your father will have our heads."

They both looked up at the stands to see King Regel sitting in the place of honor, his judgmental look burning holes into their heads. Roi Gurri turned and waved to the crowd, offering a smile that could fool the oldest among them. Susan hoped her smile could fool them as well, though there was one person who she definitely wouldn't fool.

The man next to her.

After pleasing the crowd they went back to the weapons room. Susan kept her distance from Roi Gurri, too embarrassed to bring up what had happened during the fight. She changed back into their original clothing and they left the room.

"Susan!" Caroldus's voice cheered as soon as they walked out. The energetic blonde ran up to her and hugged her before spinning her in the air. "You did amazing! You made Eludikai look like a fool!"

"As you should," William said, clearly pleased. "After what he said he should be hung."

"Harsh words, William," Roi Gurri said. "Though I can't say I disagree with you."

Susan threw her head back and laughed. "Let's just hope his insubordination was loud enough for Regel to hear," she said. "What event are we on to next?"

"Next is dancing," Roi Gurri said. "Come, we don't want to be late."

Susan gasped and smiled with joy. "Dancing? Why didn't you say so sooner? Let's go!"

The group excitedly rushed out of the arena and to their companions. The guards assigned to Susan and Roi Gurri struggled to keep up as the heirs raced William and Caroldus.

Caroldus's pegasus, Lucigor, and William's mare Stellalux easily kept up with White Star and Pure Lighting. All of the companions had been bred and raised for war, and White Star had actually seen it before. All four Zudanums were also excellent riders, so it was no wonder they lost the royal guard along the road back to the castle.

Susan, Roi Gurri, William, and Caroldus all laughed as they dismounted their companions and joined the crowd. No one was dancing, yet they all expectantly waited in a circle. It was as if they were waiting for their prince to arrive before they started.

"What now?" Susan whispered to Caroldus.

"Tradition states that the heir gets the first dance of the day," Caroldus explained. "He may pick anyone he desires, weither they be noble or common, family or stranger. There is a saying; 'the heir picks whom their heart calls to'."

Susan thought that was quite romantic, but didn't say so aloud. She watched as Roi Gurri made his way to the dance circle, but abruptly stopped and turned to face her. He extended his hand to her.

"May I?" He asked.

Susan shouldn't have been surprised that he chose her to be his dance partner, yet she was. She had thought he would want to keep his distance after being embarrased, but perhaps she was far more embarrassed than he.

"I will have no other partner," Roi Gurri whispered when he saw her hesitation.

Susan felt her face warm as she accepted his hand. He led her to the center of the dance circle, not taking his eyes off her as he did so. He turned to her and placed his other hand on her waist.

"Will I know this dance?" Susan quietly asked.

"Do you remember the Lands of Magic?" Roi Gurri asked.

"I've watched others dance it, but I haven't done it myself."

"It's easy, I promise. Follow my lead, look into my eyes, and I won't let you fall."

Susan nodded. "I trust you."

The music started. It was a beautiful and soft melody, played by wind instruments and hand drums. It reminded Susan of the old celtic music Mr. Norman had, which she would play very often.

Roi Gurri led Susan through the dance with a firm, experienced hold on her body. She never once doubted his ability to lead her, not when his movements were confident and strong. Their hands were always touching, throughout the entire dance, one way or another.

The dance was basic enough, with enough moves for it to be somewhat impressive, yet it was intimate. But perhaps what made it intimate was the intense eye contact the prince and Chosen One held the entire time. Susan thought she would be intimidated by Roi Gurri's gaze, but found it endearing that his focus was completely on her. It made butterflies flutter in her stomach, which was something she couldn't remember feeling before.

The way he looked at her made her wonder what he was thinking. She had never seen a man's eyes so focused, so full of curiosity and longing. She wished to look into his mind and see the way he saw her, for he looked like a blind man seeing the moon for the very first time.

The song ended. Everyone applauded them, yet the look in Roi Gurri's eyes never faltered. He offered Susan his arm, and when she accepted he led her out of the circle.

"Thank you," he said as he smiled.

Susan couldn't find any proper words to address him. Before she could even think to thank him back, she already had a new dance partner.

"Come, Susan!" Caroldus exclaimed eagerly, taking her hand and pulling her into the group dance. "Try to keep up!"

Susan was more than happy to dance with the Zudanum people, and more so to dance with her best friend. Even though she was still shorter than many in the group, she kept up with the dances and their many steps. She even became confident enough to dance with men and women she hadn't trained with and didn't know. It was a relief to not feel afraid of those around her, especially after the two kidnapping attempts a few months ago.

For the first time since she had arrived, Susan let herself be free to not be afraid. She was determined to not be afraid of her own people, her own long-lost family. She had seen her family tree, many in the crowd may even be her cousins or second cousins!

On Zudanum dancing was a form of self-expression. Though there were steps to be followed for each dance, every pair of dancers performed them differently. Susan, for instance, loved to add a spin to her steps whenever possible. Caroldus was just as expressive with his legs as he was with his arms when dancing, often using fancy footwork to impress his partner. Roi Gurri's movements were refined and practiced, and he enjoyed dipping his dance partner at the end of every dance.

Hours and hours of dancing went by. Susan's feet were blistered and sore, forcing her to decline her next dancing partner's offer and sit between Roi Gurri and Caroldus.

"You look like a strawberry," Caroldus commented, poking Susan's cheek.

Susan breathlessly laughed and lazily batted his hand away. "Oh, I haven't had so much fun in ages," she said. "Today hasn't even ended, and I already can't wait for next year." She looked around, her brows creasing. "Where's William?"

Caroldus hummed in thought as he looked around. "You know, that's a good question. I actually haven't seen him in a while."

"He went into town an hour ago," Roi Gurri stated. "He had something important to do."

"Should we go find him?" Susan asked.

"No, he said he'd meet us at the field of Gontron."

"The field of Gontron?"

"It's the place we go to watch the firework show every year."

"Speaking of which, we should go now," Caroldus said, glancing down at his watch. "We don't want to arrive too late and miss the beginning."

"Good thinking, let's get moving."

The trio discreetly grabbed their things and walked alongside their companions as they left, so they were less likely to be spotted. The walk to the field was far, but it gave them the chance to pick up snacks and little fireworks from vendors.

When they arrived at the field of Gontron they set up blankets Caroldus had brought, and unpacked their things before making themselves comfortable on the ground. Susan tried to focus on what Caroldus was rambling to her about, but Roi Gurri's gaze burned into her like a hot brand. She was grateful to see William approaching them.

"Hey there, long time no see," Susan jested with a grin. "Where have you been?"

"Just dropping in on an old friend," William said as he plopped down between her and Caroldus.

"You have friends beside us?"

"Hard to believe, isn't it?"

"A little."

William chuckled and shook his head in disbelief. "Believe it or not, I have a life outside the palace walls. Not many nobles would understand."

Susan playfully smacked William's arm as he laid back on the blanket, resting on his hands as he laughed. Susan turned her attention to the rapidly setting suns.

The sky sparkled as the last few rays of sunlight hit the dome covering the planet. Dusk and dawn were the only times Susan could believe in magic, despite the rational reasoning for the sparkles and rainbow of colors. Still, as the suns disappeared for the night, she was excited to see the magic again tomorrow.

"William, scoot over," Caroldus ordered, shoving his friend.

"Hey, it's not my fault this blanket isn't big enough for the three of us," William protested.

"I've got plenty of room over here," Roi Gurri commented. "Susan, will you join me?"

Susan wanted to be hesitant, but the way Caroldus was shoving William was annoying, so she quickly moved to Roi Gurri's blanket. She still kept her distance from the prince, avoiding his gaze by looking up at the sky and waiting for the fireworks to start.

"Susan," Roi Gurri called quietly, rolling onto his side to face her. "Can we talk about it, please? I don't like the silent treatment."

Susan sighed but rolled onto her side to face him. She figured she *was* being mean by not talking to him, but waited for him to start the conversation.

"I'm sorry," Roi Gurri apologized.

"You have nothing to be sorry about," Susan tried to protest.

"Yes, I do. Relationships are new for you, in both a romantic and platonic sense. I should've held my tongue. It's not right for me to suggest we kiss, let alone do anything romantic until we discuss our engagement."

"Well, then let's discuss it. I mean, it's been four months, I think we've waited long enough."

Roi Gurri glanced behind Susan, seeing that William and Caroldus were engaged in their own conversation and not listening.

"Let me ask you something," Roi Gurri said, meeting Susan's eyes. "Do you wish you weren't betrothed to me? Do you wish you could be with someone else?"

Susan thought for a moment before answering. She found it embarrassing to be talking about her feelings, but she wanted to be open and honest with Roi Gurri. After all, if she wasn't honest now she'd probably live to regret it.

"I wish I had a say in the matter," Susan said. "I think I could've grown to love you on my own, but I guess we'll never know. Though, that said, I don't wish I could be with someone else. No one else has... has caught my eye like you have."

The darkness of night hid Roi Gurri's rosy cheeks, but not his smile. "You love me?" He asked.

Susan immediately broke eye contact and pulled up the blanket to hide her face. "No, I don't," she muttered, her voice muffled by the blanket.

"Sorry, can't hear you, Little Legs." Susan groaned and smacked Roi Gurri's chest, causing the prince to laugh. "All right, all right, you don't have to say anything."

Susan took a few seconds to recover from her embarrassment before pushing off the blanket. She sent Roi Gurri a playful glare, but he smiled like the past minute hadn't happened.

"Do you wish you could be with someone else?" Susan asked, her expression turning serious.

Roi Gurri shook his head. "No. Forgive me for not having original words to say, but no one has caught my eye as you have."

"Did your father ever try to set you up with someone else in the past?"

"No, but his council did. I think my father always knew you would come back home."

"I mean, if I didn't come home who would be your Chosen One?"

An emotion flashed in Roi Gurri's eyes that Susan hadn't seen before. Was it fear? Sorrow? But as soon as she had seen it, it was gone. Roi Gurri smiled.

"You have a point," he said. "I suppose I always knew you would return as well."

"Did you love me before I was sent to Earth?"

"I was far too young to know what love truly was, so no, I didn't. But I did care for you as I do for William and Caroldus."

"Do you love me now?"

When Roi Gurri didn't answer right away Susan braced for a terrible answer. And if she was honest with herself, both 'yes' and 'no' were terrible answers at the moment.

"I will answer that question when you are ready to hear the answer," Roi Gurri finally responded. "Can you live with that?"

Susan let out a sigh of relief. "Yes, I can."

"Good. Now, I have a proposal." Susan stayed quiet, letting him continue. "If you are comfortable, let us court each other properly these next three years. I believe we're beyond the term 'dating', and too advanced for titles such as 'boyfriend' and 'girlfriend', but we can still go on dates and speak to each other with the intention of being husband and wife one day."

Susan smiled, but couldn't hold in her laughter. Roi Gurri raised a confused brow.

"What's funny?" He asked.

"The way you word things," Susan laughed. "If it weren't for the way you formally say things every now and then I'd forget that you're the king's son."

Roi Gurri rolled his eyes. "I can't help it, I speak posh when I'm in intimidating situations."

"You find me intimidating?"

"I find this *conversation* intimidating." Roi Gurri playfully grinned. "Don't think you can intimidate me when you are both shorter and of a lower class than me."

Susan gasped with mock hurt and placed a hand on her heart. "How dare you speak to your future wife in such a way. I fear you have crossed the line."

Roi Gurri gently took Susan's hand and raised it to his lips, placing a gentle kiss on her knuckles. "I apologize, my Queen," he said in a low, raspy voice. "Please, give me a chance to make it up to you."

Susan's face burned like fire, and she couldn't help looking away. "I suppose I could give you another chance," she said quietly, meeting his eyes once again. "Though, if you're going to call me such a romantic name I must find something equally romantic for you."

"I look forward to hearing what you come up with, my Queen."

Oh, if Roi Gurri only knew the way that name made Susan's heart flutter. Though, from the way he looked at her, one could suspect he already knew.

"This reminds me, I have something for you," Susan said, sitting up and reaching for her bag.

"Really?" Roi Gurri asked, sitting up.

"Yes, but know that you're not exactly the easiest person to shop for."

"I'll cherish everything you give me, Susan."

"Shh, enough lovey talk, close your eyes."

Roi Gurri chuckled but obeyed and closed his eyes before cupping his hands and holding them out in Susan's direction. Something small and metal was placed in his hand. It felt like a ring.

"Open!" Susan's voice exclaimed excitedly.

Roi Gurri opened his eyes to find he had been correct in assuming it was a ring. It was huge and gold, with amethyst stones set all around the band. He placed it on his right hand's middle finger, finding it was a perfect fit.

"Thank Jehoyam it fits," Susan said. "I got one of the biggest rings they had because your hands are monstrous."

"Hey, leave my monster hands alone," Roi Gurri said with a smile. "I love it, Susan, thank you."

"Happy birthday, my Prince."

As fireworks began to burst in the sky, so did Roi Gurri's heart as a big grin broke out on his lips. He pulled Susan into an embrace, and she immediately wrapped her arms tightly around his broad shoulders.

"Thank you," Roi Gurri whispered, closing his eyes to relish the feeling of her in his arms.

Susan couldn't find the words to respond, so instead, she pressed a gentle kiss to Roi Gurri's cheek. She closed her eyes and inhaled his strong scent of fresh, newly tilled, dirt. It made her long to be near him always.

If Susan only knew the way her kind actions made Roi Gurri's heart flutter. Though, from the way she held onto him, one could suspect she already knew.

Chapter Fourteen
A Stubborn King Makes Cunning Advisors

"My King, it is high time that we introduce Susan to the nobles and councilmen," General Fridink, Caroldus's father and King Regel's head advisor, urged during a private meeting with the King, Queen, and Scadrin. "They have seen her during Royenden, but many still doubt her authority as a noble, and her right to be Roi Gurri's betrothed."

"The nobles of this land are very closed-minded, but they will come to accept her," King Regel said. "I will not push them to accept her when she has only just arrived."

"Do you not see that they are itching for an excuse to find Roi Gurri another bride? They see Susan as too short, not strong enough, not beautiful enough, not smart enough, or knowledgeable in her own people, the list goes on and on! They need to meet her and see that she is truly one of them, that she is a Zudanium."

"She is not ready."

"I disagree," Scadrin said. "Susan has scored very highly on every test, both physically and academically, in the past four months. I know that is thanks to Roi Gurri, Caroldus, and William tutoring her. I believe she will fare well with the nobles."

"Eight months is not enough time for Susan to be well acquainted with all of Zudanum's history and culture. No, the nobles will tear her to shreds."

"My King, please-" General Fridink tried to plead.

"My mind is made up, General. I thank you for your insight, but this meeting has come to a close."

General Fridink was tempted to press the issue but knew his king was a stubborn man and wouldn't change his mind. So, he respectfully bowed and left, followed by Scadrin and Queen Sharmon.

"You know, my son Jesidor will be coming back to Zudanum next week," General Fridink casually mentioned. "I would like to have a party, in his honor."

"That sounds like an excellent idea," Queen Sharmon approved. "You will need to send invitations far and wide."

"Every noble will be invited, of course."

"Including the *young* ones," Scadrin emphasized.

"I wouldn't dream of excluding them."

***

Susan had acquired a holographic pad, or holo-pad for short, through the help of Caroldus a few months ago. She would say it was like a phone if she had one on Earth, but a hundred times more advanced.

It was a small, thin, black metal circle plate that could easily fit into any pocket. It recognizes its owner through DNA, which it acquires when the owner taps on the plate. It can then create a holographic display, which only the person directly in front of it can see. If someone watched a person look through their holographic files from afar, they would see nothing. But it could also show its screen flat on the pad, which was better for texting and note taking.

Susan couldn't claim to know how the pad worked, but it was convenient. She was able to record Scadrin's lectures, download books from the library onto the pad, access public records, keep in touch with her friends when they were separated, and so much more.

Though she missed physical books, even if she had them she didn't have a place to put them in the castle. Any physical books she happened to acquire would be brought to her family's manor when she had the time.

It was a cool evening, so Susan decided to take up some light reading outside of the training grounds. Her favorite subject to read about was Zudanum history, specifically the history of its kings.

The sound of footsteps prompted her to look up, even though she already knew who it was by her smell and weight of her steps. She smiled up at Eloziah, who returned it with one of her own.

"What're you doing out here?" Eloziah asked, motioning to the training grounds.

"Reading about King Elidam the Swift," Susan said, lifting her pad to show her.

"Ah. It's a shame what happened to him. He would've been a greater king if he hadn't died so quickly into his reign."

"Maybe, but his sacrifice is why we're here today. If he hadn't found a cure for the plague, all Zudaniums may have been wiped out. The Drago line nearly went extinct."

"But it didn't. Anyway, are you coming to my family's party on the sixth night?"

Susan wasn't surprised by Eloziah's lack of interest in history. "Party? I haven't heard of it."

"Of course you did, you're on the guest list. Check your messages."

Susan pulled up her messages and found she did indeed have a message from General Fridink. Maybe she didn't notice it because she already had two 'Fridink' names in her contacts.

"Here it is," Susan said. Eloziah pressed her body closely her so she could see her hologram. "'Esteemed guest," Susan read aloud. "You have been invited to celebrate the return of my eldest son, Jesidor Fridink, on the sixth night of the ninth month, at the Fridink Estate.'"

"See, told you," Eloziah said.

"Why am I invited?"

"Um, because you're a countess? Because you're betrothed to the heir of Zudanum? Because you own a ton of land? Should I continue?"

Susan laughed lightly, unsure if she'd ever get used to Eloziah's sarcastic attitude. "No, I get it. Is there a dress code for this sort of thing?"

"Always wear your family colors unless you're going to an event hosted by the king. Then you have to wear black or white."

"Noted, thanks. I suppose I'll have to go to my estate and see if my mother's dresses fit me, but I doubt it."

"Why?"

"She was so much taller and muscular than me. I might look decent in a very tight-fitting dress, but it would still drag it on the floor."

"Oh, that stuff is an easy fix for my mom. Our manors are close to each other, I can see if she'll stop by and help you adjust a dress."

"Really?"

"Yeah, I think she'd have fun with it. She used to love making dresses for me when I was into them. And besides, mom likes to get out of the house whenever she can. Just make sure you have tea or wine waiting, she loves to have a drink in hand when talking."

"It's a deal."

***

Susan had arrived at the Wellns manor a few hours before Duchess Fridink was to arrive. She wanted to make sure the rooms they'd be using were clean, and that she had food and drinks ready.

Hosting wasn't one of Susan's skills, but she hoped the duchess wouldn't be too picky about her choice of food. In her opinion, all Zudanum food was good, and a lot of the realms agreed.

Besides exporting technology and military aid to the realms, Zudanum also exported food. Thousands upon thousands of crops around the globe are planted with the many unique fruits, vegetables, and nuts the planet has to offer. Susan was hesitant to try a lot of Zudanum food at first, especially the very brightly colored fruit, but once she let her tastebuds explore the unknown she was hooked. The same went for their wine and alcohol.

Susan's holo-pad alerted her that a ship was approaching the manor. She went to the window and indeed found a shining blue ship in the distance. She was downstairs by the time it pulled up to the front. Before anyone could knock on the door, Susan had already opened it.

"Welcome, Duchess Fridink," Susan quickly said, like she had rehearsed in her head and in the mirror a dozen times. "Please come in."

Duchess Fridink smiled politely and curtsied to Susan in greeting. "Thank you for your invitation, Countess Wellns," she said.

"Oh, you can call me Susan."

"Then please call me Paluna. I hope you don't mind, I brought some of my attendants to assist me."

"That's fine." Susan nodded at the handful of men and women behind Paluna. "Please, come in."

Susan led the party to a guest room, where she had laid out her dress of choice from her mother's wardrobe, as well as the refreshments.

"This is what you've chosen?" Paluna asked Susan, holding up the dress.

It was a gorgeous dark purple ball gown. It's sweetheart neckline was low and it cut down to just above where the belly-button would be, though that area was covered with sheer fabric. Susan liked the low cut though, because she believed her collarbones were one of her best features. She also liked the beautiful embroidery, the softness of the fabric, the garnet stones woven into it, and most importantly the built in sheath, meant for a dagger, replacing a pocket.

From the moment Susan had began training with Scadrin, her instructor drilled into her the importance of weapons and how to keep them hidden. So when she found a dress that was practically made for hiding a weapon, it was obviously going to be her first choice to wear.

"Yes," Susan confirmed. "Is something wrong with it?"

"It's awfully... revealing."

"Is it?"

"My dear, in Zudanum culture a low-cut dress is a declaration of war."

Susan's eyes widened with horror. She knew it was low-cut, but she hadn't thought it would be such a scandalous thing. But she'd sacrifice the easy hiding spot for a weapon to avoid declaring war on the Fridink household.

"I'm sorry, I wasn't aware," Susan quickly apologized.

"It's quite alright, dear," Paluna said with a reassuring smile. "Let's find something more suitable."

"No need, I have another one in mind. Excuse me."

Susan quickly left the room. She didn't want to admit that she didn't like the idea of strangers in her parents room, even if it was her best friends mother.

She grabbed one of the more modest dresses from her mothers closet and put it on. It was a velvet garnet-red dress that pooled around her feet like fresh blood. The back of the collar reached the bottom of Susan's skull, the front went down in a v-shape to her collarbones, and the sleeves had cuffs at her wrist. It also had a built-in corset that would define her waist when tied properly.

Despite it being completely different than her first pick, Susan had to admit that this dress was just as gorgeous, only in a different way. She was glad that she wouldn't be declaring war on her friend's household, but it made her wonder why her mother had such a lowcut dress in her closet.

"Maybe she was just as rebellious as my father," she thought with an amused smile.

Paluna's expression morphed into one of awe when Susan walked in wearing the dress. "Oh, my dear, this is perfect," she said. "You look just as stunning as your mother when she wore this."

"You knew my mother?" Susan asked.

"Very well. Your father and my husband knew each other since boyhood, so when your parents wed I became close friends with your mother."

"I've read a lot about her." Susan lifted her arms, allowing Paluna's attendants to begin to draw in the loose fabric. "She seems like a strong woman."

"Very, and very independent. Now, hold still, and I'll tell you a story about her."

Paluna rambled on to Susan about her mother, telling story after story about her adventures, her highs and lows with her father, and the times they'd gossip together.

Paluna also warned her about things she could and couldn't do at the party. As the betrothed of the heir prince, she could not bow to anyone except the king, queen, or Roi Gurri. She could not wear her hair up in a braided bun or she'd be declaring war. It wouldn't apply to her at this party, but the duchess also informed Susan that any dress with a slit was a declaration of war.

"Seems like one wrong flick of my wrist could be a declaration of war," Susan thought.

Her first and last dance automatically belonged to her betrothed unless he said otherwise. Only her betrothed could kiss her, whether it be on her hand, cheek, or lips. She could nod her head or shake her hands in greeting. She could not slouch whatsoever, she could not slurp her food, and so on and so forth.

Susan quickly warmed up to the duchess. She began to recognize Caroldus's fun attitude and constant joy in her, though she was far more composed than her son.

"I can see where Caroldus gets his personality from," Susan commented.

"You wouldn't say that if you knew my husband," Paluna said with a smile. "Caroldus is definitely his father's son, and Eloziah is his daughter. Now, my boys Jesidor, Contral, and Adonis are the children after my own heart."

"I don't think I've met Contral or Adonis," Susan mused.

"Contral tends to keep to himself within the Owl Perch, so that is no surprise. And Adonis, well, he can barely walk, let alone lift a sword. It will be many, yet few, years until he is placed into a patrol."

"If I may ask, why do you have so many kids so close together? Roi Gurri told me it is rare for families outside of the royal line to have lots of kids close together because you live so long."

"Jemdi and I quite enjoy having a large family. We waited till Jesidor was out on his own before having more children because we wanted to give all of our love to him. But once the twins, Caroldus and Contral, were born, I couldn't help but want a little army running around the empty house."

Susan chuckled, regretting it when a pin stabbed her side. "In the end you got what you wanted."

"I did, and I haven't regretted a moment of it."

"I hope I feel the same way when I'm older."

"I'm sure you will. Just you wait and see."

By the time the dress fit Susan like a glove it was dusk. She escorted the party out of the manor, but before they could leave, Paluna put a strong hand on her shoulder.

"Susan, heed my words," Paluna said in a hushed tone. "The nobles will be watching you like a hawk, so keep your head held high, and never let your voice falter. I strongly advise you to memorize everything you can about your grandfather, General Karniss Wellns. Some of these nobles are old enough to remember him, and if they do not think of him when they see you, you will be set up to fail in the courts just like your father."

Susan was taken aback. "Like my father?"

"You have read his files, you know of his struggles. Why would the son of a general have to claw his way to the top? Because he was an orphan, with no great general to guide him. I want you to take command of every person at the ball like *you* are a general. Do you understand?"

Susan nodded. "Thank you, Paluna. Please continue to believe in me."

"I will, Susan. But many will only follow you because of your mother. Don't give them a reason to doubt you."

Susan's heart raced as she watched the duchess leave.

"I'll give everyone a reason to follow me," she thought. *"Just watch."*

Chapter Fifteen
Countess Wellns

The night of Jesidor's return party didn't come quick enough. Duchess Paluna's words had kept Susan on edge for days, keeping her mind sharp and focused. She read everything about her grandfather she could get her hands on, from reports of his youth to documents of battles he had won for King Quintal the Harsh, King Regel's father.

To solidify the figure of Karniss Wells in the noble's minds, Susan decided to wear some of his accessories. She found dozens of beautiful wooden canes with gold and silver heads preserved in glass cases, a collection that probably took hundreds of years to complete.

In the end, she was forced to pick the shortest cane, which was tall enough to be a short walking stick.

"My grandfather was a unit," Susan thought as she admired the cane.

The head was that of a lion, which Susan hoped would allude to her engagement with Roi Gurri. The wood was a very dark shade of red, and perfectly matched her dress.

She also found one of his capes, the same garnet color as her dress, with gold trim and a clasp with an amethyst stone in the center.

She wore gold rings on her middle fingers, large sunset-colored gems resting atop, and gold bands on every other. Atop her head lay a tiara of gold, rubies, and garnets of every shade, shaped to look like flames in the midst of her fluffy, curled hair.

Now, flames were a touchy subject due to fire being associated with A'Vaddon and his dragon. But fire had been a power in the Wellns line long before A'Vaddon tainted the beautiful gift, and Susan wouldn't let the nobles forget it.

Susan didn't mind the idea of driving herself to the party, but at the last minute William offered to be her escort. He picked her up right on time, as the two suns began to set on the horizon.

Before Susan could think of descending the stairs, William rushed out of the ship and up to her. He gave her a little bow and offered his arm to her.

"Countess," he greeted with a nod of his head. "Please, allow me to help you."

Susan laughed and smiled before accepting his arm. "Why thank you, noble knight. You look dashing this evening."

William wore a student's uniform, one that normally would be worn at graduation or a very rare formal event. The outfit was completely grey, a turtleneck tucked into dress pants with a fancy jacket that buttoned down on the side instead of the front. His sword hung at his side, leather boots clad his feet, and gloves concealed his hands.

"My looks are nothing compared to yours," William insisted as he led Susan down the stairs. "I hope tonight goes in your favor."

"Me too, William."

He opened the back door of the ship for her, and she climbed in. The short ride to the Fridink Estate was silent. Susan used this time to collect her thoughts, playing scenarios in her head about what may happen.

She hardly realized they had come to the estate until the ship came to a complete stop.

"Are you sure you can't come inside with me?" Susan asked William. "I would feel much better with you close by."

"You remember what Roi Gurri said," William responded.

Susan sighed as she recalled the prince's words.

"No, absolutely not. It would be insulting for my fiance to walk in on the arm of another man, no matter who he is. All nobles will immediately begin forming speculations, spreading gossip all night about our 'failing alliance'. You must walk in alone."

"Besides, parties aren't really my thing," William insisted. "If you need me, I'll be out here. But you'll be fine. Roi Gurri will come to find you."

"Thank you, William," Susan said with a nod.

She took a deep breath and opened the door. An attendant from outside opened it the rest of the way before offering Susan a hand.

"Welcome to the Fridink Estate, Countess Wellns," the elderly man said with a smile. "Allow me to walk you up the stairs."

"Thank you."

He walked her up the stairs before dropping his arm. "I hope you have a satisfactory time tonight."

"I'm sure I will," Susan said with a polite smile. "Have a good night."

With her head held up high and cane at her side, Susan proudly walked into the estate.

"Introducing, Countess Wellns!" A man shouted loudly.

All eyes went to Susan. She had been startled by the shouting, but didn't show it. An attendant took the robe off her shoulders and she faced the crowd.

She could feel the condemning stares of the elderly as her eyes scanned the room. When she met someone's eyes she held them for a second before moving on. She didn't want to look away for too long and appear cowardly, but she didn't want to stare for too long and initiate challenges. She found the stormy grey eyes of Caroldus from across the room and made her way to him.

He approached her with a genuine smile, bowing lowly to her. "Countess, it's a pleasure to see you," Caroldus greeted. "You look gorgeous."

"Thank you, Duke," Susan said with a nod of her head. "My beauty is all thanks to your mother's hard work and wise words."

"Please, allow me to introduce you to my father and brothers."

Caroldus offered her his arm and led her through the room. She admired his suit, dark lapis blue with silver cufflinks and earrings shining in the light. What surprised her was the tight metal breastplate, like a corset peeking out from under his vest.

"Does that hurt you?" Susan whispered, looking down at his chest.

"It's not that tight," Caroldus said. "It's like armor, but for fashion. It's only uncomfortable when I sit down."

"Well, it looks good."

Susan turned her attention to General Fridink, Paluna, and the man of the hour, Jesidor. He was very handsome, arguably more than Caroldus. He was tall, lean, with curly dirty blonde hair, a beautiful beard, and grey eyes.

All of the Fridink family were dressed in lapis blue, but General Fridink clearly stood out from the rest in his uniform with dozens of pins and metals.

"Father, mother I believe you know Susan," Caroldus introduced with a smile. "Susan, allow me to introduce Jesidor, my older brother.

"It's a pleasure to meet you," Susan greeted, offering Jesidor her hand.

"The pleasure is all mine, Countess," Jesidor greeted with a big smile. "Caroldus speaks very highly of you."

"I'm very glad to hear that. Caroldus has been a great friend to me and an even greater teacher."

"I shouldn't expect anything less from my little brother. Please, allow me to introduce my wife, Doctor Lilah Lodin."

Susan shook the hand of the woman who stood beside Jesidor. She was much shorter than Jesidor, with dark skin and buzzed hair. Her smile was kind and her grip was firm.

"It's a pleasure to meet you, Doctor," Susan said with a smile. "What field do you study?"

"I'm an anameliologist, same as Jesidor," Lilah explained. "We study animals, but specifically the rare and endangered kind. Jesidor and I have been trying to find more peryton throughout the realms, but decided it was time to come home for a little while."

"Peryton? My companion is one."

"Yes, I've met White Star. He's a unique creature, it breaks my heart that his species is almost extinct."

Susan was alarmed by this news! She had no idea peryton were so rare, it made her appreciate her companion even more. It also made her feel sorry for him. Was he lonely because he was one of the only few left of his kind?

"Doctor, if there's anything I can do to help you in your search for the peryton, please do not hesitate to contact me," Susan said. "I want to help you, for the sake of my beloved companion."

"Oh, it brings me such joy to hear you say that!" Lilah exclaimed with a big smile. "Thank you for your kind offer, countess."

"Please, call me Susan."

"We'll bring the peryton back one day," Jesidor assured. "But for tonight, let's not worry about it. Susan, please, walk the floor. We'll be seeing more of each other tonight."

Susan nodded and the family bowed to her before she walked away.

Walking the floor was a lot more intimidating than she thought it was going to be. Eyes followed her everywhere but none dared to approach her. It was as if she were a rare yet deadly creature, one that no one would approach in fear of the judging stares of the elderly.

Well, all except for a tall woman in a vibrant scarlet red suit uniform, which looked exactly like General Fridink's. She was tall, clearly strong, with braided auburn hair and kind multi-colored eyes. She looked young for a high-ranking soldier, but Susan knew she had to be over a hundred to have such a rank.

The woman strode up to Susan with confidence and saluted. "My lady," she said. "Allow me to introduce myself. I am General Joyze Havingburg, head of intelligence."

Susan was in awe at the sound of her title. "It's an honor," she said with a nod. "But I should be saluting you, general, I am not yet a knight."

"As far as I am concerned, you are my future queen, and I will treat you with the same respect now as I will in the future."

"I appreciate that."

"You seem lost, my lady."

Susan laughed. "I thought I was hiding it well."

General Havingburg offered her a kind smile. "I mean no disrespect, but there's a reason I'm head of intelligence at my age. May I introduce you to some of the nobles while we wait for the prince to arrive?"

"You may."

Susan accepted General Havingburg's arm and allowed her to lead her to a group of middle-aged men. Even through the layers of clothes the general wore, Susan could feel her bulging muscles.

"I want her workout routine," she thought.

"My friends," General Havingburg slid into the conversation. "Allow me to introduce Countess Wellns. Countess, this is Lady Agmith, who sits among King Regel's advisors."

"A pleasure," Lady Agmith, an enchanting woman with black hair and pale yellow eyes, said as she shook Susan's hand.

"Doctor Dormis, who also sits among King Regel's advisors."

The doctor only nodded at Susan. He was a very heavyset man, with a bushy beard despite his balding head.

"And Lord and Lady Tugar," General Havingburg continued. "I believe you train with their son."

Susan was surprised as she came face to face with Subaron's parents! She expected Lord Tugar to look like his son, but no, he had peppered black hair and a strong chin, but he did not appear to be in fighting shape. Lady

Tugar, on the other hand, clearly gave Subaron his narrow eyes and high cheekbones. Oddly, neither had his hair or complexion.

"Countess," Lord Tugar greeted with a nod. "My son has spoken of you."

"Good things, I hope," Susan replied.

"Naturally." Lord Tugar was an exceptional liar. "I am pleased to see that King Regel has let you out of that cage he calls a palace."

"If the palace is a cage then I am a free bird, Lord Tugar. King Regel merely observes my training progress, but outside of that I'm free to do what I please."

"And how do you spend that precious time?" Lady Tugar asked, swirling the drink in her hand.

"I travel Zudanum, for I must make up for the time I've been gone. The residents of my land, and this court, have been without a Wellns for far too long."

"I'll drink to that," Lady Agmith said, grabbing two glasses from a server's tray. "Will you drink with me, Countess?"

"I will, thank you."

Susan accepted the glass, clinking it with Lady Agmith's before taking a sip. The drink wasn't as strong as the ones she often drank with her friends, which was a pleasant surprise. It meant she would be able to show the guests she needed to please that she could hold her liquor, an important trait to have.

"My my, who do we have here?"

Susan immediately recognized Subaron's chilling voice, turning to greet him with a forced smile. "Subaron, how good to see you."

“Countess, you look lovely,” Subaron lied through his teeth, a vein popping out of his forehead. “I didn’t expect to see you here tonight.”

“Why might that be?”

Susan could see Subaron hold back every sarcastic, snarky remark he could think of under the suns, probably to save face in front of the general, but he didn’t have to when his father was right beside him.

“Perhaps it’s because you have not attended any formal events besides Royenden,” Lord Tugar stated. “Is that because of your lack of manners or lack of invitation?”

“So this is where Subaron gets it from,” Susan thought.

“I’m afraid training and overseeing my land has kept me tied up,” Susan said. “Being the Chosen One *and* future Queen of Zudanum isn’t as easy as it may seem.”

The Tugar parents looked enraged at the reminder that their son still wasn’t the Chosen One, on top of the fact Susan held a much higher title than all of them. The rest of the group, which had gradually become bigger, kept their mouths shut. Everyone knew of the Tugar and Wellns rivalry, started hundreds of years ago, and it looked like the two families were back at it again.

“Let’s hope the pressure doesn’t get to you,” Lady Tugar hissed. “After all, your family has a history of coming to early ends at inconvenient times.”

“Excuse me?” Susan snapped.

“Karniss and Falgide died before they could properly raise their son. Your parents did the same, at the hand of A’Vaddon. And, well, there is the matter we do not speak of-”

“Lady Tugar!” General Havingburg sharply interrupted. “Must I remind you of the King’s order?”

Lady Tugar flashed a furtive smile. "I apologise, General. I suppose I got carried away."

Susan was confused. *"The matter we do not speak of?"*

But her confusion was overshadowed by her anger. Clearly the Tugars were going to be a consistent problem in her life, and she hated the thought.

"Introducing the Heir Prince Roi Gurri Drago and Prince Johles Drago!"

The rage building in Susan's bones subsided as her gaze rested on the noble princes.

Everyone turned to the entrance as the two princes walked into the room. Susan had only heard of Prince Johles, Queen Sharmon's only son, but never met him. He clearly didn't like the attention he was reciving, his gaze wandering to the ground. He had the same vibrant red hair as his sister and mother, with dark chocolate brown eyes.

Susan's gaze didn't linger on him for too long, her eyes drawn to Roi Gurri. This was her first time seeing him in formal wear, and the sight made her heart flutter.

He wore a soldier's uniform like the generals did, though it was emerald green with gold lining. Pins and medals crossed his chest, thick golden rings adorned his fingers, and the same crown he wore for Royenden rested on his head. An attendant took the cloak off his shoulders to reveal a golden cape flowing down his back.

Susan met Roi Gurri's eyes and a sense of opia, a feeling that made her feel both invasive and vulnerable, rushed through her body. She hoped she wasn't blushing an embarrassing shade of red, especially with the intense stare of the Tugar trio burning into her. But their judgmental looks meant nothing compared to the affectionate look in her lover's eyes.

Instead of going to greet the host first, Roi Gurri approached Susan.

"My love," Susan greeted as she curtsied. "You look breathtaking."

"You flatter me, darling," Roi Gurri said with a smile before leaning down and pressing a gentle kiss to her cheek. "You look ravishing, my Queen," he whisp- ered into her ear before pulling away.

Roi Gurri had made it clear beforehand that in front of nobles he couldn't call Susan his queen, since she was not the one who officially held that title at the moment. But Susan didn't mind. She wouldn't admit it, but she liked the secrecy that came with him whispering that name to her.

Susan was sure her face was a red, blushing mess, but she smiled through it. She prayed the makeup she was wearing wouldn't melt.

"Please accompany me tonight," Roi Gurri said as he offered Susan his arm.

"It would be my pleasure," Susan said as she accepted his arm.

Susan let out a quiet breath of relief as they walked away from the Tugars.

"What did you say to the Tugars?" Roi Gurri asked. "They look livid."

"I simply put them in their place," Susan said with a sly smile.

"Good, they need to be knocked down a few pegs."

"Lady Tugar said something that was offputting, though. She mentioned something about a, 'matter we do not speak of'. What could she have meant?"

Roi Gurri's forearm tensed beneath her hands. "Let's discuss it later."

Their conversation was dropped as they approached the Fridink family. Unlike the Tugars, the Fridinks were always warm, welcoming, and humble. They were nothing but smiles as the couple approached.

"My friend!" Caroldus exclaimed with a huge smile as he approached Roi Gurri. They clasped arms before hugging, both smiling and laughing. "I'm glad you could make it."

"I wouldn't miss this for the world," Roi Gurri said before turning to Jesidor. "Jesidor, it's great to see you again."

"Is that really the son of Regel I see?" Jesidor asked as he firmly shook Roi Gurri's hand. "It's only been five years, and you're already almost taller than me. I distinctly remember you being shorter than my mother."

"A lot can happen in five years."

"Yes, I can see that." He glanced at Susan. "Congratulations on your engagement, it must be very exciting."

"It is," Roi Gurri agreed, looking down at Susan. "I couldn't ask for a better partner."

"I watched your fight from Royenden," Lilah commented. "You seem to work really well together."

"That's thanks to Scadrin's training," Susan said. "If it weren't for her we would've killed each other long ago."

The group laughed, both married Fridink couples nodding in understanding.

"It's a grand thing to work with your partner," Jesidor said. "It makes you stronger as a person."

"Indeed it does," General Fridink said, looking down at Paluna with a loving smile.

A distinct chime sounded throughout the manor, and the guests began making their way to a different room.

"Ah, it's time for dancing," Paluna said.

"Allow me to escort you," General Fridink said to Paluna, flashing her a dashing smile as he offered her his arm.

Paluna gratefully accepted her husband's arm and they walked to the ballroom, followed by Jesidor and Lilah.

"Have you filled anyone's dance card yet, Caroldus?" Susan asked as he followed her and Roi Gurri to the ballroom.

"No," Caroldus said, though he didn't particularly sound disappointed. "I can't say I have."

"Surely many here would be eager to dance with you."

"Perhaps, but I'm not particularly eager to dance with any of them. Even before Roi Gurri was betrothed I was receiving loads of marriage proposals, but now it's just getting ridiculous."

Roi Gurri couldn't help but chuckle. "Ah, that's why I haven't received as many letters these past few months."

"You laugh, but my head spins. Is it so much to ask for a woman whose father isn't after my inheritance?"

"I'm sure you'll find her one day," Susan assured. "But for tonight, why not have fun and dance? It's not a marriage proposal."

"I guess not."

"Besides, it's not like the women here are bad looking."

Caroldus shrugged. "True. Guess I'll find a partner before the dance starts."

"You have about fifteen seconds," Roi Gurri stated.

Caroldus speed-walked off to find a partner, leaving Susan and Roi Gurri laughing quietly.

"He's a character," Susan muttered.

"We'll probably have to be the ones to set him up with a nice girl some day," Roi Gurri stated. "I'm not convinced he could get a genuine date on his own."

"Let's have *some* faith in him."

The same chime as before went off again. Roi Gurri turned to Susan and offered her his hand.

"May I have this dance?" He asked.

"It would be my pleasure," Susan accepted with a smile.

Roi Gurri gracefully led her to the dance floor, and with only a second to spare. The music, performed by talented musicians on the other side of the room, started.

After Susan's insightful conversation with Duchess Paluna, she decided to ask Roi Gurri to help polish up her dancing skills. After all, who better to ask than the man who could never forget anything? Thanks to him, Susan knew exactly what dance went with the song that played.

The couple stayed quiet as they danced. They couldn't talk freely in such a place, especially with so many people so close to them, but that didn't stop them from intimately gazing into each others eyes.

Susan once heard that the eyes were the gateway to the soul. If that statement was true, she could say she knew Roi Gurri's soul inside and out. She had freely stared into his eyes for a total of hours, maybe even days since Royenden, and she wasn't tired of seeing them.

When the song ended she was disappointed to feel a tap on her shoulder. She was even more disappointed when she turned to see Subaron!

"I'll have the next dance," he stated, holding his hand out.

"Like sheol you will," Roi Gurri hissed through his teeth.

Before the prince could approach Subaron, Susan placed a hand on his chest to stop him.

"No, it's okay," Susan said to Roi Gurri before facing Subaron and accepting his hand. "Shall we?"

Before Roi Gurri could protest, Subaron had led Susan away from him and into the next dance.

"I'm surprised you accepted my offer," Subaron admitted.

"I accepted because I have a question," Susan said in a low voice.

"What makes you think I would answer any of your questions?"

"Because you would love to watch me cause an uproar if I were upset by what you say. Especially in front of all these nobles."

"You would like to think that, wouldn't you?"

"Are you claiming you wouldn't?"

"Don't get me wrong, I'd love for you to ruin your reputaion, but only if you weren't the Chosen One."

Susan was confused by his statement. "Elaborate."

"Being a Countess or Lord or Lady is a flimsy thing. Bankruptcy, war, famine, or death could easily take away those titles. But being the Chosen One comes with a special permanence." Subaron stared deeply into her eyes, allowing her to look into his icy soul. "You weren't *given* the title of Chosen One, you fulfilled an ancient prophecy that no other could. Even the council had to eventually face facts when they didn't want to name you the Chosen One because of your gender. Just like they couldn't *give* you that title, they can't *take it away* either. So whether the nobles like it or not, whether my parents like it or not, whether *I* like it or not, *you* are the Chosen One. And if these people lose faith in you, your journey to taking down A'Vaddon will be much longer than it needs to be, and very, very, difficult. So no, I will not let you cause a scene just because of your emotions."

Susan was too stunned to speak. Why was Subaron being a voice of reason? Why was what he was saying making sense? Was it because of their setting? Was he saving face because of the people around them?

"Do not play games with me, Subaron," Susan hissed. "If you truly believed what you say you would not have struck me with your lightning, nor would you have let me dive after the crystal ball from such a height. You have risked my life far too many times for me to ever believe you care for my well being."

"One day you will understand the things I've done for you and you will thank me."

"Doubt it."

The song ended, and Susan pulled herself away from Subaron. She didn't even allow him to escort her off the dance floor, instead marching out of the ballroom.

She found herself wandering empty hallways filled with portraits, taking deep breaths to calm herself down.

"Why should I believe Subaron when all he does is torment me?" She asked herself.

A voice of reason came to mind.

"Because he's a fellow Zudanum. Because he wants A'Vaddon to be gone more than I do. And perhaps he'd rather I be the one to face A'Vaddon rather than himself."

Susan hadn't admitted to anyone other than William that many times she had wished for Subaron to be the Chosen One rather than herself. Life would be so much simpler if she didn't have to be the one to take up extra physical training to even dream of making a scratch on A'Vaddon. All that, atop her extra academics so she could one day be queen, made her life exhausting.

Susan sighed as she looked out the large window to the starry night sky. "If only there were another."

"Another what?"

Susan turned at the voice of Roi Gurri. He approached her with a worried look and gently took her hands in his.

"Nothing," Susan said. "I was just being dramatic."

They both chuckled. Thankfully Roi Gurri didn't press Susan for an answer.

"What did Subaron say to make you storm out?" Roi Gurri asked.

"Nothing I care to repeat at the moment. Let's forget about him and go-"

Susan cut herself off as a chill went down her spine. She turned her head back to the window and met a pair of dark eyes from outside. Strangely, they looked a lot like her own, and the sight of them made her head feel fuzzy.

"Susan, what's wrong?" Roi Gurri asked.

Susan glanced up at him, and when she looked back outside the eyes were gone. She shook her head to rid herself of the chilled feeling.

"Nothing," Susan said. "Let's go dance."

As Susan danced with noble after noble, flattering their hearts and winning over their heads with her words, she felt the gazes of others become less judgmental and more endearing.

"You're doing it," Duchess Paluna whispered to Susan after a dance, the two approaching the refreshment table. "I hear positive gossip about the Wellns for the first time in a decade."

"That's a relief," Susan admitted as she took a long sip of her drink. "What are they calling me?"

"*Countess* Wellns."

Susan couldn't help but smile. "That sounds *so* much better than the things I know people have been calling me."

"Keep it up, my lady, and one day they'll be happy to call you their queen."

A sense of pride welled up in Susan's chest. Being queen hadn't excited her before, but now that she was getting the approval of those who would one day be her greatest allies she wouldn't mind being called it one day.

"Personally, I think you'd make a fine queen."

Susan jumped in surprise as she looked up to find the masked face of William! She smiled with delight.

"When did you come in?" She asked.

"Not long ago," William said. "I wanted to make sure you were doing okay. Though it seems there was no reason for me to use my skill sets to get in, with the news I just heard."

"Skill sets?"

"William, it's good to see you," Paluna said, offering her hand to him.

He took it and gently pressed it to his mask, as if he were kissing it. "It's always a pleasure to see you, Duchess."

"How did you manage to get in? I don't recall seeing your name on the guest list."

Paluna's words may have sounded harsh, but her grin and the hint of rebelliousness in her voice gave away the fact she did not care one bit if William was here.

William's eyes glimmered with mischief. "I'm sorry, my lady, but I will take that secret with me to my grave."

Chapter Sixteen
Whispers in the Halls

Susan kept up her training over the next three months, keeping a steady pace with the men of Warrior Brave and Cobra Cave. She was now a sturdy and handsome woman, with muscles climbing her arms and legs that she could be proud of.

Late one night, Susan decided to try to sneak out of the Warrior Brave room, but she only managed to walk a few steps before she was spotted.

"Who goes there?" The demanding voice of Lucas echoed.

"It's alright Lucas, it's just me, Adathir," Susan assured.

Lucas stepped out of the shadows. "What are you doing out this late?"

"I can't sleep. I'm just going to the library for a while. I won't be out too long, I promise."

Lucas peered at her, his colorless eyes haunting her.

"How do I know that you're not just going to spy on another patrol?" He asked.

Susan knew he asked because a sort of 'prank war' had been going on among the patrols for the past month. She hadn't personally partaken in the war, but she knew Caroldus had.

"Do I look like someone who would waste my time pranking another patrol?" Susan asked.

Lucas grinned a wolf grin. "Alright, just make sure not to disturb anyone. And try not to run into Doctor Almit, or he'll turn you in as a 'traitor'."

She nodded and smiled as she walked away. She walked down many halls and managed to get lost, even after living in the castle for almost a year. In her defense, usually she would walk to the library with a friend and wouldn't have to rely on her knowledge of the castle.

"Now would be a good time to have Roi Gurri's ability to never forget," she thought.

When Susan got lost she tried asking the Kindness Keep guardian for help, but she wasn't very good at giving directions. She also tried to ask Tristen, the Cobra Cave guardian, but he wasn't much help either.

"Sorry, kid, I can't leave my station tonight," Tristen apologized.

Susan nodded in understanding. "Thank you, Tristen, sorry for the disturbance."

She walked down a few more long halls until she heard voices, pausing mid-step. She peeked around the corner to find Sondman, King Regel's chief advisor, talking to a tall man in a hooded cape. She couldn't see his face, but she could hear them both clearly.

"Everything is in place, Judez," Sondman said to the man. "You should have no trouble getting Susan's trust. She's very easy to manipulate."

Susan's eyes widened, and her breath caught in her throat. She could barely believe what she was hearing. Even though she had only heard one sentence, it struck her. She was tempted to come out and expose the two men, but she decided to listen instead.

"I hope so, Sondman," Judez said. "For both of our sakes. The sooner I get out of here the better."

"Why is his voice familiar?"

"You must watch out for her friends though, they will suspect you. Especially Roi Gurri. He is betrothed to her, so you might have trouble getting close to her."

"You'll have big trouble with that."

"Don't worry about me," Judez stated. "That has never stopped me before. Now, tell me about them."

"Before? Who is this guy? He's obviously with A'Vaddon, but how does he plan to sway me?"

"They are Susan, Roi Gurri, William, and Caroldus," Sondman explained. "Roi Gurri is an anti-natural, but the others aren't. At least not yet."

"Is there a chance Susan isn't anti-natural at all?"

"It's hard to say. She doesn't have any actual powers, but she does have special abilities, like Roi Gurri's ability to never forget. She can sense things, like an animal. She is especially sensitive to smells and sounds, and she can feel someone's emotions without even looking at them. I am afraid that she won't trust you because of this, for she has been relying on this more than the normal person."

"That's because I'm not a normal person."

"That's her weakness," Judez said. "Relying on one skill or ability is like leaning your weight on one crutch. All I have to do is kick it out from under her and she'll fall like a domino. This ability won't scare me off."

"How so?" Sondman asked.

"He knows who I am, so he will try to protect the others. But he wouldn't dare point me out, he knows the consequences."

"What if the others get in your way?"

"Then I'll have to take extreme measures."

"You'd kill them?"

"I'd have to silence them somehow. What else could I do, ask them nicely not to tell anyone that I'm the head General of-"

"Don't say his name here," Sondman hushed. "Many things here that are not human have eyes and ears. But what about the Groon? Or King Regel for that matter. They can read minds."

"I am mentally stronger than both of them," Judez said confidently. "I'll be able to get in no problem."

"I wish you luck, and I will do everything I can to help. I must leave now, the king will be missing me."

"Damn Regel, and glory to A'Vaddon."

Sondman frowned, but he shook Judez's hand. Susan was shaking, covering her mouth with one hand as she broke out in a cold sweat. Her heart was beating much too loudly, and she feared every breath she took would expose her position.

"I have to warn the others," she thought, her heart racing as she thought of what Judez might do to her friends.

Susan paused, taking a moment to think. From what she heard, there was at least one spy in the patrols. Not just in the patrols, there would most likely be more in the castle as well. This new spy, Judez, had different orders than any others, she concluded from what she heard. He also wasn't afraid to harm her friends, that's what sent a shudder down her spine.

Having composed herself, she softly tiptoed backwards, but turned around to find herself face to face with Roi Gurri! He quickly covered her mouth with his hand to muffle her gasp of surprise, but it was too late, she had been heard.

Sondman and Judez stopped at the sound.

"Did you hear that?" Judez asked, alerted.

Susan and Roi Gurri froze as their eyes locked.

"Yes I did," Sondman, said. "I'm sure it was just one of the many dragon-cats that roam here. The Princess, Sutan, likes to have them around."

Judez wasn't fully convinced. He walked toward the corner where Roi Gurri and Susan were hiding.

Hearing the footsteps and not wanting to risk confrontation with Susan being so shaken, Roi Gurri grabbed her hand and ran down the hall. Judez heard them running, quickly turning the corner and blasting fire at the wall from his hands. He just missed Susan's hand and was about to pursue them, when he realized that he had made enough noise already.

"Another night, perhaps," he mused to himself. "Whoever they were, I'll find them."

Luckily he didn't see Susan or Roi Gurri's faces. Roi Gurri was ready to fight, but Susan looked so stunned that he knew she couldn't handle a fight right now. They continued running down halls until they were sure they were far from the two men.

Susan looked up at Roi Gurri, her breath slowly starting to steady as she leaned against the wall.

"What are you doing here?" She asked, catching her breath. "And how did you find me?"

"I woke up and had a sense that you were in danger," Roi Gurri replied, steadying his breath. "When you weren't in the library, I started looking around. I didn't mean to startle you."

"Well, you showed up at the wrong moment. I could've easily snuck away without you scaring me."

Roi Gurri frowned. "If you hadn't snuck out in the first place, then this all wouldn't have happened!"

"If I hadn't snuck out then I wouldn't have found out that all of our lives are in danger!"

"Keep it down," the Owl Perch guardian whispered. "You might wake up someone."

Ignoring the guardian, Roi Gurri looked into Susan's eyes.

"What do you mean our lives are in danger?" He asked in a hushed tone.

Susan told him everything she had heard, not leaving out a single detail. The prince thought hard for several long moments before he spoke.

"We can't tell anyone about this," Roi Gurri concluded

"What?" Susan asked, confused. "We have to warn your father!"

"He would never believe us. My father has always believed that our security is impenetrable, so he wouldn't believe that multiple people actually broke in. He's very stubborn in that way. We have to catch this Judez guy in the act."

"How? It kind of sounded like he was after me, so do I just stay in my room and hope he gives up?"

"Of course not, we just need to keep a close eye on things."

"Like spying on people within the patrols?"

"Exactly."

"I guess we'll never know who this guy is then, he could be anyone! Especially anyone in Cobra Cave, since apparently they're good at what they do. And anyone can pretend to be nice, even when really they're dark."

"What do you suppose we do?" Roi Gurri sighed, running a hand through his hair. "Ask everyone nicely if they're serving the demon himself?"

"I guess we'll just have to trust our instincts then," Susan said with a shrug. "From what I heard, It sounds like this guy hasn't been assigned to a patrol yet."

"Of course! We'll just keep an eye on the new guy! Susan, you're brilliant."

Susan grinned. "Yeah I know." Roi Gurri rolled his eyes in response and they both laughed. "But that sounds legit. Hopefully, he comes soon, I'd rather not sleep with one eye open." Susan thought for a moment. "Do you think this guy might also be after the Jewel of Numenera?"

"It's possible. Why did you suddenly think that?"

"I'm not sure, it just seems like something A'Vaddon would want. I keep the jewel on me at all times, I'll make sure that it doesn't get into the wrong hands."

"We also have to find this other inside person they mentioned."

"It sounds like he isn't actually on their side though. Judez said he might try to get in their way and protect us."

"Even so, if he has ties to A'Vaddon he can be manipulated in some way."

"Who do you think he could be?"

"It could be anyone, or anything. Some of the companions talk."

"So who do we trust?"

"Just Caroldus and William. No one else, not even my father. And whenever Sondman talks to you, be on your guard. He can't know we know."

"Well, that's going to be difficult. He manages most of the reports from Scadrin and the Groon."

"Well, then he can't know anything personal. The four of us can't talk about anything private in the open anymore."

"Agreed."

Susan let out a small yawn, and Roi Gurri smiled softly.

"Come on," he said, placing his hand on the small of her back. "We should be in bed. It's been a long night, and we have training tomorrow."

Susan nodded and allowed Roi Gurri to lead her back to the Warrior Brave Patrol.

Chapter Seventeen
Nightmares in Dreams

Susan found herself in a sitting room that looked like it belonged in her estate. Her long hair was brushed down to the back of her thighs, and she was wearing a white dress. She looked down at her hands to find them adorned with beautiful bracelets and rings embedded with jewels, and a necklace hung around her neck.

She looked around the room but didn't see anyone. She walked toward the window and moved the curtain to find a beautiful garden that wasn't planted there before.

"So beautiful," Susan whispered. "But where am I?"

"Susan?" A soft, song-like voice asked from across the room.

Susan turned to see a beautiful woman with long, vibrant flowing blonde hair and piercing green eyes. She wore a thin ice-blue dress that flowed onto the ground and fluttered in the breeze. As soon as Susan saw her she knew who she was. Her breathing abruptly stopped, and her hands started shaking.

"Mom?" She asked, stepping back away from the woman who looked identical to her mother. "Is- Is that really you?"

Defestri Wellns' expression was filled with worry. "Susan, what's wrong?" She asked as she slowly walked closer to her.

Tears came to Susan's eyes as she backed away.

"You're not real," Susan said, her voice shaking as she pointed at her mother.

Defestri raised a brow, looking confused and worried.

"I am real, and so is your father."

A tall, handsome man came out from around the corner and Susan gasped. He looked at her and smiled. He had Susan's brown eyes, with shaggy soot-black hair. His smile was warm and loving, like a father's smile.

"D-Dad?" Susan choked out, a tear falling down her face.

"Susan?" Marcus asked, his face washing with worry. "What's wrong, princess?"

"You're dead!" Susan screamed. "A'Vaddon killed you both!"

Defestri and Marcus looked at each other before turning back to her.

"Jehoyam is allowing us to see each other," Defestri explained as she walked toward Susan. "He is allowing us to speak through this dream."

Susan fell down on her knees and began to cry bitterly. "Why did you have to die?" She asked as her mother kneeled beside her.

"Because it was our time."

"No, it wasn't! Subaron was right. If you both were still alive, we would be a happy family living in the castle. My friends would still be my friends, and A'Vaddon would be gone!"

Defestri embraced her. Susan's hands gripped her as tears drenched her dress.

"How do you know that your friends would still be your friends?" Defestri asked, softly petting Susan's hair.

Susan frowned and looked up. "What do you mean?" She asked, but Defestri only smiled.

"My princess, everything happens for a reason."

In an instant, Susan found herself outside and she quickly stood.

"Mom?" She called. "Dad?"

Silence hung in the air, and a cold, heavy weight fell onto Susan's shoulders. She wiped away her tears and looked around, not recognizing anything around her. Was she in a garden at the castle? If she was it must be well hidden, because she hadn't seen this one before.

Susan turned to see Caroldus walking along a path, his hair shorter than she thought it was, and he was dressed in blue and silver clothing, his family's colors.

"Caroldus!" Susan cried, racing over to her best friend, her bare feet gliding across the short grass.

He turned at the sound of her voice, but he didn't smile.

"Who are you?" He asked, his brow lifting.

Susan's smile quickly faded as she came to a stop in front of him. "It's me, Susan Wellns," she said.

Caroldus rolled his eyes at her and groaned. "Oh boy, a *Wellns*," he sneered, his tone harsh. "Your parents defeated A'Vaddon, you don't have to rub it in our faces."

"Caroldus, I would never-"

"Just stay away from me, I don't care about what you have to say."

Caroldus walked off, not taking a second glance back at her. Susan couldn't help but cry as she watched one of her best friends walk away from her with hatred in his eyes. She turned to see Roi Gurri walking beside Tristen, dressed in his family colors. She ran up to them.

"Roi Gurri!" Susan called, hoping he knew her. "You will not believe what Caroldus just said to me-"

"Caroldus Fridink?" Roi Gurri asked. "Why would I care about what he said to you?"

Susan felt like she had just been stabbed in the stomach. Her chin quivered, and she became anxious.

"Because he's your best friend," she insisted. "You're both in the same patrol, Warrior Brave. You grew up together!"

Roi Gurri and Tristin gave each other confused glances and turned back to her.

"Susan, I don't have time to play pretend with you," Roi Gurri snapped, his tone harsh. "I'm in Cobra Cave, and Subaron's waiting for me to play Swarbus. *He* is my best friend."

"Subaron?!" She cried, the pain in her stomach growing. "But you hate him!"

"Did you become even more stupid overnight?" Roi Gurri asked. "Just go home to your intended, leave me alone."

"B-But... *we're* betrothed," Susan whispered in confusion as Roi Gurri tried to walk away. "Roi Gurri, you must be mistaken! My love-"

"Do *not* address me that way!" Roi Gurri snapped, turning to Susan with annoyance and anger in his eyes. "Now go home."

He turned and continued walking alongside Tristin.

Tears started to stream down Susan's face, the pain in her stomach becoming unbearable. She began running, looking for the road that led to the castle.

"William!" Susan called, running all around the palace grounds. "William!"

She tripped on her dress and fell on sharp gravel, scraping her knees and palms. Her hands and knees started bleeding, staining her white dress.

"William!" She cried out again.

She screamed in pain, clutching her stomach as she felt she was being torn inside and out. Uncontrollable tears streamed down her face.

"Do you wish your parents were still alive?"

She looked up and spun her head around, but didn't see anyone. She felt a hand on her shoulder and turned to see a man, but the brightness of the sun hid his face.

"William?" Susan asked.

The man didn't answer, he only reached down and softly wiped her tears away with his thumb.

"I'm sorry," he whispered. "I'm sorry I couldn't take care of you."

She frowned in confusion. "Who are you?"

The man didn't answer, he only left his hand lingering on her face.

"In this world, I'm no one."

Susan leaned her head against his hand, and the pain in her stomach started to settle.

"Who are you?" Susan quietly asked again, her eyes fluttering closed.

The dream started to fade away, like the dripping of water on paint.

***

Susan quickly sat up in bed, sweat streaming down her face, and she placed a hand over her mouth to keep from crying out. Her breathing was heavy and her hands and knees stung as if they were still scraped and bleeding. She tried to get out of bed, but lost her balance and fell to the floor, groaning as her head hit the edge of the dresser.

Roi Gurri was still awake, thinking about what to do with Sondman, but his thoughts were interrupted when he heard a loud thump come from Susan's room. He quickly got up and walked into her room to find her on the floor, sweat and tears pouring down her face. Her hands were held close to her chest, her nightgown bunched up around her.

"What's wrong?" He asked, worry clear in his voice as he knelt beside her. "What happened?"

Susan's head snapped up to look at him. She reached up and threw her arms around his shoulders, hugging him tightly. He was caught off guard, but didn't hesitate to return the hug.

"Nightmares," Susan whispered. "I had this dream, it was so light in the beginning, but then it got so dark. I wasn't me. My parents- I saw my parents. Caroldus didn't know me. You barely knew me. You were in Cobra Cave and you said I was engaged to someone else. And William he- he wasn't there."

Her lip quivered and tears spilled down her face. Roi Gurri held her tighter, rubbing her back.

"I feel like the whole world is resting on my shoulders," Susan whispered. "I- I don't want to let everyone down."

"I know what it's like," Roi Gurri said in a comforting tone.

She looked up at him. "How?"

He stood, carried her back to her bed, and sat with her on his lap. He reached his hand over and wiped her tears away softly.

"I'm heir to the throne," Roi Gurri said quietly. "One day, I'll have the most powerful kingdom in this realm, possibly this universe, on my shoulders. Plus, I have the responsibility of taking care of you."

“Am I a burden to you?” Susan asked, looking down guiltily.

Roi Gurri placed a hand under Susan’s chin and lifted her head so she was looking into his eyes.

“No. You’re a challenge. A puzzle with a million pieces, but I only have half of them. But, I’ll be able to complete you one day. I just need to find the rest of your pieces.”

“Maybe one day I’ll figure you out, too.”

“Even my father hasn’t done that. I’m not sure you ever will.”

“I’m not your father. I actually pay attention to you. I listen to you. I know how to catch your attention.”

He smiled softly and pressed a gentle kiss to her forehead. “When I had nightmares as a child, my nurse would tell me to think about the things I love most in life,” Roi Gurri said. “To imagine the good things that will take place in ten years. Try that, it helped me.”

Susan closed her eyes and leaned her head against his chest, going quiet for a moment.

“What are you thinking about?” Roi Gurri asked.

“I’m thinking about White Star,” Susan said with a smile. “About how he saved me. About Caroldus, how he always makes me laugh, and how he’s my best friend. How he has such a kind personality, and how he cares for his sister so much. I’m thinking about William, how he’s always there. How he’s like a brother to me, someone I can lean on. I’m thinking about you.” Roi Gurri looked down at her with more interest, her eyes still closed. “You’re different,” she continued. “I feel something different for you, in a way I’ve never felt before. I’m thinking of how one day... one day, we might have beautiful children.”

She yawned, and her voice lowered to a whisper. Suddenly she went quiet.

"Susan?" Roi Gurri asked, but she didn't answer as her hands gripping his shirt relaxed.

He realized she was asleep and stood, gently laying her on her bed. He watched her sleeping figure for a moment and covered her with a blanket. He leaned down and kissed her cheek softly, smiling to himself.

"I agree, we will have beautiful children," he whispered. "Sleep well."

He quietly walked out of her room and slipped back into bed.

"What happened?" William whispered from above Roi Gurri.

He looked up to see William looking down at him through his mask.

"She had a nightmare," Roi Gurri responded.

William looked over toward Susan's room and sighed. "Is she alright?" He asked.

"Yes, she's asleep now."

"What did she dream about?"

"What life would've been like if her parents hadn't died."

William closed his eyes and let out a shaky breath. "I can only imagine," he whispered, gazing at an empty space.

"She said that I was in Cobra Cave."

"I know that's something I can't imagine."

"Neither can I. I've always thought I would always be in Warrior Brave no matter what."

"Did she say anything about me?"

Roi Gurri paused. "She said that you weren't there."

William rolled back on his bed, letting out a shaky sigh. "Really?" He asked sadly.

"Yeah."

"What about Caroldus?"

"She said he didn't know her."

"I can't imagine that either."

"Yeah, they're basically family now."

The two men nodded. What would life really be like if Susan's parents had survived? Would it be like it was in Susan's dream? Roi Gurri broke the silence.

"We have a long day tomorrow. We should sleep."

"Alright," William agreed, lying down on his bunk. "Good night Roi Gurri."

"Good night William."

The two men lay there, but neither slept.

Chapter Eighteen
Spies in their Midst

The next morning everyone in Cobra Cave and Warrior Brave was pulled together for training, which wasn't abnormal. Susan, Roi Gurri, and Caroldus stood together, waiting for William to join them.

"Kids!" Scadrin announced. "Today we let two new people into your patrols. This is Ethim, he will be put in Warrior Brave. His patrol name is Red Falcon, and he is to be respected. And this is Acron, he will be put in Cobra Cave. His name is patrol Croflysis, and he is to be respected."

"With a name like that?" Roi Gurri mumbled, causing Caroldus to snicker.

"Yeah," he agreed.

"What does it mean?" Susan asked.

"Crafty Serpent."

"Carry on with your training now," Scadrin said.

"One of those two has to be Judez," Roi Gurri muttered and Susan nodded in agreement.

"But which one?" She asked herself quietly, her hand playing with the hilt of her sword.

"I'm betting on the one that was put in Cobra Cave," Roi Gurri decided.

"I would agree with you but this guy's smart," Susan said. "He'll want to put himself in a position that wouldn't be too obvious. I'm betting on the Warrior Brave one."

"I like your conclusions, but come on. The guy's house name is 'Crafty Serpent' in the original Zudanum language. That doesn't tip you off a bit?"

"I will admit, that does tip the scale. But still-"

"I know, I know. We need to keep an eye on both of them."

"That'll be hard since Acron is in a different patrol than ours."

"We could ask Eloziah to keep an eye on him."

Susan shook her head. "Too risky. This needs to be just you, Caroldus, William, and me for now. I don't want to put anyone else in danger. We'll just have to watch him during training and break."

"We should split up."

"What do you mean?"

"I mean you watch one person while I watch the other."

"Good plan. I'll take Ethim, you take Acron. Unless you'd rather stay in Warrior Brave territory."

"No, it's fine, I'll see you later."

Susan nodded and started walking towards Ethim, pushing past the other people in Warrior Brave and Cobra Cave. She walked up to him and put on a warm smile as he turned to her.

"Hello," she greeted.

Ethim had dark brown hair and soft brown eyes, with skin like oak wood. He smiled warmly at her.

"You must be Adathir," Ethim said. "I've heard quite a bit about you."

He held out his hand, and Susan shook it.

"Really?" Susan asked, actually curious about what he had heard about her. "Like what?"

"Just normal things. That you're from Earth, you aren't anti-natural, you don't have any family-"

Susan's expression dropped and she winced. Before her dream last night she hadn't cared about mention of her family. But after meeting her parents, it was a different story.

Ethim's smile dropped when he realized what he said. "I'm so sorry, I really didn't mean any harm," he quickly apologized.

"It's fine," Susan said with a chuckle, raising a hand to stop Ethim. "Because it's true. I don't remember enough to miss them, so I don't feel very hurt."

"Good. For a second I thought I lost your friendship."

"Are we friends?"

Ethim scratched his neck nervously. "I mean, uh... if you want to. I'm sorry, it's just that I don't have a lot of friends. And you're so special and so, uh, beautiful, I thought I might just try my luck."

Susan laughed, blushing. "You seem like a nice guy, Ethim. Maybe your luck is working after all. I didn't have a lot of friends either when I first joined. But now I have really good friends, and some fans, too. But I don't think that really counts. And besides, with your looks, you'll have a lot of lady friends soon."

Susan blushed, and Ethim grinned.

"I can't believe I just said that," she thought.

"Works for me," Ethim approved.

Her smile fell into a frown. She felt something but wasn't quite sure what. It was a feeling of danger. She looked behind her to see Subaron and Agurion, one of his close friends, standing there with some others.

"No wonder."

"What do you want?" Susan asked Subaron.

"Give me the jewel," Subaron demanded.

Susan's hand instinctively rested on her pocket, but she put on an innocent face, deciding to play with Subaron for a moment.

"What jewel?" She asked innocently. "You know, there are many jewels in this universe, some pretty, others dull. So you're going to have to give me an *exact* description of the jewel you're looking for."

Ethim bit his lip to keep himself from laughing, but a snort came from him and the wide smile on his lips was *not* discreet.

"Don't toy with me, Susan," Subaron snapped. "I know that you have the Jewel of Numenera."

"I have absolutely no idea what you're talking about," Susan replied, pretending to inspect her recently chewed fingernails.

Another snort came from Ethim and he placed his hand over his mouth to stop himself. Subaron's face flushed with anger.

"You shouldn't mock me, *Wellns*," Subaron warned.

"Who says I'm mocking you..." Susan glanced up at Subaron as if she was thinking. "What's your name again? I keep forgetting."

People around them snickered and laughed, causing Subaron to flare in anger and embarrassment, but his expression suddenly turned stoic and expressionless.

"Why should you have the Jewel of Numenera?" He snapped at her. "You're a mutt. You're not worthy. If anything, you should be bowing down to me in submission."

Susan sneered. "I bow to no one. Especially not to some jerk like you. What's gotten into you? You haven't talked to me in months, and now you come demanding my property? I knew that speech at Jesidor's party was a facade."

"Being the Chosen One is one thing, holding the universe's most powerful weapon in your pocket is another. You should learn your place, *Wellns*."

"I have no place, you should know that. Earth was no home to me, and I've only lived here for a year. I don't have a solid foundation anywhere. You should be happy that you have one."

"I'm not stupid, Susan! You're the Chosen One! Basically, the whole universe is yours and you act like it's nothing."

"The universe belongs to no man. Why? Because no mortal man would be able to keep the whole universe in harmony. The universe isn't mine, Subaron. And if it is, I don't want it."

Subaron's patience snapped like a twig. "You're just a girl!" He cried, walking up to her and looking deep into her eyes. "You know nothing about what's out there, and about what you have to protect! You shouldn't be the Chosen One, I should! It was me until you came into this god-forsaken world!"

Susan's expression fell, and silence hung in the air as everyone watched.

"I think we should make this conversation more private," she said quietly.

"Scared of a few witnesses?"

"If you don't want to talk privately, then don't talk to me at all."

She turned to leave, but Subaron's arm shot out and grabbed her shoulder.

"Fine," he hissed, before turning to the crowd. "All of you, get out of here."

No one wanted to pick a fight with Subaron, so they all started focusing on their individual training. Except for Ethim, who stayed close to Susan.

"There, happy?" Subaron sneered.

"Yes," Susan said.

"Now, give me the jewel. Someone like you couldn't even fathom controlling its power. I'm an anti-natural, I know how to subdue it."

Susan didn't say anything for a moment, looking up into Subaron's eyes. He never once broke eye contact, he didn't feel intimidated by her.

"You've been talking to your father, haven't you?" Susan asked. "Is he the reason you're acting out and making a fool of yourself?"

"I'm not stupid, Wellns," Subaron snapped. "I can't be played into one of your mind games."

"I don't think you're stupid," she whispered, her warm breath hitting his chin.

"Then what do you think I am?"

"I think that you're foolish. You work hard to get your father's approval but you never get it because of your older siblings. You're jealous of me because you might have been the Chosen One, obviously. Now you feel like you have to prove yourself because your father is enraged that you will never be what I am."

Subaron stayed quiet for a minute. "How would you know any of that?" He asked quietly.

Susan touched his hand gently as if assuring him it was alright, but he quickly snatched his hand away as if it was burned by fire.

"Your silence speaks volumes," Susan said. "I'm not blind, Subaron. I've seen the way you act around your father. You need to let go. Be you. Not your father."

"Don't tell me what I need and don't need," he snapped. "Now, give me the jewel."

Subaron reached for Susan, but before he could touch her the Jewel of Numenera's forcefield surrounded her and knocked him away! He fell on his back with a groan before looking up at Susan with wide eyes.

"If you look at the Jewel of Numenera and only see a mere stone, you have no right to hold it," Susan stated as the forcefield disappeared. "If it were just raw power, perhaps you could subdue it. But there's more to this power than meets the eye. That's why I have it, and you don't."

Subaron said nothing, and Susan knew her point had been made. She saw understanding in his eyes for a brief moment before anger and embarrassment overcame and he looked away. She turned to Ethim.

"Let's go," she said.

"I know a shortcut," Ethim said, grabbing Susan and teleporting them away.

He brought them to another part of the training center in less than a second. Susan looked around, processing what had happened before she looked up at him in awe.

"Any more surprises?" She asked.

"Not very many," Ethim said sheepishly.

"What are your powers?"

"Teleportation."

"That's it?"

"Yeah. A bit boring, isn't it?"

Susan laughed and shook her head. "Not at all! I think your gift is amazing."

***

While Susan was chatting and asking Ethim questions, Roi Gurri was checking out Acron. He had been watching him for a while, waiting for an opportunity to approach him, and was about to make his move. He walked up to Acron and extended his hand.

"I'm Roi Gurri," he said. "Welcome, your stay won't be very pleasant at Cobra Cave with Subaron around, though."

"I know who you are," Acron said, not accepting Roi Gurri's hand. "And I'm very happy to be placed in Cobra Cave. My family has been placed here for hundreds of years."

"You must be a Lukimus then. I thought I recognized you."

"Sure am, have been all my life, and I'm honored. What about you? You must be ashamed to be a Drago."

Roi Gurri did his best to keep himself from snapping at Acron. He had an image to maintain, as the prince of Zudanum.

"And why is that?" Roi Gurri asked.

"Because your family were the ones who let the Chosen One disappear," Acron stated. "If it wasn't for you then she would be ready to fight A'Vaddon by now. Don't blame yourself, it was your father who let her slip away. Or was it your mother? Oh, I forgot, she died before you were even three years old. My bad."

Roi Gurri's face turned red with anger and his fists clenched, causing his knuckles to turn white.

"This has to be Judez," he thought, feeling hate towards Acron swell within. *"No one else in the realms would be so blatantly disrespectful."*

"If you don't mind, I'm going to go see the Chosen One myself," Acron said in a snobbish tone.

He purposely shoved Roi Gurri as he walked past him. Roi Gurri followed him over to where Susan was.

"I'm Acron," Acron introduced himself to Susan. "I've been waiting for this day my entire life."

He extended his hand to her, and she shook it.

"It's nice to meet you, too," Susan said with a polite smile.

She looked over at Roi Gurri to see him slap himself on his forehead.

"I see that you and Roi Gurri have met," Susan said, a little amused with Roi Gurri's reaction.

"Oh yes, we have," Acron affirmed. "It was very interesting. Quite a guy isn't he?"

"I'm right behind you," Roi Gurri hissed.

"Oh, I'm sorry. Did I hurt your feelings? I'll make sure not to do it again."

Roi Gurri didn't want to cause an uproar so he walked away, but remained in earshot.

"You're a character," Ethim said to Acron, the two shaking hands.

"You have no idea," Acron said. "I can't believe it's taken me this long to get here. The council must've been thinking too hard."

"The council?" Susan asked.

"The council decides if you get to come into a patrol or not. They also do many other things, but I forgot most of them. Anyway, what is it with Roi Gurri? He seems pretty defensive, don't you think?"

Susan glanced at Roi Gurri before meeting Acron's eyes once again. "He usually has a reason," she said. "It's best not to push his buttons."

There was a pause before Acron laughed. "I get it, you like him so you don't want to talk behind his back."

"Well, he is my betrothed."

"Ah, of course, they want the Chosen One to breed with the heir."

Susan's mouth dropped open in shock.

"*Excuse me*?" Roi Gurri seethed, immediately at Acron's side and grabbing him by the collar of his shirt, forcing him to face him. "How *dare* you speak to her that way."

"I'm sorry, did I hurt your feelings by speaking the truth?" Acron asked, still keeping his arrogant posture.

"I demand an apology from you right now, or I'll repeat your words to my father." Acron's expression faltered and his face paled. "I wonder how long you'll get to stay in the patrols for after that. An hour? Maybe two, if you're lucky."

Acron immediately looked at Susan, his lips moving to form an apology, but Roi Gurri kicked the back of his legs and made him kneel before her before he could say anything.

"Maybe you forget your place, Acron, but she is the future Queen of Zudanum," Roi Gurri hissed. "Now apologize."

Susan crossed her arms as she looked down at Acron, who actually looked terrified as he looked up into her eyes.

"I'm sorry," Acron said in a shaky voice. "I was out of line. Please forgive me."

Susan hummed in thought, glancing at Roi Gurri before looking back down. She knew the other patrols were watching and wanted to make sure they also knew not to insult her. When they were first betrothed, Roi Gurri told her to always keep her head high and not to show weakness.

So, she wasn't going to forgive Acron so easily. She kicked him in the stomach. He gasped and groaned, bending over to clutch his stomach. She then swiftly punched him in the face, which knocked him to the ground.

"You're forgiven," Susan said.

Susan then grabbed Roi Gurri's arm and quickly walked away. A few of the Warrior Brave kids patted her on the back and cheered. Ethim smirked and walked over to Acron, who still lay on the ground.

"I guess you're not so tough after all," he said before running after Susan.

Acron grinned as he watched Susan walk off. "I like her," he muttered.

***

"Thanks for defending me," Susan said to Roi Gurri when they were far from the crowd of trainees.

"Of course," Roi Gurri said with a nod. "I won't let anyone disrespect you as long as I can help it."

Butterflies fluttered in Susan's chest as he smiled down at her. She quickly looked away and raised her fist.

"What did you think of my hit?" Susan asked Roi Gurri and Ethim.

"It was great!" Ethim praised. "You two definitely showed him who was boss."

"You can punch harder," Roi Gurri said confidently, to which Susan smiled.

"I'm glad you think so, but I don't," Susan admitted.

"With a little more training you could."

"Considering his build and height are much more significant than yours I'm surprised you could hit hard enough to get him to fall over," Ethim said.

"Personally, I was more impressed with your kick," Roi Gurri said. "You definitely haven't been skipping leg-day."

"It was the adrenaline I suppose," Susan said with a grin. "Can I talk to you for a minute, alone?"

Ethim got the idea and walked away.

"What is it?" Roi Gurri asked quietly.

"Do you need to trade?" Susan asked.

"Trade Acron and Ethim?"

"Yes."

"Why would I want to do that?"

"I saw you slap yourself in the face, one. And two, I can already tell you two are not getting along."

"You just punched Acron in the face. Do you really think you're going to get luckier?"

"Touché. Though, I still think I may have a better chance. He obviously hates you, and you hate him."

"And he obviously likes you, so out of the question."

Susan raised a brow, hearing a tone of jealousy in his words, but nodded.

"So did you get anything from him?" Susan asked, changing the subject.

"Sort of. I found out that he's a Lukimus."

"A who?"

"They're a powerful family on the planet. They turned back to our side after A'Vaddon was 'defeated'. They've been on close watch ever since, but they haven't been making contact with A'Vaddon as far as we can tell. Though, like Subaron's family, they are trusted highly."

"This all sounds like a very familiar story to me."

"How so?"

"We're the good guys, they're the bad guys, we both have allies. There's a spy among us, and we don't know who he is. A'Vaddon is the main villain of the story, and I have to stop him."

"Sounds like every story."

"Yeah, I suppose, but I was thinking of a specific story I read on Earth."

"Does your story give us any ideas on how to catch the spy?"

"In order to catch him, we need to think outside the box. We need to think as he might think."

Roi Gurri scoffed, as if it was obvious, but decided to play along in case there was a slight chance it would work.

"Well, how would a villain think?" He asked.

Susan grinned. "Thankfully, you have two very sneaky people here."

Roi Gurri raised a brow. "Being sneaky doesn't mean they're villainous."

"Well, true, but I suppose the sneaky are clever as well, and the clever think as others do."

"Good point. Who are you thinking?"

"Subaron, and myself."

Roi Gurri laughed. "You?" He asked in disbelief.

"Do you not know? I practically *had* to grow up devious. Mr. Norman wouldn't let me do a lot of things, but I worked my way around that. Anyway, now I'm glad I did. Whoever this spy is, he's probably older and smarter than we are so we have to think big. I have an idea, but it's kind of crazy."

"I suppose we don't have a choice."

"Then follow me."

Roi Gurri wished they had more choices as Susan led him over to Subaron and Acron.

"Can you give Subaron and me a moment, Acron?" Susan asked.

"Really?" He asked. "I thought I'd be the one you'd want to see."

Acron smirked, and Roi Gurri did his best to not show emotion.

"Watch it," Roi Gurri growled.

Acron flinched and glared before walking away.

"What do you want with me?" Subaron asked Susan, ignoring the other two.

"If I was trying to win over a very important person, how would I do it?" Susan asked. "I've finally been face to face with them, and I know where they live. What should be my next move?"

Subaron crossed his arms and glared at Susan. "Why do you want to know?"

"That's above you."

"If it's at your level, then it's at mine."

Thunder boomed above and rain started to fall on their head and shoulders, causing Susan to shudder. Roi Gurri made fists and took a step forward ready to 'persuade' Subaron to help, but Susan placed the back of her hand on his chest to stop him.

"Fine, I'll tell you," Susan said to Subaron. "But, you have to promise not to tell anybody."

Roi Gurri looked down at Susan with a questioning look, but she didn't look at him.

"I swear on my name as a Tugar," Subaron promised.

"That's not good enough for me, but it'll do for now. There's a traitor here, in one of the patrols, either Cobra Cave or Warrior Brave, but we're not sure who. He's a spy for A'Vaddon, and he's going to try to turn me over to their side. We know for a fact he's here, and we're just trying to predict his next move. Since apparently you're the most clever person here, I thought that you would be the best person to go to."

Subaron raised a brow. "You think I'm clever?" He asked, his tone weary as if he didn't believe her.

"Who doesn't?" Susan asked.

"More than you think."

"Then they have been deceived by your clever facade."

Subaron grinned in approval. "You made the right choice coming to me. I think I can help. If I were him my next move would be to get as close to you as possible. If he's smart he'll pose as a friend. He might even try to get closer to you romantically. Be on your guard, especially at night. The night is when anyone will try to strike. Are you sure that he's not trying to murder you?"

Susan thought for a minute. She looked up at Roi Gurri, and then back at Subaron.

"I'm not actually sure," she admitted.

"Well if he is, his first move would be to find out what patrol you are in. Once he knew that, he would make it silent and quick. But, because I don't know who this guy is, I don't know his strategy."

Susan pondered his words for a moment and nodded. "Thanks for the help, Subaron."

"I ask for one thing in return."

"Which is?"

"When you figure out who the spy is, tell me first. There's nothing I'd love more than to claim some credit for him being found."

Susan held back a grin. "It's a deal," she said before shaking his hand.

"I never thought I would say those words," she thought as she turned to walk away. *"Then again, I underestimated him when we first met. I won't make that mistake again."*

"Susan," Subaron stopped her. She turned to face him. "I'll do some looking around for you here at Cobra Cave. I want to help you take down A'Vaddon."

"If you really think that it'll make your father proud."

Susan walked away, leaving Subaron standing there stunned.

"I think Subaron is misunderstood, Roi Gurri," Susan confessed quietly as he looked down at her with a questioning look.

"Why?" Roi Gurri asked.

Susan shrugged. "Just an instinct. I have a feeling he just has a twisted personality. Besides, if he really didn't have a good side to him, why would he help us?"

Chapter Nineteen
The Questions of William and Caroldus

That morning, William raced over to the Groon's room. He knocked on the door but entered without waiting for a reply. The Groon turned and looked at William.

"By what means do you visit me now, young Silentum?" The Groon asked him, expecting what he had to say was urgent.

"I must ask you about Susan's patrol name, Adathir," William replied.

The patrol name, which is given to a person by the Groon when appointed to a patrol, signifies the nature of one's soul. If one could explain the complete reasoning behind the patrol names one would, but this is the simplest way to explain it.

"The name is not in the archives, and the council doesn't know of a time where the name was used before," William explained. "And they have access to as much knowledge as angels themselves! Why give her a name that comes from the language of angels?"

"You will know in due time," the Groon stated. "As for the name Adathir, do you remember what the name means?"

William paused to think. "Fire?"

"*Daughter* of fire."

"So she was named for her father?"

"Not exactly. She has more of her mother's spirit than many realize, but I will admit that she shares many traits with her father."

"That is what everyone is afraid of. But of course, I never personally met him. What was so bad about him?"

"He had a desperate need for power. He wasn't a bad man, but many thought he would turn out to be one. He was full of longings and ambition until he met Susan's mother. They fell in love and started a family. He then lost all ambition for seeking power, though he never lost ambition for protecting his family. Adathir is dangerous, yet very interesting. She pulls energy from a much higher power than you or me, in fact, I'd say she pulls her power from Jehoyam himself."

"I... I don't understand."

"It is not your place to understand." The Groon let out a longing sigh. "If only Marcus and Defestri were here, for they understood. Even the one who is lost understood."

"How do I protect Susan from becoming like..." William stopped and sighed. "How can I stop her from being power-hungry and full of hatred? You said her father changed, but what if she doesn't?"

"You cannot protect her from fate. She will have to make that choice herself."

"Will she ever come to peace?"

There was a long pause.

"I am not sure," the Groon admitted. "That's up to her."

William decided that it was time to go. He already had way more questions now than he did when he first entered the room, and talking to the Groon was taking a toll on his mind.

"Silentum," the Groon said as William's hand landed on the door handle. "Do not leave her side. She needs you, more than anyone in her life."

William didn't respond as he left the room.

***

After hearing about Susan's encounter with this supposed general of A'Vaddon, Caroldus decided it was time to take matters into his own hands. He always suspected that there were spies all over Zudanum, especially in the castle, but for them to meet within the walls meant they were getting bolder. They were becoming confident no one would find them.

Making his way to the throne room he turned a corner and bumped into someone, who fell over and scattered papers.

"Oh my goodness, I'm so sorry!" Caroldus exclaimed, kneeling down to help pick up the mess.

"It's alright, I should've held on tighter."

Caroldus looked into the eyes of a beautiful female servant and his face became warm. Her eyes were dark and rich like molasses, and her hair was as black as the ink he wrote with daily. He paused, not being able to stop himself from admiring her. He couldn't think of a time where he might've seen her, for surely he would've remembered such a beautiful woman.

"Please, ma'am, don't blame yourself, I wasn't watching where I was going," Caroldus said as he stood, offering his hand to help her up.

She giggled as she accepted. "Ma'am?" She asked. "You make it sound like I'm royalty."

"You most certainly look the part."

They both blushed, looking away from each other. Caroldus wasn't used to flirting with girls.

"O-Oh, here are your papers," he said.

He handed them to her, noting that they looked like reports.

"Thank you, stranger," the girl said.

Caroldus smiled and laughed. "Sorry, I should've introduced myself. I'm Caroldus, Caroldus Fridink."

He extended a hand and she shifted her papers to one arm to accept it.

"I'm Kamila, Kamila Gladtide," she introduced herself.

"Kamila... that's a beautiful name. S-Sorry, I don't usually say things like this."

Kamila giggled. "It's okay, I don't mind."

They both laughed.

"Are those captain's reports?" Caroldus asked.

"Oh, yes, I'm actually supposed to bring these to the king's advisor, Sondman."

A lightbulb clicked in Caroldus's head. "I was actually on my way to see him. He's not in the throne room?"

"No, he's in his office today."

"I see. Here, let me bring these reports on my way there."

"Oh no, it's okay, I can carry them. Besides, I need to let the king know he received them."

"It's no problem for me. Go tell the king he got them, you have my word they will be delivered."

Kamila paused before nodding, passing the reports to Caroldus. "Thank you, Caroldus," she said. "What can I do to repay you?"

He smiled softly. "You can let me see you again?" Caroldus suggested.

They both blushed and Kamila giggled and nodded.

"Alright. You can find me in the Starlight Garden at sunset tonight."

"Perfect, I'll see you soon then."

With smiles the two parted, Caroldus's heart beating rapidly in his chest.

"Did I just flirt?" He thought to himself. *"Did I just get a date?"*

He shook his head and cleared his thoughts of Kamila as he approached Sondman's office. He had to be focused on the task at hand. He couldn't be distracted now. He stopped and took in a deep breath before knocking on the office door.

"Come in," Sondman called, his eyes widening as he saw Caroldus walk in. "Caroldus Fridink? My my, it's been a long time since I've laid eyes on a son of General Jemdi Fridink. How can I help you?"

"I have a matter I wanted to discuss with you," Caroldus explained. "But first of all, here are the captain's reports."

"Ah! I've been waiting for those, thank you. Please have a seat and we'll discuss this matter you've come to talk about."

Caroldus set the reports on the desk before sitting. His expression hardened as he looked into Sondman's eyes.

"There's really no way to put this delicately, so I might as well say it," Caroldus said. "I know you're a spy for A'Vaddon."

Sondman's expression immediately portrayed how horrified he was. He tried to cover it up by laughing, but Caroldus had already seen his true colors.

"Now, now, Caroldus, who put you up to this silly little prank?" Sondman asked.

"I was the one in the hallway last night who heard you," Caroldus stated calmly. "I'm the one A'Vaddon's general, Judez, attacked."

Sondman's joking expression fell. "What did you hear?" He asked.

"Everything."

"Why did you run?"

"I didn't have a weapon to defend myself, and I had no idea if Judez was anti-natural or not. But that doesn't matter now. I came here to get you to relinquish your position as advisor to the king. Leave Zudanum now and never return."

"You may think you have power over me, but it's all merely in your head. I've been in this position for over six hundred years, advising both Regel and his father. And next, I will advise Roi Gurri. For me to leave now would be suicide, A'Vaddon will have my head."

"*I* will have your head if you don't. Roi Gurri and my father don't know yet, but if I were to go to them you know as well as I that they trust my word over yours. And Regel trusts my father's word over yours."

"That's up for debate."

"Maybe, but as soon as Roi Gurri becomes king you *will* be executed for treason. Better to flee now with your head intact, wouldn't you agree?"

There was silence, Caroldus allowing his words to run through Sondman's head for a few minutes.

"How could you betray your people?" Caroldus spat.

"It's easy when the Zudanums *aren't* my people," Sondman replied, Caroldus frowning.

"What?"

"I was adopted by a family who visited the Suparis people on planet Ender. They found me abandoned and took pity. Have you ever noticed that my hair is always long enough to cover my ears? That's because they're pointy, it would give me away. The Suparis and Zudanums have always gotten along, but I decided the fewer people knew about me the better I could blend in."

"So what now? Run back to Ender?"

"No, I think I'll stay. I still have work to do here."

In a flash Caroldus stood, drawing his two swords and crossing them at Sondman's neck. The advisor's expression immediately morphed into one of fear. He gripped the armrests of his chair as his confidence faded.

"I could kill you now and have no regrets," Caroldus said. "By doing so I'd save my friends a lot of trouble, but I'm giving you the chance to run. You can go to A'Vaddon and tell him all about me if you wish, but I can't have you running around Zudanum spreading your lies and false advice. Write out your letter of retirement right now and I will bring it to King Regel myself."

"You won't get away with this, Caroldus Fridink," Sondman spat. "A'Vaddon will go to any lengths to make sure those who interfere with his plans are severely punished."

"I can live with that, just write the letter. I also want you to tell me you and Judez's real names."

"I am Akuma, but I do not know the name of Judez. I believe A'Vaddon is the only one to know his true name."

Satisfied with the answer, Caroldus nodded. "Write the letter."

With a sneer, Sondman pulled out a form and pen. Caroldus took a step back so he could see his paper, but he didn't let down his swords. After a few minutes of writing, Sondman filled out the form, frowning as he handed the paper to Caroldus.

"If you take this to the king, you are handing him your death warrant," Sondman warned as Caroldus looked over the form to make sure it was legitimate.

"Thanks for the warning, but I can take care of myself," Caroldus responded as he sheathed his swords. "Run, quickly, Sondman. If I see you tomorrow I won't hesitate to drag you to my father."

With those words as a warning, he left, not looking back.

He felt no fear as he made his way to the throne room, though the paper in his hand felt heavy. He had no doubt Sondman wasn't bluffing, A'Vaddon *was* known for being determined and ruthless after all.

"Is it worth it?" A voice asked in his head, one he knew wasn't his own. *"I'll kill you, your family, everyone you hold dear to you for interfering with my plans."*

"Get out of my head, I'm not changing my mind," Caroldus snapped as he went to push open one of the golden doors that lead to the throne room.

"I'll kill your brothers, Contral, Adonis, and Jesidor. I'll kill your sister, Eloziah."

Caroldus paused. Hearing their names made him stop and think. Considering who his father was it was no surprise his sibling's names were known, but he still didn't like it.

"They have no involvement in this."

"They're related to you, and that's good enough for me. All you have to do is tear up the form and you can go back to your normal life, blissfully unaware anything is happening. Just do it, it's so easy."

"Maybe for you, A'Vaddon, but if I were to do that then the chances of Susan, Roi Gurri, William, and everyone in the realm dying goes up significantly. So no, I'm not going to stand by while their lives are in danger. You're not changing my mind, get out of my head."

A'Vaddon growled.

"Your family's blood is on your hands."

Caroldus felt A'Vaddon retract from his mind and took in a deep breath to recompose himself. With determination in his eyes, he pushed open the door, gripping the form in his hand as if he feared it would slip away.

"I won't let anyone die."

Chapter Twenty
The Masked Man

Susan and Roi Gurri went their separate ways as the rain began pouring down from the heavens.

"Susan!" William cried, running up to her. "You're going to be late for class with Scadrin if you don't run right now!"

"You're right!" Susan gasped in alarm, thanking William before booking it.

She ran into the castle, finding her patrol room and grabbing her shield before running toward the indoor training room. She'd learned over the past year that the patrols were essentially an elite school for training those in the higher class, or those they deemed to be physically and mentally fit. It was more than just the normal training she thought it was at first. In every culture, even if it is brute and mostly physical, there is always more to learn, such as the basics of reading and writing.

Susan swiftly ran into the classroom, breathing heavily, soaked in rainwater. Scadrin turned around, her brown eyes staring right into Susan's.

"Ah, Susan," Scadrin said, "Have you finally decided to join us?"

Susan flushed, nodding. "Yes ma'am," she replied meekly.

"And why are you late?"

"I lost track of the time, ma'am."

"I see. I will assume that this won't happen again, will it?"

"No, it will not."

"Take a seat and open your Deadly Herbs book and turn to chapter forty-five. We are preparing for the test you will be taking in two days. Now class, what poison can I make if I have one fompt of suntar roots, two sufar leaves, and a pinch of twuman herbs?"

Caroldus, who was sitting next to Susan, raised his hand, a large grin on his face. Susan looked at him surprised, she didn't know he was interested in this sort of thing.

"Yes, Caroldus?"

"I'm not Caroldus, I'm Contral," Contral rebuked with annoyance, Susan's eyes widening.

She had known Caroldus had a twin in the school, but she only saw him in passing once or twice before. Now that she thought about it, she had never properly introduced herself to him. Oftentimes she would completely forget that the twin existed.

"Wait, have I been calling Caroldus's twin Caroldus this whole time?" Susan thought. *"Is this proof of how little I've acknowleged my classmates?"*

"My mistake," Scadrin apologized. "Now, what is the answer?"

"When you mix the ingredients you can make a bottle of distopted fluid, which will swiftly kill the person who drinks it by melting their insides. Distopted fluid will also dissolve a few metals and the skin of humans. The ingredients can also make another kind of poison which can turn the human brain into mush."

Susan giggled quietly, actually quite impressed with Contral. Now that she thought about it, Contral was nothing like Caroldus, Contral was a nerd! She could barely believe it, but she did notice that Contral had blue in his eyes, different from the grey in Caroldus's eyes.

"Very good Contral," Scadrin said with approval. "Both of those answers are perfect. Now, I want everyone to read chapter forty-five on their own, and try to memorize some of it, please. The chapter is twenty-five pages long, and we have another hour left, so do not delay."

Susan quickly glued her eyes to the page, fascinated with the subject. She took in every word, memorizing various roots and herbs that made different medicines and poisons.

"Maybe all of those reading and memorization tricks weren't a waste of time after all," she thought.

She felt a tap on her leg. She glanced down to find a small piece of paper. She unfolded it.

"You really didn't know I wasn't Caroldus?"

She glanced at Contral, who was looking at her with a curious expression. She blushed before taking out her pen.

"I knew you existed, but we've never properly met. And you can't really blame me, you two are identical twins after all."

"Really? I thought I looked ABSOLUTELY nothing like him."

"I deserve that. Do you have any questions for me or do you just like to waste time?"

"I'm not my brother, Miss Wellns. My Patrol name is Aquila. And yes, I do have a question for you. Did you know that you were from Zudanum while you were on earth or were you just 'normal'?"

"Normal. Now if you don't mind, I'm not as smart as you, so I should get back to work."

She stopped writing and tried to read the rest of the chapter, but Contral kept writing.

"If you think that I'm in Owl Perch, then you're right," he wrote. *"Yes, I know, I am the opposite of my brother."*

"You are actually semi-similar. You're both very nice and funny."

"Trust me, those two things do not run in the family. My parents used to be control freaks and my cousins are just plain stupid. For the love of King Regel, I can't get them to study anything!"

"And for the love of my life, I know that I will not pass this test if you don't let me study."

"You can always study later"

"Unless either you can give me all the answers to the quiz or tell me about my family tree, then please leave me alone for now. We can talk later."

She looked over at him, and it looked like he was actually in deep thought. He didn't answer, which left Susan wondering what he was thinking about but decided to focus on studying.

After about thirty minutes, a loud siren went off and everyone got up to leave.

"Meet me in the study hall at midnight," Contral whispered to her as they got up to leave. "I might be able to find you some answers."

He quickly walked away, not looking back at her, which had her frowning.

"Find answers for what? The test? My family? It's strange he's being so secretive about it... but then again, I have yet to learn about Contral's character. I guess we'll find out tonight."

Susan stayed behind for a moment as she thought. Scadrin started to leave but she turned to her.

"Do you need something, Adathir, or are you stuck to the floor?" Scadrin asked.

Susan snapped out of her thoughts and looked up at her.

"No ma'am," she replied.

"Then let's go to training."

Susan nodded and backed out of the room, the two making their way to the indoor training facility for weapons training. Susan spotted William near Eloziah and she walked over to them.

"Did I miss anything?" Susan asked William as she approached.

"No, you didn't," William confirmed.

Eloziah looked over at Cobra Cave and sighed. "I should probably head back," she said.

William nodded, rubbing the back of his neck. "Yeah..."

Susan raised a brow and smirked as she observed the two. Eloziah flushed as she smiled and walked away.

"Something going on here?" Susan asked with a grin as she motioned to Eloziah.

William flushed under his mask and shook his head. "It's nothing," he insisted.

Susan still grinned but decided to drop the topic.

"So, we got two new people here," she changed the subject.

"Yeah. Roi Gurri told me about what you heard in the hall."

"We really shouldn't be talking about that here."

"No one else is near us, and no one here has super hearing, that I know of," he reassured, though he still kept his voice low just in case.

"Who do you suspect?" Susan asked.

"Acron. I mean, if he has the 'Subaron stamp of approval', then he's worth looking into."

Susan hummed in thought. "I think Subaron is a better ally than a foe, William."

"I've learned to never trust a Tugar."

"Well, I've decided to. I told Subaron what was going on, and he gave me some insight."

William's eyes narrowed and he sighed before shaking his head. "If he stabs us in the back, Susan, it is not on my hands."

"I know. Roi Gurri made quite a scene with Acron, I'm not sure we'll be able to get close to him."

"So did you."

She scratched the back of her neck. "Yeah, I suppose. It was actually kind of fun. I feel powerful. And I mean, who wouldn't after having a man apologize to you on his knees."

William shuddered, as if something was crawling in his skin. He wasn't afraid of Susan Wellns, but he was afraid of her father's dark side living somewhere within her.

"Don't give in to power, Susan," William warned. "I don't want to see you become the darkness of yourself."

He walked away from her before she could say anything, but she couldn't go after him. She was frozen.

"What could he possibly mean?"

***

The day dragged on for Susan. Williams's words weighed heavily on her. After the long day, she walked to the Warrior Brave Patrol room and lay on her bed, waiting for midnight. A few hours passed and then things got strange.

"I'm watching you," a voice whispered in Susan's head.

The voice sounded vaguely familiar, but she wasn't sure from where. The voice was low, but also wild like the sea. It was rich and deep, a tone that demanded respect. It filled her head with curiosity and wildness, but she knew she couldn't have come up with that voice.

"Who are you and what do you want?" Susan asked aloud.

"I am your conscience," the voice said.

"I'm not stupid, I would know if I had another voice in my head. Who are you really?"

"You are smart. I am A'Vaddon, I am your darkness."

Susan froze, feeling ice crawl up and into her skin.

"Get out of my head!" She hissed, immediately sitting up. "You have one chance."

"But I am not in your head. I am only telepathically speaking to you."

Susan groaned in annoyance. "While you're here, why don't you tell me where you are so that I can get over there and finish you?"

The voice of A'Vaddon laughed loudly, echoing in her head, haunting her. She would never forget it.

"Why don't you ask Regel? He knows where I am."

"I don't believe you. Now leave my head!"

"Why?"

Susan started to shake in complete anger and frustration.

"He's mocking me..." She thought. *"He knows I have no power over this, that damn bastard."*

Susan frowned, knowing cursing wasn't in her nature but shook it off.

"I swear, I will destroy you for what you did to my mother and father, and for what you did to Roi Gurri's mother," Susan threatened.

"I could attack you all now. I could easily kill you and all of your friends. But why should I do it when I can easily have my spy do it."

"You wouldn't!"

"Would I?"

His presence left, and Susan got up and swiftly walked over to Roi Gurri's bed on the other side of her door, shaking him awake.

"What is it?" Roi Gurri asked, rubbing his eyes.

"It's A'Vaddon," Susan whispered, Roi Gurri quickly sitting up in alarm.

"Where?"

"In my head."

Roi Gurri frowned. "What do you mean?"

"He was having a telepathic conversation with me. He told me he was the darkness within me. He also said that he was going to have his spy kill one of my friends tonight."

"Susan, relax," Roi Gurri said softly, placing his hands on her shoulders "I'm sure it was just a hoax."

"But what if it wasn't?"

"He just wants to scare you. Don't give in to him."

"Are you underestimating the man who killed several anti-naturals, including both of our mothers?"

Susan was frightened now, and Roi Gurri could tell.

"The palace is filled with palace guards, and there are the patrol guardians," he tried to reason with her. "And besides, you only really have friends in Warrior Brave and Cobra Cave. Both patrols are capable of handling themselves."

Susan thought for a moment, making sure that really all of her friends were safe. She was interrupted when the clock struck midnight. Dread washed over her as she remembered her task for the night.

"Contral!" She exclaimed, rushing into her room to grab her sword before running out of the Warrior Brave room.

"Susan!" Roi Gurri cried as he stood, but Susan ignored him as she ran.

"Where do you think you are going?" Lucas asked Susan, but she raced past him, barely hearing him.

Lucas awakened a knight statue to watch the patrol, and he started racing after her.

Susan looked behind her to find Lucas chasing her, but she ran faster. She couldn't afford to stop now, not when her best friend's brother was on the line. He was outside of his patrol, away from his guardian, therefore in her mind he was the greatest target out of all of her friends. And on top of that, Owl Perch isn't required to take up physical training, so she had no idea if he had a weapon to defend himself!

"I don't have time for explanations," Susan thought. *"I have to reach Contral before A'Vaddon's spy gets to him."*

Lucas barked loudly at Susan. "Stop!"

But she didn't respond.

Lucas was only a few feet away from Susan, her legs burning in exhaustion. Never in her life had she run so hard, or with such determination. She ran into the library and looked to find a masked man advancing towards Contral.

"Stop!" Susan screamed, running in front of Contral and drawing her sword. "Not another step," she growled at the masked man, her sword raised, ready for a fight.

The masked man drew his sword, accepting her challenge. Lucas finally understood what was going on as he observed the room, and stood next to Susan. His metal fur raised as he bared his teeth, and his claws grew longer and sharper.

"I have only one job in this palace, mister," Lucas growled. "And that job is to protect the children of the Warrior Brave Patrol. So you have one chance to surrender before I rip you into shreds."

The masked man looked from Lucas to Susan, his eyes narrowing.

"I know those eyes. I saw them at Caroldus's party, I'm sure of it!"

"I will never surrender," the masked man replied firmly.

"I know that voice! This is Judez!"

He lifted his sword and brought it down on Susan's.

Lucas barked and pounced upon Judez, but to Susan's surprise he punched Lucas and didn't flinch. She looked closer at his hands and saw they were made up of metal.

"He's an anti-natural?"

She ducked as Judez tried to punch her in the face, making a mental note not to let the metal fists connect with her body.

"Contral!" Susan yelled to the man behind her. "You need to get out of here!"

Susan dodged another attack, her breathing becoming more rapid.

"But I can help!" Contral exclaimed, determined.

"Well then do something, fast!"

Contral pulled out a mace from the side of the table and hit the masked man on the back as hard as he could.

"Why do you have a mace?!" Susan asked.

Contral flushed. "You never know in Zudanum!"

The two looked at Judez, who turned around with no signs of even feeling the strike.

"He's covered in metal armor!" Contral cried, surprised as he took a few steps back.

"That's definitely not obvious!" Lucas barked sarcastically.

Contral sent Lucas a glare and jumped back as Judez attempted to punch him.

Lucas ran and pounced on top of Judez, digging his metal teeth into the side of his shoulder at the base of his neck. Judez cried out in pain and tried to throw Lucas off, but Lucas dug his teeth in harder. Judez slammed him against the wall hard, which made the metal wolf whimper as he let go and slumped to the ground.

"No!" Susan cried, a cold sweat breaking out on her forehead.

"Lucas and Contral didn't stand a chance, so how can I?" She thought as Judez turned to her, but she put on a stern look and raised her sword.

Judez ran at Susan and their swords clashed harshly. One of Susan's hands let go of her sword and she went to punch him, but he grabbed her fist and twisted her arm behind her back. She cried out, dropped her sword, and tried to headbutt him in the nose.

Susan instantly regretted it as the metal of his mask came in contact with the back of her head. He let go of her as she collapsed onto the ground. Black spots started to cloud her vision.

"That was stupid..."

Lucas growled and pounced on Judez, slicing him across the chest. But the general of A'Vaddon only laughed as he grabbed Lucas by his scruff and threw the metal wolf into the wall.

"Stupid mutt," he muttered.

Susan sneered as she grabbed her sword. "Hey!" She exclaimed, slowly coming to her feet. "You have no right to talk to him like that!"

She ran at Judez and thrusted her sword at him, though he easily blocked it.

"You're as much of a mutt as he is," he snapped.

"We'll see about that."

Judez and Susan fought hard, their swords creating sparks as they clashed against each other. She knew that he was clearly in top physical shape and could easily overpower her with his strength, but she leveled the playing field by being swift and having animal senses.

But as they fought Susan noticed Judez was not like others she had fought before. Something about him was so familiar, though she had no idea how.

Then she realized they were both fighting the same way. For her offense he had a perfect defense. For his defense she had a perfect offense. Their swings and strikes were perfectly matched against each other. Almost like they were trained by the same person. Almost like they could read each other's thoughts.

Their swords clashed and pushed against each other. Susan planted her feet firmly on the ground so she wouldn't be pushed back. Her face was inches away from his, their swords pressed against each other as both used what strength they could muster.

"Who are you?" Susan demanded.

Her legs shook under his strength.

"I am your blood," Judez replied, his voice again sounding very familiar, like it was from a dream or a memory.

"But there's no way."

She pushed him back with all of her strength, quickly moving forward and ripping off his mask before he fell to the ground.

The air was still. Judez knelt on the floor with his face hidden. The only sound heard was the clock ticking, the only proof that time hadn't stopped.

"Show yourself!" Susan demanded.

"If you say so," Judez rasped.

He looked up.

Susan's eyes widened in absolute horror and she dropped her sword. Contral and Lucas gasped, neither saying a word as Judez stood, smirking.

He looked exactly like Susan.

Susan knew his eyes had looked like hers, but now she could see the full picture. They both had the exact same blonde hair, the same sparkle in their brown eyes, and the same facial features. They both had the same burn mark scar on their neck, the cracked diamond.

"Can't believe it, can you?" Judez asked Susan. "I look exactly like you. The same hair, the same eyes, the same burn."

Susan couldn't speak. She couldn't even ask the questions that turned in her head.

"Let me explain it to you," he continued, taking a step forward.

Susan snapped out of her trance and quickly picked up her sword and held it up in front of her, not wanting to take a chance of him attacking during his monologue.

"I am your twin brother, your opposite, and your equal," Judez explained. "We both have the same scar, because it is not a scar. It's a brand, given to us when we were little. It's the mark of the Chosen One, the diamond, and over that, the crack... Well, you don't need to know that yet. The important thing is that everyone and everything with the brand are connected. You are not the last of our family, as you have been told. You are not the last Wellns."

Susan finally found her voice, finding it unbearable to listen to him anymore.

"You're lying!" She cried. "King Regel-"

"Is the real liar! Tell me, what is the event no one speaks of, the one Lady Tugar mentioned not so long ago?"

Susan opened her mouth, but no words came.

"I... I don't know," she stuttered, her face turning pale and her expression dropping into one of sorrow. "I... I never asked again after that night."

"Exactly. What's my name?"

Her face turned hard again and she raised the sword higher.

"You're Judez, a spy for A'Vaddon!"

Judez scoffed. "I hate that name, *Judez*. How could you ever guess I was a spy? Tell me Susan, who was the one who stranded you on Earth? Did you ever find out why you were put there in the first place?"

She had no answer.

"I can tell you who put you there," he continued. "It was King Regel. They kept me in Zudanum because they thought *I* was their chosen one. The firstborn son, of course, it had to be me, right? But I discovered my powers and the lies they were feeding me. I demanded they bring you home, and what did they do? They banished me for treason! I was lied to and abandoned for years, and so were you! If A'Vaddon hadn't come back then you would still be on Earth with whoever you were with. You would still be isolated from the world that you still don't know. Come with me, and I will reveal to you the truth. The truth about yourself, and the truth about our parents."

Susan relaxed at the sound of the offer and she lowered her sword.

"The truth?" She asked quietly.

He nodded, his expression becoming soft. "My real name is Damian Wellns, though Judez was the name given to me by A'Vaddon. I'm offering you what's been denied you your entire life."

"Why should I trust you?"

"Because I am all that's left of your family."

Those words stabbed Susan, and the others knew it.

"Family stays together... right?" A voice asked Susan, but this voice was her own, no one else's. *"He can help you. He can help me."*

Susan took a small step forward, but Lucas got up and raced toward Damian, his strength back. Damian noticed his advance and pulled something from his pocket. He looked at Susan.

"You'll be able to find me," he said before disappearing in a flash of light.

Lucas skidded to a stop and growled. "Stay out!" He barked.

Susan looked at Lucas and Contral, still baffled.

"What in Jehoyam?" She thought, realizing several gazes were upon her, and several familiar smells reached her nose.

She looked at the doorway to see Roi Gurri, Caroldus, and William standing there with horrified looks.

"Were they there the whole time? Why didn't they help me?"

"Who was that?" Susan demanded to know, her eyes moving back and forward, looking at each of them. "Who was he?!"

No one said a word, their eyes danced around the room to avoid hers. Susan looked at Roi Gurri and walked up to him.

"Don't tell me what he said was true," she almost pleaded.

Roi Gurri finally looked into her eyes. His heart raced with anxiety and worry as he looked down at her.

"Susan," William said in a calm tone, kneeling down in front of her. "Some things are just too hard for you to comprehend. Maybe you should sleep on this."

Her head snapped over toward William with fire in her eyes.

"So it is true!" She exclaimed. "But I need more than just your word."

She ran out of the room, the others right behind her.

"How is she so fast?" Caroldus asked, William shaking his head in disbelief.

"She has a lot of adrenaline right now," he pointed out.

Susan burst into the throne room. King Regel sat on his throne talking to one of his servants.

"I just fought a man who looks exactly like me and claims to be my twin brother, Damian Wellns!" Susan exclaimed. "Is that true or not?"

The king waved away his servant, noticing the others behind Susan.

"Well? Is he?" Susan asked, her face red and her jaw clenched. "Don't you dare lie to me!"

"No, Susan," King Regel assured. "He is not your brother. You are the last Wellns."

"Liar! I just saw him with my own eyes! Tell me who he really is!"

"Do you dare talk to me in that manner?!"

"I dare!"

There was silence. Then, Regel started laughing! His laugh echoed through the room, surprising everyone.

"You remind me of your mother. She was always persistent, and not afraid to make herself heard. In honor of her memory, I will tell you the truth. Damian *was* your twin brother. But, he passed away years ago. The man you fought couldn't possibly be your brother."

Susan felt a pain in her chest. It tightened around her lungs until she felt like she was suffocating. She couldn't think, she couldn't move, she couldn't control her body as she collapsed onto the cold, stone floor. She heard cries of alarm and muffled voices, but not their words. She saw pools of color, but not people.

Susan felt herself drown in the pits of her own mind as she passed out.

Chapter Twenty-One
The Lost Chosen One

Susan groaned as she woke the next morning, her mind spinning as she felt a throbbing pain throughout her body. Everything from last night came rushing back to her as she sat up and looked around, confused.

"I have a brother," Susan thought, still in shock.

"I have a twin brother," she said aloud, testing out the words, but felt even more unnatural to say aloud.

She felt no pain other than the soreness of her muscles but remembered the searing pain that knocked her out. She couldn't find the energy or willpower to put on new clothes before walking into the kitchen to find Roi Gurri and Caroldus talking. When Roi Gurri saw her he stood.

"Good morning, Susan," he greeted, walking over to her and taking her hand in a comforting manner.

"Why don't I feel any pain?" Susan asked. "Last night after your father confirmed that Damian is my brother, I passed out. Why?"

"You passed out right after my father told you about him. I don't know why, but any injuries you had I healed so you wouldn't feel pain."

"Thanks. I really don't know what happened either."

"It was probably the shock," Caroldus said. "Panic attacks are no joke."

"Well it doesn't matter now," Roi Gurri said. "You woke up just in time, it's time for training."

"No, wait," Susan stopped him. "You think you can get away with keeping my brother from me?" She ripped her hand away from Roi Gurri's, hot anger stirring in the depts of her heart. "I thought you were smart enough to not keep secrets from me, especially one this big. Turns out you're a fool, and I'm a greater one for not listening to my instinct. I knew something was up after Jesidor's party! I should've kept asking you about what Lady Tugar said!"

"Susan, please, let us explain," Roi Gurri pleaded.

"Why, so you can lie more?" She gave Caroldus a pointed look. "You're not off the hook either. In fact, no one is! Was I really the only one in the twelve realms not to know I had a twin brother?"

"Regel ordered no one to speak of him after his death," Caroldus explained.

"His *death*? I *just* fought him!"

"He was officially announced dead," Roi Gurri said sadly. "None of us knew he was still alive, I swear it. Susan, I'm sorry."

"I can forgive you for not knowing he was alive, but why didn't you tell me about him anyways? I've been here a whole eleven months, I've proven myself time and time again, so why in Jehoyam's name did you think I didn't deserve to know about my own flesh and blood?! Was it really okay for me to know about my parents but not my brother?!"

"I... I was being selfish, I didn't want to talk about him. I also didn't want to tell you until the time was right, until you were emotionally prepared."

"What made you think I wasn't?"

"Because of your upbringing," William said, the three looking to find he had walked in. "You came to Zudanum with no fighting experience of any kind, no knowledge of your home or family. If you had been raised properly you would've been told about Damian, but because you weren't, we didn't know what to do. It's not exactly easy to explain that you had a brother that you never met, and never would. Or so we thought."

"Why didn't Regel or Scadrin tell me?" Susan asked.

"Because when my father realized you didn't know about Damian, he thought it best to keep it hidden from you," Roi Gurri explained. "He thinks that the less you know about your family the more he can... The more he can..."

Roi Gurri looked away from Susan, his teeth gritting and tears threatening to come from his eyes.

"The more he can control me?" Susan whispered.

Roi Gurri nodded in affirmation. "When he told me, I made sure you knew where the library was, so you could look up records for yourself, but he must've stored away Damian's files. I couldn't directly disobey him, but I did what I could to nudge you in the right direction. I'm sorry."

Susan frowned but nodded in understanding. "I probably would've done the same," she admitted. "Not to be rude, but your dad is kinda terrifying." The boys all nodded in agreement. "I'm sorry for yelling, I know this must be hard for all of you, but none of you are forgiven yet."

"None of us expect to be forgiven any time soon," William said.

"Did you all know Damian?"

"Yes," Caroldus said.

"Not really," William said. "When I first joined Warrior Brave I was pretty secluded, so I didn't get to know him.

"He was my best friend growing up," Roi Gurri said. "We did everything together, training, playing."

"It was a good time," Caroldus mused. "He, Roi Gurri, and I grew up together. I remember we were all ecstatic when we were all placed in the same patrol."

"But then he changed," Roi Gurri said. "I don't know what happened, but he accused my father of holding you back and conspiring against the Chosen One. He demanded you be brought back to Zudanum, but my father denied the accusations. Then one night, Damian took one of the training airships and ran off. Days later we found it crashed, his body burned to a crisp."

Susan's expression softened as she reached over and placed a hand on his shoulder.

"I'm sorry, I can't imagine what that's like," she whispered as a tear rolled down his cheek.

"It's much worse when you remember every single detail."

He wiped away the tear before reaching down and lacing his hand in hers. She gripped his hand and leaned her body onto his.

"Several people stepped forward and claimed they killed him, but we never found solid proof," Caroldus said.

"Why would someone want to claim to murder a child?" Susan asked.

"Because word had spread about Damian's rebellious tendencies. Child or not, many turned on him when he died."

"I can only imagine what they'd do if they heard he was alive," William mused.

"No one can know," Roi Gurri quickly said.

"Roi Gurri-"

"William, if people find out, it'll only encourage more Zudaniums to rebel and turn to A'Vaddon like Damian did. People outside of this group, except for my father and General Fridink, can't know."

Everyone stayed silent for a while. William looked at Caroldus, but he was staring down at the floor with a distant look in his eyes.

"This decision isn't up to me," William said, turning to leave. "I'll respect whatever you three decide."

William left, and Caroldus finally looked up. He looked into Roi Gurri's eyes to show he was crying.

"He's alive," Caroldus whispered.

"I know," Roi Gurri shakily said.

"After years of wondering what we could've done different, if we could've gotten him to change his view, it was really just a lie all along."

Roi Gurri walked over to Caroldus, placing a hand on his shoulder and kneeling.

"I've thought about it too," Roi Gurri admitted. "But now, all we can do is pray that he's not too far gone."

Caroldus nodded, wiping away his tears and offering Roi Gurri a sad smile. "Alright," he whispered. "We'll keep it a secret."

The boys looked at Susan and she nodded in agreement.

"I think I'd get a bad rap for having a brother on A'Vaddon's side," Susan said.

"Oh, boy, that'd be the biggest scandal in a thousand years," Caroldus said.

"How long did you guys watch me and Damian fight for?"

"We got there right before you ripped his mask off."

"Good job with that, by the way," Roi Gurri complimented. "From what Lucas said you fought really well."

"I did the best I could," Susan said with a shrug. "I think Damian could've beaten me if he really wanted to."

"Maybe, but you held your own, and that's a good place to be."

"Speaking of places to be, Scadrin is gonna kill us," Caroldus said, motioning to the clock.

"Oh boy," Susan grumbled. "Come on, we better make up a good excuse for being late."

The trio left the room. Susan spotted Lucas and smiled at the metal wolf.

"Did you have a good rest?" Lucas asked.

"Yeah, thank you," Susan said. "Thank you for fighting with me last night."

"It's my honor to protect the children of Zudanum. I would give my life for any of you."

"And for that, you have my thanks." Susan knelt down to Lucas's height. "Lucas, can I ask that you keep silent about last night?"

The wolf's eyes fell down to the ground. "Susan, I love you, and I loved Damian as my own. But how can I keep silent that there is a treacherous Zudanum out there?"

"It won't make you feel better, but he is not the first traitor, nor will he be the last. If people know that my brother, one of my own blood, is a traitor, they will surely turn against me. I can't let that happen, not yet. The Zudanum people still have to believe in me. At least until I defeat A'Vaddon." Lucas still didn't look up at her. "If it is any comfort, I will tell General Fridink. He will know how to handle this."

Lucas finally looked back up into her eyes. “That does bring me comfort. I will respect your wishes as long as you are receiving wise counsel.”

Susan smiled and nodded. “Thank you, Lucas.”

She offered the wolf a nod before following Roi Gurri and Caroldus down the hall. She wanted to say more to Lucas, she wanted to comfort him, but she feared Scadrin’s scolding and figured she would have more time to discuss it later.

“What were you two talking about before I woke up?” Susan asked, motioning to Caroldus.

“W-Well I had a sort of date last night...” Caroldus explained with a blush. “You know, before the chaos with Damian.”

Susan gasped and smiled. “Really?” She exclaimed giddily. “That’s awesome, Caroldus! I thought you’d never find interest in someone. Who’s the lucky girl?”

“A servant named Kamila. We met in one of the gardens and got to know one another. I even worked up the courage to ask her on a second date next week.”

“That’s awesome! I’m happy for you.”

“When do we get to meet her?” Roi Gurri asked with a grin, nudging Caroldus’s arm.

“Just wait till I see where this is going,” Caroldus said with a chuckle. “Dating is pretty new to me.”

They walked outside to hear a loud and horrid shriek from above. The three stopped dead in their tracks.

“What was that?” Susan breathed out.

Roi Gurri looked up and turned pale.

Chapter Twenty-Two
Spirit Reapers

"Spirit Reapers!" Roi Gurri shouted with alarm.

Susan followed his gaze up to the sky. Several terrifying creatures with large black wings flew overhead. Their faces were storm clouds, raging with no shape. Their hands were cloud-like but had long sharp fingernails. They wore black robes to hide their shapeless body, and each bore a weapon.

Susan and Roi Gurri both drew their swords and shields, and Caroldus drew his two double-edged swords.

"You can't fight a Spirit Reaper yet, you haven't been properly trained," Roi Gurri said to Susan, placing a hand on her shoulder and pushing her behind his larger form.

As he said that, two Spirit Reapers flew down toward Caroldus and Roi Gurri. Susan frowned as she turned to see another landing behind them.

"Looks like I'm going to have to," she said, raising her sword. "Eleven months of training will have to do."

"Eleven and a quarter actually," Caroldus corrected.

With a shriek of a banshee, a Spirit Reaper ran at Susan and raised its mace. She raised her shield arm just to have it struck. She shook and a sharp pain ran up her arm from the force, but she held her ground.

Susan kept her shield up, looking for a place to strike, but the Spirit Reaper wasn't giving her an opening. She pushed the Spirit Reaper back and tried to knock the mace out of its hand, but it had an iron grip. She pushed the Spirit Reaper back against a tree and tried to keep it there, but the Spirit Reaper was just as determined as the small girl was.

"What do you want?" Susan asked the Spirit Reaper, not sure if it could understand her or not.

"We want *you,* of course," it said, its raspy, whining voice haunting Susan. "A'Vaddon sent us here, he wants you back."

Susan stepped away, startled. "A'Vaddon? What do you mean he wants me *back*?"

"I don't ask questions. He wants you, and some kid dead, along with the Jewel of Numenera."

Susan swung her sword at the Spirit Reaper, aiming for its chest, but the Spirit Reaper moved forward and grabbed her by her shirt, throwing her back.

Susan landed harshly on the ground, accidentally dropping her sword. She looked up and saw the Spirit Reaper advancing toward her. She grabbed a shard of metal from the ground and skillfully threw it into the Spirit Reaper's shoulder.

The Spirit Reaper blasted a piercing scream, one louder than a banshee and sharper than a sword. It sent a jolting sensation through Susan's entire body, and in a second her right eardrum ruptured with a pop.

Ignoring her new injury, Susan used the time to scoop up her sword from the ground. The Spirit Reaper yanked the metal out of its shoulder and glared at Susan. Fear struck Susan's heart in such a way she was forced to turn and start running, the Spirit Reaper close behind her.

"Susan!"

Susan looked behind her to see William running behind the Spirit Reaper, trying to stop it before it could get close to Susan. She turned and swung her sword, grazing the Spirit Reapers' torso. William came up behind the Spirit Reaper and tried to stab it, but it heard his advances.

The Spirit Reaper turned and held up its shield, prohibiting William's dagger from hitting its target. Susan came up behind the Spirit Reaper and put her arm around its throat and her sword against its side.

"Tell me where A'Vaddon is or I swear to Jehoyam-" Susan threatened, but the Spirit Reaper laughed.

It turned invisible and elbowed Susan in the stomach. Susan immediately lost her grip, allowing the Reaper to slip away.

Susan gasped and looked around, very shocked at the sudden scene around her. It seemed like the Spirit Reapers were winning, their number too great for the caught off-guard Zudanums.

"Are you okay?" William asked and she nodded.

"Yeah, I'm fine," Susan assured. "But my ear is ringing."

"Yeah, I think your eardrum popped."

"Behind you!"

William quickly turned and raised his shield to block a blow, re-engaging with the battle.

Susan was suddenly grabbed by the wrists by long, sharp hands, her eyes widening in fear. She instantly realized they belonged to a Spirit Reaper and tried to shake them off, but the grip kept getting stronger. So strong, she had to let go of her sword and shield.

"William! Help!" Susan screamed.

Roi Gurri and Caroldus heard her cry and quickly ran towards her. The Spirit Reaper started to pull her up towards a giant, dark ship in the sky.

William grabbed her leg and tried to pull her down, but he wasn't strong enough to pull her all the way down with the force of the Spirit Reaper as well. The Spirit Reaper screamed a sonic blast at William and he let go of her with a painful cry, placing his hands over his ears.

"Susan!" He cried, his eyes widening in horror as he looked up to see the Spirit Reaper flying with her.

She kicked and yelled, but the Spirit Reaper didn't even flinch from her struggling. It flew straight up into the sky and into the ship. Susan was enveloped in darkness.

The ship was a black, twisted cube of metal. It had dark storm clouds covering it, making it look like the ship was a part of the clouds. The inside was musty and pitch black, like an untouched basement.

The Spirit Reaper shoved Susan into a cage and locked it. Susan felt around the room to find the bars, shaking them to try to break free, but they wouldn't budge. She tried kicking and pushing against the lock once she found it, to no avail. She called for help until her voice was hoarse, but nobody came. Eventually she gave up, assuming they had teleported and flown away from the planet.

Susan looked around for anything that might help her, but she found nothing. She could barely see her own feet on the ground.

"Who are you?" Susan called out. "Where are we going?"

She felt the cold, loveless stare of a Spirit Reaper pierce her skull.

"I am Bunetrio," one of the Spirit Reapers said. "I am the one in charge."

Susan couldn't see who was speaking to her, but she could hear him. She walked up to the front of the cage she was in and grabbed onto one of the steel bars.

"I thought A'Vaddon sent you here," Susan said.

"He did, but he made a mistake hiring us. Now he'll have to pay a ransom if he wants you. And if he won't, King Regel will."

Susan grinned and laughed. Bunetrio growled.

"What is so funny?" He asked.

"I thought I should be scared of you, but you're nothing more than a bunch of bandits," Susan spat. "Strolling around the galaxy looking for profit."

She really was scared but didn't want to show it. Sarcasm and trash talk was her only defense at the moment.

Bunetrio was angered at her comment. He rushed forward and grabbed the bars in front of her and she jumped back, startled. She could see him, for their faces were only centimeters apart. His hands were grey and cold, his face had no features, but it still scared her. His breath was icy cold yet smelled of rotting meat.

"We are the most feared race of aliens in the realm," Bunetrio stated. "We have destroyed civilizations, we have sent anti-naturals fleeing, and we have plundered more planets than you have eaten a meal. We are more than just *simple* bandits."

"I don't see a difference, but whatever helps you sleep at night."

"You are foolish to argue with me. I could kill you in a second without needing help. You are just a human, with no powers or alien blood. You're a mutt."

"I'm alright with being a mutt. I have my own special gifts, don't you dare underestimate me."

Bunetrio hummed and backed away from the cage, not allowing her to see his form anymore.

"Thanks for the warning, Adathir."

Susan was momentarily startled by the usage of her alias but decided not to bring attention to it.

"Just about everything about me must be known in every realm by now."

***

Susan eventually lost track of time in the darkness of the ship, but after what seemed like a few hours they landed. She was stirred awake by the sounds, getting up and feeling for the bars.

"Where are we now?" Susan asked, but no one answered her.

Two Spirit Reapers came up to her and dragged her out of the cage. She tried to break free, but they were too strong.

"Damn it," Susan thought. *"No wonder Zudaniums train so vigorously."*

Susan got a good look at the planet as she was escorted from the ship, surprised at what she saw. The whole planet was red and black, and smoke filled the air. There were tall pillars of metal shaped as dead trees with deep cuts etched into them.

Susan was led into a large building made of metal and pulled down a dark corridor. She couldn't see clearly what was in the building because they were pulling her in a hurry. But she saw several tapestries hanging on the walls of past battles and victories.

"So this is the home base for the Spirit Reapers," Susan thought as she was tossed into a cell.

The Spirit Reapers walked away, leaving her alone. She stood and walked back and forth in her cell, wondering what would happen to her.

"I suppose they'll send out their demands now," Susan mumbled to herself as she paced. "How long that'll take though, who knows. In the meantime, I should find a way out of here."

She pulled the Jewel of Numenera out of her pocket, taking off some of the cloth so that she could look at it. The jewel glowed in the dim light, its blood red color attracting her attention. Susan felt grateful that they hadn't searched her.

"Why does everybody seem to want you?" Susan asked herself, but also to the jewel as if it could speak to her.

And while she doubted it could speak to her, it could definitely hear her. In the eleven months Susan had the jewel, whenever she pulled it out to admire it she felt its undivided attention on her. It's like the jewel *wanted* to be used.

Even though Susan didn't know the jewel's full power, she figured it was on her side ever since A'Vaddon's demon tried to attack her at her manor. She took the jewel and pressed it against the metal bars of her cell, careful to use the cloth to hold it so she wouldn't die. Immediately the cell door melted away, freeing her. She looked down at the jewel and smiled.

"Thanks," Susan whispered and the jewel pulsed with energy, as if it was responding.

She wrapped it up and placed it in her pocket, looking down the halls to make sure the coast was clear before walking out of the cell.

She quietly walked up and down halls, avoiding the guards by hiding in the shadows and using her senses to detect when they were near. If the sight of the Spirit Reapers didn't already disgust Susan, their smell certainly did. She didn't know how they could stand it, the whole place smelled of rotting meat, mold, and blood.

The place was full of twists and turns and was mostly dark, though torches of red fire lit the halls dimly. How long Susan was wandering she wasn't sure. The adrenaline of always being on edge and not having her weapon made her believe she had wandered for hours before she heard voices coming from a room and decided to investigate. She quietly walked to the edge of the doorway and peeked inside.

"I have never liked humans," said one of the Spirit Reapers, a bronze crown sitting upon his head. "They are so fragile and weak. I would like to take them all out, to use them for the *project*, but those Zudaniums stand in the way."

There was a pause.

"Should I prepare your troops sir?" Another Spirit Reaper asked.

"Yes, you should. I'll show those Zudaniums what real power looks like."

"But what about the anti-naturals sir?" Another one pointed out.

"They are not as powerful as we are," the one with the crown said. "Their so-called 'council' doesn't train them at a young age like we do. And their soldiers are weak compared to their anti-naturals. King Regel is certainly favorable towards his anti-naturals. But we are more powerful, and we are stronger. And after I wipe them out I'll go for the next easy target, Earth."

"But it is against all laws to make any contact with them," one of the other Spirit Reapers said. "And the journey would take at least ten years with no teleportation to travel through space. They do, after all, have the biggest realm."

"No one will know of this plan. No one would even suspect someone of breaking the law at this moment, not with the quietness of peace, which is why now is the perfect time to strike. Prepare my armies, we will strike in the evening."

"I have to get this information to King Regel," Susan thought as she quietly slipped away.

She found an empty room and sat inside, her breath heavy from the intense humidity. She pulled out the Jewel of Numenera once again and sighed.

"I need help," she said to herself.

She looked up, her thoughts turning towards her lost Necto Blade. How she wished she hadn't dropped it during the battle, but they probably would've taken it from her anyway, so it didn't really matter.

"I can help you escape," came the voice of Damian.

Susan quickly stood. "Damian?" She asked quietly, looking around frantically, but only heard a chuckle from the inside of her head.

"Yes, dear sister, it's me."

Susan frowned and tsked. "Get out of my head, I don't want you in it."

Damian sighed. *"Do you want to get away from the Spirit Reapers or not? You have to trust that I'll tell you the right direction."*

"I don't trust you."

Part of her felt that was a lie, but she didn't want him to think he could invade her mind again.

"Well, you don't have much of a choice do you?" Damian asked.

Susan considered her options. Either she kept wandering without his help, and eventually get caught. Or she listened to him, but could end up in a trap.

"I'll follow your directions for now," Susan decided. "If you dare lead me into a trap I'll make your end more painful than whatever Jehoyam planned for you in the first place."

"Fair enough," Damian agreed.

"Where do I go from here?"

"Go out into the hall, turn left, and go straight."

Susan reluctantly returned to the hall, following Damian's instructions. "Why are you helping me?" She quietly asked, pressing herself against the wall to avoid two guards.

"If you knew anything about my past then you would know that despite being on different teams, I care about you," Damian explained.

"I have yet to see that."

"I wouldn't have joined A'Vaddon for any other reason. Turn left."

"How are you talking to me?"

"Twins with a powerful bloodline tend to have a telepathic connection."

"You never thought about using that to tell me about Zudanum and everything else?"

"I tried, but since I had no idea where you were, I didn't know where to call out to."

"You lied to me about Regel banishing you."

"He might as well have. You know as well as I that he's a harsh king."

Susan shrugged as she was led out of the building and into a warm wind. "Now what?" She asked, but there was no answer. "Damian?" She sighed with yet again no response. "I knew he would abandon me like that."

She looked around but didn't see much except some trees as she walked forward. The whole planet was dark and cold, and the ground was wet and mushy. She almost wished that she had never left her cell, but at least she wouldn't be lost or looking over her shoulder for Spirit Reapers.

A loud shrieking siren went off, filling the entire planet. Susan froze in feer, the sound filling her soul with dread. To those who weren't Spirit Reapers this call sounded like death herself.

Susan could hear dozens of Spirit Reapers replying to the call, their screams filling the air. She knew they had discovered she had escaped, so she quickly ran in the opposite direction of the large building. But, she stepped out of the smoke to find she had become disoriented and ran the wrong way. She was standing several feet away from a dozen Spirit Reapers who were standing in front of the building.

She turned and ran without hesitation. The Spirit Reapers were quick to follow. She ran into woods with big, looming trees covered in thick fog. She ducked under branches and ran past onlooking creatures with amber eyes, but didn't stick around to see much else.

The Spirit Reapers hovered over the trees. They were able to see her through the fog and the metal trees. They could hear her loud steps and heavy breathing. She heard their steady heartbeats as they chased after her. She also felt her own blood pumping vigorously, and for a moment wondered if they really had hearts.

Susan looked next to her to see a Spirit Reaper hovering beside her, it's featureless face piercing into her soul. She looked ahead as she ran out of the woods to find a cliff ahead!

She tried to stop but she was running too fast. With no other options, she threw herself to the ground, attempting to stop, but skidded off the cliff and barely managed to grab the edge with one hand.

"If this isn't cliche, I don't know what is," Susan mumbled sarcastically as she hung on for dear life.

The Spirit Reapers walked towards the ledge and looked down at her. She looked up, terrified. One of them reached down to grab her, but she quickly pulled out the Jewel of Numenera and held it in front of her.

"Jehoyam!" Susan cried.

The jewel instantly shone brighter than any light Susan had ever seen, and she had to close her eyes or risk blindness. With the last bit of her strength she pulled herself onto the ledge and held the jewel even farther from her, making the Spirit Reapers step back towards the tree line. She opened her eyes and stared at them.

"Go back to your master and tell him I don't need to be an anti-natural or an alien to be able to take any of you out," Susan ordered as she walked toward them, making them retreat back to where they came from.

The Jewel of Numenera stopped shining and returned to its blood red glow. Susan looked down at the small jewel curiously.

"You really are powerful, aren't you?" Susan mused as she put it back into her pocket, and looked around. "What do I do now?"

"Pull me back out."

Susan looked down at her pocket, hearing the jewel calling to her. Obeying the jewel, she pulled it out again and held it up into the sky. The jewel created a large beacon that shot straight up into the sky for miles. The light started to surround the whole planet, and shrieking could be heard from all directions.

"I'm killing them," Susan thought, her heart aching at the thought, even if they did take her captive.

Susan struggled to pull the jewel down, for it *wanted* to continue destroying the Spirit Reapers. But Susan couldn't have that. She couldn't live with genocide on her conscious.

She screamed and pulled the jewel down and into her chest, extinguishing the light. She breathed heavily for several minutes, feeling a wave of exhaustion.

"I'm not a monster," Susan whispered. "I won't be like A'Vaddon."

The Jewel of Numenera pulsed as if it were angry, but Susan didn't care. If they were going to work together, the jewel would have to learn not to commit genocide.

Susan heard a familiar whirring noise above her. She looked up and saw a small metal ship heading her way, the colors green and gold painted on the side, with the symbol of a lion.

It landed in front of her and she cautiously backed away from it. It looked like it could be a Zudanum ship, but she didn't want to be fooled by an ambush.

The door opened slowly, and as soon as the platform touched the ground out rushed William. He ran to embrace Susan, who was caught off guard by his swiftness. She relaxed her arms when she calmed down and realized it was him.

"Thank the stars," William whispered, holding her tighter to him. "I'm so sorry, Susan. I should've stayed by your side during the battle."

She shook her head and looked up at him, smiling.

“It’s fine, William, really,” Susan assured him softly, looking into his eyes.

A loud screech came from a distance and Susan flinched.

“We should go,” William said.

Susan nodded in agreement and they boarded the ship.

“Where did you get the ride?” Susan asked. “I’m not even allowed to ride a war ship.”

Susan looked around at the different gadgets in the ship, placing her hand on the wall as the door closed. The ship was small, only able to hold about three people for short distances, making her assume it was a fighter ship.

“I *borrowed* this from the Star-Ship Training Fleet, since it’s only supposed to be used for emergencies,” William explained. “I considered this to be one.”

The ship powered and William pushed a lever down. Susan tilted her head with curiosity and she looked around the ship, running her fingers over the metal interior.

“This is amazing,” she said in awe, and William’s eyes smiled as he glanced back at her.

“Earth technology has no idea how far behind they are,” he commented.

William chuckled and Susan nodded in agreement, her eyes still wide.

“*So* far behind,” she agreed. “Sometimes I can’t believe how advanced Zudanum is.”

“We didn’t just sit around watching stupid things on a glass screen. What is that again?”

Susan bit her lip and chuckled. “It’s called a TV.”

“Waste of time.”

"Everyone enjoys entertainment," Susan protested as she sat beside William in the co-pilot seat.

"A good book is all I need for entertainment. And maybe kids one day, but that's a whole different kind of entertainment."

Susan laughed and looked out the front as they exited the atmosphere. Her smile fell when she saw several small ships approaching them.

"William, they're on our tail," she said.

"Take the controls, I bet you'll be better at flying than shooting."

William shifted the controls from the levers he was holding to the ones beside Susan.

"Me?" She asked, her eyes wide as she looked at the levers. "But- But-"

"Susan, drive!"

He fired several beams at the ships in front of them. She quickly grabbed the controls and zoomed forward, swooping up and turning upside down over a ship and circling it.

"Keep the ship steady for the star's sake!" William exclaimed as he fired several rounds and two of the Spirit Reaper ships were hit.

"Well excuse me, this is my first time driving a war ship!" Susan exclaimed. "And you were the one who told me to move."

William killed off the last ship and looked down at a monitor to see more were closing in behind them.

"Susan, turn left and press the red button!"

"If we go left-"

"Just do it!"

She was quick to do as she was told. In a flash they were teleported into Zudanums atmosphere, under the thick layer of ice that covered the planet, but they were coming in fast!

"Slow down the ship!" William ordered.

"How the hell do I do that?!" Susan exclaimed.

William reached over and pulled Susan's levers back, the ship coming to a hover over the trees. He let out a sigh of relief and slumped back into his seat.

"I really need to teach you how to fly," William muttered, switching controls to his levers once again and going in to land the ship.

"I'm holding you to that."

Chapter Twenty-Three
The Battle of Shadows

William landed in front of the palace, letting out a sigh of relief.

"Welcome back," he said.

They quickly made their way out of the ship, heading for the palace. Susan glanced back at the ship wistfully before turning back, William chuckling as he noticed her longing look.

"You'll get to fly one the right way soon," William promised, causing her to smile and nod.

"You'll teach me right?" Susan asked.

"Promise."

Roi Gurri, Caroldus, Contral, Subaron, and Ethim were at the doors of the palace waiting to greet them. Roi Gurri rushed over and embraced Susan with relief in his eyes.

"Are you alright, Little Legs?" He whispered to her and she nodded with a small laugh.

"Yes, I'm alright," she whispered back, smiling. "You can't get rid of me that easily, my love. But I have important information for your father."

"What is it?" Caroldus asked, walking up to her and Roi Gurri.

"Follow me and you'll find out."

Subaron walked up to Susan and handed her her sword and shield.

"You really should be careful, someone could've stolen these while you were gone," he said, a ghost of a smile coming to his lips.

Susan strapped them on her, glad to have her weapons back. They had become a part of her, binding to her soul.

"Thanks," Susan said with a smile. "I wasn't sure if I'd see these again."

Subaron felt a small sense of pride, and they continued walking. Susan and the men walked into the throne room, where King Regel was talking with Queen Sharmon.

"The Spirit Reapers are preparing for war!" Susan announced. "They want to destroy all of us tonight, and afterward they're going after Earth."

King Regel looked down at her, his eyes widening and his interest immediately piqued.

"How do you know?" He asked in a tone of worry as Queen Sharmon turned pale.

"I heard their King and his generals with my own ears."

Subaron, Roi Gurri, and William all looked to one another, their expressions each holding a scowl. They had their own ties and scores to settle with the Spirit Reapers.

"Well then, if it's a war they want, then it's a war they'll get," King Regel said. "General Greenlook!"

A tall man in a dark blue robe strode into the room and he bowed to King Regel. "Your highness," the general greeted.

"Prepare your troops for a battle with the Spirit Reapers," King Regel commanded. "Take every precaution, do not underestimate them, General. I am putting my kingdom, and Earth, in your hands."

"Yes, my King. We will be prepared for when they come."

He bowed once again and swiftly walked out of the room, not wasting a second.

"What about my father, my King?" Caroldus spoke up.

"Your father is five thousand miles away, he won't make it in time," King Regel responded.

Caroldus nodded, but in his heart was disappointed that his first battle wouldn't be alongside his father. Susan looked up at King Regel.

"We will be ready too," she stated, standing straight.

"We?" King Regel asked, peering down at Susan.

"Yes, my King. I would put my life in any of these men's hands." She turned and looked up at her friends. "I will give my life if needed to protect you. I will fight in this battle, I will fight for our home. You have all become my friends, my brothers. I'm an outsider, it's not my right to call you to arms, but know that I *will* stand with you till the very end. Who will be there with me?"

She drew her sword and held it in front of her as if she was challenging them. Roi Gurri drew his sword and placed it on top of hers.

"I will fight with you," he said firmly.

William drew his sword. "As will I."

Subaron drew his sword. "I have nothing better to do."

Everyone laughed and Caroldus took out his double-edged swords, and Contral his mace.

"We would be honored to fight by your side," Caroldus said.

Ethim drew his bow. "As would I."

Susan smiled. "We are all in this together," she said. "Watch each other's backs."

They all lifted their weapons in the air and cheered as Susan turned to King Regel.

"Yes your highness, *we*," Susan affirmed.

King Regel smiled proudly and nodded. "Go then, prepare yourselves," he said, and the group bowed and left the room.

Susan went to follow the men to get armor fitted, but Caroldus stopped her.

"Come with me," he said, smiling childishly as if he was excited.

She nodded and followed him to the weapons area of the castle, curious as to what he was about to show her. He opened up a part of the wall to show a jumpsuit outfit to her.

It was white cloth with red and orange flames rising from the feet to the chest. It had a pair of burgundy combat boots that were lined with rubies, along with a pair of fingerless gloves that looked to be engulfed in flames, and a long white cloak rested upon its shoulders.

Susan turned to Caroldus, her eyes wide and her mouth dropped open in shock. "Did you make this?" She breathed out.

Caroldus nodded proudly, smiling as he flushed. "I read that on Earth every hero has their own signature uniform," he explained. "This one is yours. The flames are there to represent your patrol name, Adathir. Do you know what it means?"

"No, I've honestly never thought about it."

"It means daughter of fire."

Susan paused to think about the meaning. "So I was named for my father." Tears came to her eyes at the thought. "All this time, I never knew."

"Your father would be proud of you, Susan."

"I really hope so. Even though I've only seen him once, I carry the image in my heart and look back on it every single day. I pray to Jehoyam that I never forget it." She looked back at the suit. "You really made this?"

"Is that so hard to believe?"

"It's hard to believe that you found the *time* to make it."

"I make most of my own clothes, so it's not as hard as you think. The tricky part is sewing with metal."

"Metal?"

"The suit is completely made of a metal fiber, which means it'll be able to resist arrows and daggers. Not saying they won't hurt, though. There are built-in knee and elbow pads, and the cloth is specifically designed to withstand arrows and daggers. There's also extra armor to go with it, but it's very light, so you shouldn't have to worry about mobility. I designed it specifically with your swiftness in mind."

"At the speed I've been growing, I'm sad to say that I'll probably outgrow it."

"I can adjust the lengths, that's no problem. With this suit, everyone will know you're the Chosen One."

Susan turned to Caroldus and tightly embraced him. "Why are you in Warrior Brave, Caroldus?" She asked, chuckling. "You'd make an excellent tailor."

"Because I'm willing to die to save my people," Caroldus said, his tone of voice suddenly becoming grave. "Because I was given strength and courage."

"I wasn't given those."

Susan trembled as he pulled away and held her at arm's length. She looked up into his stunning hazel eyes and saw nothing but sincerity.

"Susan, you're one of the strongest people I know," Caroldus said. "You left Earth to come to Zudanum, a planet you didn't even know existed. You put your trust in complete strangers and a metal wolf. And even though it's only been a year, you're already going into battle. Don't you dare tell me you're not strong, Susan Wellns."

Susan laughed and shook her head. "You have no idea how much I needed to hear that. Thank you, Caroldus."

They both laughed and he patted her back.

"Put your suit on, I'll see you out there," Caroldus assured.

"Wait." Susan put a hand on his shoulder. "I don't know what's going to happen, but stay safe. I'd hate for you to miss your date with Kamila."

He smiled softly and shook his head. "Trust me, I won't."

***

Susan walked out of the palace with her new suit on, complete with the extra steel armor, walking over to William once she found him. He turned to see her in uniform and his eyes smiled.

"Your armor looks amazing, Susan," he said.

"Thanks," she said with a smile.

The suit felt weird to her, mainly because it was a full bodysuit. It clung on her like it was a part of her skin, making her feel naked, but she knew she would eventually get used to the feeling. The added armor helped make her feel secure.

"I'm going to guess that Caroldus made the suit," William stated.

Susan nodded with a smile. "How did you know?"

"Because no royal armor maker would put *that* much detail into their work, no matter if you're the Chosen One or future queen."

"Then I am grateful that Caroldus took the time and effort to make this. I'll always be proud to wear this armor."

"He should've become a tailor."

Susan laughed but nodded in agreement. She walked to his side and looked over to the orchard he was staring at.

"I wanted to say thanks," Susan said quietly.

William looked down at her. "For what?" He asked.

"For rescuing me from the Spirit Reaper planet. I owe you one."

William placed his hand on Susan's cheek and tilted her head so she was looking into his eyes.

"You're one of my best friends, Susan. You don't owe me for getting you off of a creepy planet."

Susan smiled fondly. "Thanks, William. You should probably go change into your armor. I'm sure the Spirit Reapers will be arriving soon."

He nodded and let his hand fall from her face. "I'll see you then, Adathir."

"And I'll see you then, Silentium."

William walked away and Susan smiled as she turned back to the orchard. It was planted a ways from the training grounds, meant to encourage the students to eat healthy and relax in the shade the trees gave. It was always beautiful, always alive.

"Jehoyam, please let my friends live," Susan prayed.

"Did you know White Star is almost a thousand years old?"

Susan turned to see Roi Gurri. She smiled, noting he looked handsome in his armor in the light. He was fully dressed in the same material her suit was made of, under his heavy armor. He had the Necto Blade of Earth at his side and his shield on his back, which reflected the sunlight. His own suit was a pinewood color, with forest green embroidery decorating it, though it was hard to see under the gold armor over his suit. He held a helmet shaped like a lion's head, which Susan thought was beautifully crafted. A thin pair of metal gloves covered his hand, the fingertips gone, and he wore brown, sturdy, ankle high boots.

"If I had known that, I wouldn't have asked him to join us in battle," Susan admitted. "If he's a thousand years old, then he probably knew my father *and* grandfather."

"He won't have a problem in battle," Roi Gurri assured. "Peryton are immortal as long as they don't kill anyone."

"How has he seen battle and not killed anyone?"

"White Star has seen many things, and he can't or won't tell most of them. Of course, there are stories and rumors. The best-known story is about the last time he fought the Spirit Reapers in the valley of Disent, with your grandfather Karnis Wellns."

Susan nodded, but she wasn't really listening, the distant look in her eyes betrayed the emptiness in her head. Roi Gurri looked down at her, worried.

"What's wrong?" He asked.

"I can't let the people of this planet down," Susan said. "And, that includes the people of Earth."

Roi Gurri put a hand on her shoulder and then placed the other on her cheek. The cold metal of his glove made her shiver.

"Promise me that you won't be reckless and get yourself killed," Roi Gurri pleaded softly.

His plea made her chest tighten and dysphoria fill her stomach as tears welled up in her eyes.

Susan wished she could promise she wouldn't get herself killed, but the adomania she felt told her that her wish wouldn't come true. She wished with all her heart she could just be another soldier on the battlefield. Or maybe she wished that they had been born as normal people.

Not a prince and a Chosen One, but maybe two high schoolers on Earth. Maybe they wouldn't have been forced to marry, maybe they could've been friends first and then slowly fall in love. The more she thought about it, the less it felt right. Neither of them would be the same person.

"I can't make a promise I might not be able to keep," Susan whispered.

Roi Gurri pressed his forehead to hers. "I suppose it is a lot to ask," he whispered. "I just... I don't want to see you die. I was actually just starting to like you."

"Well I should hope so, we haven't fought in a while."

They both laughed, masking the way their hearts ached at the thought of either one of them dying, even if they hadn't known each other for long. They were each other's first friends, from both their childhood and now. They didn't want to be separated again.

"I'm just starting to like him too..." Susan thought. *"In fact, I was just starting to love him."*

A loud alarm went off, the sound of battle that had the two parting and looking in the direction of the battle field.

"The Spirit Reapers are approaching," Roi Gurri said quietly. "Let's go."

They found their companions and rode to the designated battlefield, which was the plain of Gontron. It was far from the city, in a place where civilians couldn't be injured. Tents were set up, for extra weapons and medical attention.

"Why aren't we using firearms?" Susan asked Roi Gurri as they stopped by the weapons tent.

"Oh, we are," Roi Gurri assured, handing her a small firearm. "These firearms are made specifically for Spirit Reapers because normal bullets will go right through their bodies. But you've gotta be careful, if you hit a Zudanum with one of these they'll receive a nasty shock."

"Oh. Don't worry, I'm confident in my aiming skills."

"You should be, I've seen your range scores."

The two made their way to the front lines. Next to Roi Gurri stood Subaron, Contral and Ethim. Next to Susan stood White Star, William, and Caroldus, all of the boys mounted on their companions.

Susan looked at her friends, each one of them looking back at her, causing her to smile. She turned to see Lucas running towards them, her eyes widening in surprise.

"What are you doing here?" She asked the metal wolf, who made a sort of smile.

"I wouldn't miss this fight for the world," he said with his wolf grin. "I haven't fought Spirit Reapers since your grandfather was alive."

"How old are you?"

"Like I'm going to tell you."

They both laughed. Subaron looked over at Susan and they locked eyes.

"Try not to get yourself killed," he said. "You still owe me a fight."

"I'll try not to."

Susan found it much easier to make a fake promise to her once rival than to the man she loved.

She turned her attention to the other side of the field. There, the Spirit Reapers ship had landed and their soldiers came swarming out. Fear immediately struck the hearts of all of the soldiers at the sight. The Spirit Reapers moved like a storming ocean, moving up and up. It was only a matter of time until the wave crashed.

"It feels like we're outnumbered," Susan whispered to Lucas.

"Don't give up hope," he said, "I'm a living metal wolf, so anything is possible. Besides, you're carrying the Necto Blade of Hope right now. It's your job to keep hope alive as long as you live."

Susan looked down at the Necto Blade in her hand, the phantom gem in the pommel of the blade glowing just barely. She felt an energy coursing through her veins that came from the jewel itself, giving her a shot of confidence and optimism.

"Hope," the sound of many voices ehoed in her head. *"Have hope for the living."*

Susan looked up to see King Regel ride up on his horse, his sword drawn, his body covered in the same kind of armor as Roi Gurri. He looked across the battlefield and turned to his son.

"Move two squadrons to the front lines," King Regel commanded, making Roi Gurri frown.

"But father, that will leave our back exposed, and they might be able to sneak behind us," Roi Gurri pointed out.

King Regel looked at his son and placed a hand on his shoulder. "Son, trust me."

Despite his gut telling him otherwise, Roi Gurri nodded and signaled some of the men to move to the front lines. He mounted his white unicorn, Pure Lightning, and drew his sword. Susan looked at White Star and placed a hand on his side.

"You don't have to do this," she said to the peryton.

White Star nodded and motioned for her to jump on. She mounted him and strapped her shield to her back, allowing her to grip into her drawn sword tightly. King Regel rode forward and turned around to address his troops.

"We will fight to the last breath!" He cried. "We will defend our planet, our home, our families. We must not lose to the Spirit Reapers. If we do, our home and the people of Earth will suffer greatly for it. So fight with courage, fight till the end! Fight to live another day!"

"Well, I'm sure that didn't make anyone feel pressured," Susan thought sarcastically.

King Regel turned back around towards the Spirit Reapers and held up his sword. The Spirit Reaper king rode in front of his troops on a sickly, shadowy black horse, his sword drawn. Thunder roared and the lightning clashed in the black sky, causing Susan to jump at the sudden appearance of the storm.

"How did it get dark so quickly?" She asked Roi Gurri.

"Certain Spirit Reapers can summon storm clouds at will," he explained. "They make it dark because they fight better in it."

"So they're making us play on their turf."

"Yeah."

"Regel!" The Spirit Reaper King cried, his voice sending chills across the battlefield. "All of you will fall here today! No one on this planet will be left alive!"

"Not today!" King Regel exclaimed. "Your losses will be far greater than any battle the realms have ever seen! Our anti-naturals are powerful, and our armies are mighty. We also have the Chosen One fighting by our side!"

King Regel's soldiers cheered at this, but Susan had to take a deep breath to try to still her trembling body.

"You are foolish to even consider going into battle!" The Spirit Reaper king hissed. "Even with the girl, you know whose blood is running through her veins, you know that she is like him more than anyone!"

"Attack!" King Regel commanded before Susan had time to process what the Spirit Reaper King said.

White Star swiftly took off, his legs moving like a blur, causing Susan to hold on tighter to his antlers. Lucas ran after them, Roi Gurri and King Regel following. The armies of Zudanum followed Susan, their confidence building after seeing that the Chosen One was leading the charge.

King Roclash, the Spirit Reaper King, rode towards Susan, his fiery sword held firmly in his clawed hand. Their swords were the first to clash, the blow so hard it knocked Susan off of White Star.

Susan gasped as the wind was knocked out of her, but she scrambled up from the ground and quickly blocked another attack from King Roclash before his sword could hit her. He turned to hit her again, but she slashed his horse's leg and it tumbled to the ground.

"Now this is a fair fight," Susan stated, shifting her feet into a fighting stance.

"Is it?" King Roclash asked as he looked behind Susan.

She glanced back to see Spirit Reapers coming up behind King Regel's army, advancing toward the city. Roi Gurri had been right!

"Roi Gurri!" Susan cried, seeing the prince from a distance. "They're coming from behind!"

"Turn around!" He cried with alarm.

Susan turned just in time to move away from King Roclash's sword that was about to slash her back.

"You will be killed with the others," King Roclash hissed. "You are worth nothing to me without your powers."

"I'm more than just my powers, your highness." She ran and slid between his legs, slicing one if his ankles with her sword as she moved, stood up and shot him in the back with her firearm. "But to be honest, I would rather die than be your pawn."

King Roclash stood still, fell to the ground and disintegrated. Susan was surprised by the king's quick death, but moved to her next opponent, the other Spirit Reapers putting up a better fight than their king.

War was far more terrifying than training, Susan could say that for certain. Every movement she made was a life or death decision, every swing of her blade could mean a consequence. The thought of protecting her friends and their families kept her going, slaying Spirit Reapers one by one, slowly but surely cutting down the army.

As Susan finished her next apponent, she spotted Caroldus fighting a large Spirit Reaper with a spear. He was doing well, matching his opponent's attacks and making up for strength with speed. That is, until he exerted too much force and swung his swords back, leaving himself exposed for a half second. At that exact moment the Spirit Reaper threw its spear through his stomach.

It took a second for the scene in front of Susan to process in her mind. Time slowed down for Susan as Spirit Reapers disintegrated around her and denial coursed throughout her body. She could see Caroldus grip the spear protruding from his stomach, look at her in disbelief, and fall to the ground. The Spirit Reaper ripped his spear out of Caroldus's stomach, the Zudanium emitting an agonizing scream that brought Susan back to reality.

"No!" Susan screamed. "Caroldus!"

The Spirit Reaper turned to look at Susan's horrified expression and smirked tauntingly. It raised its spear, Caroldus's blood slowly dripping down the handle onto his hand.

Susan's blood boiled with anger. Her eyes turned pure amethyst as the Phantom Gem of Hope glowed brighter. She ran to the Spirit Reaper, swords clashing. Susan cried out from the strength pushing against her. Using all her strength and adrenaline, she pushed the Spirit Reaper away from her, slicing off its arm bearing the spear. It shrieked in agony as specks of black fell from where his arm used to be. She gave a cry, angrily shoving her sword in his stomach. Its expression warped with pain and shock, unable to believe it was defeated.

Susan twisted the sword in its stomach before pulling it out and lopping its head off. It disintegrated and its black, ash-like dust blew away.

Susan rushed over to Caroldus, not caring for a second about her victory. She fell onto her knees and lifted his head up onto her lap, which caused him to gasp in pain. Her whole body trembled as tears poured from her eyes. She shook her head in disbelief, unable to even look at his wound without feeling nauseous.

"S-Susan," Caroldus breathed out shakily, his words barely audible.

"No, don't say anything, Caroldus," she protested, placing her hand on his cheek. "Roi Gurri will be able to heal you, just hang on."

"Susan," Caroldus whispered, reaching up and placing a hand on Susan's cheek softly. "No healer can heal a wound this large."

She was horrified as he coughed up blood. "No, stop it! Don't say things like that, Caroldus! Roi Gurri!" She screamed. "Help! Roi Gurri!"

Roi Gurri was nearby and heard her cries. He quickly ran over to her and Caroldus. He knelt down and examined Caroldus, his hands trembling as he placed them on the gruesome wound. For several long minutes he sent his golden healing energy into Caroldus, but it was to no avail.

"I can't heal this wound," Roi Gurri said in a grave tone, his voice trembling.

Susan's eyes watered. "What do you mean you can't heal him?!" She screeched. "I thought you were a healer!"

Roi Gurri looked away, not able to look her in the eye. "Susan, the kind of healing I possess is the ability to turn tissue and parts of the human body back to its original state, but the process isn't as fast as I wish it could be. A wound like this that goes all the way through and is so damaged..." He looked into Caroldus's eyes. Tears fell as he placed a hand on his best friend's shoulder. “I’m so sorry, Caroldus,” he whispered, letting out a sob. “I can’t save you.”

Caroldus gave him a small smile. “It’s fine, Roi Gurri,” he whispered. “C-Can you cover us?”

Roi Gurri quickly turned to block the blow of a Spirit Reaper just as it was about to land on Susan.

“Anything for you, old friend,” Roi Gurri whispered. “We will see each other again, I swear.”

“At the gates of Destir, old friend.”

Thick roots shot up from the ground and covered Susan and Caroldus, making a protective dome over them. Susan looked down at Caroldus, though she couldn’t see him.

“No, stop it!” She screamed, holding Caroldus closer to her chest. “Why are you giving up? Why won’t you let him at least try longer?”

“Susan, p-please-” Caroldus tried to speak, but he was cut off by a harsh cough and blood erupting from his parted lips.

“Stop, don’t say anything. Sorry it's so dark.”

She heard Caroldus chuckle. Suddenly a light started emitting from his skin, lighting the dome.

“Caroldus...” Susan breathed out in amazement. “I thought- I thought you weren’t anti-natural.”

“Some people only find their power when they’re about to die,” he explained quietly, coughing up more blood onto his uniform, as well as Susan’s. “It’s my body’s last-ditch effort to save itself.”

Tears filled Susan’s eyes as she wiped the blood away from Caroldus’s face with her sleeve, her motherly instinct kicking in seeing his bloodied and dirty state. The young boy winced, but smiled at her actions.

“Using your power is making you worse,” Susan observed, looking into his eyes. “Please stop, Caroldus.”

"I-It doesn't matter, Susan," Caroldus stuttered, blood flowing from his mouth as he spoke. "I am glad to die f-fighting by your side."

"No Caroldus, you're not going to die. Your spirit will never die. You're going to live on in another life. You're going to get the best care, I promise. You're going to go to a place where you will always be cared for, and where you'll never die. I'll be there with you in a few years, I promise. Just please- please watch over me. Don't leave me alone."

Susan burst into sobs and she cradled Caroldus in her arms. He smiled sadly, tears rolling down his cheeks.

"I... I promise." Caroldus breathed out, and Susan smiled.

"Good."

"Susan... Your father's spirit is alive."

Susan froze. "What? Caroldus, what do you mea-?"

"I-I don't have time to explain," he cut her off. "I love you, Susan. I wish... I would've liked to have known you a bit longer. Please tell Kamila I won't be able to make it next week. T-Tell my father I fought bravely. Tell my siblings I didn't die angry or in vain. Tell my mother I love her. Tell Will... T-Tell him..."

Before Caroldus could finish what he wanted to say, he slowly closed his eyes and his head fell back limp. The light from his skin started gradually fading away as his blood drained. Susan bowed her head and tears streamed down her face as she clutched his dead body. The light faded and the dome was dark again.

"No, please!" Susan screamed, rubbing his cheeks as if that would bring back their warmth. "You can't leave me now, you can't! I still need you, please! Roi Gurri and William still need you! Don't leave me alone, don't leave me here to fight them! I still need you! I'm not ready to go on this ride on my own!"

Susan started hyperventilating, rocking back and forth sobbing. She thought back to the time they first met, that stupid song Caroldus sang saying he'd be there until the end of the ride. She thought to the times he'd carry her on his shoulders like a big brother or a father would, how she felt like she could touch the clouds. She thought back to their training. He mentored her in such a way his lessons would never escape her memory.

"I love you too, Caroldus," Susan whispered as she kissed his cold forehead. "You were the brother I needed, and I thank you for that. I'll make sure that they all pay, I promise."

She drew her sword and sliced a hole in the vines, crawling out so no Spirit Reapers got to Caroldus's body. She looked in front of her to see a hand and she looked up to see Roi Gurri, black dust covering his body and tear stains covering his dirty cheeks. He helped her up, both of them shaking.

"I don't care about heroism or stereotypes, they all deserve to die," Susan spat.

"I agree," Roi Gurri firmly replied.

"What do Spirit Reapers hate most?"

"Light."

Susan looked back at the vine dome, thinking for a minute. Her head tilted as an idea clicked.

"Then I'll give them light," Susan stated. "I need to find White Star."

"I have to find him before more people die," she thought as she ran.

***

King Regel was afar, fighting a large Spirit Reaper, who was one of the main generals of their army. Their swords clashed as they fought, hearts racing like wild stallions. King Regel thrusted his sword at the Spirit Reaper who blocked it with its shield. It sliced King Regel's abdomen, who stumbled back in pain, but quickly recovered. He raised his hand and threw an energy sphere at the Spirit Reaper who fell to the ground, paralyzed. King Regel stabbed it in the stomach and turned just as another Spirit Reaper was about to try to kill him. Lucas jumped up and knocked it away from him.

"Thanks," King Regel said, returning to the fight.

"It was my honor," Lucas said. "I haven't had this much fun in decades!"

Lucas howled as he took off running again, killing Spirit Reapers along the way. King Regel chuckled as he continued fighting, ignoring the stinging pain in his stomach.

He saw his son and Susan running, several Spirit Reapers on their heels. He ran to them, blasting the Spirit Reapers with his paralyzing energy before they could touch his son. Roi Gurri looked back at him with wide eyes.

"Father!" He cried, turning to assist.

"Go!" King Regel ordered. "Protect Susan! I can handle them."

Roi Gurri nodded, and watched with awe and admiration as his father fended off several Spirit Reapers.

He truly was a force to be reckoned with, even in his wounded state. King Regel had been trained for battle since birth, and at over five hundred years old he was one of the greatest examples of a fighter the Zudanums could ever have.

When Roi Gurri was sure his father would be okay, he turned and continued to search for White Star with Susan.

***

"Susan!" William called. "White Star is over there!"

Susan looked over where he was pointing and saw White Star using himself to lure Spirit Reapers over so that Zudaniums could kill them, since he was immortal. A Spirit Reaper ran up to Susan and clawed her face, giving her a large, deep cut on her cheek. She cried out, knocked the Spirit Reaper out of the way, and continued to run toward White Star.

"Can you fly up high?" She asked him, placing her hand on his side.

White Star nodded, kicking a Spirit Reaper away. Just as she was about to mount him someone gripped her wrist, and she turned to see Roi Gurri.

"Susan, I know what you're about to do," he said sternly. "We can win this battle without you having to put your life at risk. Don't do it."

Susan looked into his eyes, placing her other hand over his. "We have no other choice," she said sadly. "I am willing to give my life to protect the people I love. I might not have been able to save Caroldus, but I will save you."

Susan pulled Roi Gurri down for their first kiss. It was brief, yet there was more emotion in that first kiss than any other first kiss in recorded Zudanum history. Both love and mourning drove their kiss, their tears of grief mixing with their longing to say 'I love you' for the first, and possibly, the last time.

Roi Gurri's hands tightly gripped Susan's sides, as if he could keep her grounded and prevent her from doing what she was about to do.

Unfortunately, he could not.

Susan broke the kiss and mounted White Star before she could change her mind. She gave Roi Gurri one last, sorry look before White Star flew her high above the battle. His full wings flapped furiously, thunder and lighting clashing in the sky. Susan looked down at the battle one time and sighed, her hands shaking.

"Here it goes," she mumbled as she pulled out the Jewel of Numenera.

In her trembling state, she accidentally let go of the jewel. Not thinking, she jumped off White Star to grab it. Her hand latched onto the jewel, but the cloth that had been protecting her from its power fluttered far out of her reach.

Roi Gurri watched with dread.

Susan's mind instantly began to twist, the jewels power making her fly higher into the sky without White Star's help, allowing the peryton to fly back into the battle.

Susan screamed in agony as the Jewel of Numenera tormented her mind. Her skull was burning, as if her brain was being physically twisted and turned. Her eyes closed tight and her body coiled as she attempted to make the pain stop, but nothing helped. She couldn't even open her hand to let go of the jewel because it was cramped shut into a tight fist.

"Caroldus!" Susan screamed, crying out to her friends for help. "Roi Gurri! William! Please!"

"Susan!" Roi Gurri cried. "Stop! Let it go!"

"Susan!" William and Subaron called in dread as they watched their friend's torment.

But, Susan's plan was working, though she was in too much pain to tell.

The Jewel of Numenera glowed brighter and brighter, just like on the Spirit Reaper planet, making the Spirit Reapers screech in pain as the light pierced their cloud-like skin. The jewel soon got so bright their whole army disintegrated into black dust. The wind scattered them like the ashes of a roaring fire.

The soldiers of Zudanum had to lift their hands to shield their eyes from the light, or completely look away if they didn't want to be blinded. Roi Gurri grew more nervous as the light continued to get brighter.

"Let her go!" Roi Gurri cried. "You've finished the job!"

When all of the Spirit Reapers were gone the jewel stopped glowing, its power flooding back into itself, which caused Susan to stop floating in the air.

She started falling. Her body had gone limp long ago, and now her skin paled. Roi Gurri and William ran over to where she was falling, pushing past other soldiers, and latching their arms together to catch her before she hit the ground. Worried, Contral, Lucas, White Star, Ethim, and Subaron ran to where they were.

Roi Gurri panicked when he didn't see Susan breathing.

"No, no, no," he muttered, kneeling and placing her head on his lap. "I can't lose you and Caroldus on the same day, wake up!"

He rubbed her face and sent his healing into her, trying to bring her to life, but nothing happened.

"Wake up!" Roi Gurri pleaded.

There was no heartbeat.

"Please!"

No breathing.

"Please, I love you!"

As much as Roi Gurri's cries moved the hearts of those around him, it did not move the woman in his arms.

Susan was dead.

"This can't be happening," Subaron murmured, breaking the silence.

"You only want her alive because of your fight," Lucas barked.

"I don't care about the stupid fight, Lucas!" Subaron snapped in disgust. The others were shocked at Subaron's sudden outburst. "Susan is the reason I decided to join this fight, not because of my father, nor anyone else. She's the Chosen One, how can she be dead?"

"Guys," William breathed out. "Look."

The others looked back at Susan. The Jewel of Numenera was hovering above her face like it was scanning her. It shot a stream of red light at her, which disappeared into the opening of her cut from the Spirit Reaper. The jewel then fell back into her hand and stopped glowing.

The men, wolf, and peryton waited nervously as a minute passed. Soldiers also watched in anticipation. Lucas moved closer and sat beside Susan, whimpering as he moved forward and nudged her limp hand with his snout. He licked it gently, trying to soothe her.

"Guys, she's breathing!" Ethim gasped, pointing at her.

The others looked closely at her and saw Ethim was right. She was breathing, but shallow breaths. Roi Gurri cupped her face gently and brushed his thumb over her new cut.

"Susan?" Roi Gurri asked softly.

Susan groaned as her eyes fluttered open and she looked up, straight into Roi Gurri's eyes. Her brown eyes shimmered briefly before changing into a stunning emerald green color. Roi Gurri was shocked by the change, but he didn't say anything as he embraced her tightly.

"Did it work?" Susan asked, pulling back and looking into his eyes.

Roi Gurri smiled as tears slipped down his cheeks. "Yes, it worked," he affirmed.

She smiled and wiped his tears away. "I'm alive, my love."

"I can see that, Little Legs."

Susan gave a little laugh, and looked down at her hand to see the Jewel of Numenera. She gasped and threw it away before pressing herself closer to Roi Gurri, fear in her eyes as she watched the glowing jewel.

"It's okay," Roi Gurri cooed, rubbing her shoulder. "It brought you back. I don't think it'll hurt you anymore."

Susan was still unconvinced. Roi Gurri reached out his gloved hand and carefully picked up the jewel, offering it to her.

"It's okay," he said again.

With his words to encourage her, Susan slowly reached out and touched the jewel with her fingertips. When she felt no pain, she took it from his hand and examined it.

"It looks like the Jewel of Numenera has finally accepted me," she whispered to herself, smiling.

"It sure does," William said.

Roi Gurri helped Susan stand as she viewed the battlefield. The Zudaniums had taken loses, but far fewer than she had thought. She saw King Regel with a sword wound in his abdomen, soldiers helping him to the medical tent.

"King Regel?" She asked.

Roi Gurri looked over to see his wounded father. "Father!" He cried in alarm.

Roi Gurri ran to King Regel, leaving Susan with the others. She tried to run after him, but collapsed in exhaustion. Contral stopped her from hitting the ground.

"Take it easy," he said, "You were dead a minute ago."

"I was?!" She exclaimed in shock.

"You don't remember?"

Her knees buckled and she knelt down, touching the ground. In an instant, diamonds covered the ground around her hands. She gasped and brought her hands to her chest. Contral knelt beside her.

"I'm anti-natural," Susan whispered as she looked up at Contral, shocked.

"The Jewel of Numenera must've unlocked your powers when it healed you," he explained with a smile. "Or you discovered it while you were dying. The power you just showed me is called Gemstone. It's the ability to create any gem, rock, and metal out of your hand. I'm sure you have more powers, but right now isn't the time to unlock them."

Contral helped her up and they walked over to Roi Gurri and King Regel. She stood beside Roi Gurri. He was teary-eyed as he knelt in front of his father, who was lying on a medical cot.

"Roi Gurri," King Regel said quietly, placing a hand on his son's cheek. "You are now the King of Zudanum."

"Father, no," Roi Gurri pleaded. "I can't rule, n-not yet. I'm only twenty, which is still *really* young! Father-"

"Roi Gurri, please. You will rule well my son, I know you will. Take care of your brother, sister, and mother for me."

"I will, father."

He blinked rapidly to try to keep back tears from falling, but he couldn't.

"And Roi Gurri," King Regel breathed out. "Take care of Susan. She reminds me so much of your mother. All I've wished for in a wife for you."

The mighty king laid his head back and breathed his last. Roi Gurri rested his head beside his father's and started to cry bitterly. His cries pierced all the soldiers who watched.

Their prince, no, their king was in a vulnerable state right in front of them. Susan couldn't help but cry as she watched Roi Gurri. Her mind raced back to when Caroldus died, placing a hand over her mouth to contain her sobs. She softly placed a hand on Roi Gurri's shoulder and squeezed it gently.

"I'm sorry," she whispered softly.

He looked up at her. "I should've been there," he whispered. "I-I saw him wounded, and I didn't do anything."

Susan's expression fell as she knelt beside him. "Roi Gurri, there's nothing you could've done. I know this is hard. I know what it's like to lose family. But I'm here for you. We all are." He nodded as she softly wiped his tears away. "Now, make your father proud. Be the king he taught you to be."

He took a deep breath and nodded. His mourning was far from over, but he would put on a brave face for his people. He would be the strong, brave king they all expected him to be.

Roi Gurri stood and looked at his soldiers and friends. He stood tall and helped Susan up before pulling her beside him. The soldiers, William, Subaron, Contral, and Ethim all bowed to Roi Gurri. Except for Susan, who looked down at the others, before respectfully stepping away from him.

"My King," William said in a respectful tone. "We are at your service."

Susan looked up at Roi Gurri, their eyes locked in an almost unbreakable gaze. She fell on one knee and bowed her head respectfully to her new king.

"My King," she said, looking up at him.

Roi Gurri looked at his friends solemnly. Their loyalty meant more to him than they realized.

"Get up my friends," he said, placing a hand on William and Susan's shoulders. "We have a lot of work to do."

The last part he whispered so only they could hear. William glanced at Susan and realized her eyes had changed from brown to green. Maybe it was due to the power of the Jewel of Numenera, or perhaps those had been her eyes' real color all along. He took note of how her hair was loose and wild around her face, giving her the appearance of one surrounded by fire. At that moment he couldn't help but think that she was truly deserving of the name Adathir.

She really was a daughter of fire.

Chapter Twenty-Four
The End of the Beginning

A few days after the battle of Shadows, as things started to get clearer, Susan decided to take a trip to the Groon's room. She needed answers. She had wanted to come right after the battle but thought she wasn't in the right state of mind. Now, her thoughts were more crowded than ever, but waiting wasn't an option anymore.

She quietly opened the door to the Groon's. Light seeped in from behind her as she entered the dark room. His back was turned to her, but he felt her presence in the room.

"Adathir," the Groon said. "I wasn't expecting you here. Is there something you need?"

"An explanation," Susan replied, her tone low.

The Groon turned to face her, his expression blank but his eyes curious.

"I don't understand."

"Before Caroldus died, he told me my father is still alive. I need help finding him, and I know you can help me."

"How so?"

"You have the ability to communicate with every living thing in the realm. Surely you know people who could help me find my father."

The Groon sighed, sounding doubtful, and Susan bit her lip nervously.

"Please," Susan pleaded. "If he's really alive, then he's all the family I have left who might help me."

"Susan, your father is dead-" The Groon went to say.

"Don't try to feed me that crap like everyone else!" Susan snapped. "Have hope and tell me the possible places he'd be if he's alive!"

The Groon paused. They stared each other down. Neither said anything for several seconds until he finally gave in to her determination.

"The only person who would know where your father is... is A'Vaddon," the Groon answered, his voice low so she could just barely make out what he said.

Susan straightened her shoulders and took a deep breath. She was afraid, but desperate to know the truth.

"Is... is there a way I can speak to him?" She asked.

The Groon's eyes softened in admiration.

"She's chasing a fantasy, though her bravery gives me a new respect for her," he thought as he nodded.

"A'Vaddon has me blocked, but I can ask for permission to communicate with him through his mind," the Groon explained. "I can then use my power so you can communicate with him if that's what you want."

She slowly nodded. "Whatever I have to do."

The Groon nodded before he closed his eyes and called out to A'Vaddon through a mind link.

"He's letting me in," he muttered.

Susan shook in fear of what was about to happen.

"He knows," she thought, her hand clutching her sword at her side. *"He knows what I want."*

"I'll push you through now," the Groon said.

He placed a hand on Susan's forehead and the other on her heart. She felt herself entering A'Vaddon's mind, seeing swirls of black and blood red in her vision. A'Vaddon's colors!

The process was painful, a rough sandpaper texture vigorously scratching her everywhere over and over again, with the intent of grinding her down to the bone. Susan screamed. Her body collapsed and curled into a ball hoping it might soothe the pain, but she continued screaming in agony.

Susan gasped as she felt her feet hit solid ground again. She was no longer in Zudanum. She wasn't in any place, not on any planet anyway. She slowly looked up as the pain she had just experienced faded away.

She found herself in a room, lit by a blazing fireplace. On the walls hung nine skeletons held up by chains, and Susan wondered if they were real. There were black and dark grey pieces of furniture, sitting in front of the fireplace, and on the mantle of the fireplace was the symbol of a mighty dragon engulfed in flames. A'Vaddon's symbol.

"Welcome to my mind, Susan Wellns," a deep voice greeted Susan.

She looked to her side to see A'Vaddon standing right next to her, causing her to jump in surprise and back away. She wasn't afraid, she was *terrified*. This was her first time seeing A'Vaddon with her own eyes, and it was a sight. He was very tall, well over nine feet, and very strong looking.

"I wonder if he could move mountains," was her first thought.

He wore black clothes, a long cape rested on his shoulders that went to the floor, and dragon skin armor covered most of his figure. A metal mask covered his entire face, outlining his jaw, but not much else. She couldn't see his eyes, and a hood covered his hair. She tried to control her shaking and anger, but A'Vaddon could clearly read the young girl's emotions. She was terrified. She was heartbroken. Her heart was full of rage.

"What brings you to my mind, Adathir?" A'Vaddon asked, walking past her toward the fire.

"Apparently I'm not the last Wellns," Susan said, her voice shaking.

A'Vaddon grinned under his mask, but she had no way of reading him.

"Ah, so you've met my assassin, Judez," he said. "Did you enjoy your fight with him? I must say, he held back quite a bit. If he didn't, he would've torn you to shreds."

"Not Damian, my father," Susan corrected sternly. "Marcus Wellns. Where is he?"

A'Vaddon frowned and his hands turned into fists.

"Your father is dead, child," he spat. "Your brother Damian is the only family you have left, and he's under my control."

Susan didn't believe him. Why would Caroldus lie to her?

"Damian was led astray by you," Susan said.

"And who told you that?" A'Vaddon asked calmly as he turned to Susan, surprising her.

"Roi- Roi Gurri."

"Do you trust his word more than mine?"

"Of course I do! He's my friend, my king, my betrothed. You're my enemy."

"Trust me Susan when I say this, one day you'll trust me as if I were your father."

A'Vaddon growled in a serious tone that was frightening. Susan almost believed him.

"But you're not my father," she rebuked.

"How would you know? I wear a mask. You have no idea who I could be. I could be someone in the palace, a friend, for all you know."

"My father would never kill my mother! What kind of hold do you have on my brother? Is it possession? Witchcraft?"

"You're foolish to think I would tell you."

Susan's anger boiled over, letting out a cry and throwing a punch at A'Vaddon, but he easily grabbed her fist. He swiftly turned her and pressed her back to his chest. He held her with one arm across her chest bringing his other hand to her face.

"This is *my* mind, Adathir," A'Vaddon warned. "Whatever I say, goes."

In a flash his hand erupted in electricity and fear invaded Susans heart. She tried prying out of his hold, but he was too strong. He rendered her defenseless.

"You can die here, you know," A'Vaddon said. "Or, so they say. We could always test that."

Horror filled Susan's face, but A'Vaddon moved his hand and pushed her away. Her whole body shook as she fell to the floor. She unsuccessfully attempted to stop her shaking and heavy breathing. Her weakened state brought A'Vaddon a satisfied grin. Even though she couldn't see it, she felt it.

"What's stopping you from killing me right now?" Susan asked in a quiet, yet curious tone, turning and looking back at A'Vaddon.

"The satisfaction of seeing the horrified looks on your friend's faces when I do eventually kill you," A'Vaddon said. "The same look your mother had when I killed your father. You see, I get high off of others' grief and suffering. And ever since I killed Marcus, I've been chasing the high Defestri gave me."

Susan's face flared. Her shaking immediately ceased, and her eyes tinted red.

"You will never have that pleasure with me!" She declared. "I will hunt down every single one of your spies! I will find you, and I will destroy you! Just as I'm destined to!"

"You'll have to catch me first, Adathir."

"Believe me, I will, A'Vaddon."

"Then let the games begin. I can't wait to tear you to bits."

***

While Susan was visiting the Groon, Roi Gurri had other plans.

He leaned against the wall of a corridor, arms folded and dressed in his new kingly robes, the grand crown of past Zudanium kings now resting on his head. Susan had called him handsome that morning, the memory making him smile. There were some days when having the ability to remember everything was a blessing.

The sound of scurried footsteps caused him to stand, his smile falling. A figure rounded the corner and smacked right into him, but he didn't flinch. Sondman fell to the ground, dropping a briefcase. He looked up in fear, before he saw the king and smiled.

"My King, how good it is to see you," Sondman said as he scurried to his feet and bowed. "What may I do to assist you? May I say that the crown suits you-"

"Shut up," Roi Gurri snapped. "Akuma, I hereby sentence you to death for treason and first-degree murder of over five hundred thousand men, women, and children."

Before Sondman could say anything, William and Contral appeared from behind and grabbed his arms.

"W-Wait, my King, this is all a misunderstanding," Sondman pleaded. "Please, I have no idea what you're talking about."

"You should've ran when you had the opportunity," Roi Gurri said. "Caroldus may have been merciful to you, but I can assure you, you will get no such thing from me."

"On your knees, bastard," William growled, kicking the back of Sondman's knees and forcing him to kneel.

"Let the accusers state their claims," Roi Gurri said.

"I accuse Sondman, known as Akuma, of plotting and executing the murder of Caroldus Fridink," Contral stated.

"I accuse Sondman, known as Akuma, of plotting and executing the murder of King Regel Drago," William stated.

"I accuse you, Akuma, of being a spy and traitor to Zudanum," Roi Gurri stated. "I accuse you of the deaths of thousands of innocent people. I accuse you of feeding lies to my father and purposefully placing Susan Wellns into the hands of a traitor to hinder her."

"You have no proof!" Sondman screamed. "You can't kill me without proof!"

"I have all of the proof I need."

Roi Gurri pulled out a small device, clicked a button, and the voices of Sondman and Caroldus filled the hall. Horror flooded Sondman.

Caroldus had recorded their entire conversation.

"I also had your office gutted," Roi Gurri explained. "I found all of your recordings and reports to A'Vaddon behind the walls. Thought you were clever? You underestimated Caroldus, and that is your downfall. What do the accusers proclaim the accused?"

"Guilty," Contral said with a sneer.

"Guilty," William said through gritted teeth.

"And guilty say I," Roi Gurri said as he drew his sword and looked into Sondman's eyes.

"Oh, and by the way, it was *Susan* who heard you in the hall. You sentenced an innocent man to death. As the King of Zudanum and protector of the twelve realms, I must serve my people."

He brought his sword down and sliced off Sondman's head in one, fluid, motion.

"May your time in sheol be most unpleasant."

Acknowledgements

It's all thanks to God that this is happening after thirteen years of writing draft after draft. I always dreamed of publishing but never thought I'd actually do it until now. Every step was challenging, but it was certainly fun. This draft alone took six years to get out! It's always so much easier to re-work chapters than it is to write them out, but the rewards make it worthwhile.

I've used reading and writing as a means to escape reality, to find a world where I felt I belonged, for as long as I can remember. Escaping to Zudanum on a daily basis is a unique experience every time, always filled with new possibilities and adventures. Writing the story of Susan has helped me cope with a lot of my struggles, and I can admit that it helped keep me going many times when I wanted to give up more than just my writing. I hope that this story can inspire those like me to keep moving forward.

Sometimes reality isn't as bad as we think. Yes, sometimes I wish I could escape to Zudanum forever, but just like our world, it isn't perfect. There will always be war, famine, poverty, problems in any world because that's just how humans are. No system is perfect, but as I've gotten older I've learned to appreciate the things I have. No matter where I go, no matter how low my mentality is dragged down, I strive to see the bright side of my situation and where I am. Why? Because no matter what happens in the world, no matter how many friends or family I lose, and no matter if this book completely fails, I will always have hope and faith that my God will lift me up when I get knocked down.

To those who want to explore the stars, who look out of their bedroom window late at night, remember to always have hope. As long as we have hope, all is not lost.

I want to give a special thanks to my very first editor, Eldon Miller, who was the first to read this story in full and give me genuine feedback. He encouraged me to keep going, he was the one who had my back when I made mistakes. Thank you, Eldon. Without you, this wouldn't be possible.

Thank you to all of my friends and family who took the time to either read this story or be there to support me when I was feeling down. Thank you to Isaiah, who still hasn't read this book, but is always there to give me advice when I'm struggling. To Victoria, who let me read aloud my old drafts to her. To David, thank you for being my biggest fan and constantly asking for book two. To Hazel, who is basically my god-mother, for always encouraging me to read, write, and use my gifts to the best of my abilities. To Anika, Sarianna, and Kara, for letting me pick your brains and giving me genuine feedback on the many drafts I made you read. To my mom and dad, for believing in my dreams and constantly pushing me to get my story out there.

Most importantly, I want to thank my God, and my savior, Jesus Christ, because without him I'd be completely lost in life. Everything I've done is through him, and through his glory. I hope that my stories can be a testimony of my love for him, because if I hadn't walked home from church and met a black horse with a white star on its forehead thirteen years ago, this story would've never been created.

Keep hope by your side, and reach for the stars! Anything, and everything is possible to those who are willing to work for it!

Paloma Earnheart

Paloma lives and writes on a small farm in Kansas City Missouri. While she is working on the next book in the series, she can be reached, by all fans, at PO Box 271 Grandview, MO 64030 or through adventuresofadathir@gmail.com. She can also be found on all forms of social media, such as Instagram and Twitter.

Author photo @ victoriaearnheart_

www.ingramcontent.com/pod-product-compliance
Lightning Source LLC
LaVergne TN
LVHW090549110826
845146LV00001B/72

* 9 7 9 8 9 8 8 1 3 3 9 2 6 *